A wealthy merchant kingdom situated east of Cormyr on the western edge of the Sea of Fallen Stars.

❂

SELGAUNT

A haughty place, dripping with wealth and bustling with excited commercial intrigues. "Everyone comes to Sembia a-hunting coins," is the local catchphrase.

❂

NIGHT KNIVES

The most influential of Selgaunt's underworld, especially when it comes to extortion, bribery, and killing for hire.

❂

THE USKEVREN

One of the oldest, proudest families of Selgaunt. The last name is derived from an extinct Chondathan tongue, and means, "Too bold to hide."

❂

EREVIS CALE

Trusted servant, master thief—he serves two masters. Erevis and his friend Jak Fleet are the only ones that can save the city and the Uskevren family.

SEMBIA

THE HALLS OF STORMWEATHER

SHADOW'S WITNESS
Paul S. Kemp

THE SHATTERED MASK
Richard Lee Byers
MAY 2001

BLACK WOLF
Dave Gross
NOVEMBER 2001

SEMBIA

SHADOW'S WITNESS

Paul S. Kemp

Dedication
For my comrades in arms,
the Band of the Broken Bow.

SHADOW'S WITNESS
Sembia

Distributed in the United States by St. Martin's Press. Distributed in Canada by Fenn Ltd.

Distributed to the hobby, toy, and comic trade in the United States and Canada by regional distributors.

Distributed worldwide by Wizards of the Coast, Inc. and regional distributors.

The FORGOTTEN REALMS and the Wizards of the Coast logo are registered trademarks owned by Wizards of the Coast, Inc.

All Wizards of the Coast characters, character names, and the distinctive likenesses thereof are trademarks owned by Wizards of the Coast, Inc.

Made in the U.S.A.

Cover art by Terese Nielsen
Cartography by Dennis Kauth
First Printing: November 2000
Library of Congress Catalog Card Number: 00-101963

9 8 7 6 5 4 3 2 1

ISBN: 0-7869-1677-X
620-T21677

U.S., CANADA,   EUROPEAN HEADQUARTERS
ASIA, PACIFIC, & LATIN AMERICA   Wizards of the Coast, Belgium
Wizards of the Coast, Inc.   P.B. 2031
P.O. Box 707   2600 Berchem
Renton, WA 98057-0707   Belgium
+1-800-324-6496   +32-70-23-32-77

Visit our web site at **www.wizards.com/forgottenrealms**

Selgaunt

River Arkhen

Selgaunt Bay

N W E S

1. Oxblood Quarter
2. Warehouse District
3. harper Gatehouse
4. Avenue of the Temples
5. Temple of Deneir
6. Arhness Street
7. Night Knife Guildhouse
8. Stormweather Towers
9. Sarn Street
10. Raunces's Ride

CHAPTER 1

THE SUMMONING

**The month of Hammer, 1371DR,
the Year of the Unstrung Harp**

The dim light from the guttering torches in the stairwell stopped at the edge of the doorway as though blocked by a wall of magical darkness. Conscious of Riven beside him and unwilling to show the assassin the nervousness which had him sweating beneath his robes, Krollir stepped briskly through the doorway and into the summoning chamber. Riven followed, wary and apprehensive.

When both had stepped through the archway, Krollir turned and closed the door behind them. Instantly, darkness as thick and impenetrable as scribe's ink cloaked the room. The iron portal's immense latch fell into place with an ominous, resounding *click*.

Familiar from long habit, Krollir felt around

in the blackness for the wrist-thick iron deadbolt, quickly found it, and slid it home. The shrieking grate of metal against metal set his teeth on edge. He quelled the apprehensive quaver that fluttered in his gut. I will succeed, he assured himself. I *am* the chosen of Mask.

Invisible in the darkness beside him, Riven's breath came harsh and rapid. Blindness apparently made the assassin nervous. He no doubt suspected an ambush.

Krollir smiled behind the black felt of his ceremonial mask. His lieutenant's nervousness amused him. Riven's breathing reminded Krollir of the frightened pant of a wary cur.

Despite Riven's earlier protests, Krollir had forbidden the assassin from bringing a torch or candle, even while descending the dimly lit stairs. Unsanctified light brought into the Shadowlord's summoning chamber spoiled its holiness. Only certain spells and specially prepared forms of luminescence could safely light this room. His thoughts turned to the candles he had specially prepared for this night. He had spent months painstakingly crafting them and carefully instilling them with power.

Though blind in the darkness, Krollir knew his lieutenant well enough that he could imagine perfectly Drasek Riven's stance—a ready crouch with his back to the wall—his single eye darting about the darkness and both callused hands resting familiarly on his enchanted saber hilts.

Spitefully, Krollir let him simmer nervously in the soup of pitch darkness for a few extra moments. Let him wonder and fear, he thought. He had told Riven nothing; he required the assassin's presence but left his purpose unexplained. He enjoyed keeping his lieutenant off balance and making him nervous. Like all dogs born vicious, Riven occasionally had to be reminded of his master's authority.

The summoning chamber of Mask—Krollir's patron deity—fairly stank of power. Behind the stale must, the magical residue of past conjurations lingered in the dry air and ran tingling along Krollir's nasal passages. No doubt Riven sensed it too, in his own thick way.

Inhaling deeply, Krollir drank in the sheer energy of the room while letting Riven stew in the dark.

The sinister majesty of the summoning chamber served as a pointed reminder to the one-eyed assassin that Krollir Venastin—the Righteous Man—was not only the guildmaster of the Night Knives but also a powerful servant of Mask the Shadowlord. Krollir was a man not to be challenged, even by the most dangerous of dogs. Riven's nervousness indicated that he still grasped that point. The cur yet remained at heel.

Krollir allowed himself another satisfied smile that vanished when thoughts of his other lieutenant, Erevis Cale, entered his mind. Three days ago, he had sent word via messenger to Riven and Cale that they must attend him tonight. Riven had obeyed; Cale however, had sent the messenger back with word that he could not attend, that Thamalon Uskevren had an important business meeting that Cale could not miss without compromising his cover.

Krollir frowned thoughtfully. He fidgeted with a platinum coin in his robe pocket. Was Cale still loyal? The answer to that question was becoming increasingly unclear. Cale had an obvious fondness for the Uskevren, the noble family he was spying upon—an unfortunate but understandable fact—but did his ultimate loyalty still reside with Krollir and the guild?

Unsure of the answer and uncomfortable with the uncertainty, Krollir decided to put a tail on Cale. A guildsman to spy on the spy.

Though he highly valued Cale's intellect and

ruthlessness—the bald giant had served the Night Knives well for many years with his cutthroat schemes—he nevertheless realized that those same qualities made Cale a potential loyalty problem—a potential rival for Mask's favor. Far more so than Riven. But would he dare an open challenge? Certainly Cale feared little—

"How about a blasted light?" Riven's hoarse, disembodied voice interrupted Krollir's chain of thought. "It's as black as a devil's heart in here. I can't see a godsdamned thing."

The tension in the assassin's voice dispelled the disquieting thoughts of Cale and returned a smile to Krollir's face. This cur, at least, remains obedient. Perhaps I should turn *him* loose on Cale he thought. That would make for an interesting dogfight.

Riven's breath continued to come fast. Krollir fancied he could hear the assassin's teeth grinding. He waited a moment longer before replying.

"Be at ease, lieutenant. You stand in the summoning chamber of Mask the Shadowlord, in the presence of Mask's most prized servant." He smiled and mentally added, In the presence of he who soon will be Mask's Champion.

Riven replied through gritted teeth. "Grand. But I still need to see."

Krollir chose to ignore the assassin's sarcasm and softly intoned the words to a spell. Upon completion, a soft, diffuse glow filled the large chamber, enough light to create a patchwork of shadows but not enough to fully dispel the darkness.

The rough-hewn limestone walls of the chamber glowed softly in the pale light of the spell. Krollir turned to face Riven. As he had suspected, the assassin stood in a fighting crouch with both saber hilts clenched in white-knuckled fists.

"In this chamber, this light alone is acceptable to the Shadowlord."

Riven nodded but made no reply. His one good eye must have adjusted quickly to the darkness, for his gaze darted warily about the chamber, still suspicious. Krollir observed his hunting dog with professional detachment. He tried to follow Riven's thinking as the assassin's one-eyed gaze scanned the room.

The summoning chamber had but one means of entry and exit, something a professional like Riven necessarily disliked—predictable entry; predictable retreat. Thick hinges as long as daggers and bolts as thick as a man's thumb affixed the door to the limestone. The great slab of blackened, cast iron looked able to resist a siege engine.

In the center of the chamber, strips of platinum inlaid into the smooth, polished floor formed a triangle. Flesh-colored candles as thick as a man's forearm stood at each of its three corners. Riven would not know that the thaumaturgic triangle served to cage the extra-planar creatures that Krollir summoned to do his bidding.

He watched with a satisfied smirk—hidden by the felt cloth of his mask, of course—as Riven's gaze took in the binding triangle and summoning candles. The assassin's one good eye widened slightly, his fear of spellcraft evident in his expression.

I know you too well, lieutenant, Krollir smugly thought.

Riven understood little of spellcraft and its practice made him uneasy. As long as Krollir demonstrated the power of his magical arts from time to time, the assassin would never present a loyalty problem. Riven would never even *aspire* to become Mask's Champion.

A plain, mahogany lectern stood at the apex of the

triangle. An open tome sat atop it, thick with knowledge and yellowed with age—the Shadowtome—a holy book of Mask that allowed Krollir to reach beyond this reality and summon . . .

"What are we doing here?" Apparently having recovered himself, Riven now sounded strangely calm, though he remained near the door and kept his back to the wall.

"All in time, lieutenant," Krollir replied. He turned his back on Riven and walked ceremoniously across the room. The velvet of his gray robes softly whispered as he strode around the triangle and took position at the lectern. Gripping the cool, smooth wood on either side of the Shadowtome, he steadied himself for the ordeal ahead. When he felt ready, he ordered over his shoulder, "Come forward and light the candles, Riven. But do not disturb their position."

He had expected the assassin to protest—for surely Riven would fear to take a direct hand in a summoning—but after only a moment's hesitation, Riven walked calmly to the binding triangle, took a tinderbox from his belt pouch, and struck flint to steel. Krollir watched him intently; he prided himself on his ability to read a man from the subtlest of actions.

Surprisingly, the assassin's hands did not shake as he held a flaming cloth to each candle in turn. The corners of Riven's thin-lipped mouth curled slightly upward. His goatee masked what could have been either a fearful grimace or a secret smile.

Strange, Krollir thought, but not entirely out of character. He had learned long ago that Riven masked fear with a show of calm bravado. Inside, the assassin's guts were no doubt roiling like a butter churn.

Careful to disturb neither the candles nor place his hand within the platinum borders of the binding triangle, Riven soon had all three of the thick wax towers lit. Wisps of stinking black smoke snaked from the dancing flames and rose toward the invisible vents in the ceiling. The room rapidly filled with the smell of rancid meat.

"What in the Nine Hells did you use to make these candles?" Riven asked. "They stink like horse dung."

Krollir smiled softly—the materials used to craft the candles had been hard bought. He made no reply to the question. He inhaled deeply, steeled himself. He had summoned lesser demons many times before, but what he would attempt now. . .

Is suitable for Mask's Champion, he reassured himself. "Stand away, Riven," he commanded.

At his authoritative tone, the assassin shot him an irritated glare but nevertheless obediently backed away from the binding triangle. He padded back to his position near the door, behind and beside the lectern.

"You still haven't explained what we're doing here."

Angered by the incessant questions, Krollir turned from the lectern to face the assassin. He spoke in a soft voice pregnant with power and heavy with threats. "Do I owe you explanations, lieutenant?" He emphasized the last word slightly, explicitly referencing Riven's status as a subordinate; a *replaceable* subordinate.

The assassin's good eye narrowed, but he swallowed whatever angry retort he might have been considering. His gaze went to the binding triangle and the unusual candles.

See in them my power, lieutenant, Krollir silently advised, and consider well your next words. If necessary, he would kill Riven where he stood.

Riven's gaze returned to meet Krollir's. His mouth remained a defiant rictus in the hairy nest of his goatee, but his words bespoke submission. "No. You don't owe me an explanation. I was curious, is all."

Krollir smiled behind his mask. Heel, cur. He decided to drive another verbal splinter under Riven's fingernails. "It is regrettable that Cale is not here," he said, as though in passing. "I would have him share my moment of triumph."

The assassin visibly stiffened at the mention of his rival Erevis Cale—and at the implicit recognition in Krollir's statement of Cale's superior status in the guild—but he ignored the bait. Instead, he asked, "Triumph?"

Krollir ignored Riven's question. He enjoyed the assassin's discomfiture at the mention of Cale. He had long encouraged the rivalry between the two men. He had chosen them as his lieutenants for that very reason. The hate that they held for one another lessened the threat to him that either alone would present. The two could never ally to overthrow him— one would always betray the other. When the time came—and it was coming soon—Krollir would kill them both. For he alone would serve as the Champion of Mask. The Champion destined to restore the faith of the Shadowlord to the status it enjoyed before the Time of Troubles, before the coming of the pretender god Cyric the Dark Sun. All of Krollir's augurs and dreams had indicated that Mask would choose a Champion soon from among the Night Knives in the city of Selgaunt. Taking nothing for granted, Krollir had decided to assure his selection with the summoning tonight.

"Alone you will have the privilege of bearing witness to these events, Riven," he grandly announced. "With this one act, the Zhentarim will be destroyed and our guild—*my* guild—will be elevated to preeminence in Selgaunt. Mask has mandated this course, and I obey."

He waited for an appropriate reply but Riven held his silence. Krollir went on.

"With the power of the Shadowtome, I will reach beyond this reality into the darkest layer of the Abyss and summon forth a dread. I dare this in the name of Mask! I dare this for the guild I lead! Do you see, Riven?"

He had expected Riven to protest or recoil upon learning Krollir's intent to summon a demonic dread—had hoped for it, in fact—but the assassin stood his ground, expressionless.

"I see," he replied noncommittally. Though Riven spoke in a steady voice, he looked coiled as tight as a dwarf's beard braid.

He is more nervous now than ever, Krollir thought with satisfaction.

He turned from Riven to stand over the lectern and peruse the pages of the Shadowtome. He had acquired the magical artifact from an ignorant curio dealer in Arabel. The oblivious fool had not been able to decipher the script and so had not known what he possessed. Krollir had sent Riven to purchase the tome, eliminate the dealer, and escort the prize back to Selgaunt. In all of the city, perhaps in all of Faerûn, only he and Riven knew of the Shadowtome's existence, and the assassin was too unschooled in the magical arts to appreciate its significance.

Within its pages of ancient, coded text, the Shadowtome contained the description and proper name of a mighty dread, the name and nature of its abyssal abode, and the means to summon and properly bind it. The dread named in the tome dwelled in Belistor, a layer of the Abyss, a void of nothingness empty of normal life, but not empty of all life. Dreads resided there, greater and lesser, as did certain powerful undead. Because the denizens of Belistor existed in such close proximity to the negative energy of the plane, they possessed a certain power that Krollir desired to harness—their touch siphoned the souls of any mortals they contacted, killing them irrevocably. Spells that raised or resurrected the dead could not bring back those slain by dreads.

Krollir planned to command one of the greatest of the dreads to slay the leaders of the Zhentarim—the widespread organization of Cyric-loving priests, warriors, and wizards. The Zhents were Krollir's and the Night Knives' most dangerous rivals. But not after tonight. With their leaders slain, the Night Knives could destroy the weakened Zhents and rule Selgaunt's underworld.

Mask's first triumph over Cyric is at hand, Krollir thought, *and my status as the Shadowlord's Champion is assured.*

He spared a glance over his shoulder to check on Riven. The assassin stood near the door. He met Krollir's gaze.

Flushed with his soon-to-be success, Krollir smiled indulgently behind his mask. He realized now that Riven and Cale had never been true rivals for Mask's favor—by the gods, neither of them had ever even set foot in Mask's shrine. Rather, they had served as whetstones. Whetstones used by Mask to hone Krollir and better prepare him for his ordained role as Champion. Feeling razor sharp, he decided to discard them as unnecessary after tonight.

"Witness, Riven," he hissed, alive with the knowledge that Mask had chosen *him*. Riven smirked but made no response. Krollir turned back to the Shadowtome and began the summoning. Though the words of power had been scribed in a now time-corrupted form of Thorass, he nevertheless pronounced them forcefully. He had rehearsed the phrases in his mind many times before and had dreamed them for a tenday.

"*Ichilai follin vaeve . . .*" His voice resounded in the chamber, magnified fourfold by the limestone. His hands rapidly traced invisible symbols in the air above the tome. Behind him, Riven's breathing again grew rapid. It sounded in Krollir's ears as loud as a bellows.

". . . *Narven Yrsillar ej . . .*" The power in the room began to grow, and as it did the candles flickered. When the wicks began to die, a feeling of stark terror washed over Krollir, but the flames quickly rallied and stayed lit. He managed to keep his cadence steady despite the moment of terror. His hands gripped the lectern so tightly they dug depressions into the wood.

". . . *Velnen dretilylar Yrsillar . . .*" Increasingly confident, his voice grew in volume as he recited. His fingers began to leave sparkling trails of silver in the air where he traced arcane symbol after arcane symbol. The glow from his earlier spell began to dim. Shadows coalesced in the corners and thickened. Inarticulate hissing sounded from everywhere and nowhere.

". . . *Belistor om follin ej . . .*" All the hairs on his body rose and stood on end. The air pressed against him so hard he felt as though he was caught in a vise. Sweat poured from his clammy skin. The hissing grew louder. The shadows grew deeper, darker. He raised his hands above his head and shouted the final phrase in a voice gone hoarse.

". . . *Yrsillar ej wexeral Belistor!*"

Like thousands of dwarven steam engines venting at once, the hissing reached an unbearable crescendo. The sound of an unliving multitude filled his ears, pawed at his soul. Reality ripped open with the sound of tearing cloth. An expanding globe of emptiness formed in the air above the binding triangle. Krollir stared into the bottomless void and knew the beginnings of madness. Mentally gripping his sanity, he watched transfixed.

Two pinpoints of yellow light took shape somewhere back in the emptiness, feral eyes so full of hate and malice that their gaze nearly made Krollir vomit. Abruptly, the hissing ceased. All stood quiet but for Krollir's and Riven's breathing. The eyes began to draw closer . . . closer. . . .

The candles suddenly flared and in an instant burned down half the length of their shafts. The melted wax flowed along the platinum lines of the triangle inset into the floor and congealed like blood, then hardened like day-old scabs. The emptiness above the triangle writhed, solidified, shaped itself into a towering, black, demonic form that Krollir *sensed* as much as saw—a muscular biped with great batlike wings and powerful, overlong arms that ended in vicious claws. Above, an oval head formed, featureless but for yellow eyes and a darker line that might have been a mouth. It was a being that somehow seemed to occupy space and create emptiness all at the same time. The malice in its eyes burned holes into Krollir's brain. When it spoke, its sinister whisper hissed with such hate that it struck him like a physical blow.

"What *creature* dares summon Yrsillar, Lord of the Void?"

Despite his exhaustion, Krollir's heart leaped in his chest. To have summoned a demon of such power! Indeed he *must* be the chosen of Mask!

Dripping with sweat but smiling triumphantly, he unclenched his hands from the lectern and closed the Shadowtome, each motion slow and deliberate. Yrsillar's angry hissing filled his brain but he pushed it aside. He had succeeded! Succeeded where none before had even dared! Confidence lent strength to his voice.

"*I* have summoned you, Yrsillar. I, the servant of Mask called the Righteous Man. Summoned you and bound you."

At that, Yrsillar hissed. As though to test Krollir's claim, the great dread extended an arm and clawed gently at the magical barrier that extended upward from the wax-filled lines of the binding triangle like an invisible pyramid. When Yrsillar tried to reach beyond the borders of that invisible pyramid, green energy flashed. The demon jerked back as though seared. Growling low but undeterred, Yrsillar examined the inside of its cage and probed for weakness, testing in turn each side of the triangle.

Krollir knew that a single flaw in the platinum strips or the wax coating would corrupt the binding and free the demon. He felt a flash of fear despite himself, though he knew he had made no mistake. Each time the towering demon tried to reach through the air beyond the border established by the wax-coated, platinum lines, flaring green energy elicited a growl and forced it to recoil. Krollir merely watched, fascinated and horrified, gleeful that—

Yrsillar suddenly whirled on him, crouched, and tried to leap bodily through the binding. Surprised, Krollir staggered a step backward in terror, nearly tripping over his own feet.

Green fire engulfed the demon and stopped it in midleap, framing its muscular black form in a penumbra of crackling energy. Its mighty figure hung suspended in the air over the binding triangle, writhing and growling as the fire seared its emptiness. Greasy black smoke boiled from its body and filled the room with the acrid stink of ozone.

Krollir quickly regained his composure and again

stepped forward to the lectern. After another moment of growls and green flames, Yrsillar finally managed to pull his body free from the barrier and back into the triangle. Streamers of smoke snaked from its torso to mix about the ceiling with the smoke from the candles. The dread's baleful eyes bored into Krollir, but this time he refused to give ground.

He gestured at the binding triangle and the half-consumed candles burning at each corner. "The candles bind you, demon. Virgins' blood and the fat from new-born babes went into their wax. I have prepared well, and you are bound." He paused to let that sink in, then asked, "Do you agree to do my bidding in exchange for your freedom?"

Yrsillar hissed and crouched low, a predator ready to kill. His yellow eyes narrowed to hate-filled sparks. Each claw looked like a dagger blade. "I will drink your soul for this, human. I smell your fear and taste your weakness. You are food, and I will consume you slowly. Your pain will be unending. I will leave your body a dried husk. You will beg for dea—"

"Do you agree to do my bidding in exchange for your freedom? Or shall I cause you pain?" Meaningfully, Krollir reopened the Shadowtome. "I can reduce the size of the binding pyramid so that you will not be able to avoid its touch. The pain will be ceaseless."

Yrsillar screamed, a frustrated howl of rage that shook the limestone. At that moment, Krollir knew that his plan had come to fruition. Tonight, Zhentarim would die by the score, never to be raised from the dead by the foul priests of Cyric the Dark Sun.

The demon finished its outburst and spoke slowly, growling the while, the words reluctantly spilling forth. "So long as I am bound, I agree to do your bidding."

Well enough, Krollir thought, and barely managed not to laugh aloud. He spoke over his shoulder to

Riven, unable to keep the glee out of his voice. "Witness, lieutenant! You see before you the end of our enemies. The end of the Zhentarim! Witn—"

The shriek of the opening door jerked Krollir around. Riven stood in the open doorway, his squat, athletic silhouette framed by the torchlight in the stairwell. A cold chill raced up Krollir's spine. Behind him, Yrsillar began to softly hiss.

"Riven, what are you doing?"

The assassin reached into his cloak, pulled out a small token, and flung it at him. It *tinked* on the stone floor and skittered to a stop at Krollir's feet. His eyes went wide when he saw a black triangle with a yellow circle inset and a Z superimposed over the whole—the device of a Zhentarim agent. The realization crashed over him like a collapsing wall. Riven is a Zhentarim agent! They know! He looked up, goggle-eyed—

"Riven, no! Don't! You don't know what you're do—"

The assassin had already pulled a dagger from his belt sheath. "Witness *this*, fool," he snapped, and threw the dagger.

Krollir felt his next heartbeat as though it were an hour, or an eternity. The dagger toppled slowly through the air, with every turn the blade's edge glinting orange in the candlelight. It flew through space toward the binding triangle, toppling end over end. Krollir's heart stopped. His eyes threatened to burst from his skull. Point, hilt, point, hilt, toppling, toppling.

Yrsillar crouched low in anticipation, flexed his muscular, clawed arms. Yellow eyes narrowed to hungry slits.

Krollir watched in horror as the dagger's point impaled one of the candles. A few droplets of melted wax jumped into the air. The candle fell to its side and rolled along the floor. The dancing flame snuffed instantly, drowned in the remainder of the candle's wax, drowned in virgins' blood and babies' fat.

The great iron door to the summoning chamber slammed shut. Riven was gone and Yrsillar was free.

The demon began to laugh loud and long. The sound, like the opening of a hundred mausoleum doors, hit Krollir like a fist. A wave of supernatural fear flowed from the broken binding and drove him to his knees. His eyes welled with tears and snot streamed down his face as he helplessly watched the demon *flow* through the open corner of the triangle, laughing. Cold yellow eyes stared out of emptiness and pulled his breath from his lungs. The demon approached. He closed his eyes and prayed to Mask for a quick death. I'm not the Champion, I'm not the Champion, I'm not the—

Yrsillar stood before him. Fear blanked his mind. Every hair on his body stood on end. A coldness embraced him and set his teeth to chattering. He dared not open his eyes. Terror pulled inarticulate moans from his throat. He felt a disgustingly soft caress on his neck and face, like ice running over his skin. A scream rose in his throat.

"Food," Yrsillar hissed in his ear, and began again to laugh.

❖   ❖   ❖   ❖   ❖

Breathing hard, Riven grabbed a torch from a wall sconce and raced up the stairs three at a time. Though blocked by an iron door, the terrified screams of the Righteous Man still filled his ears and chased him like a specter. The hopeless sounds of a helpless animal, those screams. He felt no guilt for the betrayal, of course—Nine Hells, that's why the Zhentarim had placed him with the Night Knives in the first place.

He actually felt a certain satisfaction for a job well done, but even Riven found it mildly distasteful to leave the Righteous Man as food for a demon. No way for a man to die, he thought. He would have preferred to drive a dagger into the old man's back and have done with it.

Abruptly, the screaming ceased. He stopped running, steadied his breathing, and listened for a moment. Nothing. Satisfied, he ascended the rest of the long staircase at a walk. By the time he reached the door at the top, he had fully regained his breath. He took a moment to compose himself. Knowing that he had nothing to fear from the dread, he took his time. When he felt ready, he pushed open the door and walked into the lower level of the Night Knives' guildhouse.

The long hallway to either side of him stood empty and dim. Torches hung from wall sconces along the uneven plaster walls and cast shadows that looked uncomfortably similar to the black nothingness of the dread.

It's long gone already, he assured himself, long gone.

Still, the screams of the Righteous Man echoed in his brain and sent a cold shudder up his spine. Out of long habit, his hands fell to his saber hilts as he walked.

The lower level of the guildhouse was used mainly for storage, training, and worship. It also doubled as a final defensive strongpoint in the unlikely event of some kind of frontal assault on the guild. At this hour, the area stood empty. The main hallway Riven walked served as a spine from which branched all of the other rooms, hallways, and stairs of the lower level. At the northern end of the hallway, behind a sturdy door, stood a small storage chamber with a concealed trapdoor that opened onto a secret access route into the city's old sewer system. At the southern end of the hall is the old man's shrine, he thought with contempt. He glanced behind him down the hallway to the double doors of the shrine and sneered in derision.

Over the past three years the Righteous Man had quietly spent guild proceeds to build an elaborate worship hall dedicated to Mask the Shadowlord. Riven had seen smaller temples dedicated to so-called "legitimate" gods.

What a waste of coin, he thought. Pissing away valuable time and resources, the Righteous Man had led the guild in a service every tenth night of every tenday since. Over time, more and more of the Knives had attended and more and more had come to actively worship Mask. So much so that the worship had come to dominate the activities of the guild.

Idiots! he sneered. This place was becoming more priesthood than thieves' guild with every passing day. I did you all a favor tonight. Riven had made a point never to set foot in the shrine. He despised gods, even Cyric, the patron of many of his fellow Zhentarim. Reliance on the gods made men weak, overconfident, and willing to rely on miracles rather than their own abilities. He figured that the fate of the Righteous Man was the ultimate fate of all priests, for priests kept their eyes on a god and not on the world around them. Riven had spied on the Knives for the Zhentarim *for years*, all the while holding the implicit trust of the Righteous Man. The old fool's faith had made him stupid and blind.

Weeks before, when the Righteous Man had told him about the Shadowtome, Riven had sent word of it to Malix, his Zhentarim superior. Then, upon retrieving the book and returning to Selgaunt, he had not taken it directly to the Righteous Man. Instead, he had taken it to Malix for study. Based on the book's contents, Zhentarim mages had easily determined that the old man planned to summon a dread. Riven was told how to sabotage the delicate binding. At the time, he had thought he would have to create an excuse to be present for the summoning, or that he would have to break in during the casting of the spell, but the old fool had actually *required* him to be present! Witness this, lieutenant! Riven had almost laughed aloud. The arrogant ass!

Though Riven knew little of magic—he disdained spellcasters almost as much as priests, trusting his steel over spells any day—even he had seen the potential danger of turning a demon loose from its binding, possibly turning it loose on Selgaunt. Malix had laid that fear to rest, though. The Zhentarim did not fear the dread running amok in the city because, according to the Shadowtome, it could not long endure existence on this plane. Since negative energy made up so much of a dread's being, existence on this plane—a plane full of positive energy—caused it immense pain.

Or some such. Riven had ignored most of Malix's explanation. It was enough for him that the dread would kill the Righteous Man and then leave. He smiled viciously. Kill and then leave. He liked that. He had done the same countless times himself, was doing so again now. Killing and then leaving.

After he walked out of the guildhouse tonight, his time as a Night Knife was over. The Night Knives were over. When Riven informed Malix of the Righteous Man's death, the Zhentarim would pounce on the leaderless guild. Without someone to organize a defense, the Night Knives would be easy prey. The Zhentarim would hunt them down, recruit those who would turn, and kill the rest.

The rest will be a lot, Riven figured, with a backward look at the shrine. Too many of the Knives had become religious fanatics. Far too many. They would not be open to recruitment. Zealots didn't change sides, they were martyred.

This guild is already a cooling corpse, he thought. Other than he and Cale, everyone else in the guild had the mind of a lackey, which was why they had been led to religion in the first place. None of them could lead the guild in a fight against the Zhentarim. They all would be easy fodder. Of course, Riven was prepared to acknowledge—reluctantly—that Cale *could* lead them, were he so inclined. But he was not so inclined. In fact, Riven suspected that Cale wanted *out* of the guild, not leadership of it. The leaderless Night Knives would soon be no more, another casualty in Selgaunt's ongoing gang wars.

Still, for the next few days Riven would have to lay low and watch his back. At least until after the Zhentarim hit the guildhouse. If anyone with a grudge survived the coming purge, they might notice his absence, put the puzzle together, and come looking for him. He wasn't afraid for his safety, but he didn't want the bother of fanatics trying to hunt him down.

He smiled, appreciating the irony. The rabid fanaticism of the Knives had been the very reason the Zhentarim had decided to move against them so forcefully in the first place. While Selgaunt's underworld *was* a viper's pit of competing organizations, none of them had been fanatical prior to the radicalization of the Night Knives. Thieves' guilds acted predictably; religious movements did not. Selgaunt's underworld could not long tolerate an unpredictable actor—unpredictability drew the attention of the city's otherwise disinterested authorities. The Zhentarim could not allow that.

One more reason to spurn religion, Riven supposed with a contemptuous sneer. Where was your god tonight, old man? Holed up in the shrine, maybe? He chuckled aloud. Riven restricted his worship to only three things—sharp steel, cold coin, and warm women, in that order. Anything else was weakness.

Still chuckling, he turned his back to the shrine and strode down the hallway until he reached the oak door that opened into the storage room. Low voices from within carried through the wood. He spared one last glance over his shoulder—his last sight of this den of idiots—wiped the satisfied grin off his face, and pushed the door open.

Two men, Fek and Norwyl, decent thugs, not so decent sentries—hastily stood from their game of dice. Two small piles of silver lay at their feet, and a pair of ivory knucklebones rested on the floor between them. Asp eyes, Riven saw, and smiled coldly. Crates lined the walls. For light, Fek and Norwyl had stuffed a tallow candle into the tap of an empty keg. A filthy rug covered the floor.

"Riven," Fek said in nervous surprise. The taller of the two, Fek wore a short sword at his belt and looked as though he hadn't shaved his spotty beard in days. A wooden disc painted black and ringed with red at the edge hung from a leather thong around his neck— the makeshift symbol of Mask that many of the guild's members had taken to wearing. Riven managed not to strangle him with it. Barely.

"Fek," Riven replied with a nod. "Norwyl."

Norwyl too wore the black disc about his neck. A nervous little man even shorter than Riven. Norwyl gestured at the knucklebones on the floor.

"Join us?" he asked halfheartedly. "Fek could use a change in his luck."

"Piss off," Fek said.

"No," Riven briskly replied and pushed past them. He thought about killing them both, a sort of going-away present for the guild, but decided against it. They'd be dead soon enough. "I'm leaving for a few days," he announced. "Business for the Man."

Without waiting for a reply, he pulled up the dirty carpet—scattering the coins and dice—to expose a trapdoor with an iron pull ring. Norwyl and Fek merely watched, shifted from foot to foot, and said nothing further—they knew better than to ask him about his business or complain about the spilled coins. He had killed many men for much less.

He jerked the trapdoor open and wrinkled his nose at the stink of old sewage that raced up his nostrils. Without a glance at the two guards, he lowered himself over the side and slid down the rusty iron ladder. Halfway down, Norwyl's head appeared above him, framed in the candlelight. The guildsman's wooden holy symbol dangled from his neck, slowly twisted in the air. "Mask's favor," he called.

"Luck to you too," Riven grunted insincerely. You'll need it, he silently added.

With that, Norwyl slammed the trapdoor shut.

Riven, familiar with this exit, descended the rest of the ladder in darkness. When he reached the muck-covered floor, he took out his tinderbox, struck a flame, and lit a candle taken from his belt pouch. Surprised by the sudden light, rats squeaked and scurried for the comforting dark.

Riven pulled his crimson cloak close against the chill, shielded the small flame with one hand, and headed westward for the well exit onto Winding Way. As he walked, he replayed the events of the night in his head. *It is regrettable that Cale is not here to share this triumph,* the Righteous Man had said. Riven frowned thoughtfully. Regrettable indeed. Hearing

Cale scream as the dread devoured him would have been the sweetest triumph of all.

❂ ❂ ❂ ❂ ❂

Yrsillar pushed the squealing soul of the Righteous Man into a dark corner of the mind they now shared. He smiled in satisfaction. The feel of pliable, fleshy lips—his lips!—peeling back over spit-wet teeth exhilarated him. He disdainfully wiped the snot and spittle from his new face and held his hand before his eyes for examination. He frowned when he saw that the spotted, wrinkled flesh of this body covered muscles and bones weakened with age.

Testing their limits, he repeatedly clenched and unclenched the fists of his new body, clawed the air, bent at the knees, twisted at the torso, and finally hopped up and down. Afterward, he hissed in satisfaction.

Though old, the body remained fit. Indeed, fit enough to contain Yrsillar's being and still provide a living shell that protected his emptiness from this plane. He felt no pain! None!

He reached his hands toward the ceiling and laughed, deep and long, a sound so full of power and malice that the true occupant of the body could never have produced it. The soul of the Righteous Man squirmed helplessly in its dark corner and Yrsillar laughed the more.

He had waited long for this day, centuries. Once before he had been summoned here. Over six hundred years ago as mortals measured time, a drow mage named Avarix had called his true name and drawn him here, had bound him and required for his freedom that he slay every member of a rival household. Yrsillar had done so without compunction, reveled in the massacre, fed greedily on drow souls, but screamed in pain all the while. The energy of this plane ate away like acid at his being, burning, searing.

He had felt the scars of that first summoning for years, even after he had won his freedom from accursed Avarix. Throughout the long healing process, he had brooded, plotted. The lure of this place had pulled at him. A plane so full of life, so full of *food*. He had longed to return and gorge himself, but the unavoidable pain that accompanied his existence here had made such a return inconceivable. Inconceivable that was, until he had struck upon the simplest of solutions—possess a living mortal body and use its flesh to shield him from the poison that flooded this plane. With that plan in mind, he had nursed his hate, and waited patiently for another summons.

At last the call had come. This fool called the Righteous Man had cast a summoning and pronounced his true name. The powerful word had sped instantly through the intervening planes and resounded in Yrsillar's ears as though spoken beside him. Gleefully, he had leaped upon the power thread and traced it back to this plane, his hunger for living souls lending him speed. Again however, he had found himself properly bound! His ingenious plan to possess his mortal summoner and remain here to feed caved in around him. Or nearly so. The other human had broken the binding and freed him.

He laughed and danced a gleeful little jig. As he did, his eyes fell on the Shadowtome, the hated book that held within its pages not only his true name, but also the *proper* way to bind him. What mortal had dared scribe such a thing? Avarix? Wretched book! Wretched drow!

"Rrrar!" He kicked over the lectern and knocked the book to the floor. Enraged, he stomped on it again and again, jumping up and down in a paroxysm of rage. A tendon in his calf snapped, but he ignored the twinge.

"Never! Never again!"

He ground the book into the floor with his heel until its torn, crumpled pages lay strewn about the room like blown leaves. "Never again," he said, gasping. Fatigue was new to him. He rather disliked the sensation.

To assuage the feeling, he drank a small part of the Righteous Man's soul for the first time. The tiny, fearful thing squirmed and tried to back away when it sensed Yrsillar turn inward and come for it, but its terror only whetted his appetite. He sipped from the top of the soul as a human would a fine liquor, savoring, taking delight in the horrified squeals of the Righteous Man's being. As he drank, the memories, thoughts, and experiences of the human—the events that had shaped the soul—played out in his mind's eye. The short, irrelevant life of the Righteous Man flashed through Yrsillar's mind in the space of three heartbeats. He mocked its insignificance, enjoyed the failure of its lofty aspirations.

"A priest of Mask the *Shadowlord*," he softly said to the walls, thinking aloud. "How very ironic. And with a loyal guild at your command. At *my* command," he corrected.

The beginnings of a plan took shape in his mind. The soul of the Righteous Man sensed his scheme and squealed in protest. As discipline, Yrsillar drew off still more of the human's life-force, sucked a writhing, twisting portion of it into his being. "Mind now," he said with a vicious grin. "Mind, or I'll have the rest."

The soul retreated, weakened, defeated.

"Take heart," Yrsillar mocked. "Though you'll not become the Champion of Mask, neither will the two you had thought your rivals for the honor." He laughed aloud, a deep sinister sound that bounced off the walls. The Righteous Man's soul curled in on itself, horrified. Yrsillar thought of Mask's discomfiture in Hades and smiled. "So much too for *your* lofty aspirations, Shadow-lord," he mocked.

To execute his plan, he would need more of his kind, lesser dreads that could exist on this plane without pain. Together, they would lead these shadow mongering Mask worshipers in an orgy of slaughter. He glee-fully pictured the bloodletting to come and laughed still more.

With an exercise of will, he brought a gate to Belistor into existence. An empty hole formed in the air above the toppled lectern. Hisses and moans sounded through the gate, music to Yrsillar's ears, a reminder of his home plane.

"Araniskeel and Greeve," he softly hissed. "Come forth."

Instantly, four yellow pinpoints of light took shape within the emptiness and drew closer. Shadows coalesced around the gate, solidified into clawed, winged shapes similar to, but smaller than, Yrsillar's natural form. The two shadows streaked from the gate and screamed their malice into the air of the chamber.

"Welcome, little brethren," hissed Yrsillar.

Despite his human shell, they recognized him immediately. Obsequious as always, they bowed and fawned, flitted about his person like moths. With only slight ties to the plane of unlife, these lesser dreads felt no pain from this plane. Perfect tools to bring him power and food.

"Yrsillar calls and we answer."

"Great Yrsillar, what is your will?"

"My will is to rule and to feed," he pronounced. "And this plane is my realm and table."

"Feed," they hissed in echo. "Feed."

Yrsillar smiled, smoothed his velvet robe, and gestured expansively. "You look upon the servant of Mask," he announced.

Their yellow eyes narrowed quizzically and he began to laugh. "In good time, little brethren. For now, there is much to be done. Then we shall feed."

"Feed," they hissed eagerly. "Feed."

CHAPTER 2

JAK FLEET

Silently bemoaning his three-and-a-half foot tall halfling body as *too damned inefficient for climbing*, Jak slid over the cold stone of the inner wall and soundlessly dropped to the snow-dusted flagstones of the courtyard. There he crouched, listening. To his left, he heard the murmur of voices, though a forest of statuary blocked the source. The sounds grew steadily louder with each beat of his heart. Guards approaching, he assumed. But relaxed guards to judge from their easy tone. They hadn't seen him. He bit his lip to swallow a mischievous grin—in the darkness, a flash of teeth could reveal him to an observer as easily as a wave and a shout.

He congratulated himself on his success

thus far. The defenses in the outer yard off Stoekandlar Street had presented him with only scant challenge. The lax guards were easily bypassed and the minor alarming wards were easily dispelled. He expected things to become more difficult now that he had neared the Soargyl manse proper. To that end, he had cast a spell that allowed him to endure cold so that he could shed his heavy winter cloak. The spell would last for over an hour. Plenty of time.

With the guards drawing nearer, he ducked into the darkness behind a marble sculpture of a rearing manticore and silently waited. His heart raced from excitement, not fear, but he managed to remain perfectly still. Selune had set hours ago. Except for the flaming brands borne by the guards, only the soft gold and red light of glow spells—minor magic used to illuminate and highlight the more impressive statues—dispelled the pitch of night.

When two bobbing torch flames suddenly came into view from across the courtyard and approached his location Jak melted fully into the darkness.

The green and gold liveried guards who held the brands talked casually to one another as they carefully wended their way through the maze of fountains, life-sized sculptures, decorative urns, and ornate topiary. Moving slowly toward the raised, paved walkway that ran along the inner wall and encircled the courtyard, they drew so close to Jak that he could hear the soft chinking of their chain mail, could see the frost clouds blown from their mouths and nostrils, and could make out their conversation. He tried to sink deeper into the darkness as the guards' torchlight illumined a suggestive satyr and nymph fountain five paces to his left.

". . . didn't get much sleep yesterday," the younger of the two was saying. A scraggly, frost-covered mustache clung to his upper lip. Dark circles painted the skin beneath his tired eyes.

"Ha," laughed his companion, an older, balding guard. "Larra the cooking girl keeping you up late, I'll wager." He thumped his comrade on the back. "We should all have such problems, Cobb."

Jak mentally targeted each of them—just in case. If they spotted him, he would use a spell to immobilize them. Fleshy statues among the marbles. Then . . .

Then what? he wondered.

He didn't know for sure what he would do if this went bad, but he *did know* that he would leave no corpses in his wake. Not tonight. Tonight was a holy night of sorts, not a night for killing.

Watching the guards closely from behind the manticore's hindquarters, he prepared to cast the spell.

"No, no, it's not like that," protested the young man. "She nags, and I mean *nags*. Constantly."

Though they passed within a short dagger toss of the statue he crouched behind, they barely even looked in his direction. Swords sat idle in scabbards. Cursory glances checked the shadows. Dim torchlight passed over him. They talked so loudly they wouldn't have heard him if he snapped his fingers. Their boots beat a rhythm on the walkway as they marched away.

"With her body," replied the older, "I could tolerate some nagging. As long as . . ."

Their conversation drifted away. Watching them go, Jak shook his head in astonishment. What incompetence! If he had been the sort, he could easily have killed them both before either knew what had happened. The Soargyls need to hire better guards, he thought, and tried to ward off a flash of disappointment. Perhaps this job wouldn't be as challenging as he had hoped after all. The guards behaved as though they were irrelev—

The realization hit him like a slap on the cheek. A knowing grin split his face and he patted the manticore on the rump. That's because they *are* irrelevant.

Excitedly, he removed from his belt pouch his current holy symbol—a bejeweled snuffbox taken from a Red Wizard of Thay exactly one year ago tonight. Intoning in a whisper, he cast a spell that enabled him to see enchantments and magical dweomers. The stronger the enchantment, the brighter it glowed in his eyes. When he completed the spell, he looked around the courtyard and let out a low whistle. Trickster's hairy toes!

So many spells glowed in the courtyard that they looked like the campfires of an orc horde. Enchantments littered the grounds from end to end—this statue, this fountain, this seemingly empty patch of ground. No wonder the guards restricted their patrols to the outer walkway. It would be impossible for them to remember where all the spells lay. If they patrolled the inner courtyard, the Soargyls would have magical pyrotechnics and dead house guards nearly every night.

The two guards that had just passed him must follow a predetermined route from the manse to reach the wall perimeter, where, he saw, there were no spells. He reprimanded himself for not paying closer attention to their path. He could have followed in their footsteps and saved himself some trouble.

Ah, well, he thought with a grin, saving yourself trouble is not how you work. "Or you either," he whispered to Brandobaris the Trickster.

Many of the enchantments revealed by his spell must have served only harmless utilitarian purposes— the glow spells, for example, or spells that protected a sculpture from the weather, or made an iced-over fountain shimmer in the moonlight. But at least some of them *had* to be alarms or wards, and his spell was not sensitive enough to tell the difference. Fortunately, his spell did allow him to discern the *really* dangerous enchantments. They glowed with a bright, red-orange intensity that indicated powerful magic and promised an ugly end to anyone who triggered them. No mere alarm spells, those. Most had been cast on the valuable pieces, so that anyone moving a sculpture without uttering the safety word would trigger the spell and find himself aflame, paralyzed, or electrocuted. One such spell protected the satyr fountain beside him, he saw. It had been pure luck that he had hidden behind the unprotected manticore and not the fountain.

He grinned, blew out a cloud of breath, and tapped the agate luck stone that hung from a silver chain at his belt. "The Lady favors the reckless," he whispered, to invoke Tymora's blessing, and followed it quickly with, "and the Trickster favors the *short* and reckless." He stifled a giggle, gave his holy symbol a squeeze, and replaced it in his belt pouch. As he did, he muttered, "This is your last dance, old friend." After tonight, he would make an offering of the snuffbox to Brandobaris and use an item taken from tonight's job as a new holy symbol.

Worshiping the Trickster makes for some interesting evenings, he thought wryly. Each year, Brandobaris required him to sacrifice his current holy symbol and acquire a new one with feats of derring-do. The nature of the item itself did not matter much—though protocol and Jak's pride demanded that it be valuable—so long as he acquired it through a risky endeavor undertaken on this night.

Before tonight, he had hoped that lifting a snuffbox from the pocket of a Thayan Red Wizard in the midst of spellcasting would have earned him a year off from this divine silliness, but to no avail.

So here he was, at the Soargyl manse—Sarntrumpet Towers. He had decided to hit Sarntrumpet because of the reputed brutality of Lord Boarim Soargyl. If he were caught stealing here, he knew he would not be turned over to the city authorities—in the city of Selgaunt, the nobles wielded their own authority. No, if he were caught here, he knew Lord Soargyl would have him tortured and executed. His body would be dumped into the frozen water of Selgaunt Bay and some fisherman would find his corpse days later, if the sharks didn't get to it first.

"That risky enough for you?" he whispered into the air. He waited, but the Trickster made no answer. He sniffed in good-natured derision, gracefully climbed atop the head of the manticore he had used for cover, and studied the courtyard from above.

Though winter, only a light coating of snow dusted the flagstones. A labyrinth of fountains, statues, pillars, and decorative urns dotted the stone yard, some aglow with magic, some not. From above, the courtyard looked even more a forest of stone than it did from ground level. All of the sculptures and urns were of the finest workmanship and materials—the abundance of jade, ivory, and precious metals had Jak fairly slavering. The haphazard placement of the artwork left him with the impression that the pieces had been tossed randomly about in a snowstorm and left where they landed.

An artist with style buys for the Soargyls, he thought, but a tasteless clod does the decorating. Probably Lady Soargyl herself, he speculated. Mora Soargyl was a big woman reputed to be a bit like a dwarf when it came to fashion—lots of wealth, little grace, and even less taste.

Still, the price of any one of these urns would have

kept Jak in coin for a month. But that's not why I'm here, he reminded himself.

Surrounded on all sides by the tasteless artistic trappings of Soargyl wealth, Sarntrumpet's squat towers jutted out of the center of the courtyard like five thick stone fingers. Crimson tiles shingled the roofs of each spire, blood red in the starlight. As with everything in the courtyard, the manse was built entirely of stone—marble, granite, and limestone mostly—with wood used only as necessary and evergreen shrubbery absent altogether. The few windows cut into the stark exterior were dark—bottomless mouths screaming from the stone. Hideous gargoyles chiseled from granite perched atop the roof eaves and stared ominously down on the courtyard.

To Jak, the grounds evoked the image of a grand cemetery surrounding a great mausoleum, or one of the cities of the dead built around an emperor's tomb like those he had heard about in tales of distant Mulhorand.

He had approached the manse from the back, so he could not see the main entrance. A few outbuildings stood in a cluster in the northwest corner—a stable and servants' quarters, he assumed.

From atop the manticore, he had a full view of the perimeter walkway that surrounded the courtyard and saw that not one, but three pairs of torch-bearing guards patrolled it. Not only that, but a full squad of guards in heavy cloaks patrolled around the manse itself. The Trickster only knew how many more men were within.

Could be worse, he thought with a grin, and jumped down from his marble perch.

Still using the magical vision granted him by his spell, he determined a safe path through the enchantments. Always alert to the location of the guards, he darted from shadow to shadow, from pillar to fountain, until he stood amidst a tight cluster of tall statues within fifty paces of the manse. Close enough that Sarntrumpet itself stood within the range of his spell, he saw that the high windows also shone with enchantments, though the actual tower walls did not. He nodded knowingly, having expected as much. There was too much wall space to protect it all with spells, but windows provided access for flying wizards and climbing thieves. Only a fool left them unprotected.

He focused his attention on the central tower, the tallest of the bunch by over two stories. The great spire was windowless on this side except for three expansive, closely packed panes near its top. All three glowed with the bright, red-orange light of powerful magic. That has to be the place, he thought, while he eyed the sheer walls critically.

He had not come into this job unprepared. Though he worshiped Brandobaris—the halfling god of rogues who ran pell-mell into the Abyss itself and still managed to escape with his hide—he nevertheless made it a habit to plan carefully before taking risks.

Because you're a god, and I'm a man, he thought, and hoped his oft-repeated phrase justified his habitual caution in the Trickster's eyes.

Since he wanted his new holy symbol to be an item taken from the very bedchamber of the brutal Lord Soargyl himself—a bedchamber whose location within Sarntrumpet Towers was hardly public knowledge—he had for the previous two tendays sprinkled coins and discreet inquiries among the city's architects. When that idea had failed to produce any useful information, he had ruefully decided to rely on the unpredictable humor of the Trickster. Before setting out this evening, he had cast a divination spell and requested the location of the bedchamber. The response from Brandobaris that popped into his head had been surprisingly frank, if a bit overwrought:

> *Through darkness thick, and dire-filled gloom,*
> *Where danger lurks, and shadows loom,*
> *In tallest spire that stabs the sky, within is where the treasures lie.*

He smiled and sat back on his haunches under the watchful eyes of a marble swordsman. The Trickster had given him the location, but it was up to Jak to get in. *And out,* he reminded himself.

He sat casually under the statue, eyed the guard patrols as they circled the manse, and tried to time their routes. While he watched, he took the time to relish the moment and congratulate himself on his skills. The Trickster had set him a hard task, but he had proven himself up to the challenge, as usual.

While waiting for the guard patrol to complete its circuit around the manse, he studied Sarntrumpet and tried to guess at its internal layout from its external features. It did not surprise him that Lord Soargyl had chosen the highest spire in the manse for his bedroom. Nobles in Selgaunt were notoriously arrogant, and Lord Soargyl was reputedly worse than most. Only a room that looked down on the rest of the city's citizens would satisfy his ego.

Strangely enough, Selgaunt's rogues typically respected the city's strict social hierarchy. Thieves only rarely tried to infiltrate a noble's home. Not only was such a thing likely to fail and result in an ugly death for the thief—at least for those less lucky and skilled than Jak—it simply *wasn't done*. The manses of the nobility were treated as sacrosanct. There were exceptions, of course—the Night Masks under the Righteous Man, for example. And me, he thought with a smile.

Unlike most native Sembians, Jak resolutely refused to play by Selgaunt's unwritten rules—he ran as an independent rogue in a gang-dominated underworld. He prided himself on his halfling blood in a city that held halflings in barely concealed contempt. He thought that respecting nobles simply because of their titles and bloodlines was among the silliest things he had ever heard.

Feeling self-satisfied and pining for his pipe, he leaned back against the pedestal of a statue and blew out imaginary smoke rings. Sandwiched between the guards stationed at the manse and the guards on the walkway, the inner courtyard provided a kind of thieves' sanctuary, if one could avoid the alarm spells—which he had.

He smiled and pushed his hair back from his face. Thirsty, he took out a leather skin and had a gulp of water. Around him loomed the towering marble figures. All stood upon stocky square pedestals and had a nameplate inset. Unable to read, Jak could not tell what they said. Not for the first time, he reminded himself to ask Cale to teach him. That bald giant reads nine languages, he thought, marveling. Nine! He shook his head in disbelief.

He ran his fingers along the nameplates and imagined what they might say. Most of the statues were of armored men holding swords aloft in victory, though some seemed posed in the midst of ferocious combat with an unseen foe. Jak assumed them to be representations of past Soargyl patriarchs.

He eyed the statues critically. Judging from their heroic proportions, the Soargyls of old had been impressively built men; either that, or the sculptor had been paid to take some creative, and flattering, liberties. More likely the latter.

The green cloaked squad of twelve house guards again trooped around the corner of the manse, mail clinking, boots thumping. The moment they appeared, Jak began a mental count. Then he waited, counting all the while. By the time they had retraced their route and again come around the same corner, he had reached one hundred and forty-seven, and his seeing spell had expired. He had plenty of time.

He waited for the guards to vanish around the far side of the manse again before making his move. As soon as the last of the men disappeared around the far corner, he began his count. *One, two . . .* he bade the dead Soargyls farewell, darted from the shadows, and raced to the base of the central tower. *Seventeen, eighteen . . .* there he crouched low, peering into the darkness behind him. No one. Sarntrumpet Towers was as lifeless as a tomb.

Why would people surround themselves with nothing but dead stone? he wondered, followed immediately by a whispered oath. "Dark." He had lost his count.

He grinned sheepishly. His Harper colleagues would not have been surprised. A worldwide organization of diverse operators, the Harpers worked behind the scenes to thwart the schemes of various evil-minded factions. Though he had worn the Harper pin for over six winters, Jak still had a reputation among them as a bit of a stray quarrel. If they had known of it, they would not have appreciated his burglary tonight. It was too risky.

Ah well, he thought, and gazed up the face of the sheer central tower. The Harpers could afford to take some more risks.

Jak had joined the organization because they tried

to do *good*, and because he approved of their methods. Where possible, the Harpers tried to influence events using only political pressure. They resorted to killing only when deemed necessary and justified. Someday he hoped to sponsor his friend Erevis Cale for membership, but for now, he knew Cale was not ready. The big man turned too readily to blood. The Harpers would not approve of that. Cale would fit into the organization even less well than Jak.

For years Jak had felt torn between his friendship with Cale and his membership in the Harpers. He thought Cale a good man, but a man who killed at the slightest provocation. He disliked that about his friend. Yet he knew that Cale would *always* stand by him, and that he liked. He wasn't so sure he could say the same about the Harpers. Especially if they had known about tonight's little job.

Over one hundred feet up, the trio of windows beckoned.

Jak grimaced. He would not make *that* climb without magical assistance—risk taking was one thing, stupidity another. Hurriedly, he pulled off his boots, took from his belt pouch the snuffbox holy symbol, and began to incant. Though it seemed to take an eternity, the guards did not reappear before he finished the casting. Upon completion, his hands and furry bare feet became sticky, as though he had dunked them in cobbler's glue. "This should make things easier," he whispered, and planted his hands on the granite wall.

With his extremities now adhering to the stone, he began to rapidly ascend. Twenty feet up, he heard the boot tramp of the approaching guards below him.

One forty seven, he thought in dismay, and flattened himself against the tower. The squad rounded the corner and marched nearer.

Uncomfortably, he recalled the last time he had been caught hanging along the face of a building—he and Cale had been dangling from a rope with Zhent crossbow quarrels and lightning bolts buzzing past their ears. He hoped this time turned out better.

The guards walked right below him, the clank of their armor and an occasional spoken command loud in his ears. He held his breath and sent a silent prayer winging to the Trickster: Don't let them look up and no more wise-ass comments, I promise.

Though the face of the tower was unlit, he knew he could not be hard to see. A single keen-eyed guard glancing up the tower. . . .

They walked directly under him and he felt every thump of his heart like a drumbeat. They would see him. They had to.

They didn't! They walked under and passed him by!

He held his breath until they rounded the far corner of the manse then blew it out in a frosty, relieved sigh. Not bothering to keep another count, he sped spiderlike up the face of the tower until he reached the cluster of windows near the top. The wind ruffled his shirt and pants but his spell prevented a fall.

Unable to touch the windows for fear of triggering the protective spells, he moved from one to the other, held his nose a fingerwidth from the thick glass, and tried to peer through. Only nobles could afford glass windows instead of shutters—and Jak cursed Lord Soargyl for it. Through the smoky glass of each he could see only darkness beyond. Any one of them could be Lord Soargyl's bedroom, or the guards' mess hall.

I'll just have to pick one and trust to Lady Fortune, he thought. At that, he fancied he heard the Trickster's laughter tinkling on the night breeze. Grinning despite himself, he skirted wide of the windows and climbed up to the red-tiled roof. From there, he had a panoramic view of the city, and it astounded him.

Selgaunt stretched before him as though a giant had unrolled a great carpet made of stone blocks. Row after row of night shrouded, snow-dusted buildings extended to the limits of his vision. Braziers and street torches dotted the avenues even at this late hour, motionless orange fireflies suspended in a sea of black. He turned to see starlight glistening off the whitecaps in Selgaunt Bay. Cargo ships and icebreakers crowded the docks, their masts a forest of timber framed against the night sky and dark water. The cold breeze carried the salt tang of the Inner Sea. Again he found himself wishing for a smoke. Next time, he vowed. From now on, I bring my pipe on all jobs.

He allowed himself another moment of enjoyment before recalling his business. He willed his sticky spell to expire, freeing his extremities from the awkward magical adhesive, and again removed his holy symbol from his pouch. Intoning in a whisper, he recast the spell that allowed him to see dweomers. He lay flat on his stomach and carefully crept headfirst down the sloped roof until he had his head and neck extended beyond the overhang. The precipitous drop dizzied him momentarily, but he bore it, remaining perfectly still until his body regained its equilibrium.

"This dangerous enough for you?" he mouthed through gritted teeth. Oops, he reprimanded himself, I promised no more wise-ass comments. He muttered an apology to the Trickster and studied the windows.

Up close with the seeing spell, he saw now that all three glowed orange-red with *numerous* dweomers. There's something important in there, he thought, excited.

He dug his toes into the roof tiles for stability, freed his hands for casting, and recited the incantation for yet another spell, this one a powerful magic that attempted to unravel and dispel the magic of other spellcasters. When he completed his spell, he felt a surge of energy burst from his body and attack the spells on the windows. He watched as his own power warred with that of the caster of the protective spells, whoever that was. Jak witnessed his power triumph and the red-orange glow around the windows winked out.

"Gotcha," he chuckled. Before righting himself, he cast another spell on the now unprotected windows to create a globe of silence centered on the ornate stone sills. No sound would pass in, out, or through the area affected by the spell.

He awkwardly backed up, stood, and shook the stiffness from his arms and legs. He looked down over the roof edge to see the house guard patrol making another round of the grounds. From this height they looked like a single organism snaking around the manse. He waited for them to pass. Ready, he pulled a dagger from his belt and gripped it in his teeth.

Now, for the really hard part.

With a light touch on his luckstone and a final whispered prayer to Brandobaris, he lay flat on his belly and backed feet first toward the roof edge. His heart began to race when his feet slid off the roof and hung loose over open air, but he continued to back up, slow and easy. He bent at the waist and felt around the tower's face with his foot—again cursing his small stature—until his toes found a secure hold in the craggy wall. Carefully, he placed his weight upon it—now praising his small stature and scant weight—then did the same with his other foot. Bracing himself with his feet, he eased his upper body over the roof overhang. His fingers reached for and found cracks in the granite blocks as he went. His heart leaped in his

chest when he finally hung suspended from the wall—
no rope, no spell, no anything. A strong wind off the
bay could blow him off. He didn't dare look to the earth
below.

Burn me, he thought to the Trickster, but if this
doesn't satisfy you, I quit. He suppressed a giggle—it
wouldn't do to shake with laughter with a hundred-
odd foot drop below him—and inched down and left-
ward toward the center windowsill. When he got close
to it, he came within the effect of the silence spell. The
whistle of the wind suddenly fell silent, his rasping
breath and occasional grunt made no sound, and the
struggle of his callused feet gripping stone became
noiseless.

He lowered himself to the wide sill and steadied
himself atop it. A sudden gust of wind ruffled his hair
and rocked him. He reached for the stone, caught himself, and tried to steady his racing heart. "Dark," he
oathed. "Dark."

He waited, perfectly still, until his heartbeat slowed.
Calm now, he crouched, gripped the sill with one hand,
took the dagger from his mouth, and smashed the hilt
into the window. Soundlessly, the thick glass veined
with a spider web of cracks but remained otherwise
intact. Come on, dammit, he cursed.

He hit it again, harder this time, and the pane
silently shattered. He leaped through the opening as
quickly as he dared, careful to avoid cutting his feet on
the broken glass.

Still smiling on the foolish, Lady, he thought upon
landing, and tapped his luckstone. I appreciate that.

The window he had chosen didn't open into a mess
hall or a bedroom, where the sudden gust of winter air
would have awakened sleepers, but into a sitting room.
A single closed oak door stood opposite the window,
while a double door beckoned to his left. Soft firelight

spilled through the half-open double doors from the room beyond.

In contrast to the stark exterior of the manse, the sitting room fairly stank of soft opulence. A thick red carpet covered most of the floor. On it stood two richly upholstered divans and a leather covered sofa surrounding a carved teakwood table with a leaded glass top. Bronze candelabra taller than Jak stood in each corner, their beeswax candles unlit. A hearth with a masterfully crafted mantle of carved marble sat in the east wall, its coals still aglow. Valuable gold and silver knickknacks were piled atop both table and mantle but Jak admired them only with his eyes—he had come for just one item, a personal token stolen from under the very nose of Lord Soargyl.

Clashing linen throws lay scattered haphazardly about the furniture and floor as though thrown about by a strong wind. Jak grinned and shook his head, again stunned by Lady Soargyl's garish taste. He may have been a thief, but he was a thief who prided himself on *style*.

He lightly tapped his knuckle on the table to determine whether he still stood within the effect of his silence spell. He did. Careful to disturb nothing, he walked across the carpet to the far wall of the room. He enjoyed the feel of the thick fibers on his bare toes.

He knew the moment he emerged from the silence spell because snores as loud as a boar's snorts assaulted his ears from behind the double doors. He covered his mouth to stifle the laugh that rose in his throat. I can only hope that those are from Lord, and not Lady Soargyl, he thought mischievously.

After composing himself, he glided to the open door and peeked through. Light from a low burning fire illuminated the large Soargyl bedroom. Jak allowed himself a moment of self-satisfaction for having read

Brandobaris's augury correctly. *Within is where the treasures lie.*

A bronze-framed canopy bed sat in the center of the room. Through the hanging linens and piles of blankets, Jak could see the vague outlines of two sleeping forms. A cushion topped-chest sat at the bed's foot. To his right, a wardrobe and dressing screen. To his left, the dressing tables.

Though he knew he could have stomped across the floor and not awakened anyone who could sleep through *that* snoring, he nevertheless squeezed through the door and prowled silently around the room. Keeping his ears attuned to any change in the snoring that might indicate a sleeper beginning to awaken, he quietly hopped onto the top of the dressing table, kneeled, and moved methodically through the items he found there.

He discarded as unsuitable a silver buckle and a pair of engraved gold bracers. The item he chose had to be just right. He finally settled on a silver cloak pin shaped like an eagle's talon inset with a single tourmaline. Perfect, he thought, and dropped it in his belt pouch. Now for the final touch. He whispered the words to an incantation and the image of a long-stemmed pipe, with its embers softly aglow and smoke wisps rising gently from the ivory bowl, took shape on the dressing table—the calling card Jak left behind at all his jobs.

Style, good Lady, he thought, with a nod and smile at the bed. Style. Still grinning, he hopped to the floor—and froze in his tracks.

A feeling of stark terror stopped him. His breath caught in his lungs. Weak-kneed, he stumbled backward and bumped into the dressing table. Resisting the urge to hide his face behind his hands, he watched as an emptiness, a darkness blacker than pitch, boiled through the same bedroom door he had just entered.

His heart hammered painfully in his chest. The darkness roiled like a living thing, coalesced, and finally solidified into the shape of a tall, featureless, black humanoid. Waves of palpable hate radiated from it like heat from the hearth. Batlike wings sprouted from its back, the span as wide as half the room. Two dagger points of light formed in its face, yellow beads filled with malice.

Jak recoiled into the shadows, sinking slowly to the floor, his eyes involuntarily glued to the creature—not a creature, a demon! A demon! His breath came in short, fearful heaves that he struggled desperately to control. He tried to meld with the wood of the dresser and prayed that those evil yellow eyes did not spy him. Please, please. Some distant part of his consciousness yelled at him to do something, anything—a Harper should do something!—but his body seemed made of lead.

The demon hovered in the doorway and considered the Soargyl bed. Though it flew, its great wings flapped only occasionally and without wind. Lord Soargyl's snores continued unabated.

Shut up! Jak thought irrationally. Shut up! It'll hear you. But the demon had already noticed the sleeping couple, and it went for them.

With terrifying speed, the shadowy horror darted to the foot of the bed. It hovered outside the transparent canopy for a moment with its head cocked curiously to the side, as though studying the Soargyls. Its yellow eyes flared eagerly. Jak could sense it slavering, could sense the killer allowing its anticipation to build before the satisfaction of the slaughter. He wanted to scream but could not find his breath. He could only watch, transfixed by horror.

Two overlong black arms, each corded with shadowy muscle, formed from the demon's body. The arms ended in vicious claws as long as a man's fingers. With a gentle grace horrible to witness—for Jak knew the butchery that would surely follow—the demon extended a thin arm and parted the linens that shielded the Soargyl bed. Silent tears formed in Jak's eyes and began to run down his face.

Do something, he ordered himself. Do something, dammit! But he could not. He loathed himself for doing nothing, but fear of attracting the demon's attention froze him to inaction. He gripped his holy symbol cloak-clasp so tightly the metal dug painfully into his palm. Don't wake up, he prayed for the Soargyls. Please don't wake up. Silent prayer was all he could bring himself to do for them.

The demon glided under the canopy and hovered over the bed, looking down on the sleepers. It held its wings and clawed arms outstretched, as though to embrace the Soargyls, to envelop them in emptiness. Lord Soargyl snorted, mumbled something, and rolled toward his wife. His snores quickly renewed, an almost comical funeral liturgy.

As the demon stared down at the Soargyls, Jak could literally feel its tension building, its hate growing. Stay sleeping, he prayed. Please gods, let them stay asleep. No one should have to die staring into the face of a nightmare.

The demon reached down and extended a claw toward the sleepers. Jak sensed its insatiable hunger. The shadowy claw seemed to tremble in eager anticipation as it neared their flesh. It will finish them quickly, he thought. His guts roiled at the thought of the slaughter. They'll be dead before they ever wake up. He took some small solace in that.

The demon reared back and raised its claw high to slay—

And suddenly stopped, thoughtful.

No! No! Do it! Do it, godsdammit! He almost said the words aloud.

As though sensing Jak's silent pleas, the demon lowered its claw and turned its baleful yellow eyes in his direction. His heart stopped. He tried to sink farther into the shadows. Them first, he thought, hating himself for a coward but unable to stop the thought. Them first.

The demon turned back to the Soargyls and Jak's heart began again to beat. Cold sweat now mixed with silent tears. You're a coward, he accused himself. A damned coward.

Rather than raising a claw to strike, the demon instead reached down and gently caressed the cheek of Lord Soargyl.

Bastard, Jak cursed it through his fear. He realized then that it fed on terror as much as blood. It wanted its prey awake.

The demon's dire touch jerked Lord Soargyl from sleep. Lady Soargyl, too, began to stir. The burly lord sat bolt upright in bed to find himself face to face with hungry yellow eyes and a darkness as empty as the Void. "Huh? What the—" He reached instinctively for a nonexistent sword but found only nightclothes.

His first thought was to fight, Jak cursed himself. Mine was to hide. Tears poured unabated down his face now, for he saw terror take shape in Lord Soargyl's wide eyes. "Hel—" Lord Soargyl started to shout.

Casually, the demon flashed its claw and tore open a gash in his throat, a ragged hole so wide that it nearly severed his head. The bed should have been awash in a fountain of blood, but inexplicably the wound did not bleed. Wide-eyed with terror, Lord Soargyl gurgled and pawed futilely at the tear in his throat, trying desperately to keep his head attached to his neck. His body began to convulse.

"Ahg, arg, agh." Foam flecked his mouth and a gray vapor gushed from the wound. Eagerly, the demon devoured it. As it feasted on the vapor, it seemed to grow larger, more substantial.

It's his soul, Jak thought in terror. It eats souls.

Lord Soargyl's body began to shrink then, to implode until it was little more than an unrecognizable mass of wrinkled flesh. No sounds emerged from his open, screaming mouth.

Lady Soargyl at last came fully awake, sat up, saw the leering eyes of the demon, and began to scream. Her terrified wail pierced Jak's soul and freed him from his paralysis.

"Boarim, Boarim!" She shook the shrunken remains of her husband and Boarim Soargyl's body crumbled into dried hunks. She pulled back as though burned, screaming and crying the desperate keen of the hopeless. Before Jak could move to intervene, the demon picked her up from the bed and drew her near. A big woman, she kicked and shouted in protest, but the thing held her body aloft.

"No! Please! Please!" The demon ended her screams by tearing her open from navel to sternum and devouring the vapor of her soul, filling its emptiness with the life it had stolen.

While it fed, Jak found his wits enough to whisper the words to a spell that rendered him invisible.

The guards have to be coming, he told himself. They heard her and now they're coming. But they hadn't come yet, and the demon finished with Lady Soargyl all too soon. It playfully squeezed the husk of her body and the corpse exploded into a rain of dried pieces that fell to the bed, intermixing with the pieces of her husband. Without a backward glance, it flowed toward the door—

It stopped.

Jak's heart stopped too. It senses me, he realized. Dark, but it senses me!

The living shadow turned and raised its head, sniffing the air like a hound. Its eyes narrowed thoughtfully and it looked back toward the dressing table. Silently, holding his breath, Jak tried to back away toward the far corner of the room, near the hearth. He froze when the demon darted toward him, quick as a cat. Though it could not see him, it knew he was there. It prowled around the corner of the room, holding its arms and wings out, feeling for its prey. Jak fought off tears as the demon's claws swept through space and drove him inexorably backward. The thump of his back against the wall made him squeak in terror. With nowhere to run, he held his holy symbol to his chest, tight.

The demon continued to sniff for him, drew nearer. Sweat poured from him by the bucketful. Surely the thing could hear his heart! It stood right before him now and he could do nothing but wait for death. Fear washed over him. He watched it sniffing, sniffing, its evil eyes searching. Jak's hair stood on end and he felt so cold that his teeth nearly chattered.

Suddenly, the demon looked down on him with eyes that bored into his soul like daggers. *There you are*, said a soft voice in his head, and he shuddered uncontrollably. Gently, the demon reached out a claw, a soft caress that brushed his shoulder.

At that touch, Jak felt his soul—that essential thing that made him *himself*—come loose from its moorings and flow toward the empty shadow before him. Terrified, he wet himself.

I'm going to die stinking of piss, he thought, and would have laughed but for the tears. The demon reared back and raised its claw high for the kill. A scream raced up Jak's throat—

The door to the sitting room burst open with a crash.

"Lord! Lord!" Boots stomped toward the bedroom. The startled demon halted in midkill, whirled, and then streaked toward the door. Jak sensed it hiss in frustration. Barely coherent, Jak sagged to the floor.

The demon blew past the startled house guards as they charged into the bedroom.

"There! Get it!" But the shadow flew past them before they could bring their blades to bear—if blades could even harm such a creature. Three men in the green and gold of House Soargyl hurried to the bed and stopped cold. One turned away, covering his mouth. Horrified, the other two poked with their swords at the remains scattered across the bed.

"Gods," the taller guard oathed. "Call the priests," he ordered over his shoulder, "and get a mage in here. And send for Master—make that, *Lord* Rorsin."

Still invisible, Jak rose unsteadily to his feet. He had to get out. A thief caught in a murdered noble-man's bedroom would not be treated mercifully. Dazed and wracked with shame, he picked his way through the milling guards and into the sitting room. Shouted orders and frightened conversations sounded all around him but he couldn't make out the words. Everything blurred into an inchoate roar. Two stout guards stood near the broken window he had entered through, talking and pointing—his silence spell had expired.

He waited for them to step away, then squirmed past and jumped through the window. With a whispered magical word, his fall turned into the gentle descent of a feather. As he floated earthward, he felt his soul clinging to his body by only the merest of threads, a tattered cloak that the cold winter breeze threatened to tear from his being. A vision of living darkness, boundless emptiness, and hate-filled yellow eyes haunted his mind's eye. Again, he relived a portion of his soul being jerked from his body; relived his essence being torn in two. Halfway to the earth below he began to scream. When he hit the ground of the courtyard, he ran pell-mell from the grounds, unmindful of guards or spells, still screaming.

CHAPTER 3

EREVIS

The vast Uskevren feasthall overflowed with the glittering grandeur of Selgaunt's assembled Old Chauncel. Having completed the five-course feast, the guests, in accordance with Sembia's social custom, now stood or sat about the feasthall in small groups, laughing, drinking, smoking, and talking.

Cale despised their perceived self-importance. To him, the room seemed an ocean of arrogant faces and empty-headed chatter. He strived to keep the contempt from his expression as he maneuvered through the thick crowd and dutifully refilled wine chalices.

A bewildering array of silk gowns, jewelry, and silver-laced stomachers—the latest fashion among the city's noblewomen—shimmered in the soft, aromatic candlelight. Though he recognized the faces of many of the nobles in attendance, many more were strangers to him. It seemed his lord had invited half the city to celebrate Perivel's birthday. This, despite the fact that Perivel Uskevren is forty years dead, he thought.

Every year on the thirtieth of Hammer, Thamalon held a birthday ball to honor his lost older brother, Perivel Uskevren. Cale had never known Perivel, of course, but based on what he had heard of the elder Uskevren over the years, he thought he would have liked him. Perivel had died plying steel against three foes while the former Uskevren manse, Storl Oak, had burned down around him.

Though he would have done the family a service by leaving behind a recognizable body, Cale thought.

After the inferno, the ruins had been carefully searched and the bodies of the dead dutifully removed, but there had been no way to tell if any of the charred corpses pulled from the ruins had been Perivel. Rumors persisted to this day that he had survived.

So it seemed that at least once every few years, a man claiming to be Perivel Uskevren showed up at Stormweather's doors and asserted the rights to primogeniture. Invariably, Thamalon and Cale exposed such claimants as imposters sponsored by rival families and turned them away. Still, the problem never seemed to go away entirely.

Nevertheless, despite the problems that it created by reawakening rumors of Perivel's return, Thamalon kept his brother's memory alive with an annual celebration, a feast and ball that had become a fixture in Selgaunt's social calendar. That the invitees did business in the process seemed only natural. For such is Selgaunt, Cale thought with a smile.

Though held in Perivel's name, the birthday ball

had long ago become as much about making deals as it was about honoring the elder Uskevren. Thamalon used the fine wine, excellent food, and general good feeling as a platform to discuss trade alliances and business deals with the rest of the Old Chauncel patriarchs. Cale felt certain that Perivel would approve.

Making his rounds with a bottle of Storm Ruby, he spotted his lord seated in a sequestered corner of the feasthall engaged in earnest conversation with Nuldrevyn Talendar. Cale could guess the topic of their discussion: a contract to arrange shipment of Uskevren wine to the southern lands of Faerûn. House Talendar dealt in fine furniture and frequently shipped to the kingdoms of the far South—Amn, Calimshan, and Tethyr, where the demand for Archendale walnut and Sembian mahogany seemed infinite. Thamalon thought the Uskevren house wines would also sell briskly in the south—particularly the full-bodied Storm Ruby—and had long sought an economical way to move bottles. Renting space on a Talendar caravan would be ideal.

Seeing the opportunity Thamalon had instructed him to watch for, Cale maneuvered through the crowd and walked toward the two men. Like the other noblemen in attendance, both wore finely tailored attire—Thamalon's fit frame covered in a twelve button doublet of crimson with black under-sleeves; Lord Talendar's ample belly draped in a doublet of purple with silver under-sleeves and a lace collar. As well, both wore fitted hose and polished Sembian high boots. Neither wore visible steel. As was his custom, Thamalon had forbidden weapons at Perivel's ball—even dress blades. The agenda was business, not blood, though the two frequently crossed paths in Selgaunt.

As he approached, Cale plucked uncomfortably at

his own black butler's doublet and pants. Despite his best efforts, he had never been able to retain a tailor competent to fit his towering frame. If his clothing was too short, it exposed his ankles and made him look an imbecile. If it was too large, he looked like a pale scarecrow swimming in a sea of black cloth. With only those two options, he had finally surrendered to the god of the ill-fit and decided on too large rather than too small, and resigned himself to the mediocrity of his tailor.

He had not worn his leather and steel for over a month—since his would-be ambush of a Night Knives' kidnapping team had turned instead into a Zhentarim ambush of he and his friend Jak—and Cale had never longed for them more than now. He felt more than just uncomfortable in his ill-fitting attire; he felt *false*, as if he wore a lie for all to see. That night in Drover's Square a month ago had resurrected the old Cale, and Erevis the butler had not been able to put him fully back in the grave. The feigned civility of Selgaunt's nobility only reminded him of his own facade.

They wear a mask and hide behind a veneer, he thought, and so do I. When not serving drinks, he killed people. When not laughing at one another's jokes and complimenting the wine, they stabbed each other in the back like common street thieves. Except for Thamalon, of course.

Cale knew his lord to be honest, at least by Selgaunt's standards, and fair by anybody's standards. An uncommon man in this city, he thought. Honesty was rare in Selgaunt. Cale himself embodied the point, and the bitter taste of his own lies rankled him.

He stopped a discreet distance from Thamalon and Nuldrevyn so as not to intrude on their conversation. Music and the drone of conversation sounded all about him but he focused his hearing on only Thamalon and Lord Talendar.

Nuldrevyn Talendar, a tall, overweight man with heavy-lidded eyes, spoke in his deep voice. "An interesting proposition Thamalon. We should pursue it further."

Thamalon leaned forward in his chair, placed his elbows on the table, crossed his hands before his face, and smiled his deal-nearly-done smile. "Indeed we should, Nuldrevyn. Of course, there will be a small commission for House Talendar on every bottle."

"Of course." Lord Talendar raised his glass in a toast and Thamalon reciprocated. Cale, having waited dutifully for a pause, took that moment to interject, a timely interruption planned by he and Thamalon days before.

"May I refill my Lords' goblets?"

"Ah, Erevis. Excellent." Thamalon made a show of scrutinizing the bottle that Cale held forth. He feigned surprise. "Why, this is the very Storm Ruby of which we were speaking, Nuldrevyn. I insist you sample it."

Nuldrevyn looked receptive so Cale added, "This is the 1352 vintage, Lord Talendar. The very best in the household."

From under his bushy brows, Thamalon shot him a sidelong glance of approval that only long familiarity allowed Cale to notice.

"Well, in that case," Lord Talendar gulped down the last of the wine currently in his goblet and held it out to Cale. "I believe I will."

"Excellent, Lord." Cale refilled his goblet and looked to Thamalon. "Will there be anything else, Lord?"

Thamalon smiled. "No, thank you, Erevis."

Cale bowed to Thamalon, nodded to Lord Talendar, and walked away. With Nuldrevyn in such high spirits, favorable contract terms seemed assured.

"This *is* most excellent, Thamalon," Cale heard as he walked away. "You say you press the grapes where . . ."

Having done his duty for his lord, Cale refocused on his primary concern—the security of the family. Though Jander Orvist and the rest of the Uskevren household guards watched with ready crossbows from the second floor balconies that overlooked the feast-hall, Cale preferred to rely on his own trained eye. He acknowledged that an assassination attempt on Thamalon *was* unlikely, but he did not entirely rule it out. The Uskevren rivals in the Old Chauncel would like nothing more than to see the Old Owl dead, for then Tamlin would inherit the Uskevren holdings.

And Master Tamlin is too much a dilettante to manage even a whorehouse well, Cale thought. Much less a noble house. Guards or no, Cale would personally see to the safety of his lord, just as he had for the past nine years.

Originally, he had come to Stormweather as a spy for the Night Knives, the thieves' guild he had joined soon after coming to Selgaunt from Westgate. Though the Knives had been able to place spies as servants in most of the other noble houses, the guild had not been able to place an operative in Stormweather.

Because Cale had been formally educated—by tutors hired by a thieves' guild in Westgate—and knew the etiquette appropriate to upper society, he had sought to win favor with the Righteous Man and gain status in the guild by proposing a plan. He would eliminate the then current Uskevren butler and take the position himself. Thinking about it now made his stomach roil.

I had an innocent man killed so that I could put myself in a position to blackmail the influential Uskevren patriarch, he thought accusingly. It shamed him that he could not even remember the previous butler's name. I didn't want to know his name, he realized. And I still don't.

He hated himself for what he had been, for what he had done.

But I'm different now, he thought, with only a tinge of desperation. I'm different.

The plan had been perfect in its conception, but flawed in its execution. Cale quickly had come to respect Thamalon as the father he had never known, the Uskevren as the family he had never had. He replaced membership in a long series of guilds and shadowy organizations with the love of a *real* family. It had not taken him long to realize that he could not betray them.

Neither could he confide to them his background that he had been trained as a killer and thief by the Night Masks in Westgate, that he had been taught nine languages so as to better impersonate, forge, and decipher, that he had come to their home as a spy. He knew that Thamalon, an otherwise gracious man, would not forgive the betrayal. So he had decided to live a lie rather than give up what he had come to love.

Over the years, he had fed the Righteous Man harmless information about Thamalon and the Uskevren, occasionally threw in a useful tidbit about some *other* noble family, and in the meantime aided his lordship in running the household. His supervision of the servants was incidental. His true value to Thamalon was his knowledge of Selgaunt's underworld—an underworld intricately intertwined with the plots of the Old Chauncel. He explained his illicit knowledge as derived from a disreputable cousin who moved in underworld circles. He had never been, and still wasn't, sure that Thamalon believed in this fictional cousin, but his lord had always respected Cale's privacy.

Lie upon lie upon lie, he chided. But I've got no other options. If Thazienne ever learned what I was . . .

He feared putting a name to the feelings he had for the Uskevren daughter. He had watched her blossom from a precocious teen to the most stunning and vivacious young woman he had ever seen. The light from her innocent spirit lit the dark places in his soul like a bonfire. Without her . . .

He shook his head, suddenly tired. He did not want to think about the kind of man that he would have been if he hadn't met her.

Almost involuntarily, his eyes sought her out. Towering head and shoulders over most of the men in attendance, he could see from one end of the feasthall to the other. Groups of guests thronged the room. Chalices and goblets clinked, laughter roared, music played, and Selgaunt's nobility glittered like a dragon's hoard. On the side of the hall nearest Cale stood the long feast tables, the dishes from the last course even now being cleared by Larajin and Ryton. They noticed him watching and picked up the pace of their efforts, Larajin fumbling with a serving platter in the process. At that, she looked up nervously, saw Cale's frown, and wilted like a dying flower. He could see her slight body trembling.

Have to do something about that girl, he thought. He strived to be fair with the staff, but tolerated few mistakes. Larajin seemed all thumbs. He would have let her go months ago but Thamalon insisted he be patient with her. Cale did not want to know why his lord was so protective of the willowy girl and so did not inquire further.

Larajin and Ryton worked around a few smokers who still lingered at the feast tables. The noblemen talked softly amongst themselves through a haze of pipe smoke. The pipes reminded Cale of Jak Fleet, his friend. He smiled, and wondered how the little man fared. Probably loaded with coin, cards, and fine tobacco, he thought, and chuckled aloud.

Still desiring to catch sight of Thazienne, he peered across the hardwood dance floor—currently unoccupied. Even though Selgaunt's Old Chauncel rarely danced, it was mandatory to *have* a dance floor. Cale continued scanning the opposite side of the hall.

A quartet of musicians sat upon a raised, carpeted dais and played softly. A fat, balding man pounding a slow beat on a hand drum played next to a nondescript but exceedingly skillful harpist. Next to them Cale saw a blonde, attractive woman playing the longhorn and beside her a stocky, black-bearded man playing the shawm. Thamalon had imported the musicians all the way from Daerlun for the celebration. The unusual combination of strings, woodwinds, and subtle percussion was an innovation from Cormyr that had found popularity in the neighboring cities of Sembia. Cale listened to the quartet for the first time and found that he rather enjoyed the sound. The gentle tones of the instruments and the low murmur of the assembled guests combined to create a sleepy, melodic drone. He allowed himself to drift peacefully on the chords as he continued his search for Thazienne.

He finally spotted her standing near the wall, to the right of the musicians' dais, and she stole his breath. The music and crowd noise fell away. He heard only his heartbeat, he saw only her, and she glittered like a jewel.

Dressed in a jade gown laced with silver thread and a bejeweled silver stomacher, her beauty outshone that of the other women in attendance the way silver

Selune outshone the glowing tears that trailed her orbit through the night sky. A crowd of noble sons surrounded her, talking, smiling, eager to impress.

Even from this distance, Cale recognized the frustrated set of her strong jaw. She hated noble fops and dress balls even more than he, but her mother had insisted she attend. As he watched, she smiled half-heartedly at a young noble's joke and glanced about as though seeking an excuse to escape. Their eyes met. She gave him a quick wave and smiled at him—a smile of genuine happiness. The men around her turned to shoot him envious glares. He bit back his jealousy, returned her wave, and smiled softly in return.

He dared not watch her too long for fear that his feelings would become plain on his face. Shooting her a final longing glance, he returned to his business and tried to locate the rest of the Uskevren family in the hall.

Lady Shamur, glamorous as always in a long sleeved blue gown with a gold stomacher, sat nearby in lighthearted conversation with Dolera and Meena Foxmantle. To Cale's perceptive eyes, she looked scarcely more comfortable than her daughter—her smiles seemed forced and her slim body looked coiled—but she masked her feelings well. Dutifully, Cale walked over and refreshed the three ladies' wine glasses.

"Thank you, Erevis," said Shamur. She flashed a grateful smile for the interruption and the severity that usually masked her finely chiseled features fell away for a moment. In that instant, Cale caught a rare glimpse of his ladyship's sophisticated beauty. Small wonder that Thazienne had turned out as gorgeous as she had; they could have been sisters.

"Do you require anything else, Lady?"

"No, Erevis. That will be all."

He bowed, first to Shamur, then to the Foxmantles. "Lady. Ladies."

"My," observed Dolera in her singsong voice as he walked away. "He is so very *tall*."

Cale hurried off without looking back. He would be hard-pressed to keep the impatience out of his voice if the empty-headed Dolera Foxmantle spoke to him. No wonder Lady Uskevren has to force her smiles, he thought with an inner grin.

He spotted Tamlin near the double doors that led to the forehall. The Uskevren heir stood with a half-empty wine bottle in his hand, a smile on his handsome face, and a crowd of young men and women clustered around him. Mostly women, Cale saw. At the edge of that sea of chattering femininity stood Tamlin's huge bodyguard, Vox, watchful and alert as always. The big man's crossed arms rippled with muscle, and even without weapons in evidence he radiated dangerousness. Cale watched Tamlin throw back his head in laughter and sprinkle the floor with wine. He frowned at Tamlin's carelessness.

While Cale envied Tamlin's easy grace with women, he despised the young man's lack of discipline. As he saw it, the sole weakness of the household was the Uskevren heir. Tamlin lacked maturity, lacked judgment, and worst of all, lacked focus. He stuck his hands in whatever took his fancy from day to day, but never took the time to master anything. He needed to learn discipline. Cale would have been willing to teach him—very willing—but he suspected that Tamlin would not enjoy the lessons. Everything had been handed to the young man since boyhood. He had never had to work for anything. If Tamlin was ever forced to fend for himself, he was as likely to survive as an orc in a dwarf hold. Unless something changed, Cale knew, the preeminence of House Uskevren would last only through Thamalon's lifetime.

At that moment, Tamlin looked across the hall and met Cale's eyes, caught Cale's disapproving frown, and momentarily lost his own ready smile. Cale looked away quickly, trying to keep the disdain in his expression hidden. As he did so, he caught a dark stare from Vox. The big man was apparently displeased that Cale had so discomfited Tamlin with only a look.

Cale returned *that* dull-eyed stare unflinchingly and didn't bother to hide his contempt. He knew Vox to be a professional mercenary and no doubt a skilled combatant, but Tymora would take him before he gave ground in his own house. Any time, big man, he thought, any time.

Vox looked away after a final glare, his thick-lipped mouth moving as though muttering to himself, though Cale knew him to be a mute.

Without thinking, Cale began to search the crowd for Talbot, but then remembered that the youngest Uskevren had begged off the celebration and remained at his tallhouse on Alasper Lane. He bit his lip thoughtfully, worried for the boy. He's been begging off a lot of things lately, Cale realized. All since that hunting accident.

Boyhood pranks gone awry were the previous extent of Talbot's troubles—Cale had typically resolved those without even informing Thamalon and Shamur—but the boy was getting old enough now that he might be attracting grown-up sized troubles. Cale knew that if he *was* in some kind of scrape, he would be afraid to tell anyone—especially his parents.

I'll have to look into that, he resolved. He made a mental scribe to contact Jak and ask the little man to quietly monitor the boy for a few days.

Satisfied at last that all was in order with the family, he returned his mind to his butler's duties and made one final inspection of the floor staff. Everything seemed in good order, though he tensed when he spotted Larajin wobbling under a tray of empty wine bottles and dishes. His eyes bored nervous holes into her back as she walked unsteadily toward the forehall, but she managed to make it through the doors without incident. Cale followed her across the feasthall and stuck his head into the forehall to assure himself that she had made it to the kitchen without breaking something. She had.

The silence coming from down the hall—rather than the rattle of pans and Brilla the kitchen mistress's shouts—indicated to him that the exhausted cooking staff must have finally settled in to take their own dinner. Cale's growling stomach reminded him that the floor staff, himself included, would eat only after all the guests had gone.

Spotting a nearby wine valet, he walked over and replaced his near empty bottle of Storm Ruby with a fresh bottle of Usk Fine Old—a light, pear wine suitable for late evening—and prepared for what often proved to be his most interesting work during celebrations—information gathering.

Eavesdropping, he chided with a smile. At least call it what it is.

Surveying the hall, he noted the locations of the Old Chauncel patriarchs and planned a route from one to the other. In his time at Stormweather, he had learned that Lord Uskevren's food and drink tended to loosen otherwise tightly reined noble tongues. Especially in the presence of a mere servant. With his keen hearing, Cale had overheard innumerable incriminating facts while casually refilling after-dinner drinks. Over the years, he had been able to keep the Righteous Man satisfied with such information—information embarrassing to this or that noble family, but harmless to the Uskevren.

Generally meticulous about his posture, he deliberately slouched when making his rounds. He had found that guests went silent if the keen-eyed, towering butler approached, but did not seem to notice him at all if he shrank in on himself and softened his habitually hard expression.

The best servants are like old furniture, he thought, recalling an old Sembian adage, there when you need them, but otherwise not to be noticed.

Wearing his best furniture disguise, he wove his way through the crowd. He refilled drinks as he went, casually spoke the praises of Usk Fine Old, and kept his keen ears attuned to nearby conversations. As expected, most was simply the mundane, after-dinner chatter of silly nobles.

". . . hear Lady Baerent had taken an interest in the work of a young artist, if you take my meaning," said Lord Colvith with a laugh.

". . . the Boaters sure are a strange lot," Lord Relendar was saying to a plump young woman Cale did not recognize. "I hear they sacrifice. . . ."

Cale moved along, smiling, filling drinks, listening for anything that might be of use to the Righteous Man or to Thamalon.

In a quiet corner he noticed Thildar Foxmantle— partially drunk as usual—engaged in an earnest conversation with Owyl Thisvin, a fat mage-merchant who worked primarily in the neighboring city of Saerloon. Thildar's heavy mustache and the dim light made lip-reading impossible, so Cale approached them, wine bottle in hand. They fell silent as he drew near, further piquing his interest.

"My Lords?" Cale held the wine bottle aloft.

"None for me, butler," Owyl replied dismissively.

Cale swallowed the urge to punch the smugness from Owyl's blotchy visage and instead turned to Thildar, who acknowledged him only by holding forth a silver goblet. Deferentially, Cale refilled it, walked a discreet distance away, and pretended to observe the crowd. Only then did Thildar and Owyl renew their conversation.

This *must* be interesting, Cale thought.

He tuned out the crowd noise and focused his hearing on the two men. When he heard them speaking Elvish, he had to contain his surprise. No doubt they felt secure in speaking the language of the elves—few Selgauntans had ever even seen one of the fair folk, much less understood their tongue. Cale silently thanked them for their arrogance. He had learned the expressive, intricate language of the elves at nineteen. A long time ago, when he had been a very different man.

"Body sucked as dry as a Chondathan raisin," said Thildar, drunk and too loud. *"My man in the household guard tells me a shadow streaked out the window just as the guards burst in."*

At Thildar's overloud tone, Owyl glanced about in irritable nervousness. The mage-merchant's eyes fell on Cale but passed over and by him as though he didn't exist. Unnoticed furniture, Cale thought with a smile.

Owyl slipped back into the common tongue. "Did you say *a shadow?*"

"Yes," replied Thildar, again in Elvish. *"Or at least so he tells it."* He waved a hand dismissively and gulped from his goblet. *"But you know servants. In any case, that is neither here nor there, as they say. The important thing is this: with Boarim Soargyl and the Lady dead, you'll need someone else to move your wares*

across the Inner Sea. I can help with that. No doubt we can reach an amicable agreement. . . ."

Cale ignored the rest of the conversation, mere commercial negotiations of no interest to him. He found the news about Lord and Lady Soargyl only mildly surprising. The Soargyls had not made a public appearance in over a tenday, a rarity for them, and rumors had been flying. Through his own sources, Cale had heard a story of murder in Sarntrumpet Towers, though nothing about a shadow. He would have to relate this news to Thamalon. With Boarim Soargyl dead and his untested son Rorsin heading the family, the rest of the Old Chauncel families would scramble to take over any vulnerable Soargyl interests.

Like vultures, he thought, eyeing Thildar with contempt. Perhaps Thamalon could offer Rorsin an alliance? Cale could not hide a grim smile at the thought. Boarim would spin in his casket. The Uskevren and Soargyl lords had long been bitter enemies. But times change, thought Cale, and so do men. Despite the acrimonious history, he had no doubt that Thamalon would offer Rorsin an alliance, *if* it was in the Uskevren's interest.

Thildar's description of the bodies stuck in Cale's mind and sounded alarm bells in his head: *Sucked dry as a Chondathan raisin.* He had heard disquieting rumors recently that some of Selgaunt's underworld leaders had died similarly—three Zhentarim fished out of Selgaunt Bay, their bodies pruned by more than immersion in the sea. Zalen Quickblade, former leader of the Redcowls, found dead in an alley with his body collapsed in on itself. Too many similarities for a coincidence and too well targeted for a random predator. A new player looking to establish himself? he wondered. Or an old one grown bold?

He knew that murder within the walls of Sarntrumpet Towers would make things difficult for everyone. Such a daring attack on a noble's home indicated recklessness, stupidity, or fearlessness. Selgaunt's Scepters—the city's watchmen—would be prowling the streets for the culprit, and they wouldn't be overly careful about who got caught in the melee.

He would have to warn Jak so that the little man would know to lie low. Independent rogues always suffered the most when the Scepters went on a purge. Guilds could bribe Watch Captains and buy safety; independents had to hide or hang. Cale would also have to leave word with Riven to arrange a meeting with the Righteous Man. The Night Knife guildmaster might know more about what was going on—

His stream of thought abruptly stopped. Disbelieving, his gaze followed a blond haired, handsome young man moving casually through the crowd. Dressed in a finely cut tan doublet with green under-sleeves, black hose, and high boots, the man looked much the same as every other young noble in attendance. Except that he was *casing* the attendees. He moved among the young noblewomen, flashed a smile, laughed, and no doubt commented on the beauty of their jewelry.

He was picking his marks! Cale could not believe it. Professionally, he had to admit that the would-be thief had skills. Only Cale's long experience and trained eye allowed him to notice anything amiss.

Spotting Larajin nearby again clearing dishes, he hurried over to her.

"Larajin—"

She jumped as though he had poked her with a pin. The tray of chalices she bore shook alarmingly. "Oh! Oh." When she turned and saw him, her voice quavered. "Yes, Mister Cale?"

"Give me one of those." He nodded absently at the tray, his eyes still on the young thief.

"Mister Cale?"

"A chalice, girl," he snapped. "Give me a damned chalice."

She recoiled, green eyes wide, and he felt a swift pang of guilt. She *was* just a girl, after all, and she was trying. He softened his tone. "I'm sorry, Larajin. Something else is on my mind. Here." He removed a chalice from the trembling tray and filled it from the bottle he held. "And you take this." He placed the wine bottle on the tray. "Remove it all to the kitchen and take your dinner."

"But—"

He turned on his heel and walked across the hall toward the thief. Waiting until the boy stood alone, Cale approached with the chalice. "A drink, young sir—oops." Feigning a stumble, he bumped into the boy, quickly felt him for steel—one buckleknife beneath his belt—and dumped the wine over the boy's doublet.

"Oh, forgive me, young sir." He pulled a kerchief from his breast pocket and daubed at the stain. "Forgive me. I'm so sorry."

"It's all right," replied the blushing thief, looking about in embarrassment and trying to push Cale away. A few heads turned their way, curious, but quickly turned back to their own conversations. That the boy had not exploded at Cale for such clumsiness—as any of Selgaunt's nobility would have—only confirmed his suspicions.

Cale continued to apologize and daub awkwardly at the stain while the boy continued trying to push him away. "It's all right, butler. You can go—"

Cale looked up abruptly as though struck with an idea. "Young sir . . . that is, if the young sir will be gracious enough to allow me to escort him to the kitchens,

Brilla the cook will see to the stain. I'm sure she will be able to remove it entirely."

"That won't be necessary—"

"Please young master, I insist you allow me to correct my clumsiness. Please?"

The boy looked down at his stained doublet, hesitated, then gave a shrug. "Very well then, butler. But let's be quick."

"Follow me, young master. The kitchens are this way."

Cale led him through the double doors into the forehall, but rather than turning right to go through the parlor and into the kitchen he turned left and strode toward an unoccupied receiving room.

The thief looked about absently as they walked, no doubt noting portable valuables. "How far are the kitchens, butleaaggh—"

Without warning, Cale whirled on him, gripped him by the throat, and pinned him against the wood paneled receiving room wall. The boy kicked and gagged but Cale held him fast. He stared into the boy's wide brown eyes and slowly lifted him from his feet. Desperate wheezes squeaked from the thief's throat. His red face began rapidly to turn blue.

"I know exactly what you are and what you're doing here," Cale hissed into his face. The boy feebly shook his head in the negative so Cale squeezed harder. The wheezes stopped altogether. The boy thrashed but Cale's iron grip could not be broken. "Don't deny it. I can always spot an amateur."

Indignant at first, the asphyxiating thief at last nodded. Satisfied, Cale eased his grip, but only slightly. The wheezes returned while the thief's blue face faded back to flush red. Cale stared straight into his frightened eyes. "Boy, if your left hand moves one inch closer to that buckleknife in your belt, I promise you that you've already taken your last breath."

The boy went wide-eyed and let his hand, which had been inching surreptitiously toward his belt, dangle limply.

"Here's how it's going to be," said Cale. "You listening?"

The boy nodded, but looked on the verge of passing out.

"I don't know who you work for and I don't care, but after tonight this house is off limits. Understand?"

Another desperate nod.

Cale gave a final, meaningful glare, and released him. The would-be thief collapsed to the floor, gasping.

"Collect yourself. I'm going to show you out."

"But my coat," the boy protested. "It's cold." He realized immediately that he should not have opened his mouth.

Cale *stared* at him. The boy's eyes found the floor. "Forget it," he muttered.

He climbed slowly to his feet and Cale led him through the receiving room to a side door that opened onto the patio. He pulled the door open and the blast of cold, Deepwinter air set the boy's teeth to chattering.

"Through the gardens, left to Sarn Street. Don't let me see you again."

The boy nodded, crossed his arms against the cold, and hurried out.

After closing the door and securing the deadbolt, Cale congratulated himself for solving a problem without bloodshed. Ten years ago, he'd have taken the boy into the gardens and put him down, just to be thorough. I *have* changed, he realized with a soft smile. Thazienne would be proud.

❧ ❧ ❧ ❧ ❧

Crouching amidst the tall shrubbery, Araniskeel hungrily eyed the two humans. The tall one said something and shoved the smaller one out of the door of the great house. Light, sound, and life spilled from the open door like blood from a wound. Araniskeel growled, low and dangerous, and a soft chorus of snarls sounded behind him in answer. The power of the two humans' souls glowed in his eyes, tempting him, whetting his appetite to *feed*. The tall human's soul shone with power, half of it white, half of it shadow, as though it fought a war with itself. The smaller human's soul, though a mere gray spark in comparison, elicited an anticipatory purr from the demon.

The fifteen former humans hidden in the gardens with him sensed his pleasure and shifted eagerly. "Feed us," they whispered. "Feed us."

Araniskeel turned to face them. *Silence*, he thought to them, and they fell on their faces to the dirty snow, abject. He regarded them with contempt, as he did all humans. Araniskeel's master Yrsillar had possessed the leader of these humans—these Night Knives—and named himself the avatar of their god. Now these ignorant fools literally fell over themselves in their frenzy to serve. Yrsillar had taken their zeal and used it— used it to twist their bodies, warp their minds, and pollute their souls until they had become tools suitable to his purposes. Now, not even Araniskeel would feed upon the twisted, black things that served as the corrupted humans' souls.

The door to the house slammed closed. The sound jerked him back around. The tall human had retreated within, but the short one remained outside. *Silence*, he projected again to the corrupted humans. As always, they obeyed. They soundlessly rocked back and forth, hungry for flesh, their claws alternately clenching and unclenching fistfuls of frozen earth.

Patience, he thought. *Soon you will feed*.

The small human, his arms crossed against a cold Araniskeel did not feel in this form, muttered to himself and walked from the house toward them. Araniskeel allowed his hunger to build, savored the growing anticipation that would soon be sated. The small human neared and walked past unsuspecting. Araniskeel stepped from the shrubs and reached for him.

The human's startled gasp ended almost as soon as it began. Araniskeel flashed a claw and opened the human's throat. His wings beat in ecstasy as the paltry soul pulsed screaming from the wound and into his being. Araniskeel's black form swallowed and utterly devoured the small human's life-force.

"For Mask," the corrupted humans chanted into the dirt. "For Mask."

Finished with the feeding, Araniskeel let the dried body fall to the pavement. *Feed*, he ordered.

Growling eagerly, the corrupted humans leaped to their feet, dragged the corpse into the bushes, and began to feast on the dried flesh. Their mindless gobbling delighted Araniskeel, so he allowed their frenzy to continue until only the tattered clothing remained of the corpse.

As the corrupted humans fed, he savored the lingering sweetness of the human's soul. In all the world, only humans had such a complex, delicious life-force capable of sating the perpetual hunger of his kind. Yrsillar, Araniskeel, and Greeve would turn this city of humans into a slaughterhouse. Tonight's feeding would be the first of many.

More souls resided within the house, he knew. Many more. He could sense them through the walls even at this distance. He sensed their essence on the winter wind. Araniskeel did not know why his master had chosen this house as a target and did not care. There was food within. That was enough.

Come, he said to the corrupted humans. *There is more food within.*

Their long, purple tongues lolled over gray lips and needle-sharp fangs. He took pleasure in their anticipatory slavering. "Food," they hissed. "Food."

CHAPTER 4

THE FEAST OF SOULS

Pleased with himself for not harming the would-be thief, Cale walked back through the receiving room hall and into the parlor. The thick Thayan floor rugs—each depicting red dragons in flight—felt wonderful beneath his sore feet. The cozy feeling of the parlor tempted him to kick off his boots and collapse into one of the richly upholstered chairs and retire for the night, but he resisted the urge. Instead, he strolled around the room and admired the thematic oil paintings that adorned the walls. The first painting depicted a roiling sky, against which elf knights mounted on hippogriffs warred with orogs mounted on wyverns. Each subsequent work represented a different point in the aerial battle, with the elves finally defeating the orogs in the last painting. Cale smiled as he moved from one to another, captured by the artist's skillful rendition of the combat. Thamalon had commissioned the half-elf artist Celista Ferim to paint the works two years ago. Ever since, Cale had found himself drawn to them.

Apart from his own sparsely furnished bedroom, the parlor had become his favorite room in Stormweather. Rarely used by anyone else in the family, at night it seemed his own private refuge—just he and the elves. When his troubled conscience kept him awake and he did not feel like reading, he often came down here to think, to lose himself in the unblemished heroics of a war that had occurred only on canvas.

Bathed in the dim light of a single candle and the soft glow of embers in the fireplace, he collapsed into his favorite overstuffed chair, put his feet up on the hassock, and allowed himself a moment to enjoy the solitude.

This would be a good time for a smoke, he thought wistfully. If only I smoked. He thought fondly of his pipe-toting friend, Jak Fleet, and smiled.

The distant bustle of the ball carried through the hall and nearby double doors, but the parlor itself was quiet, removed from the celebratory tumult. The candlelight flickered off the four suits of ceremonial armor that stood silent guard in each of the room's corners—each suit was engraved with a crossed hammer and sword on the breastplate, the arms of some long forgotten Selgaunt noble's house. The parlor's decor reflected his lord's love for the history of other peoples, places, and times.

Maybe that's why I like it so much, he thought. Because *I'm* from somewhere else.

Unlike most of Selgaunt's Old Chauncel, Thamalon did not consider the city such a beacon of cultural superiority that other cultures were not worth studying.

Though most obvious in the parlor, the whole of Stormweather fairly brimmed with unique antiquities drawn from the four corners of Faerûn. The library alone was stocked with treatises from all over the continent, some written in languages even Cale did not understand. Though he despised Selgaunt generally, he loved Stormweather.

He allowed himself a few more moments of peace before forcing himself to rise. He adjusted the cast bronze dragon figurines atop the walnut mantle, walked the short hallway to the adjacent main kitchen, and pushed open the doors.

As he had suspected, the kitchen staff sat eating and chatting around the cleaver-scarred butcher's block. The moment he entered, the eight young women on staff—Brilla tolerated *only* women on her staff—gave a start and the talking fell abruptly silent. Cale smiled knowingly. Because he allowed Brilla a free hand in running the kitchen, he usually only made an appearance when something had gone wrong with the meal.

Eight pairs of exhausted, apprehensive eyes stared at him and nervously awaited his next words. None of them said a word.

"Everything is all right," he assured them, but the apprehension written in their expressions did not change. He looked from one pretty face to the other and realized that he did not know most of their names. Have to remedy that, he thought. He had always made it a point to know everyone in the household, even kitchen help.

When at last he found a familiar face among the girls, he grabbed her with his gaze.

"Aileen, where is Brilla?" Aileen gave a slight start when he spoke her name.

"In the pantries, Mister Cale," she responded immediately. A slight, very attractive girl with wispy blonde hair and bright green eyes, Aileen had been on staff since the summer. "Shall I go and get her?"

"Thank you, Aileen."

She jumped down from her stool and hurried out the other side of the main kitchen, toward the pantries. Cale winced when she began to shout.

"Brilla! Brilla! Mister Cale wants you! Brilla!"

While he waited, the rest of the young women half-heartedly picked at their plates and studiously avoided eye contact. They must have heard that he was an ogre.

After a few minutes, Brilla waddled defiantly into the main kitchen, a dead chicken clutched in one thick-fingered hand, an apprehensive Aileen clutched in the other.

"Mister Cale," she acknowledged with a nod. She scooted Aileen back to her stool. "Go, girl, finish your meal. I told you he doesn't bite."

Blushing, Aileen took to her stool. Brilla turned her sour gaze back to Cale.

"I hope this is important, Mister Cale. I was just preparing to pluck the chickens for tomorrow." She held up the dead chicken for emphasis.

In a good humor, Cale barely suppressed a smile. Brilla stood almost as wide as she did tall, her thick legs as sturdy as tree stumps. With her long black hair pulled back and tied into a sloppy bun, she reminded him of the archetypal dwarven *oerwen*, the esteemed house matron, but without a beard.

Careful, man, he reminded himself jovially. You'd be as dead as that chicken if she knew you were comparing her to a dwarf.

Unlike most of the household staff, big Brilla was not and never would be intimidated by him. He respected her for that. That's why he left her alone to run the kitchens.

"Mister Cale?"

He swallowed the last of his smile and put on his expressionless, head butler's face. "I wanted to congratulate you." He crossed his hands behind his back and nodded to include the kitchen staff, "To congratulate all of you, for work well done. Lord Uskevren has informed me that the meal received numerous compliments." He paused dramatically before adding, "Particularly the dessert torte."

At that, Brilla beamed. She had created the recipe for the torte herself and had personally selected the Calishite barkberries. She turned her broad smile on her staff, the eight of whom were sharing tired smiles of their own.

"Did you hear that, gir—" A high-pitched scream cut short her praise. Brilla cocked an eyebrow. "Now what was—" Another wail rose and fell.

At first, Cale thought the screams merely the giddy squeals of an empty-headed noblewoman, but another terror-filled shout, this one from a man, changed his mind. Something was wrong.

Instinctively, he fell into a fighting crouch, though he had no weapon. The kitchen girls jumped down from their stools.

Loud thumps suddenly sounded through the walls and startled the girls. They began to chatter fearfully. The heavy stomp of boots and angry shouts joined the frightened screams and carried down the forehall from the feasthall.

With his keen ears, Cale thought he caught the sound of the savage snarls of an animal intermixed with the shouts. What in the Hells? With the girls clamoring beside him, he could not make out any other details.

"Quiet down," he ordered.

Nine mouths clamped shut. He walked to the

kitchen door, pushed it open a handwidth, and listened.

The distant but distinctive sounds of shouting men, plied iron, and panicked screams filled the air. A battle!

Suddenly, from close by, he heard a man shout in surprise, then a loud scream of pain followed by vicious snarling. The sound made the hair on the nape of his neck rise. That had come from the parlor.

As though reading his mind, Brilla observed nervously, "That sounded like an animal loose in the parlor." As one, the girls gasped and clustered together fearfully.

Cale let the door close and turned to the women. "Get in the herb pantry," he ordered, as calmly as he could. Judging from the sound, the source of the growls was a *big* animal. "Block the door and don't come out unless I say so."

They stared at him blankly, dumbfounded.

"Move! Now."

That got them going.

"Yes, yes, of course," said Brilla. "Mister Cale is right. Come along, girls. Hurry now."

While casting nervous glances back at the wall through which the sounds of combat were made, Brilla quickly led the fearful staff out of the rear of the main kitchen toward the herb pantry. Cale waited till they had gone, then barreled through the kitchen door and raced toward the feasthall. He stopped cold when he reached the parlor, his favorite room.

Shouts, screams, and the crash of breaking dishes sounded loudly through the feasthall's double doors. Across the parlor near the archway to the forehall, dimly visible in the candlelight, a bipedal form in tattered clothes hunched over the body of a slain household guard. The wet chomping sounds of a feeding animal filled Cale's ears. When he gasped in surprise the creature looked up from its meal, wide eyed and startled. Cale's stomach roiled. He had expected an *animal*, not . . . this.

Strings of flesh clung to the creature's dirty fangs and inch-long claws. Yellow eyes stared out of a blood soaked, feral face. When those eyes found Cale, they narrowed to ochre slits. A purple tongue half as long as a man's forearm wormed out of its mouth, swept its lips, and slobbered up the last bits of flesh that clung to its face. It gave a low growl, a sound as savage and merciless as the fiercest animal, yet inexplicably human. It left the corpse and took one step toward him. His stomach fluttered nervously.

It registered in his mind that the creature had *eaten* the fallen guard. Ghouls, he realized. Ghouls are in the house! He had never before encountered undead, but he had heard enough tales to recognize the warped body of one of the creatures. No wonder the monster's growl had sounded vaguely human.

The panicked shouting from the feasthall grew louder, increasing in intensity. Men screamed, ghouls snarled—lots of ghouls—and women shrieked in terror. Cale, however, could spare no thought for the events in the feasthall. The ghoul before him began to prowl across the parlor toward him.

Involuntarily, he backed up a step. He reached for a weapon, patted himself for anything, but quickly realized that he had nothing. He cursed himself an idiot for leaving the kitchen without at least a carving knife. Think before you act, he rebuked himself.

Picking its way through the eclectic collection of furniture, the ghoul stalked closer. It moved in a hunched crouch, a vile, sickly-gray predator ready to pounce. As it approached, it tensed its clawed arms, smacked its lips, and gave a *thoughtful* snarl. Cale could have sworn it actually leered at him.

It knows I'm unarmed, he thought, and he realized that this savage, flesh-eating monster still retained some intelligence.

What in the Nine Hells is happening? Where's the house guard?

He knew the answer the moment he thought the question. One of the house guards already lay dead on the parlor floor; the rest were fighting in the feasthall. Judging from all the screaming and breaking dishes, he did not think that Jander and his men were faring too well.

For an instant, he considered making a dash for the kitchen to retrieve a weapon, but dismissed the idea. He could not risk leading the ghoul to Brilla and the kitchen girls.

With his gaze never leaving the yellow eyes of the ghoul, he sidestepped along the wall. As he moved, he tried to keep furniture between himself and the ghoul. It seemed to enjoy his efforts. It playfully circled to cut him off and pawed at the air, content for now merely to toy with him.

Up close, Cale nearly gagged on the creature's stench. It stank like the rotted remains of a corpse baking in the sun. He tried to breathe through his mouth to keep from vomiting. With only a high backed wooden chair between them, he got a good look at the creature for the first time.

A spider web tracery of purple veins showed through its gray, leprous skin. A bit of blood from the dead guard still glistened scarlet on its sunken cheeks, and its fanged mouth and feral eyes promised a similar end to Cale. The remains of its befouled clothes hung in tatters from a hunched, twisted body. Its claws, filthy knife blades caked with dirt and gore, clenched and unclenched reflexively while it stalked him. A strange mark on its shoulder caught the candlelight and grabbed Cale's eye.

He stopped and stared, stupefied.

The ghoul had a tattoo inked into the flesh of its shoulder, a familiar tattoo, two crossed daggers superimposed over a cracked skull.

A wave of nausea and dizziness washed over Cale. He fought it off and studied the twisted, savage face of the ghoul. The clothes that might once have been the favorite blue cloak of a man Cale had known.

"Krendik," he whispered in disbelief, the words drawn involuntarily from his constricted throat. He tasted bile and swallowed it down. "Krendik?" he said again, louder this time.

The ghoul stopped snarling and stood upright for a moment, as though hearing Cale say its name recalled the memory of its former humanity. In that instant, the feral gleam in its yellow eyes fell away. Its mouth softened from the rictus of savage hunger and a familiar face revealed itself. Behind the blood, the stink, and the twisted form, Cale recognized with certainty the face of Krendik, once a fellow Night Knife.

"Gods, man," he breathed. "What happened to you? What has the Righteous Man done?"

Krendik the ghoul crouched low, threw its head back, and snarled into the rafters. All traces of its former humanity vanished. He returned his gaze to Cale, insane eyes narrowed conspiratorially, and hissed, "Maassk."

Cale stared, dumbfounded. Mask? He did not understand. He knew that the Righteous Man was trying to convert everyone in the guild to the worship of Mask but that didn't explain *this*.

"Feed," Krendik mouthed, and a foul brown slaver dripped from between its filthy fangs. "Feed."

The ghoul lunged at him.

Cale shoved the rocking chair into Krendik and

frantically backpedaled. His eyes scanned the parlor for a weapon. Nothing! Cale scooted to his right.

Krendik bounded nimbly over the toppled chair and lashed out with a filthy claw.

Cale stumbled backward. Inadvertently, he crashed into one of the suits of armor and nearly tripped over the display pedestal. Unthinking, he grabbed at the armor to steady himself. It toppled. He flailed to keep his balance while the mail crashed to the floor and sent bits of armor skittering across the floor.

The ghoul pounced on him.

Krendik crashed into him like a battering ram, claws flailing maniacally. The force of the charge drove Cale backward into the wall and blew the breath from his lungs. Snarls rang in his ears. The stink of rotted flesh and fetid breath filled his nostrils. Claws tore through his clothes and raked again and again at his unprotected flesh.

Reeling, and with no weapon at hand, he tried to pull it close and throttle it with his bare hands. The squirming ghoul pulled him off balance and the two tumbled to the armor-strewn floor in a chaotic pile of limbs, fangs, and claws.

Surging with adrenaline, Cale used his greater size and strength to roll atop the snarling beast and slam a knee into its abdomen. It squealed in pain and slashed at his chest and shoulders. Filthy claws tore gashes through his doublet and into his flesh. Warm blood ran down his arms. The ghoul sank its teeth into Cale's bicep and shook its head to rip his flesh open.

Through the pain, Cale felt his muscles begin to grow thick. The snarls of the ghoul became distant. His vision began to blur. Some kind of venom . . .

If his body did not resist it, he would be immobilized and the ghoul would eat him alive. He tried to punch at the squirming thing but with sluggish muscles he managed only a few feeble blows. Fight it, godsdammit! Fight!

The ghoul took advantage of his weakness and squirmed loose. Once free, it tore into his flesh with a manic flurry of raking claws. Cale awkwardly rose to his feet, stumbled backward, and tried to fend off the blows with his limbs. The ghoul ripped into him without mercy. *His* blood dribbled from the ghoul's filthy fangs now. Snarling, slashing, and biting, Krendik tore into Cale's body. Stinking, brown saliva pelted Cale's face and drove him backward. He felt himself growing weaker. Stubbornly, he tried to fight back, but he knew his efforts to be futile. He was too weak. Soon he would not be able to move at all.

Distantly, he noticed that the chaotic noise from the feasthall had grown to a fever pitch. It sounded as though every dish in Stormweather was being shattered and an army was fighting on the dance floor. He had a sudden vision of the entire house guard slain and rampant ghouls feasting at leisure upon paralyzed victims. Thazienne! Thamalon! Shamur! In his mind's eye, he saw his family being devoured alive, like him.

No! Anger heated his blood into a bonfire. A flood of rage washed away the ghoul's paralyzing poison like a cleansing rain.

"No!" he shouted into the ghoul's face, mere inches from its shark-toothed mouth. He caught it by the wrists and forced them out wide.

"No!" He pulled it toward him and at the same time kicked the ghoul square in the chest. Bone cracked and it squealed in agony. Its jaws snapped reflexively and brown spittle flew. Still holding it by the wrists, Cale threw it to the ground and landed on top of it, knees first. More cracking bones; more pain-filled squeals.

He released the ghoul's arms, endured repeated retaliatory claw rakes, and closed both his hands around its throat. Blood flowed freely down Cale's sides but he did not feel it. He felt only hot rage.

"No!" he shouted again. Gagging, the ghoul left off tearing at his sides and aimed for his forearms. Cale endured the pain and only tightened his grip.

With a grunt, he jerked the ghoul's head forward and promptly slammed it back against the hardwood floor. *Thud*. Stunned, its eyes rolled backward for a moment.

"No!"

Its tongue lolled from its mouth and lay between its fangs. Cale released its throat only long enough to slam his palm under its lower jaw. Impaled between rows of fangs, the tongue exploded in a spray of stinking purple blood. The ghoul squealed in agony, squirmed desperately, but Cale held it pinned. Spit foamed between its teeth and blood continued to pour from its tongue. In desperation, it slashed into Cale's ribs, but he maintained his hold.

"No!" He slammed its head against the floor.

It shrieked and clawed like an angry cat, but Cale had long passed the point where he felt pain.

"No!" *Thud*. Again and again, he slammed its head into the floor. "By . . ." *Thud*. Its squeals of pain gave way to stunned whimpers. ". . . the . . ." *Thud*.

Incoherent, it clawed weakly at his chest and arms. He pounded it mercilessly.

". . . gods . . ." *Thud*.

Its head cracked open like a Yule nut. Reeking gore poured from its broken skull and formed a puddle of wet stink on the parlor floor.

Gasping, weakened from blood loss, Cale collapsed on top of the corpse. The rush of rage fled his body as fast as it had come, and the vacuum left him quivering and exhausted. Blood and putrescence covered him but he hardly noticed. As his lungs heaved for air, he tried to gather himself.

The desperate shouts coming from the feasthall gave him no time to rest. The terrible sounds pulled him to his feet and refueled his anger. Thazienne! Nearly slipping in the ghoul's brains, he bounded over the corpse and sprinted for the feasthall.

He stopped cold in the double doorway. Perivel's birthday celebration had been transformed into a chaotic melee of blood, screams, and death. Cale took it in, horrified.

Near him, the oak feast table and most of the dinner chairs lay overturned. Broken dishes lay scattered across the floor. Toppled candles and spilled oil lamps had started a few scattered fires. Cale watched Shamur's tablecloths burn and the plush velvet curtains smolder. Wispy clouds of black smoke filled the room and gave the whole scene the look of some surreal vision from a nightmare. From everywhere, a horrid cacophony of terrified screams, hungry growls, and angry shouts filled his ears. Smears of blood stained everything red.

A pack of at least ten ghouls rampaged freely amidst the chaos. They bounded haphazardly through the clutter, attacking anything that came within their reach. Many guests were already paralyzed. He winced when he saw the wounds torn in their bodies. The ghouls had devoured hunks of their bodies while they stood helpless. His eyes moved frantically from victim to victim, looking for the members of his family. He didn't see them.

Corpses lay scattered about the floor amidst the dishes and dining furniture, their bodies desiccated and unrecognizable. Not ghoul work, Cale realized, but he had no time to give it further thought.

He saw that the ghouls had herded most of the surviving guests to the far side of the feasthall, away from the double doors. Away from any means of escape. Though a few guests had tried to break the large, leaded glass windows, the beautifully crafted metal veins that depicted dragons in flight and men in battle imprisoned the guests as effectively as a jailer's cell. Outside, the safety of the patio and gardens tantalizingly beckoned, just out of reach. Inside, the slaughter continued.

Here and there about the feasthall, groups of cornered noblemen fought the ghouls as best they could. The men pushed the women behind them and used table knives or heavy platters as makeshift weapons and shields. Cale watched transfixed as a ghoul leaped past the feeble weapons wielded by one elderly nobleman, knocked him to the floor, and began to feed. The man's pathetic screams ended when the ghoul tore open his throat.

The three old women the elderly nobleman had been trying to protect screamed in terror and tried to flee. Two other ghouls bounded after them, pulled them down from behind, and began to feast.

Cale pushed aside his nausea and fear and looked frantically through the smoke for his family. *Where are they, dammit?*

At last he spotted them, across the hall standing behind a protective screen of the surviving house guards. Jander Orvist and the rest of his blue uniformed men had backed the family and many of the guests against the back wall and formed a semi-circle of flesh and steel around them. Each house guard brandished a long sword and stout buckler. They made no move to attack but lashed out at any ghouls that came near.

Through the smoke, Cale could make out Shamur

and Thamalon. The pair were struggling to get free of the ring to return and protect the rest of their friends, but Jander personally held them back.

Good man, Cale thought. The only safe place on that side of the feasthall was right where they were, behind Jander's men.

He saw that Tamlin, too, stood within the ring near his parents. He looked pale from fear, but still held his ground near the perimeter of the ring shielding two young women. Vox, Tamlin's huge, hairy bodyguard, had somehow produced a wide-bladed short sword and now stood alongside the guards, a grim scowl on his face. Many of the house guards, their uniforms stained black with blood, had already fallen to the ghouls' claws. The ghouls now looked to be keeping their distance. Captain Orvist was waiting for an opportune moment to make a run for the double doors.

For now, the ghouls seemed content to attack only the groups of guests left outside the ring of Jander's men. Selgaunt's noblemen fought, shouted, and died by fang and claw. Ghouls devoured the soft skin of the city's noblewomen. The macabre feasting was within view of the horrified guests being protected by Uskevren house guards.

Despite the protests of Lord and Lady Uskevren, Jander Orvist let no one break from the ring. Cale searched the faces behind Jander's men—he saw Lord and Lady Foxmantle, and Lord and Lady Talendar, among others—but didn't see Thazienne.

Jander, in the midst of trying gently to restrain Thamalon, suddenly threw Lord Uskevren behind him, shouted something to his men, and pointed with his blade to the ceiling. Cale's eyes followed his pointed blade.

He saw nothing but black smoke—

Sudden motion among the ceiling rafters drew his eye. Quick as an arrow shot, a huge, bat-winged shadow with long, clawed arms swooped down from the smoky ceiling toward the house guard perimeter.

"Look out!" Cale shouted, but knew they could not hear him through the noise.

The crowd of guests had also followed Jander's pointed blade. They backed up and cowered as the shadow dived toward them. Jander stood over Thamalon and brandished his long sword. Two other guards flanked Shamur. Vox edged toward Tamlin.

Difficult to distinguish from the smoke, the shadow darted over the flashing steel of Jander's men. A few quick-thinking house guards had readied crossbows and fired on the creature, but the bolts passed through its body without effect. It swooped into the crowd like a kingfisher and scooped up a young nobleman. The nobleman dangled and squirmed from the shadow's clawed grip. Cale did not know the young man's name. The creature hovered over the terrified crowd of guests. Its eyes flared yellow in the black oval of its face. Several of the women fainted. Many of the men cowered in fear, even some among the house guard. Meantime, the young man in the shadow's clutches screamed and kicked frenetically but his blows passed harmlessly through the creature.

Cale watched in fascination as the shadow, hovering only two armspans above the crowd, placed a claw on the scrabbling man's chest and slowly tore open a hole in his torso. Inch by inch the man's body split open. He screamed, convulsed, and died.

Cale expected a rain of entrails to shower the terrified crowd below, but nothing spilled from the wound but a whitish vapor streaked with swirls of gray. The mist flowed toward the shadow's mouth like iron shavings to a lodestone. The creature drank it in greedily. As it did, the nobleman's body began to collapse in on itself as though sucked empty—eyeballs shrunk and fell back into the collapsing sockets. The jawbone fell open in a soundless scream.

When only a dried husk remained, the creature threw the body into the cowering crowd below and began to scan the hall below for its next victim.

Cale's gaze swept the feasthall near him and took in the many desicated corpses that littered the ground. The shadow had already fed well. No wonder Jander had been forced into a corner. How could the house guard hope to fight off such a creature? He had to find Thazienne!

He searched the hall, but through the smoke Cale couldn't see her anywhere. With one eye, he kept a watch on the shadow. It continued to lazily circle near the ceiling. Cale searched for Thazienne. Where was she, godsdammit?

"Thazienne!" he shouted from the doorway, heedless now of whether ghouls noticed him or not. "Tazi!"

Through the smoke, he spotted her across the feast-hall. She stood opposite from him, near the musicians' dais, fighting a ghoul. It toyed with her the way the one in the parlor had toyed with him.

She had torn her jade gown off at the thighs and now skillfully brandished a softly glowing dagger. Cale thanked the gods she had defied her father and worn the dagger under her dress. Her short hair hung wildly about her face and her eyes glowed with the fire of combat. Behind her, tiny Meena Foxmantle cowered against the wall, wide-eyed with fright.

The ghoul backed off, circled wide, then suddenly bounded over a toppled chair to try to get at Meena. Thazienne jumped in front of it and slashed open its forearm with her dagger. The gray-skinned beast recoiled with a growl, blood from previous victims still dripping from its claws. It backed off and again circled, less playfully now, then rushed in to attack her with a flurry of claw rakes. Despite his concern, Cale picked his way toward her cautiously, trying to avoid the attention of the rest of the ghoul pack.

Thazienne leaped backward and nimbly dodged a claw attack. She ducked low and lashed out with the dagger, this time to the ghoul's abdomen. The creature staggered backward. She shouted something, reversed her stroke, and slashed it backhand across the throat. Purple blood sprayed from the wound. The ghoul clutched at its neck and fell writhing to the floor. Without hesitation, she pounced on it and drove her dagger through its chest.

"Thazienne!" Cale shouted, to get her attention. "Thazienne!"

She didn't hear him. There was too much shouting. Several ghouls did hear him though, and eyed him hungrily.

After making sure the ghoul was dead, Thazienne grabbed Meena by the hand and began to lead her across the feasthall toward Jander and the protective circle of guards.

Smart girl. Cale headed that way as well.

He looked up and caught the shadow creature's baleful yellow eyes. They fell on Thazienne and Meena. It stopped circling and hovered.

"Thazienne!" Cale shouted, but still she did not hear him through the tumult. The shadow began to flow sinuously earthward.

Cale threw caution to the wind. Leaping chairs and tables, he ran across the hall and through the carnage. He ignored the paralyzed but still living guests, even those being fed upon by ghouls. He ignored the hungry slavers of the ghouls, loud in his ears as they bounded after him. He saw nothing but the need to get to her before the shadow did.

Something crashed into Cale's back. A ghoul buried its fangs into the muscles of Cale's shoulder and its claws tore at his face. Off balance, he skidded into an overturned table, a snarling ghoul astride his back.

Tableware, broken dishes, and the ghoul's fangs and claws bit into his flesh. The charnel reek of the creature filled his nose and he swallowed bile. Fueled by his fear for Thazienne, he flipped the ghoul over his back and slammed it onto the table. It squirmed and slashed but he held it fast with one hand and a knee. His other hand frantically fished the debris nearby for the first sharp thing he could find. His hand closed on the hilt of a carving knife.

With a grunt, he drove the blade through the ghoul's throat and into the wood of the table underneath. Pinned, it gurgled, kicked feebly, and died.

Tazi! He wiped the blood from his face, ignored the pain in his shoulder and sides, and jumped to his feet.

The shadow had landed on the floor to cut Tazi off from the ring of house guards. Now only twenty paces from Cale, Tazi shoved Meena Foxmantle behind her and held the enchanted dagger before her in a trembling hand. The shadow flowed toward Tazi, faster now. Beyond her, Cale saw Thamalon and Shamur struggling frantically to get free of the house guard ring, but Jander refused to let them go. Cale raced for her, leaping over and through debris and corpses.

"Thazienne!"

As the shadow neared, Meena Foxmantle swooned and fell to the floor at Thazienne's feet. With its long clawed arms outstretched, the shadow darted in for her.

"Tazi!" He realized how stupid it was to shout the moment he did it. If he distracted her—

She showed no sign of having heard him and he

thanked the gods for her single-mindedness. She paid attention only to the living darkness that swirled around her.

When the shadow drew near enough, she slashed with her dagger. Incredibly fast, the creature easily flowed out of the reach of her small blade. She did not pursue it, instead standing protectively over Meena.

Cale was almost there.

Suddenly, with blinding speed, the shadow darted in and flashed a claw. Thazienne leaped to the side but the blow still tore a gash in her shoulder. Immediately, her face turned ashen. She staggered, clutching her shoulder, and fell to her knees.

"No!" Cale shouted, but knew his cry to be futile. Thazienne stood perfectly still and the suddenly vacant look in her wide, haunted eyes burned holes into his soul. Her dagger clattered to the floor.

"No!"

Before he took another stride, the shadow slashed again, tore open her gown, and opened a wound in her chest. Gray vapor began to pulse from the gash toward the shadow's waiting mouth. Thazienne's mouth fell open.

Cale could *feel* the creature's eager anticipation. The thing radiated hunger like heat from a fire.

"No, gods damn you!"

He leaped over the last chair in his way and charged into the shadow at a full run. Flailing wildly with his fists, he ran right through the insubstantial body of the creature and felt nothing but a pitiless cold, as though he had stepped unclothed into the freezing air of a cold Hammer night. Unable to halt his charge, he crashed into Thazienne and knocked her flat. Forcing his numb limbs to answer his commands, he turned to fight, turned to protect Thazienne. He faced the shadow, filled with the heat of rage, and charged it again, fists first.

Taken aback by Cale's fearlessness, the creature darted backward, out of his reach. Cale did not pursue. He stood his ground over Thazienne, fists clenched. His breathing came in labored gasps and his body shook with emotion. He stared without fear into the shadow's flaring yellow eyes.

"Come on!" he shouted, and beckoned it toward him.

The shadow circled around him, watchful, curious, *predatory*. He turned as it moved, kept his eyes on it all the while. The shouting and growling all around him seemed to fall away. There was only Cale and the shadow, nothing else mattered.

He sensed its amusement with him, the same way he had felt its hunger, but he felt no fear. Let it come.

Weaponless but for his hands, he dared it with his eyes to try again for Thazienne. He momentarily lowered his gaze from the shadow to her and saw that the vapor that had bled from her wound still clung in wisps around her body. The creature had not yet fed. And it never will, he vowed. Not while I live.

"Come on," he challenged. "Come on."

Meena Foxmantle, now awake and trembling with sobs on the floor behind him, pulled pathetically at the leg of his breeches. When he tried to reassure her with a quick glance, his eyes fell on Thazienne's dagger—Thazienne's *enchanted* dagger—lying on the floor only a few feet away.

Without a moment's hesitation, he dived for the blade. As he did, he noticed with his peripheral vision the shadow darting in to strike. He grabbed the steel, rolled to dodge the shadow's attack, and jumped up with the now glowing dagger held before him. The moment he stood, the cut of a shadowy claw tore open his side.

His body went instantly numb, as though he had been immersed in ice water. He kept his fingers wrapped around the dagger's hilt only by sheer force of will. No blood flowed from the deep cut in his ribs—he would have welcomed the warmth—rather, he felt a nauseating yet seductive tug on his soul. In his mind's eye, he saw a horrible vision of his desiccated, pruned body falling in dried pieces upon Thazienne and Meena. In that terrifying instant, he realized that he faced not merely an undead creature, like the ghouls, but a demon from the Abyss—for only a demon could drink a man's soul.

Seeing his vulnerability, the demon's yellow eyes flashed in the void of its oval head and it raised a second claw high to strike. Again, Cale felt waves of hunger coming from the emptiness of its body. Its overlong arm extended high and seemed to Cale to reach all the way to the ceiling rafters. The claws looked as long as broadswords.

Desperately, he willed his numb body and thick brain to answer his command to move. Move! Move!

The claw sped downward for the kill.

At the last possible moment, he dived under the demon's arm and reflexively stabbed upward with Thazienne's dagger. Unlike his punches, the blow from the enchanted dagger actually bit into the demon's shadowy substance. Cale felt resistance as the blade penetrated the demon's being—soft tension, then sudden give—as though he had poked a hole in a wineskin. His hand hurt from the cold.

The demon jerked back and Cale *sensed* rather than heard a surprised howl of rage and pain. Black, foulsmelling smoke hissed from the wound in its arm. It jerked back and circled him at a distance, leaking foulness. Its yellow eyes narrowed. Cale sensed it hiss. It was no longer amused.

His eyes fell on Thazienne, motionless on the floor, and he charged it with a roar.

Startled, the demon's yellow eyes went wide and it flowed backward. Cale chased after and stabbed maniacally with the dagger. Heedless of the creature's claws, Cale attacked. He was interested only in killing the thing that had harmed Thazienne.

With each telling cut, the demon's shrieks of pain and surprise thumped in Cale's brain and fed his anger. He stabbed, ducked, rolled, and stabbed again. Shadowy claws flashed about him but he kept moving and avoided them all. He spun, ducked, and cut again. As he fought, he shouted incoherently, bellows of primal rage.

Reeking shadow stuff streamed out of the demon from a handful of dagger wounds. Cale pressed it relentlessly.

Without warning, the wounded demon suddenly took wing and streaked, still bleeding, from the feasthall. Cale sensed its pain and shock. He chased after it on foot for a few paces, waving the dagger and shouting challenges.

When it left his sight, he came back to himself.

Except for some soft crying and pained moans, the feasthall was silent. Cale looked around.

The ghouls had ceased attacking and now stood idle, as though the defeat of the demon had left them stunned. Their faces hung slack. Their expressions were vacant.

Jander Orvist needed no better opportunity. His voice boomed from across the feasthall. "Now!" he ordered, and the house guard charged, blades held high.

The ghouls did not even move to defend themselves. The surviving Uskevren house guards brandished their long swords and began to chop them down like farmers harvesting wheat. Cale dropped the ice-cold dagger and rushed to Thazienne's side.

As though freed to return by the absence of the demon, the white vapor that clung in wisps around her body—her soul, Cale now knew—flowed back into the slash in her chest. Immediately, the wound knitted itself shut to leave only an ugly pink scar. He knelt beside her and brushed the hair from her forehead. She looked so pale. Her body felt as cold as Deepwinter snow.

Ignoring the pain of his own wounds, Cale pulled her limp body close and cradled her to his chest. She still breathed, he realized, but only barely. His eyes welled as he rocked her back and forth. Please, gods, not her, please.

"Thazienne," he murmured. "Please come back, Thazienne." He buried his face in her dark hair and tried to warm her cold body with the heat of his own.

Moments later—it seemed an eternity to him—Meena Foxmantle's sobs brought Cale back to himself. She lay on the floor near him, curled into a fetal position, trembling so badly that she looked as if she were convulsing. Her terrified eyes stared vacantly at him. He reached out and gently placed a reassuring hand on her shoulder. She grabbed at his arm like a drowning person clutching a lifeline and held so tight that he lost all feeling in his hand within moments.

"It's all right," he said. "It's going to be all right." He wasn't sure if he was trying to convince her or himself.

While Captain Orvist and the house guard finished with the remainder of the ghouls, Thamalon and Shamur charged across the feasthall, the Foxmantles close behind.

Cale saw them coming and lifted Thazienne from the floor.

"Tazi!" they shouted in shared alarm. They rushed forward and touched her hands and face. Upon feeling the coldness of her flesh, Thamalon recoiled in shock. Shamur's already tear-streaked face went white. She clutched her husband's wrist with one hand, raised the other to her mouth, and looked upon the limp form of her daughter.

"Gods," Thamalon oathed, and tears formed in his eyes.

Cale's knees trembled. Tears welled in his eyes. A house guard tried to relieve him of Thazienne but he refused to let her go.

"Send for a priest, Lord," he said to Thamalon, his voice quavering with emotion. "Send for a priest *now.*"

❦ ❦ ❦ ❦ ❦

Riven glared at the gate guard of the manor house and stormed past without a word, violence on his mind. The sleepy, bearded house guard took one look at Riven's scowl and apparently thought better of challenging his entrance to Whitebirch.

Fortunate for you, Riven thought. He would have welcomed an excuse to vent his anger by gutting one of Verdrinal's lackeys.

His foul mood only worsened as he strode through the neatly landscaped, illumined grounds and approached Whitebirch Manor itself. Verdrinal's manse exuded decadence, which of course fit the man perfectly. The front was bedecked with winter shrubs, perfectly hedged, statues of nude women frolicking with leering satyrs, snow dusted benches, and a wooden veranda. Riven found the whole sight vaguely offensive, as though the very air here somehow *soiled* him. Not for the first time, he marveled that a fool such as Verdrinal could have risen so far within the Zhentarim. The bastard actually equaled him in rank!

You get born to the right family and anything's possible, he supposed with a scowl. The only heir of the Isterin family fortune, Verdrinal Isterin provided a legitimate face for many otherwise illicit Zhentarim operations. Apart from his wealth and family name, Riven thought Verdrinal a useless, incompetent man. Equal in rank or not, Riven held him in contempt.

Not bothering to use the bronze doorknocker, he kicked open the main doors and walked into the foyer. Not a guard in sight.

"Verdrinal!" he shouted up the main stairway. "Get out of bed and get down here!" He deliberately had come in the small hours, just to inconvenience Verdrinal the more. He must have caught the house guard unawares as well—Hov usually did better work.

Muffled voices and a shuffling from upstairs told him that he had been heard. In a few moments, a dark-haired young man in the purple uniform of an Isterin house guard emerged from the hallway and leaned over the banister. He scowled when he saw Riven.

"What do you want?"

"Get out of my sight," Riven retorted. "And tell Verdrinal to get down here, now."

The house guard's eyes narrowed. Riven assumed he was trying to be intimidating. "He'll be along soon enough."

Riven said nothing. Verdrinal was no doubt upstairs with a woman. The nobleman went through women the way other men went through clothes. The man's insatiable tastes made him weak—he lacked focus, lacked discipline.

"Why don't you fetch Hov, *boy*. Keeping an eye on me is no job for a little puke like you."

The house guard snarled and stepped back from the landing. He stomped down the stairs, a white-knuckled grip on his sword hilt. He walked up to Riven, face to face.

"Don't *ever* burst in here again or *I'll* put you down. I don't need Hov for the likes of you."

Before the guard could move, Riven whipped free a dagger and stabbed him through the gut.

The surprised house guard grunted in pain, tried to draw his own blade, but doubled over instead. Warm blood coursed over Riven's hand and stained the house guard's purple uniform black. Riven jerked the dagger free and kicked the guard to the floor.

"Never say *don't* to me, boy." He knelt and wiped his blade clean on the dying house guard's uniform.

"Drasek!"

Verdrinal's voice from atop the stairs pulled his gaze upward and wiped the satisfied smile from his face. The tall, brown-haired Zhentarim nobleman had taken the time to don a shirt and blue pantaloons. He pointed a long finger at the groaning house guard.

"What have you done? Do you have any idea how hard it is to find good men?"

Riven ignored both the question and the house guard's dying spasms. He stared into Verdrinal's eyes.

"If he was a good man, he wouldn't be dying on the floor. And if you ever call me *Drasek* again, Verdrinal, I'll leave you bleeding beside him."

Verdrinal smiled distantly at the threat and descended the stairs. "But *Riven* sounds so formal," he said with a phony smile. "And the two of us such old friends."

Riven spat on the foyer floor, sheathed his dagger, and said nothing.

The house guard gasped and finally expired. Verdrinal looked down at the expanding pool of blood on the hardwood floor. His smooth, handsome face creased with a flash of anger. "What a blasted mess." He stared ice at Riven. "Varra," he shouted over his shoulder. "Varra!"

After a moment, a pretty brunette maid in a white nightdress scurried into the foyer through an adjacent doorway. Upon seeing the corpse, she gasped.

"Clean this up please, Varra dear." He shot Riven an ingenuous smile. "Mister . . . *Riven* and I will be in the study."

The girl gave a frightened nod, whirled in a cloud of white nightdress, and ran from the foyer. Riven watched her go, aroused by the way the thin cotton hugged her slim hips as she ran. Verdrinal's voice stopped her at the doorway.

"Oh, and Varra . . ." She turned, eyes wide. Riven leered at her.

"Please let Hov know that I have company." She nodded again and ran off.

Riven glanced at Verdrinal and didn't bother to hide his derision. Hov, a brick wall of a warrior with a two-handed broadsword and a mean temper, headed Verdrinal's houseguards.

"Afraid?" he asked Verdrinal.

"Merely cautious, *Riven*, as always."

Cautious or not, Riven knew that he could put Hov down one-on-one, but the big bastard probably would bring along additional men. That could create problems.

Stay sharp, he reminded himself. Though Verdrinal *was* incompetent, he was also reasonably cunning, and he resorted to bloodletting almost as readily as Riven. He'd turn the house guard loose if Riven pushed him too hard.

Taking a deep breath, Riven struggled to quell the anger that had brought him here. Killing one of Verdrinal's house guards had helped.

Verdrinal strolled into the study off the foyer and lit an oil lamp. Plush chairs and expensive rugs covered the floors. Beautiful, Riven acknowledged, but decadent and useless, like Verdrinal himself. Bookshelves towered from floor to ceiling, filled with leather bound tomes and ribbon-tied scrolls. Riven doubted Verdrinal had read many of them. He collected books just as he collected women—pretty things to decorate his home and impress visitors.

Verdrinal pulled forth a decanter of liquor from a cherrywood hutch and poured himself a glass. "Drink?" he asked Riven.

"No."

Verdrinal shrugged and sauntered back to where Riven stood in the study's doorway. Neither man sat. Verdrinal eyed him over the rim of his glass.

"What is it you want, *Riven*? What time is it? Second hour? By Cyric, it'll be dawn in five hours." As if to make his point, he staged a theatrical yawn.

Riven forced down the urge to punch Verdrinal in his open mouth. No doubt Hov and his men were already watching from some secret room nearby.

"What I want is an explanation. And since Malix has gone underground, that leaves only you." Malix, Riven's handler and the highest-ranking Zhentarim agent in Selgaunt, had vanished soon after Riven had sabotaged the Righteous Man's summoning of the dread. "You know anything?"

Whirling the liquor around in his glass, Verdrinal regarded Riven shrewdly. His green eyes reminded Riven of a viper's.

"Malix has returned to headquarters to personally report recent events to Lord Chembryl. In the meantime, he's left *me* in charge."

Riven stiffened. "You!"

"Me."

"Temporarily, no doubt."

"Temporarily," Verdrinal said, conceding with a nod. He quickly added in an arrogant tone, "But until then, I'm your superior."

At that, Riven's anger boiled over. He no longer cared about the Zhentarim hierarchy or whether Hov and the guards were watching. He stepped close to Verdrinal and hissed into his face, "Well then, you arrogant little bastard, if you're the one in charge, then you can explain to me *what in the dark is going on!* I've lost six operators to this demon. Six! And every one of them sucked dry as a prune. Malix said the dread would kill the Righteous Man and then *leave.* Leave!" He clenched a fist before Verdrinal's handsome face and barely restrained the impulse to beat the man to pulp. "Godsdamned mages never know what they're talking about!"

Verdrinal endured the tirade without expression, even the insult and fist in his face. He waited to be sure Riven had finished, then replied in the tone of voice used to explain something to an angry child. "Things have changed, Riven."

Riven stared at him, amazed that Verdrinal could say something so obvious, and so stupid. "Really."

Verdrinal winced at the sarcasm, took a sip from his glass.

"The dread has somehow managed to remain on our plane. Malix is not sure how. He *is* sure that it has summoned lesser minions," here he smiled, "and is now doing what demons do."

Riven found Verdrinal's self-satisfied tone infuriating. The man was speaking casually about *demons*, as though they prowled Selgaunt every other tenday! He forced down his anger only because he needed information. "So what are we going to do about it? I can't keep losing men to this thing."

Verdrinal gazed at him condescendingly. "Malix's orders are to do *nothing* about it."

"Nothing! Did his brain turn to dung? It's killing my men. Our men. Good operators."

"True, but it is also killing the heads of certain noble families and a multitude of rival leaders. It appears to have taken the Righteous Man's enemies as its own." He smiled and waved his hand, a weak gesture. "Don't you see? It's doing our work for us. We'll let it purge the underworld and only then move against it. That's why Malix went to see Lord Chembryl personally, to determine when to take the next step."

Riven had to admit the logic of the course. A few dead low-level Zhentarim operatives were copper pennies to the gold fivestars of dead patriarchs and rival guildmasters. Malix had been hoping merely to eliminate the Night Knives with the dread, but the creature was doing far better than expected; it was single-handedly securing Selgaunt's entire underworld for the Zhentarim.

"How do we know we can get rid of it?"

Verdrinal ignored the question. "It attacked Stormweather earlier tonight." He grinned smugly, took a sip of his drink, and said nothing more. Verdrinal knew Riven's hate for Erevis Cale. He wanted him to *ask* for details.

Riven could not help himself. "And?"

"And at least twenty guests present for one of Thamalon's balls were slaughtered." Casually, he took another sip from his glass. "Did you know that I was invited to that ball?"

Riven ground his teeth together. You should've attended, he thought, but didn't say. "Cale?"

"Lives. Apparently drove the dread off himself, though the Uskevren daughter was gravely hurt. Quite a man, this Erevis Cale. Quite a man, indeed."

Riven realized that he had been clenching his fists. He released them and said, "I'll take that drink now."

"You know where it is."

Riven walked to the cabinet and surveyed the many bottles Verdrinal kept there. Able to read only with difficulty, he could not tell the vintage of any of the wines, but he'd be damned before he let Verdrinal know of his illiteracy. He grabbed a bottle at random and poured himself a glass. "He'll be looking for a cause," he said, and gulped the wine in a single drink. "Cale, I mean."

Verdrinal nodded. "I hope so. If all goes well, he'll find his cause. That'll solve another of our problems, won't it?"

Riven nodded stiffly and poured himself another glass of wine. He gulped it down too.

A month earlier, Cale and that little halfling rat Jak Fleet had ruined Riven's otherwise perfect plan to kidnap the youngest Uskevren whelp, Talbot. In the process, they had marked Riven with a scar on his back that had yet to heal fully. More importantly, the failed operation had dealt a harsh blow to Riven's aspirations for rising within the Network.

Now I find myself answering to a decadent dolt, he thought.

Since then, the Zhentarim had been keeping a close eye on Cale. They would have done the same with the halfling, but Jak Fleet had vanished into the underworld. Riven had known ever since that Cale's death was simply a matter of time, but he had hoped to kill the bald overgrown butler himself. A man like Verdrinal would not understand that.

Still angry, he walked back to face the nobleman and jabbed a finger into his chest.

"What about my men? I can't afford to lose any more."

Verdrinal backed up a step and placed a finger to his lips in affected surprise. "Dark! You've just reminded me of something. Oh my! Oh, this won't make you happy."

Riven's stare bored holes into him.

Verdrinal feigned dismay, but Riven saw the mirth in his eyes as he spoke. "Before Malix left, he told me to tell you to have your men go underground. To avoid the dread. That way—"

Riven smacked the drink out of his hands and gripped him by his fish-white throat. "You dog!" He slammed his head into Verdrinal's nose. Verdrinal exclaimed and staggered backward, clutching at a broken nose streaming blood.

"You want to play games *with me!* I lost six men while you sat on that warning!" He jerked free a dagger, grabbed Verdrinal by the robe, and waved the blade before his dazed, watering eyes. "I should split you right now."

"If you do, you'll never get out alive," Verdrinal mumbled, and smiled through the blood pouring out his nose.

Behind him, Riven could hear the hurried boot stomps of Hov approaching alone. He spat into Verdrinal's face. "Won't be long and the time will come for you and me." Riven pulled Verdrinal's bleeding face close. "Just not tonight."

Verdrinal, recovered now from the blow to his nose, and actually *grinned*. Disgusted, Riven threw him to the floor.

"Our time can come tonight, *Drasek*," Verdrinal taunted. "If you want to stay. I'm sure Hov would appreciate some company."

Riven turned and found himself staring into the wide, leather-armored chest of Hov. He took a step back and looked up into the big man's dull brown eyes. Hov glared down, right hand on his sword hilt, left hand clenched in a fist.

"Anytime," Riven whispered. "I've already left one of yours dead on the floor. What's one more to me?"

Hov smirked but said nothing.

Riven stalked past and headed for the foyer. Behind him, Verdrinal's mocking voice rang in his ears. "Praise to Cyric," the nobleman said, the standard Zhentarim words of greeting and farewell, but only among *compatriots*.

Without breaking stride, Riven shouldered over a delicate nude female statue. It shattered into hundreds of pieces on the foyer floor, chunks of marble splashed into the pool of blood that Varra had yet to clean up. Verdrinal squealed in protest.

"You bastard! You—"

Riven smiled and strode out the door. "Praise to Cyric," he said mockingly over his shoulder.

CHAPTER 5

Aftermath

Cale waited anxiously in the carpeted hall outside Thazienne's room. Sweat beaded his brow and a lump sat in his throat. When he had left her side to organize the cleanup, she still had been unconscious and barely breathing. Her face had looked so pale and drawn.

Behind the closed door of the bedroom, he could hear Thamalon, Shamur, and Tamlin praying with High Songmaster Ansril Ammhaddan, Priest of Milil. Talbot had not yet arrived. Cale had sent a servant for him several hours ago, and was growing worried by his continued absence. Talbot would never forgive himself if something happened to her and he was not here for it.

Though Thazienne still treated her little

brother as if he were an adolescent—much to the rapidly maturing young man's annoyance—Cale knew that brother and sister still shared a close bond. He hoped Talbot arrived soon.

Through the thick door Cale listened to the soft, melodic murmur of the High Songmaster's song spells and the teary, answering chorus of the grief-stricken Uskevren. Thamalon had invited Cale to accompany the family in prayer of course, but Cale had gently declined. He was not a religious man. His presence would be a hindrance to them, not a help. Prayer and priests made him uncomfortable. Gods made him uneasy. He thought people of faith often to be overly gullible—followers not leaders. Only Jak had shown himself an exception to that rule. Religion distracted men, made them blind to the true nature of events around them. The Righteous Man embodied the point. His obsession with the worship of Mask had made the old man vulnerable. Cale would never allow himself to fall into such a trap. No, Cale preferred to rely not on divine assistance, but on his brains, his body, and his blades. Now more than ever before, however, he realized that those three things could not solve all problems. He saw in his mind Thazienne lying unconscious in her bed, weak and stricken, barely breathing. His wits and steel could do nothing for her, he knew, but he still could not bring himself to offer prayer.

Of course, his brains and blades *could* solve other problems. The need for payback, for example.

Later, he reminded himself, and swallowed his rising anger. For now, Thazienne's well-being was all that mattered. Besides, at the moment he felt too exhausted and worried to plan vengeance. For an instant, he wished he could allow himself to find solace in faith.

Instead, he found solace in a high backed armchair. His anxious pacing did nothing but wear out the carpet and his nervous fidgeting only fed his worry. Trying to calm himself, he crossed his long legs, clenched the carved arms of the chair, took a deep breath, and tried hard to remain still. He had ordered the staff away so that they would not see the family distraught, but he would have welcomed someone to talk to now. Even Larajin. Anything to distract him. He felt so damned useless!

The praying within Thazienne's bedroom stopped. Cale waited anxiously. After a moment, the door to her room slowly opened and the High Priest shuffled out. A heavyset yet stately looking old man with a thick beard and a neatly combed mane of gray hair, High Songmaster Ammhaddan looked so somber that Cale's stomach hit the floor. He tried to rise from the chair but the strength had gone out of his legs.

Tamlin, eyes red and swollen, followed the High Songmaster out. Thamalon and Shamur came last. Both still wore their attire from the celebration, the fine clothes now stained, wrinkled, and disheveled.

With tears streaming unabashedly down his clean-shaven face, Thamalon gently pulled the door closed. Beside him, Shamur struggled to hold back her own tears, but finally lost the fight and wept openly. Her slight body shook with sobs.

Awkwardly, as if unsure of himself, Thamalon took her in his arms. She stiffened immediately, haltingly returned his embrace, and quickly disengaged. Though grief-stricken, she still insisted on maintaining her distance from Lord Uskevren.

Cale saw the hurt on his lord's face. The wound in his heart of a stricken daughter salted by the coolness of his wife. At that moment, Cale detested Lady Uskevren.

"It will be all right," Thamalon whispered to her. He lifted a hand as though to touch her face, but let it fall to his side without contact. "It will be all right."

Caught up in their emotion, Cale felt his own eyes begin to well. He lowered his head and looked at his hands. She can't be dead! he inwardly protested. She can't.

He had to hear it explicitly before he would believe it.

He stood on legs still weak and walked over to the solemn High Songmaster, who looked on the grieving Thamalon and Shamur with an understanding, fatherly expression. High Priest Ammhaddan turned to see him coming and regarded him with the same paternal warmth. Cale's legs gave out and he nearly fell to the floor. The High Songmaster, strong despite his years, caught him by the arm and helped him to stand upright.

Cale gave him a grateful smile through teary eyes. His voice caught when he spoke. "Well?" he asked, and winced in anticipation of the answer. "How is she?"

Still holding him by the arm, the High Songmaster scrutinized his face with a look Cale found ominous. "Mister Cale, is your first name Erevis?"

His throat constricted and he could barely find his voice. "Yes." He felt as though he were floating.

His distress must have been plain on his face for Ansril Ammhaddan softly patted his shoulder. "She'll live, son. Rest easy. She'll live."

Cale's vision instantly went blurry. She'll live!

Tears of joy replaced those of grief and streamed down his face. He smiled like a buffoon until he saw that the High Songmaster still wore a somber expression. He clutched a handful of the priest's crimson robe so hard that he pulled Ansril forward a step.

"What? You said she would live. How is she? Will she—" He could not bring himself to mouth the words. A thousand terrible possibilities flew through his mind but he could give voice to none. He stared into

Ansril Ammhaddan's wrinkled face and tried to read the priest's eyes.

"What is it, Ansril?" Thamalon asked. "I thought you said she would be all right." Thamalon and Tamlin closed in around them, apprehensive. No longer crying, Shamur seemed to be holding her breath.

High Songmaster Ammhaddan gently disengaged Cale's fingers from his robe and turned to Thamalon. "I did say that she would live, Thamalon . . ." he began to say.

Immediately, Shamur began again to laugh and cry all at once. Thamalon smiled like a fool through his own wet eyes. Cale gave Tamlin's shoulder a squeeze and the heir patted him on the back.

"*But,*" the High Songmaster's baritone cut through their relief. Their smiles vanished and the hallway fell silent. When Ansril had their full attention, he continued. "I did not say that she would be all right. She is severely wounded. Severely. Whatever this creature was, this shadow, the wounds it inflicted have attacked her soul and drained her life-force." He looked to Thamalon and Shamur with sympathy. "Her recovery will be long, and she may not be the same afterward. Wounds like these could affect the spirit as much or more than the flesh . . ." He trailed off thoughtfully and stroked his beard.

Shamur's eyes went wide. She visibly fought down her grief, looked to Thamalon, and spoke with certainty. "But she's so strong, Thamalon. She'll be all right. I know it. She will."

Thamalon gave her a soft smile. "She will. She has her mother's strength."

To that, Shamur finally gave Lord Uskevren an appreciative smile, though she did not reach out to him. Instead, she folded her arms across her chest and rubbed thoughtfully at her shoulders.

Finally unable to contain his own grief, Tamlin began to cry. He stood stiffly beside Cale with tears slowly falling down his face. Even if they had been close, Cale could have offered him nothing, his own sorrow cut too deep. *The spirit as much as the flesh,* Ansril had said. Shamur too began to weep anew.

Thamalon's eyes alone remained dry, his mouth a thoughtful grim line. Cale could see in his lord's expression grief warring with anger—anger at the parties responsible. Cale knew the reason for the attack but dared not speak it. It tore him apart inside to not immediately confide in Thamalon.

"I'm sorry, Thamalon," said High Songmaster Ammhaddan sincerely. "I'll do everything I can, of course."

Thamalon gave him a forced smile and shook the Songmaster's hand. "I know you will. Thank you, Ansril."

The High Songmaster indicated Thazienne's bedroom with a nod. "She needs undisturbed rest. The work of the Lord of Song is done. Sleep will heal her now as much as spells."

"I'll see to it she's undisturbed. Thank you again."

High Songmaster Ammhaddan bowed to Lady Uskevren. "She *is* strong, Lady. I can see that. Do not lose hope."

Shamur nodded and forced a smile of thanks.

Ansril turned and nodded to Cale and Tamlin. "The Songlord's voice bring you peace and keep you," he said, and with that took his leave.

When he had gone, Cale, Tamlin, Shamur, and Thamalon stood about in the hall, grief-stricken, exhausted, and unsure of what to do with themselves.

Tamlin broke the awkward silence at last. Embarrassed, he wiped at his tear-streaked face. "I think I'm going to try and get some sleep." He nodded goodnight to Thamalon but the two did not embrace. "Father." He did, however, hug his mother with genuine affection. "Good night, Mother. It's going to be all right. You heard the High Songmaster."

"I know," she whispered, as though trying to convince herself. "I know."

He wiped a tear from her face and smiled at her. When she returned a wan smile of her own, he patted her shoulders and turned away from her to face Cale. "Goodnight, Mister Cale."

"Goodnight, Master Tamlin."

After he had gone, Thamalon kissed Shamur on the forehead. Unusually, she did not shrink from his show of affection. "I think our son has the right notion, Lady. Let me take you to your bed. Erevis and I will wait up for Talbot."

At first hesitant—Thamalon only rarely set foot in her quarters—she at last nodded, dabbed her nose, and allowed him to lead her off toward her suites. As he passed, Thamalon said to Cale, "Erevis, I'll meet you in the library in a quarter of an hour." His serious expression told Cale that he should be ready to discuss business.

"Yes, Lord," Cale replied. He would not have been able to sleep anyway.

Though only a few hours from dawn, the halls of Stormweather still bustled with activity. The surviving house guards scoured the manse. They searched and re-searched every room in the manse and every outbuilding on the grounds for ghoul stragglers.

A pair of weary-eyed guards dressed in blood-spattered, Uskevren blue thumped up the stairs as Cale padded down. They looked exhausted, but nevertheless went about their duty with the stolid, seemingly limitless endurance possessed by all professional soldiers.

When they saw Cale, both immediately snapped to attention. Cale gave them a half-hearted smile. He had always had the respect of the house guard—once, when he had been delegating duties to the staff for an upcoming dinner, Captain Orvist had walked by and complimented him by saying that he gave orders like a field general—but his battle with the shadow demon had elevated him to the rank of honorary commander. He thought he might as well take full advantage.

"Lady Uskevren has taken to her rooms," he said. "Pass the word and see that it remains quiet upstairs. And under *no* circumstances is Mistress Thazienne's bedroom to be disturbed." The High Priest had ordered undisturbed rest for Thazienne, and Cale would see to it.

"Yes, Mister Cale," snapped Darven, a big, muscular veteran who towered over most of the guards but still stood a handspan shorter than Cale. "We'll inform Captain Orvist right now." Darven gave the guard beside him an elbow and both men spun and hurried back down the stairs. Cale followed at a more leisurely pace, thoughtful.

The members of the household staff had already cleaned up most of the carnage, though Cale could still hear voices and the occasional clatter of dishes coming from the feasthall.

Thank the gods for Brilla, he thought with a tired smile. While he had personally organized the cleanup, he had left supervision of the effort in the kitchen mistress's pudgy, but still very capable hands.

After the attack, the families of the slain had been notified immediately. All of the corpses and the pieces of corpses had been removed hours ago. No doubt some fortunate few already had been raised from the dead.

Cale knew that with enough coin for the temple's coffers and a powerful enough priest, not even death was insurmountable for the richest of the Old Chauncel nobility.

Thinking of the raised dead reminded him of Krendik, a former living man twisted into an undead monster, and sent a shudder up his spine. The dead should be left dead, he thought, and knew as soon as he thought it that those murdered by the shadow demon *would* be left dead. Cale himself had felt that black horror's touch pull sickeningly at his soul. No matter the coin a family paid the temple priests for those the demon had slain, there would be no coming back. There was nothing to bring back. The demon had devoured their souls.

Shuddering, his hand went to the faded gash in his shoulder. Strangely, the physical damage from the demon's claws had almost entirely healed. The same was true of Thazienne's chest. It was as though the demon's claws opened the skin only to free the soul, and if the soul was not loosed and devoured, the wound quickly healed. The *physical* wound, at least. The emotional wounds would heal much more slowly.

Cale still did not know the total number of guests that had been killed. In truth, he didn't want to know, but it had been a lot. The number of distraught relatives that had come by coach and carriage to Stormweather's doors to retrieve their dead had seemed to him an unending stream. With Thamalon, Shamur, and Tamlin tending to Thazienne, the duty to assist the grief stricken relatives in sorting through the corpses had fallen to Cale and Captain Orvist. He had seen up close the gory wounds inflicted by ghoul fang and claw. He had also witnessed the desiccated remains left in the wake of the demon's attacks. The images from the slaughter's aftermath would haunt his mind for a long while. The fact that it was his fault would haunt him longer.

It *was* my fault, he frankly admitted. It had to be. He felt too tired now even to feel anger at himself for the attack. He admitted the truth of it as he would any other self-evident fact. Thazienne's wounded spirit, Meena Foxmantle's wounded sanity, all the dead guests and house guards—his fault. He was not sure how, but he *was* sure that the Righteous Man had finally learned that he had been protecting the Uskevren, not spying on them. The Righteous Man had meant the attack to send a message—*I know*.

After driving off the demon, Cale had carried Thazienne up the stairs to her room and placed her in bed to await a priest. Thamalon, Shamur, and Tamlin had remained with her. Cale had reluctantly left her side and hurried back to the feasthall to examine the ghoul corpses. He had to know for sure.

As he had suspected and feared, all of the ghouls had been former Night Knives. Beneath the gray skin, rotted fangs, and charnel reek, he had recognized the twisted faces of his former fellow guild members. Somehow, they had been transformed from living men into flesh-eating, undead monsters. The realization had sickened him, but he had swallowed his nausea and tried to put together the pieces of the puzzle.

After learning of Cale's ten-year deception, the Righteous Man must have decided to repay the betrayal by hurting the people Cale loved most. To accomplish that, the Righteous Man, not only a guildmaster but also a powerful priest of Mask the Shadowlord, had summoned the shadow demon. After using his black magic to warp guildsmen into ghouls, he had turned them loose on Stormweather to slay its inhabitants.

While it seemed an extreme measure, Cale put

nothing beyond the sadistic guildmaster. He was a priest, and therefore a fanatic by definition. Even as that thought crossed his mind, he realized that he was mistaken, that anger was causing him to over generalize. *Many* priests might be fanatics, but not all. Not Jak, and not Ansril Ammhaddan. For them at least, religion had not meant fanaticism.

But it had for the Righteous Man. Once, Cale had watched him burn down an entire guild warehouse, *with eleven guildsmen trapped inside*, just to ensure that he had eliminated one among them whom he suspected to be a traitor. It would be just like him to try to hurt Cale before killing him.

Cale's thinking had gone no further, then. At that moment, High Songmaster Ammhaddan and three other underling priests had walked huffing and wide-eyed into the feasthall. The priests insisted on healing Cale's wounds and he had reluctantly stood still for a few moments while their song spells closed the numerous cuts in his chest, back, and shoulders. Afterward, he had dispatched three of the priests to tend the wounded among the house guard and had escorted High Songmaster Ammhaddan from the slaughterhouse to Thazienne's room.

She had looked worse than when he had first left her, so he had waited apprehensively in the hall while the High Songmaster had used song spells to try to heal her.

Now that he knew her to be safe—or at least knew that she would live—he began again to consider the depths to which the Righteous Man would sink. The masked dog had dared attack him *here!* Had dared harm Thazienne!

Rising anger began to wash away his fatigue—anger at himself for adopting this selfish, asinine plan ten years ago, anger at the Righteous Man for using

Cale's family as a way to get at him. As he stomped through Stormweather's carpeted halls, he gritted his teeth and clenched his fists in rage.

If the Righteous Man had targeted him, as he now suspected, then he was already a walking corpse. He could admit that forthrightly—his death was only a matter of time. Sooner or later the Righteous Man would come to finish him, or more likely still, send Drasek Riven to do the job. Unfortunately, at least as far as Cale was concerned, Riven had not been among the ghoul corpses. Given that situation, Cale could not remain in Stormweather and risk another attack on the family. But where to go?

He knew the answer almost as soon as he posed the question—the Night Knife guildhouse. Thinking of it gave him a focus for his anger. He would take the battle to them.

I'm coming for you old man, he silently vowed. I may be a dead man, but I'm taking you with me.

He stalked into the library and began to pace and think. The smell of burning ghoul corpses carried through the shuttered windows. Spells that allowed High Songmaster Ammhaddan's priests to magically communicate with the dead ghouls had revealed nothing. Cale had therefore directed the house guard to pile the dead creatures near the stables, cover them in lantern oil, and burn them to ashes. The lingering reek of the burning pyre only fueled his anger.

Seething with rage, he hardly noticed the blazing stone hearth. He barely saw the shelves of valuable, leather-bound books that he so loved. He paced the floor, thinking, planning, stewing. His lord's chess set, the pieces skillfully carved from imported ivory, the board itself crafted of aged mahogany, stood untouched on a walnut end table. He restrained the urge to shatter the valuable pieces against the wall.

He tried to calm himself.

He lit a single candle, carried it to the end table, and fell into one of the accompanying chairs to await his lord. He could feel his pulse pounding in his forehead, every beat of his heart feeding his rising rage. Get yourself under control, he ordered.

With a supreme effort of will, he calmed himself and remained still.

After a time, Thamalon walked into the room and pulled the door shut behind him. He had shed his doublet and now wore only a light shirt, blue pants, and cloth slippers. He looked exhausted—the events of the night understandably weighed heavy on his mind—but his blazing eyes could fire a torch. When he entered, Cale immediately climbed to his feet, but Thamalon ordered him to sit down.

Grim faced, Thamalon walked to the small wine rack he kept near his oak work desk and pulled out a bottle of Storm Ruby. He stabbed the cork with a screw, jerked it out, and poured two glasses. Cale could see the barely controlled anger in the tense set of Thamalon's powerful shoulders.

He and I are much alike, Cale realized. We both understand that uncontrolled anger works against us, not for us. Both men had to struggle mightily to control that anger. Of course, guilt did not pollute Thamalon's anger. That burden was Cale's alone.

Thamalon strode over to him, handed him a silver goblet, and sat opposite in his favorite rocking chair. For a time, they sat in the dim light of the fire and silently regarded one another, two friends who took comfort in each other's company. Riddled with guilt, Cale found it difficult to look Thamalon in the eye. Uncomfortable, he placed his wine untouched onto the table beside him.

"You wanted to talk, Lord?" He managed to keep his

voice level, though he thought his guilt must be plain on his face.

Thamalon gazed at him from beneath bushy brows for a long moment before replying. "I wished to thank you again for your bravery tonight—"

"Unnecessary, Lord," Cale interjected with a dismissive wave of his hand.

"Without you . . ." Thamalon trailed off and took a gulp from his goblet. He gripped the metal so tightly his fingers went white, "Without you, things would have ended much differently."

Cale nodded but held his tongue. Where was Thamalon going with this?

Thamalon set the goblet down on the table. "I did not know you were capable of such things, though I've long suspected. " His discerning eyes pierced Cale like blades.

If you knew what I was really capable of, Cale thought, *you'd have thrown me out years ago.*

After a moment of awkward silence, Thamalon spoke, "It's time we played a match, Erevis."

"Lord?"

Thamalon sat forward in the chair and indicated the chessboard with his eyes. "A chess match. We have never played. It's time we did."

"Tonight? After—"

"Tonight." Thamalon took another gulp from his goblet and slammed it down on the table so hard it knocked over several chess pieces. "I'll have the heads of *everyone* responsible for this, Erevis! Everyone."

Cale stiffened at that. *Everyone responsible.* A wave of fear and self-loathing drowned him. He looked across the end table and met Thamalon's angry gaze, fearful of what he would see there.

Thankfully, his lord's eyes held no accusations. Anger blazed in those gray orbs, but not anger directed at Cale.

Thamalon continued, "To do that, I will need to call upon *all* of my resources. Including you." He leaned forward, placed his forearms on his knees, and shot Cale a meaningful stare. "I need to know the *full* range of your . . . chess skills." He nodded at the chessboard. "I don't need to know where you learned to play."

Cale swallowed a sigh and immediately felt shame for the relief he felt. Thamalon did not suspect that Cale was responsible for the attack. He only wanted information about Cale's past and skills. He wanted to know what Cale could do to help find the guilty parties.

At that, he felt his face flush red and looked away. *I* am the guilty party, he thought. If Thamalon ever learned that his secret life had been the cause of the attack, he would never forgive him. Hells, Cale would never forgive *himself*, but he didn't want the last conversation he had with his lord to end with the revelation that he had been living in Stormweather as a spy.

Still, Thamalon obviously realized that Cale was more than a butler with a knowledgeable criminal cousin. Butlers didn't drive off demons. His lord had suspected—no, not suspected, *known*—him to be a former criminal and yet had trusted him enough to allow him to continue on as Stormweather's butler. Thamalon had even respected his privacy and asked no questions. His trust had gone that deep. Cale could never repay that debt, not fully.

For the first time in his life, Cale had gotten a taste of legitimate work. Work that did not require him to mistrust everyone. Work that did not require him to keep his eyes on the exits and his hands on his blades. Work that had allowed him to put his darker side to rest, at least for a time. But most importantly, he had done work that had resulted in the love and trust of a family. Though the lie laid heavy on his soul, now more than ever he could not reveal that he originally had been sent to Stormweather to spy. He would not pollute their memory of him, though he knew it meant polluting himself by keeping it secret. Still, he wanted them to remember him the way he would remember them—with love. He was determined to leave with their trust. The trust he had earned from years of loyal service.

Look where their trust has gotten them, he thought bitterly. Thazienne near death. His lord and lady shamed, plus a multitude of murdered guests and guards. His presence here had put them all in danger. Previously, he had always told himself that by being here he actually decreased the risk they faced in Selgaunt's backstabbing world of secret plots and scheming nobles, not increased it. "I can handle the Righteous Man," he had told himself again and again, as he had struggled to quell the pangs of conscience that tore at him. He now realized that he had been lying to himself, just as he had lied to everyone else.

No more, he vowed. No more. Abruptly, he came to a decision.

Everything changed, starting now. He would no longer put the Uskevren at risk. Either he got out of the life altogether or tonight was his last night in Stormweather; his last night as Erevis the butler. Resolved, he looked across the chessboard at Thamalon. If his lord wanted to know who he was, he would tell him.

"Let's play," he said.

Over the next hour they played and talked.

Thamalon opened with a standard cleric gambit. Cale countered it in three moves.

"You play well, Erevis," observed Thamalon with raised brows. "I find myself unsurprised."

Cale smiled.

"I was taught by the best players in Westgate two

decades ago. My instructors did not forgive mistakes, so I learned well."

Thamalon nodded sagely.

"I understand Westgate to have been that way. Still is, most say."

A city comparable in size to Selgaunt and likewise on the coast of the Inner Sea, Westgate had a long history of being run by powerful thieves' guilds. Though no longer dominated by guilds, the city still harbored more thieves than a brothel did whores.

Move. Countermove. Cale felt lighter for having finally revealed some of his past to his lord. He had kept too many secrets for far too long. Once started, he found it hard to stop. With his face turned down to look upon the board, he revealed still more.

"Of course, my instructors as such no longer exist in Westgate. Other players allied and forced them out of business."

At that, Thamalon gave a barely perceptible start. His lord knew the history of the region. Years ago, an alliance of smaller guilds and the Westgate city authorities had allied to destroy the powerful guild known as the Night Masks. The guild that had formerly run the city. The guild to which Cale had formerly belonged.

So now you know, Cale thought. Your butler was a Night Mask operative. "I found chess to be a very cutthroat game, then," he added. "Fine for me as a younger man, but not a life I wanted to live forever."

Thamalon cleared his throat as though to speak but said nothing. Instead, he moved a vicar into position to threaten one of Cale's clerics. Cale countered and attacked with his second cleric.

"I understand," Thamalon managed at last, but he looked upon Cale with different eyes now. A mixture of surprise, respect, and fear. Cale didn't much care for the change. "That answers many of my questions."

While they had existed, the Night Masks had earned a reputation for violence and assassination. Even Thamalon apparently had heard of it. When Cale had fled Westgate and the guild, he had tried to leave that life far behind, but he had never seemed fully able to escape it. Soon after arriving in Selgaunt, he had fallen in with the Night *Knives*, another guild of thieves. *That* fact he could not reveal to Thamalon. It was enough that his lord now knew him to be a former thief and assassin. Cale would not add spy to the list.

Move. Countermove. Cale had the advantage in the chess match.

"Your schoolmaster," Thamalon asked while trying to counter Cale's attack, "what did he look like?"

Cale smiled grimly but did not look up. Thamalon wanted confirmation.

When Cale had been in the Night Masks, the guild had been headed by a secretive guildmaster who called himself The Faceless—a man whose identity had been and remained to this day a mystery—to most everyone but Cale.

He looked up from the board and into Thamalon's eyes and said meaningfully, "I never saw his face."

Thamalon nodded slowly, his brow furrowed. *Move. Countermove.*

They played in silence for the next quarter of an hour. Cale knew Thamalon to be working through the implications of everything he had learned. His chess suffered for the inattention. Cale's attack soon had Thamalon's high monarch in retreat.

"You play aggressively, Erevis," Thamalon remarked, and removed his high monarch from immediate danger. Cale followed up with his archer and threatened anew.

"That is the only way I learned to play, Lord. Check."

Thamalon interposed a cleric, but both knew the game to be soon over.

"Unbridled aggression can sometimes be an enemy."

Cale halted in midmove to offer Thamalon a nod. "My Lord speaks truly. But the demands of the game frequently require it. When that is so, only the most cutthroat of players can win." He moved his low monarch into position and looked up into Thamalon's face. "Checkmate."

Thamalon smiled thoughtfully. He lay down his high monarch and sat back in his rocking chair. "A most enlightening game, old friend. Thank you, for everything."

It warmed Cale to hear Thamalon still call him *old friend*. Cale downed his wine in a single gulp, stood, and bowed.

"May I take my leave, Lord? I have . . ." he smiled without mirth, "I have another game yet to play tonight."

Thamalon raised his bushy brows and gave Cale a piercing stare. "Do you already suspect the name of your next opponent?" He sat forward in the rocker and his eyes blazed beneath his fatigue. "Tell me if so, Erevis."

Cale's lie came easy to him; too easy. "No Lord, not yet. But I will learn it."

Thamalon eased back into the chair but his eyes never left Cale's face. "Everything I have is at your disposal—coin, men, magic. You don't need to play alone, Cale."

Cale raised his eyebrows at that. Thamalon had never before called him *Cale*. This conversation had changed their relationship. "Chess is not a team game, Lord."

Thamalon smiled softly and nodded in acceptance. "No, I suppose it's not."

Cale prepared to leave but Thamalon stood and seized Cale's arm. "If the circumstances of the game change, and you require something, anything, you need only ask."

"I know, Lord." Cale smiled. He wanted to embrace Thamalon, the man who had been friend and father for ten years, but could not bring himself to do it. He cleared his throat and stepped away from his lord.

"I keep my chessboard and pieces in my room. That's all I'll need for now. I'll leave immediately. When I learn something certain, I'll send word." He wanted to tell Thamalon that he likely would not be coming back, but feared the inevitable questions that would follow. Cale knew leaving without saying good-bye would be something he would regret forever, but he also knew that if he told Thamalon the truth, his lord's pained expression would also haunt him forever. If Thazienne learned of his past, she would despise him. He could not endure that. Better they thought him dead or vanished. Better they remembered him as Erevis the butler.

"My lord should retire," he said, still playing the role of butler. "I will give this matter my full atten-tion."

Thamalon seemed to notice his exhaustion for the first time. He nodded and gave Cale a tired smile. "I will, soon. I need some time yet to think. And I still want to wait for Talbot." He patted Cale on the shoul-der. "You should rest too, old friend. Dawn is only hours away."

Cale returned his lord's smile with a hard smile of his own. "My Lord," he said, "I play chess best by night."

CHAPTER 6

CALE

Cale left Thamalon alone with his thoughts and strode purposefully out of the library. The household still bustled as the house guard and staff finalized the cleanup. Some quietly hailed him but he ignored their greetings. His mind was focused on only one thing—making the Righteous Man pay for hurting his family.

He took the steps of the spiral staircase two at a time. When he reached his room, he gently closed and locked the door behind him. For the briefest instant, doubt reared its head and caused him to hesitate. The realization that he would likely never again see his home and family, and that he would probably be dead before tomorrow, hit him like a fist. Cale stubbornly blinked away the tears beginning to well in his eyes.

I'll do it because I have to, he told himself. Ten years of my selfishness nearly killed Thazienne tonight. One way or another, it had to end. The lies, the schemes, the cover up—all of it had to end, tonight.

Resolved once again, he glanced around the safest room in which he had ever lived and tried to fix its image in his memory. The extra-long, wrought iron bed Shamur had thoughtfully acquired especially for him. The leather bound chair in which he so often fell asleep while reading. The worn oak night table with its tarnished oil lamp. In contrast to the rich but tasteful decor of the rest of Stormweather, his room looked like the spartan cell of an Ilmaterite monk.

Thazienne always tells me I live like a cloistered priest, he thought, smiling. His smile dissolved into a frown when he realized that after tonight, he would probably be dead and she wouldn't tell him anything again.

Unconsciously, he had kept his belongings to a minimum. So he could easily run away, he supposed. His room contained nothing personal.

Except for one thing: the locked pine trunk that stood at the foot of his bed. That trunk *was* personal. The lone link to his past in Westgate, it held his blades, enchanted leather armor, and his prized necklace of missiles—the gear of Cale the assassin. The gear that had saved them when thirty Zhents had ambushed Cale and Jak a month ago. That escape had been close and had cost him all but one of the explosive globes on the magical necklace. He had told himself afterward that it didn't matter because he would not need it again, even while a part of him secretly had hoped for the opportunity.

And now I've got it.

He realized now the self-deluding nature of the fiction he had maintained. He had told himself that he would not wear his equipment again, yet he had kept it and lovingly tended it through the course of ten years. Why?

Because I'm a killer playing at a butler, he realized. A killer trained by the best killers the cities of the Inner Sea have ever seen. He smiled, glad now for his Night Mask training. Cale was thankful to the gods for the character that allowed him to kill a man without remorse. Tonight, he was laying the fiction of Erevis the butler to rest. Tonight and forever after, he was Cale.

He walked to the night table, pulled out the drawer, and removed a small iron key from an ingeniously hidden recess he had carved into the wood backing. He carried the key across the room gingerly, as though it was hot, and knelt before the trunk. There he stopped—

His hand shook uncontrollably. He understood that opening the trunk and donning his gear *inside Stormweather*—something he had never before done—signified the end. The end of his life as the Uskevren butler. The end of his life as a member of a family. The end of the happiest period he had ever known. He hesitated—it also meant the end of a ten-year lie, he harshly reminded himself. And the end of putting the people I love in danger.

With a snarl, he shoved in the key and turned it. The click of the lock sounded the death knell of Erevis the butler. Cale was back, this time for good. He threw back the lid and removed his gear.

Like a viper shedding its skin, he stood and peeled off his butler's attire. Out of long habit, he neatly folded his doublet, pants, and hose before placing them on top of the bed. Surprised at himself, he smiled.

Perhaps the butler isn't altogether gone out of me, he thought, and hoped.

He pulled on his leather armor—still strong and supple despite the passage of years due to its powerful enchantment. It was the first thing he had worn in a month that fit him correctly. The smell of it reminded him of Westgate and of all the corpses he had left in the wake of his escape from the Night Masks.

Grimly, he strapped on his weapons belt. The weight of his long sword and daggers hanging from his hips felt *right*. He welcomed the feel of steel at his belt, easily adjusted his stance and movements to the familiar burden. Carefully, as though unveiling a jewel, he drew forth from a velvet bag the necklace of missiles. He thoughtfully rolled the delicate links and final explosive globe between his fingers before clasping it about his throat. He threw on a lightweight, midnight blue, hooded cloak, loaded his pockets with some fivestars, a tinderbox, and three wax candles, then made ready to leave. He walked to the door, turned to take one last glance around the room, smiled sadly, and strode into the hall.

He made a line straight for Thazienne's room. He knew that Thamalon, Shamur, and the two boys would no doubt miss him when he was gone—Tamlin perhaps less than the others, he supposed with a wry smile—but they would move on easily with their lives. He and Thazienne, however, shared a special relationship. Not having him around would be hardest for her.

Though he knew it would be difficult, he would not leave without seeing her one final time and telling her goodbye.

Darven stood guard outside her door, no doubt ensuring the undisturbed rest Cale had ordered. The big guard took in Cale's attire and his eyes went wide with questions.

"Mister Cale?"

Cale patted him reassuringly on his bulky shoulder. "Everything is all right, Darven. I need to see Thazienne. I'll only be a moment."

"Of course." Still wearing an expression full of unspoken questions, Darven pushed the door open for him and closed it behind.

Cale stood just inside the door, suddenly shaking, wary of approaching Thazienne's bed for fear that his resolve would falter. He realized now that she had been the primary reason he had stayed for so long at Stormweather, and now she was the reason he had to leave. So long as the Righteous Man wanted him, his presence here made her unsafe.

Because Thazienne disdained Selgaunt's fashion trends, much to her mother's dismay, her room exuded a unique kind of strong but still vulnerable femininity. Delicate lace doilies and silks decorated her otherwise sturdy dressing table and wardrobe. Pastel paints covered an unadorned, but rough textured wall. A stalwart yet graceful wooden sleigh bed stood in the center of the room. In it, she lay, still unconscious.

Cale saw that she had thrown off her heavy wool blanket—it had landed in a crumpled heap of purple on the floor beside the bed. Thazienne lay covered only in white sheets. Outlined by the thin linen, he could see the slight rise and fall of her breast. Her breathing seemed stronger now than it had been earlier in the evening.

She's too strong to lose, he thought, and smiled. It was the fire of her spirit that had drawn him to her in the first place. No demon's touch could quench its flames.

He steeled himself and crossed the room.

Remembering the unearthly cold that accompanied the shadow demon's touch, he retrieved the wool blanket and gently covered Thazienne's slim body. Some color had returned to her face and she felt warmer to the touch. He pulled a sitting chair close to the bed, covered her small hand with one of his own, and softly caressed her smooth cheek with the back of his other hand. He had never before touched her in that way.

I'll miss you if I don't come back, he thought, and brushed a few stray strands of dark hair from her smooth forehead. Of everything, I'll miss you the most.

He tried to fight back the tears but they came anyway. For a long while, he simply sat there, held her hand, and wept. As usual when it came to his feelings for her, he could bring himself to say nothing.

Struck with an idea, he wiped away his tears and walked to her small writing desk. He pulled a piece of parchment, a vial of ink, and a writing quill from a sliding drawer. Scribing in his light, precise script, he wrote, *Whatever good is in me exists because of you*. He thought for a moment, then wrote a verse from one of his favorite elven poems—*Ai armiel telere maenen hir. You hold my heart forever*. He signed it, stood, and stopped—

What would it do to her to learn his feelings if he never returned? Equally important, what would it do to their relationship if he did?

Doesn't matter, he resolved. She has to know. I can't die and not have told her.

He turned and walked for the door. When he reached it, he again stopped.

After a brief inner struggle, he turned again and walked back to the bed.

Though he knew her to be unconscious, his stomach still fluttered and his knees felt weak. Shaking with pent up emotion, he bent over her and gently brushed her lips with his own—the only kiss they had ever shared. Likely the only kiss they ever would share.

"I love you," he whispered. "I'll always love you."

He had wanted to say those words for years. He only wished he had done it sooner.

He turned and walked from the room.

When he stepped back into the hall and pulled the door closed behind him, Darven shot him a wink. "We all knew you were more than just a butler, Mister Cale. The house guard I mean. We all knew."

Cale nodded. "Just *Cale* from now on, Darven."

Darven cocked his big head quizzically. "Mister Cale?"

"Forget it. Be well, Darven."

He turned and walked down the hall. With each stride away from Thazienne's room, he grew more and more focused, more and more angry. His love for her gave way to hate for the Righteous Man. His hands clenched and unclenched reflexively as he walked. By all the gods, he would make the Righteous Man pay.

Korvikoum, you black-hearted bastard, he thought, invoking a term from dwarven philosophy. You chose to harm the ones I love. The consequence of that choice is that I put you down.

When he descended the stairs, the servants and house guards froze in the midst of their duties and stared in amazement. He offered them no explanations for his attire and weapons—time enough to explain *if* he returned—and walked purposefully toward the forehall. Thamalon emerged from the library and watched him from the doorway, grim approval in his exhausted eyes. Cale gave his lord and friend a nod as he passed, then walked out of Stormweather, probably for the final time.

❧ ❧ ❧ ❧ ❧

He wrinkled his nose at the faded but detectable stink of the Oxblood Quarter. The slaughterhouses that used to fill the block had been moved out of the city decades ago and the buildings converted to the services associated with caravan trade, but still the smell remained. Even the swirling breeze and moderate snowstorm could not eliminate it.

Blue cloak whipping in the wind, Cale crouched low on the roof eave of Emellia's House, a low-class brothel that served mostly wagon drivers and caravan guards. The steep pitch of the roof and snow slick shingles forced him to grip a stone rainspout for balance. He felt the cold of the stone through the leather of his gloves and his breath formed clouds before his face. Through the shuttered windows beneath him, despite the whine of the wind, he could hear the low murmur of male voices and female laughter. Brothels never closed, even in the small hours before dawn, and neither did thieves' guilds.

A dagger toss across Ariness Street, dimly visible through the swirling snow and sputtering light of the windblown street lamps, stood the Night Knife guildhouse.

Masquerading as a Six Coins trading office and storehouse, the Knife guildhouse looked much like all the other storehouses that lined the street and served Selgaunt's thriving caravan trade. Cale knew otherwise, of course. The actual Six Coins trading coster no longer even existed in Faerûn. It had dissolved years ago.

Because it had a basement level and easy access to Selgaunt's old sewer system, the Righteous Man had purchased the two-story brick building from the then money-strapped trading group over a decade ago. Since that time, the guildmaster had refurbished it with guild coin into a combination training facility, safehouse, and fortress.

To perpetuate the illusion of a going coster house, a few of the old Six Coin offices and storerooms had been left intact in the front of the building on the first floor, though most of the structure had been long ago converted to guild use. Night Knife guildsmen who were paid and trained to behave as normal merchants staffed the offices and furthered the ruse. The Righteous Man even used guild coin to fund a small amount of legitimate caravan trade, a practice that deflected suspicion by keeping a flow of wagons and drovers moving in and out of the building.

Because Cale knew what to look for, and the facade now seemed painfully transparent to him. Hardly standard in the typical coster house, the reinforced, iron bound, oak double doors that provided entry looked capable of withstanding an orc battering ram. Unusual too were the thumb-thick iron bars that backed all of the second story windows. The first story glass had been pulled out and bricked over years ago. Cale knew that a careful observer would have noticed the surprisingly small number of employees who arrived daily for work through the front doors, though the building itself was quite large. A careful observer would also have noticed the caravan guard uniforms worn by the hard-eyed rogues who typically guarded the entry were out of place.

I don't know how we managed to keep this location a secret, he thought. To Cale, now on the outside looking in, the building fairly screamed *guildhouse!*

No guards presently stood watch outside the front doors. No slingers on the roof, either. All the second story rooms were dark, an unusual state even at this late hour.

Strange, he thought with a frown, because of the snow, maybe?

He considered simply storming the front doors,

bluffing his way through the guildsmen to the Righteous Man, and taking the old man down, but dismissed the idea as the ill-conceived product of anger. *Unbridled aggression can sometimes be an enemy*, Thamalon had told him. He smiled and thought: True enough, Thamalon, true enough.

He observed for a few minutes more to assure himself that he had not missed anything. He hadn't. There were no guards. The whole situation stank like an ambush. He blew out his breath in a cloud of mist and rubbed the day's growth of stubble that peppered his cheeks.

Abruptly, he made his decision—he would enter the sewers at Winding Way and come up through the guildhouse basement. No doubt that entrance would be trapped as well, but going in that way would put him closer to the basement shrine, and thus closer to the Righteous Man. Survival had ceased to be his primary concern. Cale had already said goodbye to everything that he had to live for. Killing the Righteous Man was all that mattered anymore.

I'm coming for you, old man.

He lowered himself over the side of Emellia's and nimbly climbed down to street level.

The falling snow melted the moment it hit the cobblestones, so the street was covered in a slushy brown muck. Cale pulled his cloak tight against the wind and sloshed a block to Winding Way. The snowfall made visibility difficult, so he relied on his keen ears to alert him to an ambush. He heard nothing. No one was on the street.

When he reached Winding Way, Cale ducked into an alley and looked through the falling snow to make sure no one was behind him. Still no one. He sprinted to the dry common well that the guild had "mistakenly" dug, and that now provided access to the sewers.

Using his height to good effect, he climbed over the well wall and straddled the top. He braced his heels against one side, braced his upper back and shoulder blades against the other, and began slowly to descend. As he did, he kept his ears focused on the sewer bottom forty feet below. Snowflakes fluttered down the well and landed on his face. They melted instantly in the heat of his exertion. Despite the cold air, sweat beaded his forehead and his raspy, labored breathing echoed off the walls. The stink of waste and organic decay rose up the well to fill his nostrils. He inhaled deeply as he descended, trying to dull his senses to the smell.

He let himself drop the final few feet. Hitting the ground in a crouch, he instantly pulled his long sword from its scabbard. Faint in the distance, he heard the high-pitched squeaks of rats and the scurrying sounds of other vermin. Though too dark to see much, he knew the sewer tunnels branched off in three directions. He wanted east. He pulled forth his flint, steel, and tinderbox, and lit a candle. In the damp air, its small flame sputtered dim and orange off the crumbling walls.

Long sword and candle in hand, he headed down the east tunnel. He tried to ignore the muck that sucked at his feet. Tales abounded in Selgaunt about the dire creatures that lurked in the city's sewers—creatures such as flesh dissolving slimes and intelligent algae men—but Cale had concern only for an ambush by guildsmen. This portion of the sewers had been sealed off from the main tunnels a few blocks away, and the guild regularly patrolled to keep it clear of anything, or anybody, unwanted.

He had walked less than fifty paces when he began to smell rotting flesh. Shielding the light of the candle with his hand, he crept forward and strained to listen.

He expected to hear the growl of approaching ghouls, but instead heard nothing. Warily, he advanced.

The stench grew increasingly stronger as he neared the turn in the tunnel that led toward the guildhouse. Still hearing nothing, he hugged the tunnel wall and stalked forward, blade at the ready. When he rounded the turn, he saw the source of the stink. Vomit raced up his throat but he gritted his teeth and swallowed it down.

Ahead of him, at the base of the ladder that ascended into the guildhouse, lay a pile of rotting corpses. Black rats, some of them as large as small dogs, feasted on the bodies. Most of them squeaked indignantly at his approach, left their feast, and scurried off.

"Dark," he softly oathed. He shooed away with his long sword two stubborn rats that had not fled with the rest and knelt to examine the corpses.

A ghastly pile of decomposing flesh, the bodies lay heaped atop one another like cordwood, so rotted and intertwined that Cale could hardly tell where one corpse ended and another began. Fifteen or twenty men maybe, he couldn't tell for sure. Dead a tenday at least, maybe two. The stench made his eyes water.

Torn and naked, the corpses had been tossed down from the trapdoor above like garbage. Partially eaten by ghouls—Cale recognized the ragged wounds of ghoul claw and fang—the rats had been at what remained. Puss and blood assaulted his eyes. He tried to scrutinize the mangled faces more closely but could not recognize any of them before he had to turn away or vomit. The grotesque image of a half-eaten arm sticking out of the base of the heap, the limb seemingly reaching for release, stuck in his mind and made him sweat in the chill.

He tried to steel himself, for he knew he would have to disengage the tangle of bodies to clear a path to the ladder. It was either that or try to climb over.

Shuddering, he immediately dismissed climbing as a bad idea. A big man, he would likely find himself sinking into the midst of the corpses rather than walking on top of them. The thought of wading chest deep in rot made him gag.

Holding his breath and stifling retches, he set to work. He pulled the bodies loose from the pile and hurriedly cast them to the side. Many came apart in his hands. Others leaked so much fluid as he picked them up that pus and blood soon soaked his cloak. He worked as fast as he could. Grab, throw, gag. Grab, throw, gag.

When he finally cleared enough of a path to the ladder, he grabbed desperately at the rusty iron rungs and began to climb. Halfway up he vomited down the front of his cloak. At the same time he realized that he had left his candle sputtering on the sewer floor. He didn't care. He could not go back down, at least not right now.

When he reached the trapdoor, he shouldered it open with a grunt and climbed into the storeroom.

Darkness, but surprisingly, no guards. Light trickled in from beneath the only door out and provided a dim luminescence. Crates and bags lay broken and torn open. Spilled grain and splintered wood littered the ground. Only tattered scraps remained of the filthy rug that once had covered the trapdoor.

Relieved, and in no danger of imminent attack, Cale took a moment to strip his befouled cloak and use a torn burlap grain sack to wipe clean his blood-soaked arms and chest. After transferring his coin and tinderbox into his pants pockets, he tossed the cloak, the sack, and his leather gloves into the sewer below and closed the trapdoor. Still reeling from the sights and smells of the sewer, he put his hands on his knees and allowed himself a moment to recover. He inhaled deeply and enjoyed a breath of cleaner air. The charnel smell of nearby ghouls lingered in the air, true, but that seemed clean compared with the foulness of the sewers.

After a few moments, he stood upright and mentally prepared himself. He did not know what he should expect. The guild seemed to have undergone some kind of purge in his absence. He felt certain that the corpses in the sewers below were former Night Knives. Dabbling with the demonic must have finally driven the Righteous Man insane. The guildmaster was purging the guild of unbelievers and transforming Mask's faithful into undead. The realization caused Cale to despise religion all the more. A man lost himself when he took the rites. The Righteous Man had lost himself. The attack on Stormweather had not been an attempt to get at Cale through his family. It had been merely a ham-handed attempt to get at Cale, an unbeliever. Thazienne's injury and all the dead were incidental.

Doesn't matter, he told himself, he did what he did and he goes down anyway.

Ready, he knelt before the door and listened. Nothing. He had the benefit of surprise then. Slowly, he pulled the door open—

A body slammed into it and knocked him backward. He caught a glimpse of gray flesh and dirty fangs. Ghoul!

He leaped back with a shout and brandished his blade, expecting a flurry of claws, fangs, and stink. Instead, the ghoul inexplicably halted in the doorway. It growled softly, almost a purr, then stepped *backward* into the hall, out of Cale's sight.

Stupefied, Cale stood there, blade ready. He waited for a tense moment, but nothing happened. What in the Hells?

The ghoul—Cale now recognized it from its long black hair as Tyllin Var, a former pickpocket specialist and Mask believer—reappeared in the doorway. It snarled impatiently and waved a clawed hand, beckoning Cale forward.

Cale's heart thudded in his chest but he quieted his fear with anger. *Seems I'm expected after all,* he thought. Gripping his blade in a sweating fist, he advanced cautiously out of the room.

As with the storeroom, the guildhouse was in a filthy, chaotic shambles. The long main hall stretched before him, dotted with open doors and littered with debris like the aftermath of a street riot. Broken weapons, half-eaten bodies, shredded clothing, rotten food, overturned chairs and tables, all lay strewn haphazardly about. Behind Tyllin, who flashed Cale his fangs in an evil grin, stood a ghastly formation— pair upon pair of ghouls lined the hall at even intervals, a grisly formation of twisted gray bodies that marked a processional path directly to the shrine. The double doors to the Righteous Man's sanctuary and worship hall stood open, but from where Cale stood, he could not pierce the dimness of its interior.

Tyllin stood aside, regarded Cale with slitted eyes, gave a snarl, and waved him forward. Presented with no other option, he stalked cautiously past Tyllin and made his way down the hall. Cale realized how futile his resistance to an attack would be at this point.

Eyeing him hungrily, each pair of ghouls growled softly as he walked between them. Some pawed the air and snarled, unable to conceal their insatiable desire for his flesh. He kept his long sword ready and watched them all like a hawk, but none of them made an aggressive move.

As he passed each pair, they fell in behind him and herded him toward the shrine. Only a third of the way down the hall, he already had a small crowd of ghouls behind and still more before him. He could feel their hungry eyes boring into his back. Surprisingly, he felt unafraid. He felt the liberation of a condemned man being led to the gallows. He *knew* now that he would not get out of here alive, and the realization freed him from fear. Neither of us is coming out of that shrine, old man, he vowed.

Though many of the ghouls still wore clothing or had tattoos that Cale recognized as belonging to a one-time comrade, their feral yellow eyes no longer contained anything recognizably human. Magic and religious fanaticism had mutat—

A yellow-eyed shadow flitted in the corner of his vision. He whirled on it, blade high. Nothing was there.

Nothing but the gaming parlor where guildsmen once had bet their take from jobs on the chance deal of cards and the random fall of knucklebones. Human vices that Cale could understand.

Still scanning the darkness of the parlor for the shadow demon, his eyes fell to the floor and he gave a start. He stopped walking and looked more closely to be sure his vision had not deceived him. The crowd of ghouls behind herded closer. The floor just inside the doorway of the parlor appeared to be slowly boiling, like simmering soup. He felt the hairs on his arms rise and bend toward the weird floor, as though pulled. Had the shadow demon vanished into that? Before he could consider further, a chorus of impatient growls sounded from the ghouls.

"Maaassk," they mouthed as one, and the press of their vile, stinking bodies forced him forward.

Mask indeed, he thought as he walked. This is where your fanaticism has brought you, old man. He kept his eyes away from the half-eaten corpses scattered along his path.

More doorways yawned to either side as he walked the rest of the long hall. The rooms beyond the doorways had once been familiar to him—here a meeting room, there a dining hall, there a training room—but like the gaming parlor, all of them now stood warped in some way. The familiar furnishings he had known lay toppled, broken, befouled, or missing altogether. Horrors had replaced them. A wall in the dining hall dripped what looked to be blood. Drops of crimson seeped through the plaster near the ceiling and ran down the wall in rivulets. Two ghouls crouched at the base, purring, and licked up the blood like children eating sweetened ice. The steady rasp of their tongues had worn grooves in the wall. Cale forced down the vomit that tried to climb up his throat. He sidestepped a patch of floor before him that oozed a thick, black liquid and walked on.

"Mask," the ghouls behind him murmured.

Instead of the familiar oak table and chairs standing in the center of the main meeting room, a sickly gray colored whirlpool now churned, as though the floor had become a thick liquid. Again, he felt a strange pull from the maelstrom. Streaks of ochre and viridian swirled a slow path into gray oblivion. Cale found the motion hypnotic. With an effort of will, he forced himself to look away before the urge to leap in overpowered him. As he turned away, he thought he glimpsed a pair of baleful yellow eyes peering at him from within the whirlpool.

He drew nearer to the shrine. The crowd of ghouls behind him grew as each pair fell in line.

He passed what had once been the training room for pickpocketing and climbing and saw that portions of the wall and floor seemed *absent*. Not hewn out or dug up, but *absent*, as though reality had been slashed open to reveal nothingness beneath. Again he thought he saw a pair of yellow eyes staring at him from the emptiness in the wall, but when he blinked, the eyes disappeared. Disconcerted, he turned away and focused his gaze forward on the open double doors of the shrine.

This is utter madness, he thought, and struggled to keep a tight grip on his sanity. The *wrongness* of the guildhouse made him dizzy and nauseated. A man could lose himself quickly. The living do not belong here, he thought. He now knew for certain that the Righteous Man had gone mad—summoning demons, turning guildsmen into ghouls, transforming the guildhouse into a seething den of vileness. There could be no other explanation. He no longer cared for the *why* of the Righteous Man's behavior—how could he hope to understand the reasons of the man who had done *this*—he only cared about stopping him.

That resolution brought him an odd, detached calm. He reached for his throat and felt the reassuring coolness of the necklace of missiles, rolled the last explosive globe between his fingers. He would kill the Righteous Man with his steel, then start a blaze with his globe that would incinerate the entire guildhouse and everything in it.

Resolved, he picked up his pace and strode unafraid for the shrine. The crowd of ghouls behind him loped to keep up.

He walked through the ornate doorway, turned to glare at the ghouls, then slammed the doors shut in their faces. He held the doors fast for a moment, expecting the ghouls to push them open and pile in behind him, but they made no effort to follow. They waited just outside. Cale could hear their low growling through the doors. They were only the escort, it seemed. He turned to survey the shrine.

"Erevis Cale come at last," said the Righteous Man, the contempt evident in his voice. The guildmaster stood near the front of the large shrine room, atop a raised dais, behind the block of basalt that served as an altar. Black candles burned in tall bronze candelabra but shed only dim light. Shadows filled every corner. Cale quickly glanced through them for the yellow eyes of the shadow demon but saw nothing.

Wooden pews lined the room from the back wall up to the altar. Ghouls filled those in the rear. Rocking gently and growling low, they held their hands clasped as though in prayer, a macabre mockery of piety. They watched him sidelong out of slitted eyes. They licked their fangs hungrily but kept their seats.

Already holding his long sword at the ready, he filled his other hand with a dagger. At that, the ghouls began to growl and rock faster but still remained seated. He walked straight down the center aisle, through and past the ghouls, halfway to the altar. He kept his eyes locked on the masked face of the Righteous Man.

"That's right, I've come," he said. "What in the name of the gods have you done here?"

The Righteous Man stepped out from behind the altar and spoke in a soft, menacing tone. "You've come to do Mask's bidding, perhaps?"

"Maaasssk," the ghouls in the pews echoed. "Masssk." They rocked and rocked.

The guildmaster's voice sounded different, Cale noted, but he attributed it to the guildmaster's obvious insanity. Only then did the Righteous Man's question strike him—Mask's bidding? What does that mean?

He shook his head and forced himself to stay focused.

"I've come to do *my* bidding, not a god's. I'm here for you, old man. It ends tonight, all of it. You hear me?"

Still rocking in their pews, the ghouls gave a soft, prolonged hiss. Cale attuned his hearing behind him but kept his eyes locked on the Righteous Man. Casually, he pulled the explosive globe from his necklace and cupped it in his dagger hand. If bad went to worse, he'd blow the whole place immediately.

Favoring his leg, the Righteous Man stepped down from the dais. He stood only a dagger toss away. Cale could feel the intensity of his stare even through the black felt of the mask. He looked normal beneath his velvet robes—tall, thin, slightly stooped—but something about his mannerisms struck Cale as odd. He moved stiffly, herky-jerky, like a marionette. Palpably radiating contempt, he seemed to have more . . . *presence*. His ominous silence made Cale uncomfortable.

"I asked you a question, old man!" He gripped the dagger and globe in his now sweaty hand.

At his harsh tone, a cacophony of hisses sounded from the ghouls. Cale heard their leathery skin rasping against the wood of the pews as they rocked faster and faster. "Mask," they whispered, "Mask."

"I heard you, Erevis Cale," said the Righteous Man, and again Cale noticed the odd inflection and cadence. The guildmaster limped forward a step. Involuntarily, Cale found himself backing up. The hissing of the ghouls grew louder. The rasping of their skin on the pews sounded like a carpenter's plane on wood.

"You enter my guild and utter bold words. Bold words indeed for but a *pre-incarnate* Champion of Mask." He fairly spat the name of the Shadowlord, and when he did the ghouls hissed their echo.

"Maaasssk."

Pre-what? Cale took another step back as the Righteous Man approached. Seized with an inexplicable fear, Cale struggled to keep it out of his voice.

"*You're* the servant of Mask, priest, not me. And he can't save you from me. It's over." He held forth his blades to demonstrate a defiance he didn't feel.

When the Righteous Man replied, his voice sounded oddly distant, and Cale realized that he was speaking to someone who existed only within the realm of his madness.

"No, he *isn't* going to save you now, is he Krollir?" the Righteous Man whispered to himself, and began to laugh. The sound was so thick with evil that it sent shudders along Cale's spine. After a moment, the guildmaster returned his attention from wherever it had gone and refocused on Cale. "Nor will he save *you*. I sent servants to seek you out, Erevis Cale, to draw you forth and bring you here, you and the other. *He* knew that one of you would become the chosen of Mask, if not him. *He* feared and hated you accordingly." The guildmaster took another step toward Cale.

With difficulty, Cale held his ground.

"*I* do not share his concern. You cannot stop *me*. You or the other, paltry servants of a paltry god." The Righteous Man raised his hands to the ceiling. "I *will* feed!"

Cale stood stupefied. Who is *he?* he wondered. Me *and the other?* The Righteous Man had admitted to the attack on Stormweather. But to draw Cale out? What was going on here?

Even as he wondered, the answer began to crystallize—the shadow demon, the ghouls, the corpses, the warping of reality. No *man* could have done this, not even a priest with the power of the Righteous Man. No human could live in this pit.

He suddenly realized that the real Righteous Man was dead and the thing that now looked upon him was not human, couldn't be human. The realization multiplied his growing fear. His resolve to avenge the attack on Stormweather melted. He wanted nothing else but to get out of here, and get out of here *now*.

The . . . *thing* apparently sensed Cale's fear, for it inhaled deeply, sniffed the air as though searching for spoor. "Ah, you know now, don't you?" It inhaled again. "You do—I smell your fear."

The ghouls fell silent. Cale heard only his own breathing and the voice in his head screaming for him to *run!* The thing took a step closer and the ghouls rose as one. Cale tried to fight off a wave of supernatural fear that rooted him to the floor.

"What are you?" he managed to mouth, but wasn't sure if he said it or merely thought it.

"Not what," the thing responded. "Who. I am Yrsillar, master of Belistor, keeper of the Void, Lord of the Nothing. Now the avatar of Mask as well. Would you see his face and mine?"

His face and mine. A demon had possessed the Righteous Man. Cale's knees went weak. His tongue felt too dry to form an answer.

The thing reached up and peeled off the black felt mask. Cale recoiled in anticipation of a nightmare, but the face was merely the drawn, wrinkled visage of an old man. Except for the eyes. The sockets looked empty. Not merely without eyeballs, but empty, a pair of holes that opened onto nothingness. Their gaze hit Cale like an ogre's club. Gasping for breath, he staggered backward, suddenly free from the paralyzing fear that the demon projected.

Yrsillar began to laugh, and behind the thin body of the old man Cale sensed a towering, awful shadow— the demon Yrsillar, lord of the nothing.

"His soul for me and his flesh for you," Yrsillar said to the ghouls. "Mask commands you." He began to laugh, loud and long.

"Massk," the ghouls snarled through drooling fangs, and leaped over the pews to reach him. At that exact instant, the doors to the shrine burst open and the ghouls from the hallway streamed in.

Without thinking, Cale threw the explosive globe at

their feet. The room exploded in a ball of fire and scorching heat. Ghouls shrieked. Flesh and wood blew apart and sprayed the room. Too close to fully avoid the blast himself, the explosion blew Cale backward into the pews and painfully charred his exposed skin. Throughout, Yrsillar's laughter boomed loudly in his ears.

Though wounded, Cale regained his feet in an instant. He refused to go down easily. The blast had caused his vision to go gray and blurry, as though he peered through light fog. Corpses, fire, and rampaging ghouls tore about the room. Screams, growls, moans, and Yrsillar's haunting laughter resounded off the walls. The ghouls ran about and clawed wildly at the air, growling and snarling confusedly, as though blind. Some walked right into the blazing fires and leaped back with a scream. Cale did not understand it, but then he did not understand most of what had happened already tonight.

A ghoul prowled forward in a crouch and stood beside him, probing the area before it with its claws, but unable to see him. Without a thought, he used his dagger to gut it. The chaos in the room drowned out its dying screams.

Drawn by Yrsillar's voice, Cale turned to see the demon now standing atop the altar.

"His flesh for you, my servants! His flesh for you!" The demon's empty eyes passed over and beyond Cale. Realization dawned on him. Yrsillar could not see! Neither could the ghouls! Cale had to staunch the fit of hysterical laughter that threatened to burst from his lips.

Seeing Yrsillar vulnerable, his desire for revenge fought a war with his better sense. Better sense quickly won out. He took advantage of the blindness of his enemies, picked a clear path, and ran from the shrine.

When he crossed the doorway, the grayness in his vision instantly cleared. The hallway was vacant. All the ghouls were searching for him within the shrine. He spared a glance back and saw that the shrine stood cloaked in blackness as thick as pitch. The torchlight from the hallway simply ceased at the shrine doors, swallowed by darkness.

I saw through that!

He didn't have time to consider it further. The ghouls could burst from the darkness at any moment. Without looking to the warped rooms on either side, he grabbed a torch from a wall sconce and sprinted down the hall for the storeroom. It, too, stood empty. He jerked open the trapdoor in the floor and slid down the ladder into the stink of the sewers.

He avoided looking at the pile of corpses at the base of the ladder and raced back through the tunnel. When he reached the well opening on Winding Way, he pulled himself up into the shaft and climbed back toward the surface.

CHAPTER 7

REUNION

When he reached the top of the well, Cale climbed over the side and sprinted as fast as he could down Winding Way, away from the vileness of the guildhouse, away from the evil of Yrsillar. Minutes or hours later, he finally stopped, exhausted. The cold air stung the tender skin of his charred face. His heart raced and his gasping breath formed great clouds of frost before his face.

Get yourself under control, he ordered himself. If they were coming, they'd already be here. With an effort, he calmed himself. He had to use his right hand to peel his left fist from the hilt of his sheathed long sword. Only then did he remember that he had no cloak. Adrenaline had warmed him, but now he began to feel winter's chill. His armor and clothing held off much of the cold, but he would have to buy a cloak when Selgaunt's shops opened.

They're not coming, he assured himself again, and crossed his arms against the cold. At least not yet.

Back in control of himself, he bent against the wind and sloshed through Selgaunt's empty streets. He looked about with mild surprise—the towering brick buildings of the Warehouse District loomed on all sides. He had run halfway across the city—and it was no coincidence he had run in the direction of Stormweather. The Uskevren manse stood only blocks north of him, on Sarn Street.

At that moment, the fact that he could no longer return to the familiar comfort of his room hit him hard. He could not return to the welcoming warmth of Thazienne's smile. He had nowhere to go.

I can't go back, he reminded himself again, reaffirming his decision. At least not yet, and especially not now. The risk to the family was too great.

While Cale did not yet fully understand everything that had happened at the guildhouse, he understood enough to know that Yrsillar had targeted him *personally*. The demon's words rattled around in his head like a pair of knucklebones—*Champion of Mask. You and the other*.

What did that mean? If anyone, the Righteous Man was Mask's Champion, or had been. *He* was the priest, not Cale. Cale invoked the gods only to oath by their names. He had never even prayed to one, had been in a church only twice in his lifetime. He consciously kept gods and temples at a distance. He stayed out of their business and they stayed out of his.

Still, Cale could not deny the magical darkness that had suddenly appeared in Mask's shrine. Only he had been able to see through it. That certainly seemed a divine blessing of sorts.

Perhaps it was, he reluctantly acknowledged. But how can I be the servant of a god? Much less a god's Champion?

He found the idea so improbable as to be laughable, and yet thinking of it brought him a strange exhilaration and a peculiar fear. He had no desire to surrender himself to the whims of a god. Still . . .

Would it be *so* improbable? He had been the servant of someone or other most of his adult life—the Night Masks, the Righteous Man, Thamalon. The difference, of course, was that with all of those masters he had maintained a certain amount of independence. Could he serve a god and still be his own man?

Doesn't matter, he thought grimly. Tonight's not the night for taking rites. Rather, tonight was a night for retribution. He knew now that the paralyzing fear he had felt back in the guildhouse—the fear that had stolen his resolve and frozen him into inaction—had been supernatural in origin, a function of Yrsillar's demonic nature. Cale would be ready for it next time.

He also knew that it had been Yrsillar, and not the Righteous Man, who had ordered the attack on Stormweather. The attack that had nearly killed Thazienne. For that, Yrsillar would pay, demon or no. Cale only had to figure out how.

He *could* go to the authorities—after the carnage at Stormweather, even Selgaunt's ruler, the idiotic Hulorn, would not be able to laugh off Cale's claims. Even as he considered it, he dismissed it. It would take the Scepters days to act. It always did. Cale did not want to wait that long.

This is personal now, you bastard, he thought to Yrsillar. Cale's nature did not allow him to turn the problem over to the city authorities. This is between you and me, he mentally reiterated. If Mask wanted to protect his interest in this, he could come along for the ride, but Cale would owe the god nothing.

To the east, the slate sky began to lighten. Dawn was breaking. He had been walking the streets for over an hour. As though awakened by the winter sun, Selgaunt's shops began slowly to come back to life. Lights burned in the occasional window as a shopkeeper went about preparing his wares for the day. Cale ducked into the nearest clothier, dug a few five-stars from his pocket, handed them to the startled shopkeeper, and grabbed a blue cloak from among the wares. Too short, as usual, but far warmer than nothing at all.

He emerged onto the street and decided to take a room at the first inn he found. He had nowhere else to go.

Jak. The halfling's name popped into his head as though by divine inspiration. Jak! Of course! Though he hadn't seen the little man since their run-in with Riven and the Zhentarim a month ago, Jak had always stood with him. Jak had also made it clear that he always would. He—

Cale's assuredness melted like the snow in the street when he remembered that the little man belonged to the Harpers. Cale had learned *that* during their escape from the Zhentarim. The Harpers, a secretive organization that ostensibly strived for the good, might frown on Cale hunting a demon alone.

Demons, he corrected himself, plural, *Ecthaini*. He now knew there to be at least two demons in the guildhouse—Yrsillar, and the shadow demon that had attacked Stormweather.

Still, he had to consider the possibility that the Harpers *might* offer help in the form of intelligence, magic items, or protective spells. If they wouldn't, Cale knew that Jak would help him anyway. The little man had bucked Harper orders before to help him, and would no doubt do so again. He didn't relish the idea of getting Jak into trouble, but the little man *was* his best friend. Cale's *only* friend outside of Stormweather. He had nowhere else to turn, and probably only a little time. No doubt Yrsillar and his minions would be searching for him by tomorrow night. He had to find Jak now.

You and the other.

Yrsillar's words floated up from the depths of his mind. Is Jak the other? he wondered. The little man was a priest, after all, but of Brandobaris, not Mask. From what little Cale knew of organized religion, the relationship between the halfling god of thieves and Mask the Shadowlord was not an especially friendly one. Could a priest of one god serve the interests of another?

He shook his head in frustration. He was allowing himself to get distracted. It doesn't matter, he thought. Whether Jak had some special divine role to play or not, Cale needed his help, and he thought he knew where to find the little man.

He turned his face into the snow and headed for the gambling dens of the Wharf District.

In Selgaunt, the gaming houses along Nedreyin Street remained open all day and all night. People of all social backgrounds—nobles, transient adventurers, merchants, rogues—gambled as much as their schedules and finances permitted. Even now, despite the dawn hour and cold weather, Nedreyin Street still had its denizens eager to test Tymora's favor on the throw of knucklebones or deal of cards. As Cale watched, a crowd of five loud men in heavy cloaks and winter boots strode past the burly doorman and into the Leering Basilisk, a low quality establishment without an attached eatery. At the same time, a pair of noblemen—probably second sons, not heirs—walked hangdog out of the Scarlet Knave two doors down, no doubt lighter by a few fivestars.

Not yet extinguished by the city's linkboys, the street lamps sputtered fitfully in the wind blowing off Selgaunt Bay. The smell of sea salt and the reek of the nearby fishmongers' stalls filled the cold air—the bay did not entirely freeze over until early in the month of Alturiak, and the city's fishermen habitually worked the waters to the very last. After the horrors he had witnessed on the other side of the city, Cale welcomed the sight of human beings involved in mundane human affairs and vices.

He walked down the snow-coated street, wary of the shadows in every dark corner. Despite the cold, sleeping drunkards and men who had gambled away their lodging coin lay huddled and shivering under building eaves. Cale eyed them all with a sharp gaze, sure that their cloaks covered gray skin and sharp claws. His concern proved unwarranted—all of them were harmless.

Searching for word of Jak, he moved quickly from gambling house to gambling house and dropped some fivestars to loosen the tongues of the circumspect bartenders and taciturn doormen. Surprisingly, his coins brought no result—no one had seen the little man. He checked Jak's usual haunts twice—the Scarlet Knave, the Bent Coin, the Cardhouse—and heard from the regulars that no one had seen the halfling for weeks. At that, Cale began to worry. While he hadn't expected to find Jak actually gambling at this hour, he *had* expected to find his friend collapsed in a suite somewhere. That Jak hadn't been seen at all set off alarms in Cale's head. He knew that Yrsillar and his servants already had hit several players in Selgaunt's underworld—no doubt to draw out or find

Cale and this *other*. If Jak was *the other*, perhaps the demon had already gotten to him?

Unwilling to consider the possibility, Cale sat at the polished bar of the Cardhouse and spent a silver raven on a cup of warm spiced wine. He drank it down before he headed back outside. By then, dawn had fully broken and the city's red-cloaked linkboys had appeared. Nimbly, they scaled the street torches and snuffed the blazing coals with metal hoods. Though overcast, the light of morning dispelled the shadows of night and Cale breathed easy for the first time since fleeing the guildhouse. He thought it unlikely that Yrsillar would dare make any moves in the full light of day.

Now as much worried for Jak's well being as wanting the little man's help, Cale made a hard decision. Though he had promised not to return, he knew where he had to go for information about Jak—the Harper safehouse to which Jak had taken him after the affair with the Zhentarim. Brelgin and the Harpers there would know how to reach Jak. *If* they still used the safehouse. They had not been pleased when Cale had learned of its location and might have decided to abandon it as compromised.

There's only one way to find that out, he thought.

He walked back through the quickly crowding, snowy streets and headed for the Warehouse District. Once there, he navigated from memory a maze of back alleys, cul-de-sacs, and small storehouses until he reached the one-story Harper safehouse. The ramshackle brick building looked like any number of similar, unnamed office buildings in the district—inconspicuous for its mundanity. Having once fled with Jak up from Selgaunt's sewers into its basement, Cale knew the structure to have a secret lower level three times the area of the surface.

Through the falling snow, he could see two heavily

cloaked men lounging casually against the wooden porch posts. Neither wore visible iron, but their over-sized winter cloaks could have concealed a dwarven great axe. Alert expressions and wary eyes belied their uncaring stances—Harper guards. They had to be. So the Harpers *did* still use the safehouse, and he might still find Jak. He breathed a sigh of relief.

He walked out from the alley and toward the sentries with empty hands in evidence. They stiffened at his approach and stepped down from the porch onto the narrow, unpaved street. Though the guards' cloak hoods shadowed most of their features, Cale still recognized one of the two from his encounter with the Harpers in the sewers. A thin, short fellow with slanted green eyes that indicated an elf ancestor not more than two generations removed. The other guard, a heavyset man of medium height, Cale did not remember. He wasted no time with idle greetings.

"I need to see Brelgin," he announced when he drew close. From his previous encounter with the Harpers, Cale knew Brelgin to be in charge of the safehouse. "Now."

"Brelgin?" said the heavyset guard, "There's no Brelgin here—"

"Save it," interrupted Cale. "I know what you are and what this building is." He turned to the half-elf, threw back his own hood to reveal his bald head, and asked in elvish, *"Do you remember me?"*

The half-elf's almond eyes flashed recognition. "I remember you," he replied in common.

"Good," Cale said. "Then maybe *you* can answer my question and save Brelgin and I the agony of a meeting. I'm looking for Jak Fleet. You know I'm a friend. Where can I find him?"

At the mention of the little man, the half-elf's expression grew thoughtful. Cale didn't like his silence.

"What?" Cale asked, alarmed. He advanced a step on the half-elf and barely resisted the urge to grab the smaller man by the shoulders and shake him. "What's happened?" Cale had a terrible vision of Jak's small body sucked empty by the shadow demon.

The half-elf's eyes found the street. "You'll have to ask Brelgin, Erevis Cale. It's not my place." He poked a finger into Cale's chest. "Wait here."

"Wait—"

Both Harpers turned, bounded up the porch steps, and vanished into the safehouse.

Concerned, but knowing better than to follow them unasked into the safehouse, Cale walked to the porch, sat on the rail, and awaited Brelgin.

Within a few minutes, the tall Harper leader emerged, hastily wrapped against the cold in a green cloak. Brelgin had shaved his blond beard since last they had met, but Cale could not mistake the arrogance in the Harper leader's eyes. He stood to face him.

"You were told never to come here again, Cale." Brelgin spat Cale's name like a curse. "You could've been followed by one of the snakes you chum with. If you've compromised us," he looked up and down the empty back street, advanced a step, and stared into Cale's face, "I'll see to it you're made sorry."

Cale bit back the urge to choke this arrogant ass where he stood. For Jak's sake, he ignored the threat, swallowed his anger, and managed an even tone. "I'm looking for Fleet."

"I know."

Cale scrutinized his face. "Where is he?"

Brelgin hesitated an instant too long before answering. "He's away on organization business."

Cale knew he was lying. He grabbed the Harper leader by the cloak and jerked him close.

"You're lying, and I don't have time for this kind of nonsense. I need to see him. I'm his friend, Brelgin. Even you know that. Where is he?" He shook the Harper leader like a doll.

From within the safehouse, footsteps thumped toward the front door—Harpers rushing to Brelgin's aid. Looking impassively into Cale's face all the while, Brelgin waved them back just as they appeared in the doorway. They backed off.

"Let me go, Cale," he said, softly.

Cale stared at him a long moment, and released him.

Brelgin readjusted his cloak, studied him for a moment, and apparently came to a decision. "I'll get my gear. You want to see him that bad, I'll take you to him."

❧ ❧ ❧ ❧ ❧

Brelgin led Cale north through the city. Despite the snow, cold, and early morning hour, Selgaunt had now come fully back to life. Nobles' carriages slowly navigated the slush of the streets. Patrols of the city watch, Selgaunt's Scepters, trooped past in their red tabards. Merchants hawked their wares from shop doors to passersby. Street vendors pushed their carts through the slush. Customers rich and poor shopped, haggled, and bought. To all appearances, the city seemed perfectly normal. Except for the demons that murdered by night.

Despite his dislike for Brelgin, Cale felt obligated to let the Harper leader know about Yrsillar. He drew close to avoid eavesdroppers and spoke in a low tone, wasting no words.

"Listen, Brelgin, the Righteous Man is dead." At that, Brelgin raised his brows thoughtfully.

"Some kind of demon has taken over the guild. It has turned the guildsmen into ghouls." When he said it aloud, it sounded so far-fetched as to be ridiculous, but he plowed on. "I don't know how it happened, maybe one of the Righteous Man's summonings went wrong. But whatever the cause, I think all the recent hits in the underworld have been this demon's doing. It has another demon serving it, a shadow that does its killing. I'm not sure—"

Brelgin cut him off in a tone colder than the winter air. "Sounds like a problem for you and yours, Cale. None of mine have been hit by this *shadow*. And if it's killing criminals, I don't want to stop it. I want to *recruit* it."

Cale could not believe his ears. He grabbed the Harper leader by the arm, jerked him around, and pulled him to a stop. His voice rose with his anger.

"Can you possibly be that stupid? This thing isn't going to stop with criminals. It's not ever going to stop, not unless someone stops it. Blast you—" He lowered his voice as a fat, middle-aged housewife and her young son passed by and looked at them askance. "Nine Hells, man, it hit Stormweather last night. There aren't any criminals there."

"Except you," Brelgin snapped, and jerked his arm free of Cale's grip.

That hit Cale square in his gut. Trying to mask his shame with anger, he advanced on Brelgin until he stood nose to nose.

"Listen, you arrogant ass, there's no telling what this thing will do next. But you can be damned sure that it'll be coming for yours soon enough. You think the Harpers are immune?" He scoffed. "If you've avoided it up to now, you've just been lucky."

Brelgin returned Cale's glare and didn't retreat a handspan. "Until it does," he said tightly, "it's your problem." He spun on his heel and walked off. Stewing, Cale followed.

For a long time, they walked through the crowded streets in silence. Cale could not understand the Harper leader's indifference. Yrsillar might eventually pose a threat to the entire city.

Is it just personal antagonism? he wondered. Or orders from higher up in the organization? Either way, he found it incomprehensible. Seething more and more with each step he took, he finally could no longer hold his anger at bay.

"You and the Harpers are a bad joke," he snapped, walking beside Brelgin but not looking at him. "You've got everyone thinking that you work for the *good*—whatever that even is—but when I tell you about a *demon* running rampant in the city, you tell me that I'm on my own." He shook his head. "You think that's working for the *good?* I know thieves with more courage and more sense. You and your crew are nothing more than a bunch of little boys trying to protect your reputations and play at being men."

That stopped Brelgin cold. He whirled on Cale, a snarl on his face. "What do you know about anything good, Cale?" he spat. "You're a Night Mask murderer."

At that, Cale recoiled a step. Surprise wiped away his self-satisfaction.

"That's right, we know all about your background, all about your past in Westgate." He jabbed a finger into Cale's chest. "I don't need to hear lectures on what's good from an assassin." Brelgin turned and stomped off.

Too stunned and angry to speak, Cale continued on silently after him. It doesn't matter who knows now, he thought bitterly. Thamalon already knows. It's all ending soon anyway, one way or another.

It hurt Cale to think such thoughts, but there it was.

He no longer had anyone he needed to hide his past from—though his deepest secret remained his own. Brelgin and the Harpers knew only that he had *been* a Night Mask. Not his relationship to the organization. If they had known *that* . . .

He pushed through the crowd at a jog and fell into step beside the Harper leader.

Tension hung thick between them, and neither man said another word as they continued northward through the city. Expecting to be led to another Harper safehouse, Cale felt surprised and worried when the tall, beautifully crafted churches of the Temple District came into view.

"The Temple District?" he asked Brelgin.

"You'll see soon enough," grunted the Harper leader. They turned onto the Avenue of Temples.

Though a few shrines had been raised in other parts of Selgaunt, most had been built on the north side of the city, in the five large blocks known as the Temple District. For as far as Cale could see, spires, domes, bell towers, gold gilt work, statuary, and stained glass dominated the horizon. In the distance, the festive bells of the towering temple of Lliira pealed forth and sent the cheer of the Revelmistress speeding into the sky. To his right, the soft ring of chimes sounded from within the small shrine dedicated to Lathander the Morninglord. A crowd of faithful thronged the avenue. The low murmur of their voices mixed with the bells, chimes, and gongs created an unintentional but strangely harmonious orchestra of the devout.

Having deliberately avoided ever setting foot on the Avenue of Temples, Cale found the architectural variety of the temples surprising. The structure of the churches varied so much that the street looked a bit of a hodgepodge. Some had been crafted of granite, some of limestone, and still others of brick. Each had a different layout—here a dome, there a tower, there a squat rectangle. Still, Cale had to admit that the architectural dissonance had a symbolic beauty all its own—the various churches of the gods co-existed in peace on the Avenue of Temples. If only Selgaunt's underworld were so understanding.

At many of the church doors, worshipers already gathered for morning services. Monks and priests greeted the faithful as they entered. Clouds of incense smoke wafted from open doors and dispersed in the cool air.

Cale noted that few carriages drove the avenue and most of the worshipers awaiting entry wore the clothes of commoners. He would have expected as much. Typically, the nobility had private shrines built within their manses, and when necessary, they could *buy* direct access to a high priest. In Selgaunt, wealth bought blessings as easily as it did bread.

Shaking his head ruefully, Cale trekked up the avenue behind Brelgin.

When the smooth marble walls of the temple of Deneir came into view, the Harper leader veered directly for it. Cale followed, his worry growing for his friend.

Shaped from slabs of gray granite and green marble—both stones quarried from the majestic Thunder Peaks twenty miles to the north of the city—the Godscribe's two-story, rectangular temple stood open to the street. Though it wore a welcoming stair and beautifully columned portico, no worshipers waited outside to be allowed entry.

Unsurprising, Cale thought. As part of his Night Mask linguistic training back in Westgate, he had been tutored by a mage who had worshiped Deneir—a half-blind academic named Theevis who spoke as many languages as Cale had birthdays. From Theevis, he had learned that the faith of the Godscribe appealed mostly to scholars, not commoners.

A marble frieze ran along the top of the temple wall, inscribed with Deneir's praises in more scripts than even Cale could recognize. Two marble statues, each of an intense, elderly man poring over an open tome, flanked the closed double doors. Above the doors, a phrase had been inscribed in the common tongue—*To Preserve Knowledge is to Serve Men and Gods*. Brelgin jogged up the stairs, pushed open the double doors, and walked through. Cale followed.

Erevis Cale had been in only two temples in his life, and both of those had been furnished with pews, an offering box, a raised pulpit, and an altar. As far as he could see, Deneir's temple had none of those. The place looked more of a library than a worship hall. Desks and worn tables filled the carpeted room, each covered in papers, scrolls, inkpots, and open tomes. Tall shelves filled with books stood along the back wall. Chandeliers and three blazing hearths provided heat and light by which to study. The place smelled of ink, leather, and allorath leaf, an herbal paper preservative used by scribes and sages.

Of the handful of faithful who sat at the desks and studied lost lore, none so much as glanced up when Cale and Brelgin entered.

A tonsured acolyte in a black and white diagonally striped cloak cleared his throat and smiled at them from his table just inside the doors.

"Do you require a table, sirs?" he softly asked.

"No, thank you," Brelgin replied in equally soft tones. "We're actually here to meet someone." He gave the acolyte a smile and they walked past.

As they navigated the maze of tables and readers, Cale quietly stated, "This isn't like any temple I've ever seen."

Brelgin harrumphed as though he found it surprising that Cale had seen the inside of any temples at all.

"This isn't the worship hall, Cale. This is only the lending library. The Deneirrath grant anyone access to these writings and charge only what the borrower can afford."

Cale nodded appreciatively. If times had been different, he could have enjoyed himself greatly here. It reminded him of Thamalon's library in Stormweather.

He followed Brelgin across the library floor to the rows of tall shelves that lined the back of the room. There, they found seated at a desk a middle-aged priestess clad in a turquoise robe. She pored over an ancient book, muttering to herself as she read, and occasionally wrote furiously on a separate piece of parchment. Cale and Brelgin stood before her for a few moments before she finally noticed them and looked up.

A striking woman with short blonde hair, a strong mouth, and crows' feet around her intelligent eyes, she took them in and raised her eyebrows in question. Before she could speak, Brelgin bowed slightly, indicated Cale, and said in a whisper, "Priest Librarian Elaena, this is Erevis Cale."

She set down her writing quill, rose with austere dignity, and nodded solemnly at Cale. "Well met, Mister Cale."

"Priestess."

"*Priest*, Mister Cale. Our titles are the same, irrespective of gender."

Cale bowed. "Of course."

Brelgin continued, "Forgive the intrusion during your study hours, Priest Librarian, but Mister Cale wishes to see Jak Fleet. He's . . ." Brelgin cast a sidelong glance at Cale, "a friend."

Surprised by Brelgin's acknowledgment and soft tone, Cale gave him a grateful nod.

Priest Librarian Elaena smiled and looked right through Cale. "Of course he is." She covered the inkpot she had been using, marked her place in her tome with a flat, silver rod, and started to walk off. "Follow me, gentlemen, we've moved him to a room usually used for transient brethren traveling through the city and staying for only a short while." Cale and Brelgin followed.

Walking with a deliberateness that wasn't quite grace, the priest librarian led them through a confusing maze of narrow, candlelit corridors and rooms. Books, scrolls, and tapestries abounded. The place seemed near to bursting with the written word. Cale would have loved to stop and look, but couldn't for worry for his friend.

Elaena took them down a flight of spiral stairs until they reached what Cale took to be the residence hall of the temple. She walked to one of the paneled doors that lined the hall at intervals and knocked softly. After a moment, another tonsured acolyte opened the door and stuck his head out.

"Greetings, Aret," the priest librarian said. "Only knowledge is lasting."

"Greetings, Priest Librarian," the acolyte responded. "Only learning is worthwhile."

Apparently satisfied with the acolyte's ritual response, the priest librarian indicated Cale and Brelgin. "They have come to see Mr. Fleet."

Aret the acolyte, a slightly overweight young man with a soft face and softer eyes, nodded and stepped out of the room. "I'm afraid there hasn't been much change," he said to Brelgin.

The Harper leader nodded solemnly but otherwise made no reply.

"We'll leave you alone," announced the priest librarian. "Stay as long as you like. Come with me, Aret."

With that, the priest turned and walked back down the hall, Aret in tow. Apprehensive, Cale walked into the room. Brelgin followed and closed the door behind them.

Covered in sweat-soaked sheets, Jak lay unconscious on a plain wooden bed and straw-filled mattress. Cale took a deep breath and approached the bed slowly. The little man's ashen face looked drawn and thin. The Deneirrath must have been force feeding him bread and water, but little more. He looked to have lost considerable weight. His red hair lay pasted by sweat against his scalp and his breathing came in irregular, ragged heaves. The little man's plight reminded Cale so much of Thazienne lying stricken in her bed at Stormweather that he had to steady himself with the headboard to avoid falling down.

"What happened to him?" Cale asked, though he already suspected the answer.

Brelgin stood beside him and looked down on the bed. "He stumbled into the safehouse a tenday ago, incoherent, babbling about the night with yellow eyes. Then he fell unconscious. He's been like this ever since. The priest librarian says his body is whole. It's his soul that's wounded. They haven't been able to do anything for him."

Cale heard the genuine concern for Jak in Brelgin's commanding voice. The tall Harper leader cared for the little man. He also heard in Brelgin's description confirmation of his theory. Jak had been attacked by the demon, too.

"The night with yellow eyes, Brelgin," Cale observed. "A wounded soul. That can only be the shadow demon. I've seen it. It has yellow eyes and it feeds on human souls." He banished the image of those hate-filled, ochre orbs and turned to face the Harper leader. Cale tried to keep the self-righteousness out of his voice. "Looks like the demon is a Harper problem after all."

Brelgin looked taken aback at that. His gaze went back and forth from Jak to Cale, his face flushed red. Abashed, he fumbled with an explanation.

"It's not that I don't want to help you, Cale. Really. I would if I could." His voice lowered to an intense whisper and he unconsciously made helpless gestures with his hands. "But I've got only a handful of agents in the city." He nodded knowingly when Cale shook his head and began to protest. "I know what the rumors say, Cale. I helped spread most of them. We need our rivals to think our numbers large, but the truth is I've got less than ten operators at my disposal." He shook his head as though inwardly reaffirming his decision. "I just can't risk them hunting a demon. This city has too many other problems."

Cale considered that. He stared at Brelgin thoughtfully, took a new measure of the man who just had taken such a great risk by offering sensitive information to an outsider. "I understand," Cale said after a moment, and gave him a friendly pat on the shoulder. "We all do what we have to."

Brelgin nodded but said nothing.

I'll do it alone, then, Cale thought, and tried to ignore the nervous flutter that churned his stomach. He only now realized how much he had been counting on Jak's assistance, and company. I would have welcomed your sense of humor, my friend, he thought with a smile.

He bent over the little man's bed and wiped the sweat from his forehead. Despite the perspiration, Jak's skin felt ice cold. Cale fluffed the feather pillow and pulled the coarse wool blanket up under the little man's whiskered chin. There was nothing else he could do here.

This is one more debt I'm going to make you account for, Yrsillar, he vowed.

He stood, but placed a hand on Jak's clammy forehead before leaving. "Get well, my friend." With that, he turned to leave. Brelgin grabbed him gently by the bicep.

"What now?" asked the Harper leader.

Cale almost laughed aloud. "Now," he replied grimly, "I'm going back to the guildhouse and collecting on a debt."

"Alone?"

"Alone. I've got no one else." And nothing more to lose, he thought.

He had a brief flash of hope when he thought Brelgin might change his mind and offer him Harper aid. After a brief inner struggle that Cale could see written on his stern face, the Harper leader merely nodded. He did not meet Cale's eyes.

"Tymora favor you," Brelgin said, obviously uncomfortable.

Cale chuckled mirthlessly. "I'll be looking for the blessings of darker gods than Lady Luck, Brelgin. I appreciate the thought, though." He turned and strode for the door.

A weak, hoarse voice stopped him.

"Cale."

Jak! He whirled around to see the halfling's eyes flutter open. Jak struggled to blink away a tenday of sleep from his eyes and focus on Cale.

"Little man!" Cale exclaimed.

"Fleet!" Brelgin shouted. Both rushed to Jak's bedside.

Seeing the surprising sight of Brelgin standing beside Cale, Jak gave a weak smile. "The room doesn't seem big enough for both of you at once." His green eyes fixed laughingly on Cale. "You become a Harper while I was out?" He chuckled, but his laughter turned into a fit of wet coughing. Alarmed, Cale shoved Brelgin toward the door.

"Get the priest librarian, man!"

"Right," the Harper leader agreed, and shot out of the room.

After the coughing fit had passed, Jak's hand came out from under the blanket and fumbled for Cale's wrist. The skin of his hand already felt warmer. "There was a shadow, Erevis," he croaked. "It . . . t-t-touched m-me." Jak began to shudder, uncontrollable trembles that shook his small body from head to toe.

"Easy Jak, easy." Cale tucked the blankets tighter about the halfling. He placed a comforting hand on Jak's shoulder and waited for the shuddering fit to pass. When it did, Cale looked his friend in the face.

"I've seen the shadow too, Jak," he said. "It attacked Stormweather last night. And it touched me too."

He had been prepared to leave it at that, but Jak's eyebrows rose with an unspoken question.

"It was bad," Cale acknowledged with a nod and a sigh. "Right in the middle of a celebration. No weapons allowed, the house guard ill prepared, lots of drink. The demon came with a pack of ghouls and swarmed the house. Lots of people were killed . . ."

He trailed off, remembering. Jak squeezed his hand to bring him back to himself. "But none of the Uskevren, thankfully. Thazienne was hurt by the demon, like you. But she's going to be all right. And so are you." By saying it aloud, he hoped he made it more likely.

"Dark," Jak breathed. "I'm sorry, Cale. I know how you feel about her." He patted Cale's hand sympathetically.

"I know where the demon is. I'm putting an end to it tonight."

Jak's tired eyes went wide at that, but before he could say anything, Brelgin and Priest Librarian Elaena ran into the room.

Surprised, Elaena stopped halfway to the bed. "The Scribe's quill," she oathed. "It truly is a miracle. Even the High Scrivener's prayers have been unable to help. What did you do?" she asked Cale.

"Nothing," he replied. Cale looked at his hand, the hand he had touched Jak with and wished him to be well. "Nothing . . ."

"A miracle then," she said perfunctorily. Her hand went to the golden holy symbol of Deneir that hung about her neck. She caressed it lightly, mouthed a prayer under her breath, and approached the bed.

Stepping in front of Cale, she began immediately to fuss with Jak like a mother hen tending her chick— she felt his forehead, held his wrist, put her ear to his chest, pulled up his eyelid—

"Hey!"

Cale smiled. Jak would recover fine.

After a few more prods and protesting squeals, Priest Librarian Elaena stood, placed a finger to her lips, and cocked her head thoughtfully. "I can't explain it," she said with a smile. "But he *is* recovered. He still needs rest but—don't sit up, young man," she ordered Jak, who had kicked off the blankets and was trying to sit upright.

Stubborn as always, Jak ignored her and sat up. His green eyes found Cale. "I'm with you, Cale. When you go after this thing, I want to be with you."

Cale started to deny him but stopped before the words reached his tongue. If their situation had been reversed—if he had been wounded but knew that Jak was going into danger alone—Cale would have made the same offer. That's what friends did for one another. He would not diminish their relationship with a refusal.

Besides, deep in his heart, he *wanted* Jak with him.

"I'm with you," Jak insisted again.

Cale looked to Brelgin. The Harper leader did not meet his eye and kept his stern face expressionless. Cale looked back to Jak.

"All right," he said with a grateful smile. "You're with me."

Instantly, he felt lighter. He would not have to face Yrsillar alone. Jak would stand with him.

Jak smiled and hopped to the floor. His legs wobbled but he steadied himself with the bed and kept his feet beneath him.

"Stop right there," commanded Elaena in the stern tone of a person used to being obeyed. She shot a glare at Cale. "I will not allow him to leave here and go running about the city doing gods-only-knows with *you*. He is still not well." She turned and pushed a protesting Jak back into the bed. "You still need rest, young man."

"Priest—" Jak objected.

"Enough, woman," Cale said firmly, and interposed himself between them. "Enough. He's not a boy."

"That's right," Jak piped.

Jak's high-pitched, indignant tone brought a smile to both Cale and Elaena. "We'll wait until tomorrow," Cale assured her, "but we've got business after that. All right?"

She must have seen the resolve in his face. "All right," she reluctantly agreed.

Brelgin, too, must have seen Cale's resolve. Without a word, he walked from the room.

❧ ❧ ❧ ❧ ❧

Now dressed in his street clothes and equipped with his gear, Jak stopped talking in order to shovel in more of the bread, cheese, and dried meat the Deneirrath acolytes had set before him on a small table. Famished, Cale helped himself to some of the board as well. Brelgin had considerately left them alone.

"You know," Jak said around a mouthful of goat cheese, "I could use a spell to summon up a better meal than this."

Cale shook his head while tearing into a piece of peppered jerky. "This is fine. Save your strength."

Jak nodded agreement and continued to eat. When only crumbs remained, he eased back in his chair, pulled his pipe from a belt pouch, tamped, and lit up. Cale found the smell of the little man's tobacco comfortingly familiar.

"Yrsillar," Jak said thoughtfully. He pronounced the name as though it left a bad taste in his mouth. "And he's in the Night Knife guildhouse? With another demon?"

Cale nodded and the little man let out a low whistle.

"It'll be a hard go," Jak said softly.

Cale nodded again. "Harder than you think, even." He related to Jak the details of his experience in the warped guildhouse—the gore, the stink, the palpable evil that polluted the place like a vile fog.

"Dark," Jak oathed, and blew out a smoke ring. "Dark."

Though Jak tried to hide it, Cale saw the haunted look in his friend's eyes. He knew what Jak was feeling—he too had felt the demon's nauseating touch, he too had felt his soul come loose from its moorings and begin to drift. It was terrifying.

Jak blew out a smoke ring and looked him in the face. The little man wore a concerned expression. "They're evil, Cale. Right? The ghouls, I mean. They used to be men, but now they're just evil."

To Cale, it sounded as though Jak were trying to convince himself. Cale had not bothered with the niceties of distinguishing good from evil. Yrsillar had hurt his family, had hurt him. As far as he was concerned, anything that got in the way was fair game. Still, he wanted to put his friend's mind at ease. Jak *did* concern himself with distinguishing good from evil, and he needed to know that whatever they did in that guildhouse was *right*.

"They're evil," Cale said with an unequivocal nod. "And they aren't men anymore. We'll be doing them a favor."

Jak gave a soft nod, then blew out another smoke ring.

"You sure you're capable of this now?" Cale asked. "I'd understand if—"

"I'm in, Cale," Jak reassured him. "I'm in." He took a deep, thoughtful draw on his pipe. "But if we're not moving on this until tomorrow, we should involve Brelgin. One day is enough time for him to gather some manpower. We've got some good operators in the organization, Cale. We could—"

Cale raised his hand to cut Jak off. "The Harpers aren't helping."

The little man's chatter instantly stopped and his mouth hung open in disbelief. "What?"

"They're not helping."

"But it's a demon!" Jak protested.

Cale found it odd to be defending Brelgin but did it nevertheless. "He knows it's a demon. I told him everything I told you. I think he would help if he could, but the organization can't spare the men or resources."

"They're sparing me!"

Cale smiled. "I think he knows that you'd come with me no matter what he said."

"Damn right," Jak said, and thumped his small fist against the table. He looked up at Cale with narrowed eyes. "What about the authorities?"

"No. This is between Yrsillar and me," Cale grimly pronounced. "I'll leave word for Brelgin as to the location of the guildhouse. If we fail, he can do whatever he sees fit."

Jak nodded slowly. Thoughtful, he pulled from his shirt pocket a platinum, jewel encrusted cloak pin and rubbed it between his fingers. "It was only chance that I was there that night. In the Soargyl manse, I mean." He held up the cloak pin for Cale to see—it was in the shape of an eagle's talon, with a single tourmaline inset. Cale's mind appraised it automatically—one hundred fivestars, or thereabouts.

"This is what I went to get," Jak said. "But what I took out of there was the memory of what that demon did to the Soargyls. Gods Cale, I'll never forget his face while that thing ate his soul . . ." He fought off a round of the shudders and looked across the table. His green eyes burned with intensity. "We do this your way."

Cale nodded, pleased that the little man understood. He considered telling Jak about Yrsillar's reference to *the other*, but decided against it. If Mask was working through the two of them, then Cale and Jak would have to deal with it when the situation arose. There was no reason to burden Jak any further.

They sat in silence for a time. Cale picked at the crumbs of his dinner. Jak balanced his chair on its rear two legs, crossed his hands over his head, smoked his pipe, and studied the ceiling.

Abruptly, as though he had reached some sort of decision, the little man leaned forward, let the chair legs thump against the floor, and snuffed his pipe.

"Let's get out of here, Erevis." Without explanation, Jak rose and threw on his gray cloak.

Surprised, Cale did likewise. "Where to?"

"I don't care, but I can't stay here anymore."

Cale asked no questions. He led Jak out of the room,

through the residence hall, up the stairs, and back into the lending library. There, they found Brelgin and Priest Librarian Elaena seated at a desk, conversing softly. When they saw Jak, both looked up in surprise.

"Jak, I'm glad to see you up. What are you doing?" said Brelgin.

"Mister Cale," accused the priest librarian, "you assured me he would remain bedridden until tomorrow."

Before Cale could respond, Jak reached inside his cloak and removed something from an inner pocket. He set it down on the table with a smack.

When he removed his small hand, Cale saw the item—a silver pin in the shape of an exquisite harp. The symbol of Jak's membership in the Harpers.

"He's my best friend, Brelgin. If we can't help him, then *we* no longer includes *me*. I'm out."

Without another word, Jak turned and walked out of the temple, a stunned Cale following and a speechless Brelgin left in their wake.

CHAPTER 8

THE RETURN

Neither man said a word when they emerged onto the Avenue of Temples. Worshipers thronged the street. The smell of incense hung thick in the cold air. Simultaneously, the bells of several temples began to sound the noon hour.

Jak turned and looked at Cale, his eyebrows raised in question.

"East," Cale replied above the din. "Toward the docks. Good a place as any to spend the rest of the day."

Jak nodded agreement.

Picking their way through the crowd, they sloshed through Selgaunt's bustling streets and headed eastward for the Wharf District.

Cale smelled the fish market a full block before they reached the bay. By the time they had reached the next intersection, he could hear the dull, inchoate roar of the market in full swing. Now midday, the bayside fish stalls teemed with people and overflowed with the winter bounty of the bay—steelfin and cod, mostly. Customers haggled loudly for the day's catch. Fishmongers affected pained expressions and counter-offered. Coins clinked and moved from hand to greedy hand. Selgaunt went about its business.

Ships crowded the piers, the winter-cloaked crews busy about the decks and rigging. Sails snapped in the salty wind. Frost-covered ropes creaked in their pulleys. The shouts of sailors and the bellowed orders of captains filled the air. Though he had lived along the Inner Sea his whole life, Cale had been aboard ship only once, and that had been a harrowing adventure. Cale had fled Westgate aboard *Wave Runner*, a schooner captained by a one-armed, vulgar pirate named Gros Fallimor. Though he and Gros had become fast friends on that voyage, after debarking in Selgaunt he had never seen the old pirate again.

Thoughtful, Cale's gaze drifted out to sea. The still water of the bay mirrored the gray of the overcast sky. In the distance, working to keep the shipping lanes clear of floes, he could see powerful icebreakers plowing through the water like iron-plated dolphins.

"Let's get a room somewhere. I need a bath and some rest," said Cale. The filth of the guildhouse still lingered on his clothes, and he suddenly felt the effects of a day and a half without sleep. "We'll move on the guildhouse an hour or so before dawn."

Jak looked surprised at that, and nervous. "You want to move against Yrsillar at night? That soon?"

Cale nodded firmly as they skirted the market and walked along the pier. "I'd go after him right now if I didn't think fatigue would make me sloppy. We can't delay any longer than necessary." He stopped and looked his friend in the face. "There's no predicting what that bastard will do next. He wants me, but I'm not all he wants. He's going to keep killing unless someone stops him. And if he can continue turning men into ghouls . . ."

"He'll have an army soon enough," Jak finished solemnly. "We go at night, then."

Cale began again to walk, his mind on revenge. "Don't be worried, Jak. Darkness is as much our element as it is his."

To that, Jak said nothing. After a few moments of silence, the little man seemed to reach a decision. He pulled Cale to a stop and looked into his face, embarrassed but determined.

"Cale, when I first saw the shadow demon in Sarntrumpet, I froze. It scared me so bad I just froze." He paused and added softly. "I wanted you to know."

Cale stared at him a long moment. "So now I know. It doesn't change anything. There's no one I'd rather have with me."

Jak smiled gratefully.

"It scared me too," Cale confessed. "But it's a magical fear, supernatural. Since we know that now, it'll be easier next time."

Jak did not look totally convinced. Cale wasn't sure that he was entirely convinced himself.

"Let's get a room," he said.

❖ ❖ ❖ ❖ ❖

They took a room at the Winsome Wench, a low-cost flophouse used mostly by transient sailors and operated by a weather-beaten old woman named Matilda who looked as tough as boiled leather. She was a wench, but hardly winsome. Cale paid her an extra fivestar for the luxury of a bath and laundry service.

Afterward, he took a glass of hot spiced cider in his room, climbed into the lower bunk of the tiny bed, and quickly fell asleep.

❧ ❧ ❧ ❧ ❧

He awoke to find the room dimly lit by a single candle set in a tin candleholder. Jak sat cross-legged on the floor beside it, eyes closed, holy symbol in hand, meditating. Cale knew him to be praying to Brandobaris for spells, committing magical words to memory in preparation for the confrontation with Yrsillar.

Surprisingly, the small window in their room that overlooked the bay was dark. The sounds of commerce, cargo, and shipping had fallen silent. The wharf seemed eerily quiet.

He cleared his throat to get Jak's attention and asked in a whisper, "What time is it, little man?"

It took Jak a moment to come out of his prayer trance. When he did, he opened one eye and cocked an eyebrow at Cale. The soft glow of the candlelight made him look like a sinister, red-headed pixie. "A few hours past midnight," he softly replied. "Selune will be setting soon."

"Dark," Cale oathed in surprise, and sat up in the bed. He had slept away the whole day and most of the night. "Sorry about that, Jak," he said, while pulling on his freshly laundered shirt. The laundry girl must have brought in his clothes while he slept. "I didn't mean to sleep that long."

Jak pocketed his holy symbol, stood up, and used the candle to light the wick of the room's single oil lamp. Cale squinted as his eyes adjusted to the sudden brightness.

"Not a problem. It gave me time to come to terms with Brandobaris. Just in case." He laughed casually, but Cale thought it sounded forced. "Besides, while you slept I had some of Matilda's fish stew and home-made ale. Quite good actually. Wouldn't have been my choice for a last meal, though." He tried to smile at his joke but managed only a pained grimace.

Cale could think of nothing to say to ease his friend's uneasiness. He too felt less than sure that he would see another sunrise. He tried to change the subject. "You should've gotten some sleep, Jak. Elaena said you needed rest."

The little man snorted as he belted on his short sword and daggers. "Are you kidding? Burn me, Cale, I feel like my skin is on fire. I couldn't fall asleep if a mage used a sleep spell on me." Seeing Cale's concerned frown, he hurriedly added, "But I'm still ready for this. I'm not . . . it's just the *waiting*."

Cale nodded. He understood. Had he not been absolutely exhausted, he doubted he would have been able to sleep either. He stood and stretched his long frame and belted on his weapons.

"Let's get a quick meal and get this over with. No more waiting."

"A meal? You hungry?"

Cale donned his enchanted leather armor and threw on his new blue cloak.

"Not especially. But I need to do something . . . *normal* beforehand. You understand?"

"I understand. Definitely." Jak smiled. "I'm hungry again, anyway."

They gathered up their gear, took the candle in hand, and walked down the hall to Matilda's room. After a round of firm knocking, the sleepy, grumbling old woman opened her door a crack.

"What is it?" she croaked.

"We're leaving," Cale announced. "Now, and we won't be back."

She nodded, grumbled something obscene under her breath, and tried to shut the door. Cale stuck his boot in the opening to prevent it from closing. "We would like something to eat before we go, old woman. It's important."

At that, her eyes narrowed angrily. "It's too damned late," she protested. "You'll have to—"

Cale shut her up by flashing a handful of fivestars. "One meal, Matilda. It's not a lot to ask. I said it's important."

She studied the coins, torn between sleepiness and greed. The gold in Cale's hand represented more than a tenday's rent. After only a moment, greed won out. She gave a brisk nod and grabbed the fivestars in a wrinkled hand. "I'll get dressed and be down in a moment. You'll set your own table though, you hear? There's bowls and spoons in the cabinet."

"Fair enough," Cale said, and headed downstairs to the dining room with Jak.

They took bowls, cups, and semi-clean tableware from an ancient wooden cabinet and sat at the sturdy common table. Within a few minutes, Matilda, now dressed in faded nightclothes, descended the stairs and walked into the kitchen to start a fire. She was still grumbling.

"Stew, bread, and ale is all I got," she announced over her shoulder.

Cale shot a longsuffering smile at Jak. "Looks like you're getting fish stew as a last meal no matter what you do, little man."

"So it seems," Jak replied, and distractedly passed his finger back and forth through the candle's flame. "It's fate, Cale, and there's no point fighting fate."

Before long, Matilda emerged from the kitchen. In her gnarled hands, she held a serving board set with a pot of steaming stew, a loaf of day old black bread, and a pitcher of ale. After setting the whole on the table, she filled both their cups with ale and ladled their bowls full with the chunky fish stew.

"You have as much of this as you want," she told them. "Leave the mess and I'll get to it in the morning." She took a step back and eyed Cale determinedly. "But I'm going back to bed now, gold or no gold. This ain't no time for *decent* folks to be up and about."

"No, it's not. Thank you, Matilda, and goodnight."

Startled by his considerate reply, she muttered under her breath, walked away, and slowly walked back up the creaking stairs.

Jak and Cale sat in silence. They picked at the food, their minds on other things.

As he spooned in another mouthful of the stew—it *was* tasty, as Jak had said—Cale looked around the seamy dining room. Empty now, the morning would no doubt find the dirt-stained floor populated by seedy men with dirt-stained souls. Anyone, including fall-down drunks, thieves on the lam, assassins on a job, and whatever other dregs had managed to stumble into Matilda's boardinghouse with enough coin for a night's lodging. Back in Westgate, Cale had taken pre-dawn breakfasts in rooms exactly like this more times than he could count.

This is who you are, he thought, and felt no sadness, only resignation. He had tried for years to deny it, to be nothing more than a butler and a kind man, but he was too tired to deny his nature any longer. His soul, too, was dirt-stained, and this was where he belonged.

"Dark," Jak oathed. He set down his spoon and stared at Cale with wide eyes.

Cale waved the candle smoke out of his face. "What?" His hand went to his sword hilt and he half rose from the chair. His eyes searched the dark room but he saw nothing. "What?"

Jak's hand went to the pocket where he kept his holy symbol. "Just now," he said, still shocked. "The smoke. It . . . formed a mask around your eyes."

"You're mistaken," Cale instinctively protested, but his flesh goosepimpled.

"I'm not," Jak insisted. "Blast. Something's happening here, Cale. With Yrsillar. With us. Something big. Dark and empty, but I can feel it." He pulled his holy symbol from his pocket and rolled it along his knuckles.

Cale decided then to tell Jak everything. Maybe the little man could shed some light on what was happening.

"Jak, listen. When I faced Yrsillar, he called me a Champion of Mask." He felt stupid saying it aloud, but there it was. "That mean anything to you?"

Jak shook his head, but his knowing eyes studied Cale intently.

"He also said that there is another, that there are two champions of Mask." He looked questioningly at the little man. "Could that be us?"

Jak immediately shook his head and held his holy symbol up between thumb and forefinger. "Not possible," he said. "You could be one, I suppose, but I couldn't. I'm a priest of Brandobaris. I can't also be the servant of another god, much less the servant of Mask. If there's another Champion, it's someone other than me."

Cale accepted that with a nod. He sat back in his chair and gulped his ale.

Jak leaned forward and looked at him earnestly. "That confirms it though, Cale. The gods *are* involved here. Or at least Mask. Cale . . . I think you're being called."

"You're crazy." Cale sipped from his ale and tried to keep his hand from shaking.

Jak laughed softly. "It's hard to get your hands around, I know." He sipped from his own ale. "You know how I became a priest of Brandobaris?"

Cale looked up and shook his head. They had never discussed Jak's entry into the Trickster's priesthood. Cale welcomed the opportunity to learn more about his friend.

"It was Year's End Eve in the Year of the Serpent," Jak said, "just after the Time of Troubles. I was twenty-six then." His voice grew distant as he journeyed far back in his memory. "I was doing a fourth-story job in Hillsfar—I was solo then, too," he added with a playful wink, and took a gulp from his ale.

"Cale, I got in and out of this noble's villa without a hitch, loaded with swag. I had enough king's pictures to last two years." He chuckled and shook his head. "But I was young and stupid. Really stupid. I took too much, and it was way too heavy. I got ten feet down the wall, lost my balance, and fell."

"Fell! You?" Halfling rogues notoriously lacked climbing skill, but over the years Jak had repeatedly proven himself an exception.

Jak nodded, smiling. "I should've left nothing more than a bloodstain and a pile of coins on the pavement." He gripped his holy symbol and leaned forward intently. "Instead, I drifted to the ground like a feather."

Cale knew what that meant—he had heard similar stories before. "Divine gift."

"Divine gift," agreed Jak with a nod. "I turned over that whole take to the first priest of Brandobaris I could find. Took the rites right there. I was called. You see?"

Cale took a draw on his ale. "I see . . . but how'd you know it was Brandobaris that had called you? Why not some other god? Why not luck? Or the whim of a passing mage?"

"No, it was the Trickster, all right." Jak nodded thoughtfully and stroked his whiskered chin. "How can I explain? I think it's different for everybody, Cale, but I just *knew*, you know? The same way you know your mother is your mother, even though you didn't see her give birth to you." He crossed his hands and eyed Cale shrewdly. "Has something like that already happened to you?"

Cale sipped thoughtfully from his ale and recalled the mysterious darkness that only he had been able to see through. "Maybe," he said. "Maybe." He felt himself being pulled along through events he didn't fully understand, the marionette of a divine puppeteer. He didn't like it. He would be no one's puppet, not even a god's. Especially not a god's.

As though reading his mind, Jak said, "You're always your own man, Cale, even after you accept your calling, and you *can* reject it. Most don't though—the gods seem to call only those ready and able to accept. Kind of a convergence of mortal and divine interests."

It pleased Cale to learn that a call could be rejected. He wasn't sure Mask had tried to call him, but if so, he reserved the right to refuse.

I'm not changing for you, Mask, understand? He had tried changing for Thamalon and Thazienne, and it had only made things worse. He was through with trying to be something other than what he was. A skilled killer.

He put Mask out of his mind and finished his stew. "You ready?" he asked Jak.

The little man's face fell slightly but he rallied quickly. "Ready." Hurriedly, Jak slammed back the last of his ale and enjoyed a final spoonful of stew.

"Then let's do this."

✥ ✥ ✥ ✥ ✥

Verdrinal awoke with a start. His heart thumped so hard in his chest that he thought it would surely explode. The residuum of the sound that had awakened him from his nightmare played at the edge of his still sleepy consciousness and promised him an ugly death.

There's someone in the room! his mind screamed.

Slowly, he slid his hand under the sheets and patted the space to his right—nothing. Dark, he inwardly cursed. For the first night in the last five, he had not taken a lover. He was alone.

Terrified, but unwilling to die without trying to take *some* action, he jerked upright in bed and peered around the opulence of his bedchambers. He saw only darkness—the hearth had burned itself out. It must be several hours past midnight.

Heart racing, he waited for the sleep to clear from his eyesight. Within a few moments, he could make out varying shades of gray—his dressing table, armoire, work desk, divan, dressing screen, chairs—

There! A shadowy figure stood near his wardrobe. His breath left him, his body went weak, his intent to fight to the last vanished under a tidal wave of fear.

"Dark!" he screamed.

He threw off his sheets in a cloud of silk, rolled across the bed, and reached for the nightstand drawer where he kept a poisoned knife. He couldn't control his fingers—he fumbled clumsily with the drawer latch. He couldn't breathe—he wanted to scream for Hov but his constricted throat would make no sound. He would be dead in a heartbeat.

Damn this drawer! Damn this drawer! He stared over his shoulder in terror. The figure didn't move. He froze, cocked his head, and peered intently through the darkness. The figure didn't move because . . .

It's my damned night cloak, he realized. He had thrown it over his wardrobe before coming to bed.

"My cloak," he muttered. He would have laughed but he still hadn't recovered his breath. His sweat-soaked body shivered in the night's cold. He collapsed back into the bed and stared up at the ceiling until his heart ceased pounding.

"There's no one here," he announced to the night. He had imagined the sound, had imported the terror of his nightmare into his bedroom.

He had dreamed of the dread, or what he imagined the dread to be. He had run and run through a featureless, unending maze, all the while dogged from behind by a clawed black vision of unspeakable evil. He had heard it sniffing for him, chuffing like a hound. Periodically, it had called out to him. "Little puke," it had hissed. "Little puke."

"Puke," he breathed, and chuckled in relief. He had scared himself witless!

No longer afraid, but still flushed from the rush of fear, he pined again for Arlanni, the slim, taut young woman who had been warming his bed for the past few days. She had left in a huff after a spat over the dinner roast.

Too bad Arlanni was so damned difficult. It made her all the more appealing, of course, he thought with a smile. Thinking of her long blonde hair and firm thighs, he grew warm with excitement. I should send a messenger for her this instant, he resolved.

He sat up again and reached for the small bronze bell that sat on his nightstand. Increasingly eager for Arlanni's body, he shook it urgently. Its soft chime reverberated through his large bedroom. Hov would be along in a moment.

The big man had taken to standing watch outside his door since the incident with Riven.

Such a diligent worker . . . a pity, Verdrinal thought, too much work makes a man a dullard. He again shook the bell. "Hov," he called, "Hov."

Before Verdrinal took another breath the darkness to his right suddenly came to life. A shadowy figure rushed him. A fist grabbed him by the hair and jerked him roughly down on the bed.

"Aiiee—" The feel of cold steel at his throat silenced his scream.

A body slithered close, stinking breath felt hot on his cheek. "Hov can't help you," said a voice.

Drasek Riven's voice.

A shudder shook Verdrinal's body when he heard the coldness in the assassin's tone. This was not the emotionally volatile Riven that had argued with him yesterday in his study. This was Drasek Riven the professional killer, one of the best assassins the Zhentarim had ever trained, and he was on a job.

Verdrinal heard clear as a bell the promise of blood in Riven's sinister, emotionless voice. He knew with certainty that the assassin had come to kill him. Instead of growing strong with adrenaline, Verdrinal's body froze with fear.

"Hov can't help anyone anymore," Riven continued. Still holding the dagger at Verdrinal's throat, he held up with his other hand a jagged piece of meat and dangled it over Verdrinal's eyes.

Hov's tongue.

Warm droplets of blood peppered Verdrinal's cheeks and mouth. He twisted his face to the side and clamped his mouth closed. His eyes fell on his bedroom door—Hov's cooling body must be slumped on the floor just outside.

"You don't like that, eh?" Riven chuckled spitefully and laid Hov's tongue on Verdrinal's chest. "Well, he didn't like it much either. But he had it coming."

Riven's laugh made Verdrinal want to vomit. He thought about fighting back, but couldn't bring himself to move. Fear paralyzed him. He knew he was going to die, but he found himself unwilling to do anything that might speed the inevitable. He clutched desperately to every heartbeat that remained in his chest.

"Why?" he peeped at last.

"Why!" Riven leaned over him and looked him in the face. "Because you're a liability, and I lost six men." All in one lightning fast motion, Riven stabbed Verdrinal through the cheek, withdrew the blade, and replaced the tip against Verdrinal's throat.

"Aargh!" In agony, Verdrinal kicked and flailed with his legs. Riven's blade forced him to keep his neck motionless.

The assassin grinned and cuffed Verdrinal across the face. Verdrinal, a nobleman of Selgaunt, began to cry. Riven cuffed him again, harder.

"Shut up. The fact that you didn't see this coming only makes my point—you're a liability."

Eyes watering, Verdrinal lay motionless. Blood ran down his face from the hole in his cheek and collected in a warm pool on his pillow.

"I've killed good men for less," Riven said. "Did you think I'd let this pass from *you,* an incompetent little puke?"

Verdrinal made no answer. Little puke. He hadn't been dreaming. Something dark *had* been hunting him, a shadowy thing that had called him a *little puke.* Not the dread though, Drasek Riven.

The blade pressed harder into the flesh of his throat. He closed his eyes and waited for death. It didn't come.

Riven's free hand clamped painfully on Verdrinal's cheeks and jerked his head sidewise. Verdrinal looked into the assassin's eerily calm face, stared blankly into the hole where Riven's eye should be.

"I thought all night about what you said, about how the dread was doing our work for us, and how we would kill it afterward. But then I asked myself why Malix would leave the city without telling me and leave *you* in charge? Do you know what I realized?"

Verdrinal didn't make a move, didn't dare reply.

"I realized that he didn't tell me because I would recognize that explanation as *dung!* Malix doesn't know what to do, you idiot! That's why he went to Zhentil Keep. To get help. This demon is running rampant in the city and he doesn't have a godsdamned clue as to how to deal with it." Riven's voice lowered to a hiss. "So he left *you* in charge, because you're too stupid to see it."

Verdrinal would have protested but knew it would be futile. Riven's one black eye looked colder and emptier than the hole in his other socket. There could be no explaining to that eye. Verdrinal kept silent and tried to stop the tears from flowing down his face. He didn't want to die while crying.

Riven leaned in close. "I lost six men because of Malix's idiocy and your incompetence. Malix will answer to me later. You'll answer to me now."

"The Zhentarim will force you out of the organization," Verdrinal desperately whispered.

"Maybe," Riven conceded. "But I don't care."

A sharp stab of pain raced across Verdrinal's throat, followed by a cascade of warmth that spilled down his chest and poured down his windpipe. He coughed and gurgled, but strangely, felt no pain. He reached for his throat and felt his life pouring through his fingers from the open gash in his neck.

I'm dying, he thought. Spots exploded in his head. He tried to squirm from the bed but his body would not move. He reached a weak hand up to grab at Riven but the assassin seemed too far away. His vision started to go black.

He heard himself gurgling away the last of his life. He felt the soaked sheets sticking to his body. Riven's voice carried across the void and filled his ears.

"I'm in charge now," he said.

Verdrinal tried to laugh, gurgled instead, then died.

❧ ❧ ❧ ❧ ❧

The snow and wind had stopped. Breathless, Jak and Cale stood in the shadows of an alley beside Emellia's. The sounds of that most human of pastimes carried through the brothel's shutters.

"Not exactly shy, are they?" Jak observed with a soft chuckle.

Cale smiled despite himself. Now that they had begun to work, Jak seemed to have shaken his trepidation and regained his usual carefree sense of humor. Still, they needed to stay focused. Across Ariness Street was the guildhouse. The street itself was empty.

"I don't see any guards," Cale observed. "Didn't last time, either. You?"

"No. No one on the roof, either."

Cale continued to study the guildhouse, thinking. Assuming things had not gotten markedly worse, he knew what to expect in the basement. He also knew from his combat with the shadow demon in Stormweather that they would need enchanted weapons to destroy the demons. Jak had nothing but a luckstone. Cale had nothing at all. He rebuked himself for not keeping Thazienne's enchanted dagger.

"There's an armory on the first floor, toward the back of the building. The guild keeps a few magical weapons there, in case they are ever needed by a guild member for a job. They aren't very powerful. The Righteous Man kept anything of power for himself. But they'll be better than nothing."

Jak blew out a misty-frozen sigh and nodded. "Good idea. We'll need magical weapons to face the demons." He turned and looked at Cale. "What's the play, though? How do we get in?"

Cale knew there to be only two entrances to the guildhouse, the sewers and the front doors. Before, when he had come in by way of the sewer entrance, he had barely escaped with his life. While not superstitious, he would not go in the same way twice.

"We're walking through the front doors," he said, and started across the street.

Halfway to the guildhouse's porch, he pulled his long sword from its scabbard. Beside him, Jak jerked free a short sword and dagger.

Come on, you bastards, he challenged the cold night air, but nothing happened. They gained the porch without incident and faced the sturdy double doors.

"The hairs on my arms are standing up," Jak softly observed.

"You're just cold," Cale said, though he knew the statement to be false. His hairs also stood on end. The air around the guildhouse tasted polluted. He felt an ominous prickling in his body that made him shudder. He tried to ignore the feeling and placed his hand on the door handle. If it was locked, even Jak would have difficulty picking it.

The handle turned. Cale and Jak blew out frozen breaths simultaneously. They shared a look.

"It opens in," Cale whispered. "To better expose as a target anyone trying to force their way in." Jak nodded. Cale began to push against the oak slab. It wouldn't budge. Something blocked it.

"There's something on the other side," he said, and prepared to throw his body against it. "Ready?"

Jak sheathed his sword and dagger, drew three throwing knives, and positioned himself to the left of the door. "Ready."

With a grunt, Cale slammed his shoulder into the door. Whatever blocked it slid clear and the door flew all the way open. Jak leaped into the opening behind Cale, daggers ready. Cale, long sword before him, slid sidewise to give Jak a wide berth to throw.

Enough light from the street spilled into the room to depict a scene of terrible destruction. Tables, chairs, beds, and piles of unidentifiable debris lay scattered about. A pile of four mildewed straw mattresses had blocked the door. A musty, rotten smell wafted from the door. The smell of smoke lingered in the air—the aftereffect from Cale's earlier missile explosion in the basement.

"Stinks," Jak said. He sheathed his throwing knives and again drew his short sword and fighting dagger.

"Get used to it," Cale replied.

Jak stepped fully through the doorway and poked the mattresses with his short sword. "Why the mattresses? How're they getting in and out?"

Cale shrugged off his backpack and pulled out a torch. "Sewers, probably. Hells, I don't know. There's no making sense of what's going on in here, Jak."

Before Cale could remove his tinderbox, Jak stopped him. "Here." The little man pulled forth the metallic rod that he had used to illuminate their way through Selgaunt's sewers a month ago. As he held it, a blue light sparked in its tip and grew to a soft glow.

"I'm surprised to see you still have that thing," Cale observed.

"I don't use it much."

"Does it do anything else?"

Jak frowned thoughtfully and studied the rod. "I

don't think so." He crouched and aimed it purposefully across the street. "Kill!" It did nothing.

"Just the glow, it seems," Jak said with a smile.

"Lucky for the girls at Emellia's," Cale said grinning. "Give it here then. You can't carry it and fight two-handed."

Jak handed it over. His hand trembled slightly. Cale pretended not to notice.

He knew how Jak felt but they could not turn back now.

"Let's go," he said, summoning his own courage. They walked into the guildhouse.

The smell of corpses permeated the stuffy air. Within a few moments, Cale's nose became inured to the smell. Moving warily through the ruined offices, Cale and Jak had to pick their way through the overturned chairs, desks, and scattered papers.

"Keep your eyes on the shadows," Cale said tensely. He tightened the grip of his sweaty palms on the sword hilt and rod.

"Right," Jak said with a nod, his eyes watchful of every corner, both blades held high and ready.

They cautiously navigated room after room, but apart from the toppled, broken furniture, the offices seemed to have escaped the warping and foulness that had occurred in the basement. No corpses, no voids, no blood, no demons. Only the ubiquitous charnel reek that announced the presence of ghouls nearby.

Silent as specters, they prowled farther into the house. When the two reached the end of the offices, Cale held up a hand to signal Jak to stop.

"That door," he said, and nodded at the oak door before them, "leads into the guildhouse proper. To reach the armory, we go down the hall to the right, then left down a flight of stairs, then right down another hall. Can't miss it."

Jak nodded as he memorized the directions. He mopped the sweat from his forehead with the back of his hand. "Do you think they've abandoned the upper floor?"

"Maybe. No way to tell. We'll find out soon enough." Cale stared into Jak's eyes. "Ready?"

"Ready," Jak replied. "Let's hope the Trickster and Lady Luck are in a good mood."

Cale stepped forward, knelt at the door, and listened. Nothing in the hallway beyond. He stood and tried to turn the handle. It was jammed.

"Dark," he oathed. He held the rod before the keyhole and peered in. Jak crept close and looked over his shoulder. "The locking mechanism's been deliberately mangled." He looked back at Jak. "Can you pick it?"

"Not if the tumblers are bent," Jak replied. "But I can still get it open." He reached into his breast pocket, pulled out his holy cloak-clasp, and muttered the words to a spell. The air around his small hands began to grow charged. Cale backed a step away from the door.

When Jak finished the incantation and pointed his holy symbol at the lock, the magic of the spell forced the twisted metal in the mechanism to disentangle itself. Tumblers fell into place, metal ground against metal and shrieked like a dying man. Cale winced at the sound. If anything stood nearby, it would have heard them.

In three heartbeats, the door popped ajar. Cale pulled Jak behind him and jerked the door open, his blade ready.

The narrow hallway stretched to the left and right, dark beyond the limits of the wand's blue light. As with the rest of the guildhouse, debris lay cast haphazardly about on the floor, the ghouls and demons seemingly intent on destroying or befouling any semblance of normalcy.

Despite the chaos, Cale now felt surprisingly calm. Either he would succeed or he would die.

The little man, on the other hand, seemed balanced on a sword's edge, at one moment his cocky, adventurous self, at the next moment frightened beyond words. Cale could hear the nervousness in Jak's harsh breathing, though the halfling tried to mask it.

I shouldn't have brought him, Cale thought guiltily. Jak had not come to succeed or die. Nor had he come to avenge Thazienne. He had come because Cale was his friend and Cale had asked him to come.

I don't want him to die for that, he thought. He resolved to ensure Jak's safety no matter what.

"You feel that?" Jak asked nervously.

Cale nodded. He felt it. The air in the hallway seemed as heavy as an autumn fog, pregnant with the stink of something vile. A distant pulsing, felt rather than heard, thumped at intervals like the beat of a giant, foul heart.

"What is it?" Jak asked.

"I don't know," Cale softly replied. He tightened his grip on the long sword.

Jak looked at him sharply, eyes wide, but said nothing. The little man's hand went to his holy symbol.

"This way," Cale said, and headed right.

After walking only fifteen paces, they encountered the first signs of warping. The blue light of Jak's wand illuminated a vacant spot in the hallway floor. The emptiness utterly swallowed the light. The pulsing seemed to originate from somewhere within the void. With each pulse, Cale's loose clothes and the hairs on his arms were pulled toward the distortion.

" 'Ware that, Jak. I don't know what it is, but we can expect more of them. Lots more. I think the shadow demon can move through them."

Jak walked past Cale, stood at the edge of the emptiness, and peered within.

"Careful," Cale warned again. He recalled the hypnotic effect one of these *vacancies* had on him in the guildhouse basement. He also recalled the malice-filled yellow eyes he had seen staring at him out of one.

"I think it's a gate," Jak ventured.

Cale stepped forward and peered within. The pull never got too strong, but it was nevertheless disconcerting. "A gate? To where? Yrsillar's plane?"

Jak could only shrug.

Snarls suddenly erupted from somewhere behind. Jak gasped and whirled, blades ready. Cale leaped before him in a fighting crouch.

As suddenly as they had begun, the snarls died out and vanished.

Cale held the wand aloft and walked a few steps back the way they had come. Nothing. Inspired, he knelt and placed his ear to the floor. From below, the distant sound of snarls carried through the floorboards.

"Came through the floorboards," he said, and stood. "They must have been right below us."

Jak let his weapons sag and visibly relaxed. "Dark," he oathed. "Startled me."

"Me too."

"They coming up?" Jak asked.

"I don't know." He walked past Jak, faced the emptiness of the gate, and estimated its width—five feet, maybe six. "Can you jump over this?"

"Easy." Without another word, Jak sheathed his weapons, backed up a few steps, raced forward, and leaped over the gate. He cleared it easily and landed in a crouch. In a flash, he had his blades redrawn and stood at the ready, waiting for Cale.

Cale quickly jumped the gate as well. Dodging debris, they continued forward. Two more gates— empty holes in reality—blocked their path, one in the floor, easily jumped, and one in the wall, easily side-stepped. They reached the short flight of stairs that descended to the lower level of the guildhouse.

"Down here," Cale said.

Jak nodded. "I don't smell it anymore," he observed softly. "The rot, I mean."

Cale nodded. He didn't smell it either. The smell of decay had become so commonplace to him that he no longer noticed it.

That's why I don't feel afraid, he realized. Fear, too, had become so commonplace for him over the last two days that he noticed it only rarely.

A soft growling from down the twisting stairs interrupted his reverie. He looked questioningly at Jak. The little man nodded grimly. He had heard it too. Cale covered the cool tip of the wand with his palm so that only a little light trickled out between his fingers. In hand cant, he signaled to Jak, *I lead. Be cautious.*

Jak nodded and they silently descended the twisting stone stairs. When they reached the landing at the bottom, they discovered the source of the growls.

A ghoul dressed in green tatters sat at the base of the wall and stared dazedly into the emptiness of a gate. A slowly swirling mix of gray and black, the gate pulsed periodically, and with each beat of the unholy heart the spider web tracery of purple veins beneath the ghoul's translucent gray skin beat in time. The dazed horror rocked back and forth, rhythmically growling softly into the emptiness. Its yellow eyes looked as vacant as the hole into which it stared. The ghoul, oblivious to the pain and purple blood that coursed down its arms, mindlessly dug its claws into its own rotted flesh.

Jak gave a slight gasp and Cale signaled him to stop and stand still. Cautiously, blade before him, he walked toward the ghoul.

Enthralled by whatever it saw in the gate, the creature showed no sign of noticing him. It simply kept rocking and gouging itself. Cale moved directly behind it. It continued to mutter and stare, oblivious to all but the void.

Up close now, Cale could make out muttered words interspersed with its bestial growls. "He is among us, among us."

Cale swallowed his disgust. Though twisted and warped, he recognized the skinny body and short brown hair of Willen Trostyn, a boy the Righteous Man had recruited no more than a month ago. Willen couldn't have been more than twenty, and now Cale had to kill him.

Without further thought, he raised his long sword high to strike. He stopped in mid-stroke and looked at Jak. Eyes filled with horror and disgust, the little man met his gaze and gave him a short nod of approval. Willen showed no sign of noticing anything. He rocked, dug his claws deeper into his arms, and muttered mindlessly.

"Among us. Among us—"

With an overhand chop, Cale laid open Willen's head. Purple gore sprayed the wall and soaked the floor. Willen died instantly, collapsing into a stinking heap at the base of the gate.

Seemingly of its own accord, the gore flowed toward the void. Like the mouth of some unimaginable beast, the emptiness drew Willen's blood within and devoured it. Swirls of purple intermixed with the black and gray of the gate and spun toward nothingness. Cale turned away to find Jak. The little man's face had turned white.

"Dark," mouthed the halfling soundlessly, as he stared at the wall. He looked as though he might lose Matilda's fish stew at any moment.

Cale stepped forward and gripped him by the shoulders. "Don't look into the gates, Jak. Don't look."

The little man peeled his eyes away and stared at Cale with eyes full of horror. "It's hungry, Erevis. The gate. It's hungry."

"I know," Cale replied. "It's empty. Emptiness is always hungry." He gave the little man a slight shake. "Jak! The demons are the same way. You see? They're always hungry and they'll never stop. That's why we have to stop them. You see? Jak!"

The little man gave a nod, seemed to come back to himself some. "I see," he said, and clutched for his holy symbol.

He's close to losing it, Cale realized. He placed a gentle hand on Jak's shoulder. "Go back, my friend. Right now. Go back and get out. Get Brelgin and—"

Jak shook his head and pushed Cale's hand away. "I'm not going back, Erevis. I just . . ." He waved his blades to indicate the guildhouse. "Trickster's toes, it just takes a moment to digest all of this." His eyes fell on Willen's corpse, then returned to Cale. "I'm not going back. I'm here until this is over."

Cale accepted that. "Then let's get to the armory."

Growling suddenly erupted behind them and died away. The scratching of clawed feet on the hardwood planks of the floor was loud to Cale's ears.

"They must have come up from the basement," Jak calmly observed.

Pleased to see Jak in possession of his faculties, Cale nodded agreement. "Yrsillar must know we're here. Let's move."

With Cale leading, they sped down the debris-strewn hallway until they reached the armory. The open door hung crookedly, having been torn loose from its upper hinge.

"Here," Cale said, and ducked in. Jak followed.

Weapons lay cast about the floor, many broken or chipped, but some intact. Comically, a few broken swords had been replaced on their wall mounts after being destroyed. All the wooden tables and weapon racks had been turned over and the legs broken off. Loose sling bullets covered the floor. Of the six suits of leather armor and three suits of studded leather that hung by their straps from the wall, all had been torn into uselessness by ghoul claw. A stack of broken crossbows lay piled in the near corner. Against the right hand wall, the large wooden chests and barrels that had once held the crossbow ammunition had been broken open and the quarrels scattered. Shanks of silk rope, crowbars, and lock picking tools had been tossed about randomly.

Cale's heart sank when he saw the thorough destruction. They had to have enchanted weapons! He scanned the wreckage for the pair of long, thin, iron strongboxes that once had held the guild's small store of magical weapons—

Growls again sounded from the hallway behind them. It rose to a crescendo and then devolved into wet gibbering. Cale shared an alarmed glance with Jak. From the sound, *many* ghouls had come up from the basement.

"Probably feeding on the body of the one we killed," Cale softly observed. "Let's get this door closed. Quietly."

Ashen faced, Jak gave a nod. "Right."

With Cale reaching over him to hold the heavy oak door in position near its broken upper hinge, Jak carefully pushed it closed.

"We're looking for two iron strongboxes," Cale whispered to Jak, and started to kick through the debris. "Hurry. They'll finish with that body soon."

Jak began searching the debris.

Cale quickly found the boxes against the far wall,

buried beneath an overturned weapon rack, a wooden stool, and a pile of broken broadswords.

He gave a short, soft whistle to get Jak's attention. "Here." The little man hurried over. Cale could no longer hear the sounds of the feeding ghouls.

He saw right away that ghouls had been at the strongboxes. The surfaces had been scratched with claws and beaten with something heavy. The lock and hinges had been pried at but they hadn't been opened. He felt a flash of hope.

"I don't have a key," he said to Jak. "Can you get them open?"

Jak eyed the locks professionally and nodded. "I don't have another spell for it, but I should be able to do it the hard way." He reached into one of his pouches and pulled forth a small leather case. After loosing its strap, he unfolded it to reveal a bewildering array of lock picking tools—from a bent copper wire to a hardened steel pry for tumblers. He pondered for a moment, selected a tool Cale did not recognize, and set to work.

"Tough lock," Jak observed after working on it for a moment. He exchanged the first tool for his tumbler pry. "But I'll get it."

Tense, Cale said nothing. He could hear the growls of the ghouls from somewhere down the hall.

"Hurry, Jak."

"Mmhmm."

The growls grew louder. Through the thick door, Cale could hear the thump and scrape of clawed feet on wood, closer now.

"Jak . . ."

"I know." Jak's fingers worked rapidly. Cale heard click after click in the lock but the damned thing didn't open!

The maddened snarls of the rampaging ghouls drew

nearer until they sounded right outside the armory door. There had to be ten or more! Their footfalls sounded like a stampede of market cattle. Heart thumping, Cale stood over Jak and turned to face the door, blade ready.

"Hurry up, godsdammit," he whispered over his shoulder. He would rather face ten ghouls with an enchanted blade than without.

"Almost . . . got . . . it . . ." replied the little man. "There!"

He lifted the lid of the strongbox just as a ghoul body thumped into the door. Jak gave a start and dropped the tumbler pry. The sound of the tool clanking on the wood floor made Cale wince. Surely they had heard that. He expected a flood of ghouls to rush the room in seconds.

"Cale—" whispered Jak.

Cale waved his hand sharply. "Hssst."

The little man popped his mouth closed, drew his blades, and stood beside Cale, waiting.

Seconds passed and the door stayed closed. Gradually, the sound of the growls began to grow fainter. The ghouls were moving past them! Cale could not believe their luck!

They waited in nervous silence as the sounds of the rampaging pack grew fainter and fainter, until finally the growls disappeared altogether. They exhaled as one.

"Dark," Jak whispered.

"Dark indeed," Cale said, and shot him a hard smile. "We got lucky there."

Jak returned the smile with a grin and tapped the luckstone that hung from a chain at his belt. "The Lady *does* favor the foolish, Cale." He turned and knelt before the open chest. "Here, look at all this."

Lined with black velvet, the first iron strongbox

held two long swords, a gilt mahogany case, and a small, plain maple box. Each long sword had a large onyx set into the pommel, a hilt wrapped with silver wire, and a flawless, shining blade.

Cale reached for the blades but Jak stayed his hand.

"Let me check for magical traps," he said. "I'll also confirm that they're enchanted."

"Good idea," Cale replied, then added some good-natured ribbing. "Must be nice to have spells at your disposal on a job."

Jak winked at him as he pulled forth his holy symbol. "Very nice. The Trickster takes care of his own." He looked up at Cale sidelong. "Mask does too, I suspect."

While Cale thought on that, Jak softly intoned the words to a spell. Afterward, he carefully scrutinized the chest.

"No traps," he said with assurance. Still holding the bejeweled cloak-clasp, he mouthed the words to a second spell. "The swords are magical, plus whatever is in the box and case."

Without further ado, he lifted out the case and popped it open. Within its red, felt-lined interior sat four silvery sling bullets, each inscribed over their entire surface with tiny, intricate runes. He set that aside and pried open the maple box. Three glass vials sat within, cushioned by packing rags. The translucent liquid within the vials shimmered azure in the blue light of the wand.

"Potions," Jak announced, followed quickly by, "No good to us now though, unless you know what they do."

Cale shook his head in the negative. "Bring them anyway," he said, and knelt to pick up one of the enchanted long swords. He tested its heft. Though somewhat wider than his normal blade, the enchanted long sword felt lighter and perfectly balanced. He smiled appreciatively, though he knew it mustn't be too powerful a weapon or the Righteous Man would not have stored it in the common armory. Even a weak enchantment was better than none. Thazienne's dagger had wounded the shadow demon and he did not think it had been particularly powerful. He discarded his own ordinary blade and sheathed the enchanted one.

Jak pocketed the potions and placed the magical sling bullets in his ammunition pouch. He slid over to the other strongbox, pulled out his tools, and set to work on it.

While he waited, Cale paced apprehensively. His eyes fell on the open strongbox.

"Jak . . ."

"Hmm?" The little man didn't turn around. "Nearly got it."

A tingle ran up Cale's spine. He knelt before the first strongbox, throat constricted.

Within, nearly invisible against the black velvet, lay a black felt mask, the symbol of Mask the Shadowlord. Cale stared at it, motionless, afraid to touch. Was this a sign? He felt himself standing on the edge of a cliff. Touching the mask would be to step off and fall, or fly. He wasn't sure if he was ready to fly.

We must have overlooked it, he thought, but didn't really believe it.

Beside him, Jak popped open the lock on the other strongbox. "Got it," he said, and lifted the lid.

Cale grabbed the mask and stuffed it into his cloak pocket. He told himself he did it for the sake of Jak's safety, but knew it to be untrue. For the first time in his life, he was *hoping* for help from a god. The events of the last two days had changed him. Yrsillar had to be stopped. Tonight, Cale would take help from wherever he could get it.

"No traps," Jak said. He whistled and pulled out a wide-bladed, mundane looking short sword. "Looks plain, but the aura shows it as enchanted. I'll use it." He lifted out another maple box like the one they had found in the first strongbox. "Nothing special." Liquid dripped from the seam between the lid and the bottom. "The potion vials must have been broken when the room was tossed. They're no good." He pulled out a small leather bag, loosed the drawstring, and dumped the contents onto his palm, two rings, one a plain electrum band, one a silver band inset with three small black opals.

"No way to know what these do, either," said Jak. "You take this one." He tossed Cale the bejeweled silver ring. "I'll keep this one." He slipped the electrum ring into a belt pouch. "We'll figure them out later."

Cale pocketed the ring. When he did, his hand brushed the felt of the mask and a charge raced through his body. He had difficulty deciding whether he had imagined it or not. For an instant, he felt a part of something larger than himself. He felt a newfound confidence. Maybe they *would* get out of this alive.

Jak stood and took a few practice stabs with his new short sword, seemed satisfied, and looked at Cale. "Let's get moving."

Pleased to hear the confidence in Jak's voice, Cale nodded and moved for the door. He knelt and placed his ear against the door. The ghouls were gone.

Knowing that the loosely secured door would fall if he simply released the latch, he sheathed his blade, gripped the handle with both hands, and used his strength to steady the door while he opened it—

The instant he turned the handle, something flew into the door and blew it open, nearly knocking it entirely loose from the wall. Cale staggered backward, stunned. Savage snarls and bestial growls filled his ears. Ghouls! The smell of rot filled his nostrils as ghoul after ghoul poured into the room.

"Cale—" Jak screamed. The growls of the ghouls drowned out the rest of what the little man said.

Cale fumbled to get his sword clear of its scabbard. Gray bodies milled around him, snarled and tore at his flesh. He couldn't distinguish individual creatures. The whole pack seemed a single mass of gray flesh, black fangs, filthy claws, and wretched sewer stink. Beside him, invisible through the press of rotted skin, he could hear Jak shouting defiance.

Claws and teeth thumped off Cale's enchanted armor. Tatters of his blue cloak came loose and floated to the floor. Snarls filled his ears, surrounding him on all sides. He grabbed one ghoul by the throat while jerking his blade free with his left hand. Another jumped on his back and nearly bowled him over.

"Arrgh," he grunted. He ran his blade through the sternum of the ghoul he held by the throat. It screamed and died but others instantly rushed to replace it. The damned things were everywhere! He threw the rabid creature from his back and swiped wildly about with his blade. They pressed him so closely that he couldn't help but strike a ghoul with every blow. Again and again the enchanted iron *chunked* into ghoul flesh. Squeals of pain joined the savage growls.

A multitude of raking claws bloodied his arms and face. He ignored the pain and chopped. Purple blood sprayed the floor to join the red of his own.

A claw tore across his chest, penetrated his armor, and bit into flesh. Terrifyingly, his body began to grow sluggish, the venom of ghouls' gashes doing its work. He continued to swing his long sword while he tried to fight off the poison. His body grew heavy, slowed. He wanted to call out for Jak but his tongue weighed a hundredweight. Claws tore into him. He couldn't move. Ghouls pressed closer, bit into his flesh and *fed on him*. He felt their fetid breath hot on his skin, felt their foul saliva mix with his blood as they tore loose morsels of his exposed flesh. The excruciating pain set off a spark shower in his brain but he could not move or scream, could not even blink, could only watch helplessly as ghouls fed on him and he died.

Not like this, he desperately prayed. Mask, not like this! If the Shadowlord heard his plea, he made no response. Cale thought he was dead.

Jak suddenly leaped into his field of vision, bloody blades held high. The little man snarled challenges and lashed out with both blades at the ghouls biting at Cale. They pounced after him, but the little man ducked, whirled, and ran one through the chest with his dagger and short sword. It squealed and fell over dead. Jak had his blades free in an instant.

Three ghouls surrounded the little man. They lashed out with claws and teeth. Jak whirled, dodged, fought like a rabid badger. Cale could do nothing but watch. Jak bled freely from many wounds—the little man wore no armor—and Cale knew that if he succumbed to the paralyzing poison they would both die.

The three remaining ghouls charged the little man at once.

Like a red-headed whirlwind, Jak ducked, spun, and rolled. Claws flashed and tore into his exposed back, but he rolled away and retaliated with an upward dagger thrust through the groin of one ghoul. It screamed in agony and fell writhing to the floor. The little man jumped to his feet, jerked free another dagger, and rushed the last two. Rushed them!

Cale had never seen Jak so . . . savage. Teeth gritted in a snarl, the halfling tore open the gut of one ghoul, then finished it with a stab through the face. The last gray horror tore into his exposed flank. Red blood sprayed and Jak buckled. The ghoul leaped for him, jaws wide. Jak had nothing else to do but fall back, hold his short sword vertically like a pennon pole, and let the creature impale itself. The thick blade of his short sword burst through the back of the ghoul in a spray of purple. It squealed once, convulsed, and moved no more.

He'd done it!

Covered in purple and red blood, the little man squirmed out from under the dead ghoul. Gasping, sweating, he tried to stand but wobbled and sagged to his knees. Cale could see his small body trembling. Whether from exhaustion, rage, or fear, he could not tell. After taking a moment to recover, Jak rose and pulled out his holy symbol.

"Hang on, Cale," he said. He took a deep breath, gathered himself, and intoned the words to a healing spell. Instantly, the wounds on his back, arms, chest, and face closed to pink lines, then vanished altogether. He sheathed his blades, recovered his dagger from the body of a ghoul, and picked his way through the carnage to Cale.

"Dark and empty," he softly oathed, upon studying Cale's wounds. "You're as cut up as one of my mom's stew carrots." He giggled at that, and Cale thought he heard in the laughter the beginnings of hysteria. The little man recovered himself quickly, however, and returned to business.

"First the wounds," he said, and repeated the magical syllables of a healing spell while touching Cale's hand. The pain vanished instantly. Cale's torn skin knit itself back to wholeness. The horrible wounds closed. Jak had cast a powerful spell.

"Now the paralysis." Jak mouthed a more complex prayer while waving his holy symbol before Cale's frozen body.

Like the wounds, the paralysis suddenly vanished. Free to move, Cale sagged, lowered his blade, and found his right hand buried in his cloak pocket, clutching the felt mask.

Odd, he thought. When the ghouls had surprised him, he had drawn his blade and unconsciously reached for the mask. Very odd.

"Feel better?" Jak asked.

"I do," Cale said, and pulled his hand from his pocket. He examined his flesh. No trace remained from what had been a multitude of wounds. "Thank you, my friend."

Embarrassed, Jak waved away his gratitude and smiled awkwardly.

Cale surveyed the carnage. The corpses of eleven ghouls lay amidst the broken weapons on the blood soaked floor.

"You need a few minutes?" he asked Jak. "We can wait." The little man had to be taxed after all that.

Jak turned to face him, fire in his green eyes. "No, I'm ready now."

"Let's move then."

Jak nodded. "Where?"

"The basement," Cale said.

CHAPTER 9

STALKING DARKNESS

Cale walked out of the armory, turned left, and headed back toward the short flight of stairs that led back up to the main hallway.

"We can't access the stairway to the basement from this level," Cale said over his shoulder. "We'll have to go back up to the first floor. It's not far from there."

Not far at all. Where before they had walked out of the offices and turned right into the main hall to reach the armory, now they would go left to reach the stairway down to the basement.

Jak nodded and they continued on, wary.

After a few minutes, they reached the base of the stairs where Cale had killed Willen. The ghoul pack had reduced the corpse to a virtual skeleton. What little flesh remained hung from the twisted body in frayed ribbons. Everywhere purple blood stained the floor. Cale could only imagine the orgy of feeding that had occurred here. The odor made his eyes water. He swallowed bile and kept down the vomit by sheer force of will.

Willen's femur—nearly torn from his pelvis—stuck out at a grotesque angle and extended into the void in the wall. It vanished into nothingness just above the knee. With each pulse of the gate, a bit more of the body inched into the emptiness.

Like the ghouls, the gate too seemed to be gulping down portions of the corpse. Thick streaks of light gray and dull white—the color of Willen's skin and bones—now swirled amidst the dark gray and pitch black whorls of the void.

After taking in the scene and no doubt having thoughts similar to Cale's, Jak began to heave. He covered his mouth to hold back the vomit, but quickly lost the battle and retched Matilda's chunky fish stew onto the planked floor. As with Willen's blood, the vomit began a slow migration across the floor toward the ever-hungry void.

Though the sight of it flowing for the gate disturbed him, Cale nevertheless welcomed the vomit's acrid smell, a human smell that overwhelmed the inhuman reek of rot and death. He waited while Jak emptied his stomach and finished retching.

After a few moments, Jak gathered himself. He stood bent over with his hands on his knees, breathing hard. He looked up at Cale through watering eyes and wiped his face sheepishly.

"Dark," he said. "Sorry, Cale. Ate too much, I guess."

"I guess," Cale said with a half-smile. Seen too much, more likely. Cale could sympathize. It had been an eventful day-and-a-half. Hang on, little man, he thought.

Recovered now, Jak studied Willen's corpse and eyeballed the gate with an appraising gaze. "It's bigger," he announced after a moment. "The gate . . . it's bigger."

Jak was right. The gate *was* bigger, marginally so, but definitely bigger. Cale had missed it. "How?"

"I don't know," the little man said thoughtfully, and stroked his whiskers. He approached the gate and peered in, careful to avoid stepping on Willen's corpse.

"It drinks the life-force of the living," he said. "Like the shadow demon. Probably the more it eats, the more powerful it gets." He stepped back from the gate, shrugged, and looked over at Cale. "Maybe with each pulse, it consumes a little bit of our plane and thereby grows larger. . . ."

Cale waited. The little man was still working it through.

"I don't know how it's occurring," Jak said at last, his mouth a grim line in a nest of red whiskers. "But I know that we better stop it. If it gets too big . . ."

Cale nodded once, firmly. "Let's go." Without another word, he turned and strode up the stairs. Jak followed.

Stopping periodically to listen for any sign of ghouls, they made their way up the short stairway and back into the main hall. It stretched before them, dark and threatening. They shared a look and continued on.

After jumping or sidestepping the few gates that stood in their way—all of them also slightly larger than before, Cale observed—they made it back to the door that opened onto the offices.

The hall continued on in the opposite direction, beyond the limits of the glow wand. The pulsing from the gates continued to beat in the rotten smelling air, but Cale had become accustomed to it and barely noticed. At a run, they could be back out on Ariness

Street in less than a minute. They could be out of the guildhouse and out of this insanity. They would be safe.

He turned to face Jak. He had to give the little man another chance to get out of here.

"There will be more ghouls downstairs," he announced, and studied Jak's reaction. The little man nodded gravely, but gave no sign of fear. Cale went on, "Probably more warping too." He thought of the bleeding wall and the procession of ghouls and couldn't hide his grimace. "There will be more horrible sights."

Jak nodded again. "I understand."

"You can get out of here, Jak," Cale said. "The street's right out there." He pointed with his blade toward the offices, toward the door out. "This will probably be the last chance either of us has to turn back. I won't mention it again."

Cale didn't really want Jak to leave, he desperately wanted him to stay, but felt obligated to make the offer. The madness would only get worse in the basement, and worse still in the shrine.

To his credit, Jak didn't even look toward the offices. He shook his head emphatically and gave Cale a hard smile. "We're hip-deep in a pile of dragon dung, Cale. I'm already as dirty as I can get. There ain't no going back."

Cale smiled and gratefully squeezed Jak's small shoulder. "Thanks, my friend."

They started cautiously down the hall. Cale felt only mild surprise when he realized that his right hand was in his pocket, clutching the felt mask. *There ain't no going back,* he thought, echoing Jak. Had he already taken some first, hesitant steps toward Mask?

Fifteen paces down the hallway, the floor grew spongy, like rotten wood. The first signs of increased warping. He held the glow wand close to the floor. With each pulse of the gates, the wooden planks flickered between translucence and solidity.

"Dark," Jak observed. "This whole place is becoming one giant gate."

Cale nodded and they continued on. They gingerly trod the increasingly soft floor until they found their path blocked by another swirling hole of emptiness in the floor, this one bigger than any previous.

"I can't jump that, Cale. Too wide."

"I know," Cale replied. The jump would be tough even for him, especially with the spongy floor. The sheer walls of the hallway would make climbing around it a difficult option.

"If I can get across and throw back a rope—"

"No need," Jak interjected. He sheathed his blades, plopped down on the floor, and removed his gloves and soft boots.

"What are you doing?"

"You jump over it," the little man said. "I'll climb around it."

"That's a tough climb."

"Not to worry," Jak interrupted with a smile. "I've got a spell." He shot Cale a mirthful wink. "Nice to have spells at my disposal on a job, remember?"

Without hesitation, Jak pulled forth his holy symbol and began to chant. When he finished, a whitish paste seeped from the pores on his palms and feet. His feet sucked at the soft floor as he padded to the wall and placed his hands upon it.

"Wall is soft too," he observed. "Shouldn't be a problem though." He placed his feet against the wall—

"Wait, Jak," Cale ordered. He inched forward to the edge of the gate, blade held ready, and peered down into it. The seemingly endless void nauseated him but he fought it off and forced himself to search the vacancy for a pair of yellow eyes. He saw nothing. Satisfied, he eased back from the edge. "All right."

Immediately, Jak ascended a few feet. Despite its

softness, his hands adhered to the surface of the wall and he moved along easily. Spiderlike, he began to slide sidewise. Beneath him, the emptiness of the void beckoned.

Cale watched him nervously for a moment, but the spell seemed to be working. Now nearly halfway across, Jak showed no sign of problems. Cale now had to worry about getting himself across.

He sheathed his blade and backed off a bit. He would need running room to clear the gate. Jak's alarmed voice turned him around.

"Cale! It's *bleeding*." The little man's voice trembled with horror.

Cale hurried back to the edge of the gate and held the glow wand high—

"Dark," he breathed.

The little man hung suspended on the wall halfway across the gate. Where Jak had touched the warped wall, the pressure apparently had forced blood from the stone. With each pulse of the gates, a trickle of gore dripped from the wall where he had placed his hands and feet. A path of seeping wounds marked the route behind him.

"It's warped more here," the little man said, his voice rising in sudden alarm. "It's sticking to me. Dark, Cale, my hands are starting to slip." He tried to continue his move across, but when he attempted to pull free from the wall, the surface adhered to his hand and came away in thick, fleshy strings. Cale caught a disgusting flash of pulsing blue veins and glistening red tissue beneath the warped wall surface before the new tear began to vomit forth a steady gout of blood.

"Burn me!" Caught in the fountain of blood, the little man cursed and tried to slide aside. His abrupt movement only tore open more holes in the wall. Streams of blood ran down to the floor, drained into the gate, and quickly turned its swirls crimson.

"Cale!" Jak peered over his shoulder, spattered with gore. "Help." His fearful eyes fell to the churning gate below. "Help," he said again.

Cale heard the beginnings of panic creeping into Jak's voice.

"Hold still." Without another word, Cale backed off, sprinted forward, and leaped the gate. He hit the spongy floor in a ready crouch.

"Don't move," he again said to Jak.

"I'm *not* moving." Jak clung desperately to the warped wall, kept his face down to shield his eyes and mouth from the crimson fall. Gore-soaked, his cloak hung heavily from his small body.

"Don't look into the gate," Cale said. He set down the glow wand, shook free of his pack, and pulled out a coil of silk rope.

"Godsdammit, Cale," Jak snapped, "I'm not moving and I'm not looking! Hurry up. This is disgusting."

Cale smiled despite himself—the halfling kept his sense of humor even when terrified.

Deftly, Cale tied a slipknot into one end of the thin but strong line. He opened some play in the loop, gathered it in, and prepared to toss it to Jak.

"Catch this."

"Catch it!" Jak eyed him incredulously over his shoulder. "How?"

"Let go with one of your hands."

"But—Dark and empty!" he said, and nodded in resignation. "All right." He gingerly pulled his left hand free of the wall. Despite his care, the wall's *skin* stuck to his hand and tore loose. Blood spurted from the rip. He hung on the wall with only two sticky feet and a sticky hand.

"Throw it!"

Cale stood at the edge of the gate, let eight or so feet of line play out, and swung it up toward Jak. The little man caught it on the first try. He stuck his arm through the loop, draped it over his neck, and tried again to get a grip on the wall. Slippery with gore, his hand no longer stuck.

"Blast," he oathed. "It won't stick." Before Cale could say anything, the little man reared back and slammed his fist *into* the wall, wrist deep. "Ugh," he exclaimed in disgust.

Quick thinking, Cale thought. "Get the rope around your torso," he said. "I'll give it a jerk at the same time you jump toward me. It's only about eight feet. You'll make it."

"I know what the plan is," Jak muttered irritably. "Easier said than done, though. I don't know if this hand," he indicated with his head the hand buried in the wall, "will hold me if I let go with the other."

Cale made no reply. He waited for Jak to come to terms. They had nothing else, and Jak had to know it. The fleshy, bloody wall offered no handgrips. Jak was stuck, and if he tried to move farther, he would certainly fall into the gate.

"Let's do it now. With the rope like this."

Cale shook his head. "Can't. I think it'll slip right over your head and off when I pull. Won't work."

"Dark," Jak sighed. "All right, let's do it. But if my hand won't hold and I start to fall, you pull right away. Try to, at least." He glanced down into the bloody gate. "I don't want to go wherever *that* leads."

Cale nodded, braced himself, and pulled the rope as taut as he dared. He had to leave some play so Jak could get his other arm through, yet he had to be ready to give it a sharp pull if the little man started to fall.

"Ready," he said.

"Here goes." Jak jerked his hand free. Blood spurted from the wall and poured past him into the gate. Cale tensed. Jak dangled dangerously but didn't fall. His other hand held! Quickly, the little man threaded his free arm through the loop. He turned and shot Cale a grin.

"All right, Cale—" The little man's green eyes fell on the gate and went wide. "Pull, Cale! Now! Now!"

Cale jerked at the same moment that Jak jumped free of the wall.

The snap of the rope pulled the breath from the little man in a *whoosh*. He flew through the air, just cleared the edge of the gate, and landed in a heap on the spongy floor beside Cale. He leaped to his feet.

"The shadow demon! I saw it looking out at me from the gate!"

Cale dropped the rope and had his blade out in an instant. Without hesitation, he stepped to the edge of the gate and looked down. From deep within the void, two hate-filled yellow sparks looked out at him and narrowed balefully. The eyes of the demon that had nearly killed Thazienne.

"Bastard!" He reversed his grip on the long sword, dropped to one knee, and drove the blade hilt-deep into the void, directly between those demonic yellow eyes. The stuff of the gate gave way before the iron like water. A distortion rippled across its bloody surface. When it cleared, the eyes had disappeared. Cale snarled and pulled the weapon free. He didn't know if he had hit the demon or not.

Jak approached and stood beside him, blades bare.

"It's gone?" he asked.

"It's gone."

"Good," Jak said. "Close one, Cale. I wouldn't have wanted to fall in there with that thing, at least not without you." The little man stripped off his bloody cloak and threw it into the gate. "Here," he said to the gate, "you get this instead."

The bloody cloak swirled into oblivion and vanished.

Jak took an extra cloak from his pack and wiped himself as clean as he could. "Disgusting," he muttered as he worked. He threw the newly soiled cloak into the gate as well. "That's better," he said afterward. "I feel like a new man. We moving?"

Cale nodded and turned reluctantly from the gate. "We're moving," he affirmed.

"What's in your hand?" Jak asked.

"Huh?"

Surprised, Cale realized that he held the felt mask in his hand. He must have pulled it out of his pocket after jerking his blade out of the gate. Or had he done it before?

"What is that?" Jak asked again, and gently gripped Cale's hand by the wrist.

"It's a mask," Cale said. He shook free of Jak's grip and stuffed it back into his pocket. "I picked it up in the armory. You overlooked it in the strongbox."

Jak looked skeptical at that. "I didn't overlook it," he said thoughtfully. "A mask? Cale . . ."

"I know."

Jak smiled and patted Cale's forearm. "Seems the Shadowlord wants an answer sooner rather than later."

Cale dared not reply to that. He thought some part of him might have already given his answer. Without another word, he knelt and retrieved the glow wand. "Let's keep moving. The stairs to the basement are just ahead."

With Cale holding the glow wand high to best illuminate the darkness and Jak keeping a watchful eye behind for the shadow demon, they moved warily through the narrow halls. The floor solidified as they distanced themselves from the gate, the warping seemingly localized around the void. Still, the whole guildhouse fairly reeked of *wrongness*.

With only the dim glow wand for light, Cale relied more on his hearing than his vision to warn him of danger. He was alert to any sound, but heard nothing—nothing but the dull, thudding pulses emitted from the gates as they grew larger and ate away at the world.

He wondered briefly whether proximity to the gates would somehow change he and Jak, warp them into unspeakable horrors like the ghouls. Uncomfortable with the thought, he dismissed it as useless speculation. He reached into his pocket and felt the comforting touch of the felt mask.

I'm already changed, he admitted to himself. He was finding comfort in a god. Only time would tell if he also had been warped.

Doors dotted the hallway as they moved. The gates had warped some into saggy slabs of wood with the consistency of candle wax, while others seemed normal. Where the doors stood closed and solid, Cale left them closed. Where ajar, he kicked them open and stalked into the room, blade ready. Always the rooms beyond stood empty but for the occasional gate, broken furnishings, torn paintings, and of course, the smell. They moved forward, cautiously alert.

Jak's hand suddenly closed over Cale's wrist and pulled him to a stop. "There's something behind us," the little man whispered. "I can feel it."

Cale didn't feel it, but Jak's words caused the hairs on his nape to rise. He nodded and set the glow wand on the floor. "We'll wait for it here," he whispered into Jak's ear. It could only be the shadow demon. He had cleared the previous rooms to make sure that no ghouls could attack from behind.

The little man nodded and both took positions along opposite sides of the wall. Cale held the enchanted long sword in a two-handed grip. Jak held his short sword and dagger in trembling hands. They stood just outside the blue light of the glow wand and peered back into the darkness, ready, waiting. Cale's heart thudded in time to the unholy pulses of the gates.

Nothing happened. They stood there for twenty heartbeats, still nothing.

"Trickster's toes, Cale. I felt *something*."

Cale didn't doubt it. He felt sure that the shadow demon was lurking somewhere nearby. Even if he *had* wounded it back at the gate, he certainly hadn't killed it. He picked up the glow wand. "We keep moving. Stay close, and keep your eyes and ears alert behind."

Jak nodded agreement. Cale saw that in his dagger hand, the little man held both blade and holy symbol. Cale fought off the urge to draw forth the felt mask from his pocket.

I don't have a holy symbol, he inwardly averred. Cale didn't know if he believed himself.

They trekked on. Ahead, the hall branched into a T-shaped intersection. Moving forward in a ready crouch, wary for an ambush, Cale turned right. Illuminated by the glow wand, the door to the main stairwell came into view.

"There," he said over his shoulder, and pointed with his blade at the door. Jak mouthed the words, *Let's do it*, and they stalked ahead.

After assuring himself that it wasn't warped, Cale knelt at the door and listened. Though he heard nothing, he did not assume the landing beyond unoccupied. He hadn't heard the ghouls outside the armory, either, and had nearly died as a result. He turned to face Jak. The little man was staring into the darkness behind them, alert. Cale snapped his fingers to get his attention, and signaled in hand cant, *Ready yourself*.

Jak turned toward the door and moved in close behind Cale. When he felt ready, he gave Cale a nod.

Cale slowly turned the handle. *Click*. He shared a glance with Jak then jerked the door open and jumped back, enchanted blade before him.

There was nothing there. Only the upper landing of the stairs.

He didn't allow himself the luxury of a relieved sigh. He knew that from this point onward, there would be no rest. Yrsillar must know that they were in the guildhouse. Since the demon hadn't set up an ambush here, Cale figured he had marshaled his forces in the basement.

"Get's ugly from now on," he said to Jak.

"It's been ugly since the day we met," Jak joked, and gave him a friendly shove in the shoulder. "Why change now?"

Cale couldn't bring himself to smile. "The first flight descends ten feet or so, leads to a second landing, then to a second flight of stairs." He paused, then added, "Those go down about another fifteen feet and open into the basement."

Jak's face remained emotionless. "You lead."

Placing his right hand on the iron banister, Cale started down the narrow stone stairway. The smell of rancid meat and rotting corpses wafted up from the depths of the guildhouse as though from the bowels of the Abyss. Cale steeled himself and walked on, prodding each stair with his blade before putting his full weight upon it. He rounded the first curve in the stairway and stopped cold.

Before him, the stairs shimmered in the light of the glow wand like shallow water in moonlight. Each dull pulse of the gates sent a distortion wave rippling along them. Below, the entire landing had been transformed into a gate, a hole that led to nothingness. Leaping over it would be impossible.

"Dammit," Cale muttered.

"Dark," Jak echoed.

He turned around to face Jak. "We can turn around, go out of the guildhouse, and try to come back in through the sewers." He paused for a moment, then added, "Or we can climb around it."

At that, the little man's expression fell—Jak had apparently had enough of climbing around gates—but he rallied himself quickly. "We climb," he said. "We've come too far to turn back now. Besides, the sewer entrance could be blocked too."

He turned away from Cale and tapped along the wall with his short sword. "Wall seems unaffected this time, if not the floor. It's a good thing too, because I don't have another spell to help me get across. Seems the Lady is still with us."

Cale nodded absently and studied the walls for himself. Like everything in the guildhouse, they had been built sturdy and sound, but without regard for cosmetics. Their rough, unfinished, and unwarped surface provided plenty of handholds. The real problem, however, wasn't the absence or presence of handholds, it was that he and Jak would have to slide not just sideways along the wall, but *sideways and down*, a difficult maneuver under the best of circumstances. Thankfully, the ceiling provided plenty of clearance. They wouldn't have to climb with the gate mere inches below their feet.

We can do this, he thought, and believed it.

Jak had already sheathed his blades. Cale did the same.

"Same side or different?" asked the little man.

Cale considered. Even if they did follow each other along the same side of the wall, they wouldn't be able to help one another if either ran into difficulty. "Different," he said. "If only one side proves impassable, we don't both want to have to double back. This way, when one of us gets across safely, he can throw a rope to the other to help him across."

Jak gave a nod, turned, and started to feel the wall for handholds. Cale stuck the glow wand in his belt and did the same. He quickly found a likely route.

With a soft grunt, he began to climb. Behind him across the stairwell, he could hear Jak's breathing as he struggled to move his hands and feet over the stone. Cale ascended five or six feet vertically.

"You all right?" he asked Jak. He had to contort his neck so that he could turn far enough around to see the little man.

Jak had climbed to about the same height as Cale. His short arms and legs stuck out at all angles as he gripped the available protrusions. "I'm all right," he said. "You?"

"Fine," Cale replied. Bracing himself with his feet and left hand, he reached out sidewise for a grip. After finding one, he shifted his weight and probed the wall with his right foot for another step. He found one and slid a foot or two sidewise.

We can do this, he mentally reiterated.

Cale was breathing hard now. Sweat poured down his back, trickled down his brow and pooled in his eyebrows. Behind him, Jak's breathing had also grown loud and raspy. With his short limbs and fingers, Jak would find the climb even more difficult than Cale.

But he'll make it, Cale affirmed hopefully. He called over his shoulder, "How's it going?"

"It'd be going better if you'd stop distracting me," Jak retorted. Cale could hear the smile in the little man's voice.

Cale smiled and continued the slow sidewise climb. For the next few minutes, he focused only on the wall, his weight, and his next movement. Reach, feel for a protrusion, grip, extend his leg, plant his toe, delicately shift his weight. He made steady progress.

From the sounds of his breathing, Cale could tell that Jak lagged a bit behind him. Shorter by half, the little man could not move as quickly as Cale across the wall. Nevertheless, Jak made steady progress.

Halfway across, Cale spared a glance down between his feet at the gate. Emptiness opened beneath him. He seemed not to be climbing a wall only four feet above the surface of the stairs, but instead clinging to a cliff face that overlooked a fall into infinity.

Dizziness sent his head reeling. Gasping, he snapped his head up, clenched his eyes closed, pressed his cheek into the cool stone of the wall, and held on to let the dizziness pass. Jak must have heard his distress.

"You all right, Cale?" the little man asked, concern in his voice. "Cale?"

"I'm all right," he managed at last, eyes still closed. "Just a little dizzy." He felt like the wall he hung on was spinning. "Just don't look down."

Jak chuckled, a laugh that gave way to a grunt as he climbed another step. "Dark, Cale, that's the first ru—"

The hairs on Cale's neck rose and a wave of cold like an icy wind sent shudders through his body. An otherworldly moan of hate rose from within the gate to fill the stairwell. Though he could not turn to see it, he knew the shadow demon had burst from the void like a black arrow shot. He could feel its evil presence behind him, could feel its unearthly cold radiating into his flesh, could feel its malice-filled, yellow eyes burning holes into his back. He and Jak were helpless on the wall. They were dead men.

"Cale!" Jak shouted. "Watch out!" Cale could hear the terror in the little man's voice. The *shhk* of a drawn blade sounded. Jak had somehow drawn a weapon.

Cale struggled to fight off the dizziness. Hang on, Jak, he thought urgently. Hang on.

"Cale! Dark, Cale!"

Despite the dizziness, the fear in Jak's voice pulled his head around. Careful not to look down, he opened his eyes and looked over his shoulder. The cold from the demon hit his face like a gust of Hammer wind. The creature hovered gracefully over the center of the gate, facing Jak. Its great wings—which beat only rarely—stuck out behind it and hung in the air so close to Cale that he could almost reach out and touch them. Though it seemed composed of nothingness, the nothingness somehow had substance. Cale could see the sleek muscles that rippled beneath its skin, vicious claws at the end of its long, graceful arms. Streamers of darkness, empty ribbons of shadow, floated about its being like a black mist.

The little man had drawn his short sword and hung precariously by his feet and one hand. Looking over his shoulder with wide green eyes, he tried to wave the blade defensively to keep the demon at bay. The pathetic effort did nothing to deter the dark horror. It flitted back and forth around the little man, outside the reach of the blade. Playfully, it threatened again and again with its claws. Cale could sense its hunger building as it whetted its appetite on Jak's fear.

Cale could not clear his damn head!

"Cale," Jak cried. He frantically waved the short sword as the demon feinted an attack. The swing unbalanced him and his hold slipped. Desperately, he twisted back to the wall and tried to save himself with his blade hand. The short sword clanged into the stone, fell from his fingers as he clutched the wall, and dropped into the oblivion of the gate.

"Dark," Cale heard Jak mutter into the wall.

The demon hissed in triumph, an otherworldly sound that Cale felt more than heard, a shriek of pure hate that sounded as though it had originated from deep within the earth.

Jak clung to the wall, helpless and trembling. "Cale, help," he cried.

It tore Cale up inside to do nothing, but if he moved, he would surely lose his balance and fall into the gate.

With Jak defenseless and terrified, Cale sensed the demon's hunger rise until it reached a crescendo, felt its desire to feed radiate in palpable waves from its being.

Jak, desperate now, reached into his pocket and searched for his holy symbol—whether for comfort or for spellcasting, Cale could not tell. The little man released one hand from the wall and twisted his head so that he could see the demon. The black horror reared back with one of its claws, slowly, teasingly, prolonging the inevitable. Jak's eyes looked past it and met Cale's.

"I can't go like the Soargyls, Erevis," he announced. "I can't."

With those words, he let go his hold on the wall. Staring at Cale the while, he fell soundlessly into the emptiness of the gate and vanished into the void.

"No!" Cale shouted, and nearly leaped in after him. "No! Jak!" The dizziness gave way before a wave of grief and anger. "No, godsdammit!"

With its meal now gone the demon howled in frustration. It faced down toward the void and began to dart into the gate after the little man but it stopped cold in mid-air, seeming suddenly to remember Cale. Its head turned slowly upward and its baleful yellow eyes narrowed to sparks.

Cale looked down over his shoulder and met that gaze unflinchingly. Anger fed his courage. He no longer feared this demon.

"Do you remember me, you black son of a whore?" he snarled. Though he nearly fell as a result, he freed one of his hands to awkwardly draw his long sword. "I'm the one that cut you before, remember?"

Its eyes widened and it cocked its head thoughtfully.

"You do remember, don't you?" He waved the enchanted blade in challenge, tried to find a way to plant his feet so that he could somehow fight, somehow avenge Jak. He realized immediately that it was impossible. His gaze fell to the void below him to the emptiness that had swallowed his best friend.

A voice in his mind screamed accusations. Jak was only here because of me. He was only here because of *me!*

Though the little man's final glance had held no blame, Cale couldn't help but berate himself. Once again his selfishness had led someone he loved to be harmed. First Thazienne and now Jak.

All because of me . . .

The demon drifted nearer, a mere armslength away. Cale ignored the cold that radiated from it. His rage lent him warmth, his self-loathing insulated him and made the demon's malice for him seem paltry by comparison. He sensed its hungry anticipation but gave it no terror to feed upon. It flapped its wings once and screamed hate into his face.

He stared back into its malice filled yellow eyes and made the only decision he could. He had to go after Jak. The little man had always stood with him, come what may. Cale could not desert him now, not if there was any chance he still lived.

"But first you, you bastard," he angrily muttered.

The demon hovered directly behind him. It flitted about him and tried to make him afraid. Cale no longer felt fear, only hate. Hate for what had happened to his friend Jak.

Without another thought, he summoned his strength and leaped backwards off the wall. Spinning around in mid-air, he dexterously reversed his grip on the long sword and held it before him in a two-fisted grip, a unicorn horn of enchanted steel.

Startled, the demon's eyes flashed with surprise. Cale sensed it hiss. Lightning quick, it lashed out with a claw. Cale didn't know if it hit him. He flew into the demon and lashed out with a terrible strength fueled by rage. Even as he fell toward the void, he drove the enchanted iron between the demon's eyes and pierced its head. The long sword bit deep into the demon's shadowstuff. Black mist exploded from the wound. Its scream resounded in Cale's ears like the cries of slaughtered cattle. He kept his grip on the long sword's hilt as he plummeted toward the gate. The enchanted iron split the demon from head to groin, the tension similar to cutting a bed sheet in twain. A cloud of shadowstuff exploded around Cale, the stench overwhelming. The demon's scream of agony sounded loud in his ears—a death scream for certain.

He felt satisfaction for only a fraction of a heartbeat before he and the remains of the demon fell into the gate. When he hit the surface, he felt a brief tension followed by sudden give, as though he had jumped through the skin of one of Brilla's day-old soups. A charge raced through his body and he felt like he was swimming in syrup. A weight pressed against his chest. He gasped for breath but his constricted throat could draw in only the reeking stink of the dead demon's shadowstuff. His body went numb and he passed out.

CHAPTER 10

SOMETHING FROM
NOTHING

Jak regained consciousness. Apart from the soft
rush of an uncomfortably warm wind, Jak
heard only silence. He lay on his back and
remained perfectly still, afraid to move, afraid
to dispel the illusion that he was still alive.

Still alive? How can that be? he wondered.

He had expected to awaken in whatever
happy afterlife awaited servants of the Trickster. Brandobaris's teachings were frustrat-
ingly, and Jak suspected, deliberately, vague
on this point—but he knew from the aches in
his body that he was still composed of flesh
and bone, not spirit.

Surprising, he thought. He knew the gates
in the guildhouse to be voids, empty pits in
reality that ate away at his home plane like

pools of acid. He had assumed that flesh-and-blood beings could not withstand contact with them, and had figured physical death in the gate a better fate than the death of his soul at the hands of the shadow demon. But he hadn't died, and here he was.

Wherever here was.

He dared not open his eyes, at least not yet. He knew from the smell in the air and the coarse earth beneath his body that *here* had to be some demonic wasteland of the sort he had heard of in adventurers' tales. He was not yet ready to face that.

He took mental stock of his body and realized with alarm that breathing came only with difficulty. His muscles, his body, and his very *soul* felt *dulled*, like a once-colorful painting faded by time and sunlight to drabness. His brain felt sluggish, his thoughts thick and muddy. A side effect of passing through the gate, he assumed. Yet he was alive! His hand fumbled ineptly for the luckstone at his waist.

The Lady still favors us, Cale—

His happiness at finding himself alive vanished. Jak had left Cale back in the guildhouse, left him alone with the shadow demon helpless on the wall, left him alone to feed the demon with his soul.

I'm sorry, Erevis, he thought, and tears trickled out from under his closed eyelids. I couldn't die like the Soargyls. I couldn't be drained by the demon into dried hunks of soulless flesh. I just couldn't.

But I left Cale to die that way, he accused. He hadn't planned it that way, he just hadn't wanted to die that way himself. He realized now what he had done and the realization pained him beyond measure. Cale could not have survived on that wall.

More tears leaked out, ran along his hairline, and pooled in his ears. They did nothing to quiet the accusatory voice he heard in his head. He didn't try to fight the grief and the guilt. He couldn't fight it. He had abandoned his best friend to an ugly death.

I'm sorry, Erevis.

He had known Cale for over ten years, and had never met a man more loyal to his friends, or more fearless in the face of danger. Cale had lived for so long on the fine line that separated life from death that he walked it with the practiced ease of a festival acrobat on a tightrope. Jak had loved him like a brother and abandoned him like a coward.

I'm sorry, my friend.

He lay still and let the tears flow until the pangs of guilt began to dull. He had to get up, to try to find a way back. If their situations had been reversed, Cale would have carried on. Jak would, too. He would take up Cale's cause as his own. Yrsillar had one more death to account for.

He forced his sluggish lungs to draw in a deep breath. The acrid air left a foul grit on his tongue that tasted sulfurous and smoky. He cleared his throat to fight off a fit of coughing. Ready, he sat up with a slight grunt and snapped his eyes open.

I should've kept them closed, he immediately reprimanded himself.

As he had suspected and feared, a wasteland of coarse gray ash surrounded him in all directions. It rolled in dunes in the ceaseless breeze like sand in a great desert. Jagged slabs of basalt as sharp as spear tips occasionally jutted through the ash, tombstones in a graveyard that extended for infinity. No plants and no life. A wasteland of emptiness. There was no sign anywhere of the gate he had traveled through. The trip here was one-way. He was trapped.

I'm in the Abyss, he thought. Yrsillar's home plane. The realization hit him hard and made him weak.

He looked skyward to see an unbroken blanket of

soot-colored clouds as lifeless and gray as the sea of ash under his feet. Occasionally, flashes of sickly blue—the color of ghoul flesh—backlit the sky. Rather than enlivening the sky, the sudden, silent bursts of color served only to accent the drab desolation of the gloom.

Low on the horizon hung a gigantic vortex of swirling nothingness. A maelstrom that was a mirror image of the gates in the guildhouse but magnified in size a thousandfold. Streaks of ochre and viridian mixed with the gray and churned toward the empty center of oblivion. No sun or moon hung in the slate sky. Jak felt certain that this hellish realm had *never* seen the light of a sun, that it stood forever illumined in only perpetual twilight. He clambered to his feet and brushed a stray hair out of his eyes. When he did, he saw— "What in the . . ."

Wisps of white vapor steamed from his exposed skin like smoke from a leaf fire. Dumbfounded for a moment, he merely stared. Contrary to the direction of the wind, the vapor rose from his flesh and floated inexorably toward the vortex in the sky as though drawn by a lodestone. Then the realization dawned on him. My soul is slipping away.

Small wonder he felt so torpid. The negative energy of the maelstrom would eat his life just as surely as the demons that dwelled here. Thankfully, he had prepared for something similar back at Brilla's place.

Hurriedly, he pulled forth his holy symbol. The green tourmaline in the eagle's talon looked so dull as to appear nearly black. He began to incant the syllables to a spell that would protect him from negative energy. He had memorized the spell several times to protect himself and Cale when they fought the demon, but he thought it would work equally well against the pull of the maelstrom.

He began to cast, but stumbled over the incantation. His voice sounded strangely muted. The unnatural gloom and ash-laden air strangled his voice the moment he made a sound.

Jak's life-force leaked through his skin. He felt himself grow weaker with each heartbeat.

He cleared his throat and began again, louder this time. The vigor in his voice warred with the torpidity of the air. With great effort he forced out each magic-pregnant word, moved his holy symbol through the gray air to trace the appropriate sigils. His lungs heaved and sweat beaded his brow but he stubbornly plodded on.

At last he finished, and when he did, a golden glow took shape around him and sheathed his entire body. It crackled and popped energetically as its positive power held the negative energy of the void at bay.

"Interesting," he observed, and held his arms before him for examination. Now protected by the golden aura of the spell, the white vapor no longer seeped from his pores. His flesh had lost its gray pallor and returned to normal. Equally important, he felt himself again. His mind and body once more moved with their habitual deftness. As long as his protective spell stayed in effect he would be safe from the draining effects of the energy maelstrom.

But how long will it last? he wondered nervously. The spell was supposed to protect him from *creatures* that used negative energy in a single concentrated attack, not from the persistent, slow-draining negative energy of an entire plane. He couldn't know for certain, but from the way the golden aura sizzled, he did not think the spell would last long. He could cast it again, of course, but sooner or later, he would run out of protection.

"Unless I can find a way out of here." Within the

protective aura, his voice again sounded normal. He allowed himself a smile and enjoyed his small victory over an impossibly grim situation.

I'll take them where I can get them, he thought, and ran his thumb over his holy symbol. You got anything to say? he thought to the Trickster.

"I didn't think so," he muttered irritably. "Have to rely on Lady Luck then." He tapped the agate luckstone at his belt and scanned the landscape in all directions. Partially buried in the ash nearby, he spotted the short sword he had dropped through the gate back in the guildhouse. Smiling, he hurried over, picked it up, and sheathed it at his belt. Lady Luck had granted him another boon. It heartened him.

"There has to be another gate," he softly chanted. "There has to be."

Other than his blade, all around he saw nothing but wasteland. Only the jagged black points of basalt that jutted from the ash broke the infinite expanse of gray. Nothing that looked like a gate. Nothing that looked like anything.

His good spirits began to fail him and despair began to threaten. He was alone, had never been more alone, and he could see no way to get out. The maelstrom hung threateningly in the soot sky like the mouth of a beast, twisting, churning, ready to grind his life into oblivion, waiting for his spell to expire so it could feed.

Tears began to well but he blinked them away. He struggled to quiet the hopeless voice in his head that told him to curl up in the dirt and accept death. By all the gods, he would not surrender!

"To the pits of the Nine Hells with giving up," he said aloud, as much to steel his resolve as anything. He clutched the luckstone in his fist like a talisman of hope. "Anything more from you, Lady?"

Nothing.

He nodded, swallowed his despair, and began to walk. The direction didn't matter.

One way is as good as another, he thought. He had to find a gate back to his plane soon. Otherwise, his soul would feed the beast.

He hadn't taken five steps before an explosive surge of energy from behind blew him face first into the ground and made his ears ring. Clouds of ash whipped around him like a sandstorm.

Spitting the filth of the void from his mouth, Jak shielded his eyes from the onslaught of ash and looked over his shoulder. A sudden sound like tearing cloth broke the stillness. From a point six feet in the air above where Jak had been standing, the empty air split open. A hole the size of a door formed. Colors poured through.

The gate! his mind registered. He scrambled to his feet and ran for it. Before he could reach it, however, two bodies fell through the rift and hit the earth in an explosion of ash. Instantly, the gate collapsed in on itself and vanished with a soft pop.

"No!"

❂ ❂ ❂ ❂ ❂

Cale stared up into a sky the color of slate. He lay on his back unmoving. The earth beneath him felt coarse, like the sands of the desert kingdom of Calimshan.

Where am I? he wondered.

He tried to move but his limbs felt like lead, too heavy to lift. His mind seemed muddled. He must have hit his head. A light mist steamed from his face, like that of a lathered steed in winter.

Am I sweating?

His mind was fuzzy. He remembered jumping from a wall and stabbing a shadow—

A distant voice pulled at him. "Cale! Cale!" He tried to lift his head but couldn't. The voice remained insistent. "Erevis Cale!"

Suddenly, a form bent over him and a red-whiskered face took shape above. Jak! He tried to smile a greeting but his mouth didn't work.

"Dark," the little man oathed. He gripped Cale rudely by the face and looked with concern into his eyes.

Cale tried to say, *I'm all right*, but only managed to say, "Amgahh." His damned mouth didn't work right! What was wrong with him?

Piece yourself together, he ordered, but that seemed easier thought than done.

"Hang on, Cale," said Jak, and let his head fall back to the soft ground. The little man pulled out his holy symbol and moved it over Cale's body while mouthing a series of magical syllables. Abruptly, Jak jumped back in shock.

"How—"

A golden light took shape before Cale's eyes. He came back to himself almost immediately. His mind cleared and his body felt lighter. He had killed the demon and fallen through the gate.

He sat up. Jak rushed forward and embraced him, nearly knocking him back down.

"Cale!" the little man happily exclaimed. "Dark, but I'm glad to see you." A sparkling golden glow surrounded the little man and crackled like sizzling meat. Cale, as pleased to see Jak as Jak was to see him, returned his embrace.

"I'm glad to see you too, my friend." He disengaged himself and stood. Only then did he recognize that he too was sheathed in a golden aura.

"What is this?" he asked Jak, and indicated the

aura. While he watched, it sparked and sizzled like a bonfire in the rain.

"It's a protective spell," Jak replied. "Without it, this place would kill you. The whole plane drains souls, just like the shadow demon."

Cale nodded. "That was quick thinking, little man, thanks."

Jak gazed at him solemnly. "I didn't cast it, Cale. I started to but didn't finish." He paused a heartbeat before adding, "You must've cast it." His green eyes went to Cale's right hand.

Cale's gaze followed Jak's. There in his hand, he unknowingly held the felt mask.

His stomach went topsy-turvy. His knees turned so weak he nearly fell down. Cast a spell? He couldn't! He had made no commitment to Mask, had he? He looked to Jak, astonished.

"I don't know how to cast spells."

He sounded unconvincing even to himself. He *didn't* know how, but he also intuitively knew that somehow he had. Or that the Shadowlord had cast it for him. In the end, he wasn't sure if the difference was of any significance, and that thought made him *very* uncomfortable. He would not surrender himself to a god. He was his own man. Defeating Yrsillar was *his* task. His task alone.

Jak stepped forward and placed a small, commiserating hand on his shoulder. "Mask wants you badly, Erevis. You must be his Champion. It's the call."

Angry and frightened, Cale stuffed the felt mask back into his pocket. He couldn't quite bring himself to discard it, though the temptation was strong.

"Feels less like a call and more like an order." He clenched his fists and looked up into the churning maelstrom of nothingness that dominated the sky. "He's saved me twice, Jak. Once in the shrine and once now. But I won't bow down to him out of some sense of obligation. You understand?"

Jak smiled softly. "I do understand," he replied. "I do. But in the end it's not about obligation. You'll come to realize that. Just . . . give it some time."

Cale lowered his gaze from the soot sky. "I feel like I'm changing despite myself, Jak—" He fell silent when his eyes fell on the grotesque body that lay in the ash nearby. He swallowed down his gorge. Twisted and malformed, the flesh of the thin, winged carcass looked the bluish-gray color of something long dead. Long, wiry arms ended in a set of terrible, steel-gray claws as long as knife blades. A thin slit in the hairless oval of its head marked a mouth, and its round, milky eyes stared vacantly into the gray sky. A deep, bloodless gash—the wound from Cale's enchanted long sword—split the corpse nearly in two, from its oval face to the center of its torso. Bloodless entrails hung from the hole like a ship's rigging.

"The shadow demon," Cale realized.

Jak gave a start and stared at the corpse in amazement. He poked it with his toe. It didn't move. "You killed it. Back on our plane?"

Cale nodded grimly. "As I fell through the gate. It didn't look like this, though. Didn't feel like flesh, either." He knelt and retrieved his enchanted long sword, which lay beside the corpse.

Jak studied the macabre corpse and stroked his whiskers thoughtfully. "This is how its body must appear on this plane. Or at least how it chooses to appear on this plane." He shook his head in bewilderment. "Something from nothing. The shadow form must be how its kind manifests on our plane." He poked it again with his boot. "Dark, but its uglier like this."

Cale gave a hard smile. "It is," he softly agreed. "Looks better dead, though."

Jak giggled at that, but when his laughter died away he turned serious. His eyes found the ground and he kicked his boot in the ash.

"Cale, back at the guildhouse . . . I feel bad about . . ." he trailed off, took a deep breath, and started again. "I thought we were dead, Cale. I mean, I wasn't trying to abandon you, I just—"

Cale knew what Jak intended to say. He stopped him with an upraised hand and a raised voice. "Dark, Jak, I know why you did it." He gave the little man a reassuring pat on the shoulder. Cale knew full well that Jak, of all people, would never abandon him, at least not out of fear. Cale would not have the little man feeling guilty for doing something that most any man would have done. Cale knew too well the way guilt burdened a man's soul.

"I'd have done the same thing," he said, and meant it. "I thought we were dead too. I got lucky."

Jak looked up and gave him a grateful, sheepish nod. "But we aren't," he said with a smile. "Dead, I mean."

"No, we aren't." Cale looked around, took in for the first time the desolation that surrounded them. On all sides, a wasteland of gray extended for as far as he could see in the gloom. A whirlpool of emptiness hung in the gray sky just over the horizon line. A giant gate, he realized.

"Where in the Nine Hells are we?"

"Not the Nine Hells," Jak replied matter-of-factly. "The Abyss. At least I think." He nodded at the demon's corpse. "This is its home plane. Yrsillar's home plane too, I assume."

Hearing Yrsillar's name sent a wave of anger through Cale. He quelled it and tried to absorb what the little man had said.

He knew of the Abyss only through adventurers' stories. Stories which always portrayed it as a chaotic place teeming with demons and alive with unspeakable horrors. This place, on the other hand, seemed utterly dead.

Jak pulled out his ivory-bowled pipe and chewed its end, though he didn't light it.

"This isn't what I would've expected," Cale said after a moment. "Where are all the demons? The tortured souls writhing in agony? Surely Yrsillar and this thing," he pointed with his blade at the demon's corpse, "can't be the only creatures that live here?"

Jak shrugged thoughtfully. "Maybe they are. The Abyss is made up of lots of different planes and this is an unusual one. The energy here seems to drain away life the instant it appears. Most everything that travels here would be dead in minutes, even most demons." He nodded at the shadow demon's corpse. "Creatures like that can obviously live here, or like Yrsillar. Certain kinds of undead too, I suppose. Those kinds of creatures don't live like you and I live. They *unlive*. We'd be dead long since if not for the protective spells."

Cale winced, once more reminded of Mask's seeming beneficence, once more reminded of the call. The felt mask in his pocket weighed like a stone.

Only when and if I'm ready, he thought to the Shadowlord. Stop pushing.

"Can we get out of here?"

Jak took his pipe from his mouth and regarded Cale with raised eyebrows. "I don't know."

Cale appreciated the frankness. "The gate?"

Jak eyed the empty air above Cale's head. "That's where it materialized, but it must be one-way only. It doesn't even appear on this side unless someone is passing through from the other side." Seeing Cale's frown, he added, "Maybe there's another one somewhere else."

Maybe. Frustration and anger rose in Cale like a red tide. That they could have come so far only to die in this damnable extra-planar desert enraged him. He would not let Yrsillar win, he could not. Not after what had been done to Thazienne and Stormweather. The demon would pay, by Mask.

By Mask? He gave a slight start, surprised at himself.

"You all right?" Jak asked.

Cale took a deep breath, quelled his frustration and his surprise. Anger would not get them out of here. "I'm all right," he replied.

Jak nodded, pulled his pipe from between his teeth, and placed it back in his belt pouch. "Cale, whatever we're going to do, we've got to do it soon. I don't think our protective spells are going to last very long. At least mine won't."

Cale ignored the implication in Jak's last statement. "Let's get moving then," he said. "We've got to find a way back to the guildhouse—"

Without warning, the earth buckled and roiled like the storm-tossed whitecaps of Selgaunt Bay. Cale's vision blurred. The world spun. The landscape dissolved into a gray haze. Unbalanced, his stomach churned and his knees buckled. He struggled to stay upright. He felt himself streaming forward through space, out of control. The blurry landscape whipped past, a continuous sheet of indistinguishable gray. He felt sure that at any moment he would be slammed into the side of a basalt slab and pulverized. He tried to speak but his tongue stuck to the roof of his mouth.

"Jaaalllkk!"

As though through a howling wind, he heard Jak's poorly articulated reply. "Caaeelllc!" The little man was still with him.

He couldn't turn his head to look at Jak, could hardly keep his feet under him.

Without warning, the sensation of motion ceased.

Cale bent over double from the abrupt stop, gasping, but managed to keep his feet by catching himself with a palm on the ground. Beside him, Jak stumbled willy-nilly across the planked floor and slammed against the wall. He recovered himself quickly and looked around, wide-eyed and gasping. Only then did their location hit Cale.

Floor? Wall?

Floor and wall indeed. He looked around in disbelief. "What in the Hells?"

"Burn me," Jak oathed.

They stood in the guildhouse. Or at least, they stood in something that looked very much like the guildhouse. Planked floors, rough-hewn stone walls and stairs leading down to a basement. The whole building was composed of the drab, gray color of the void, as though the guildhouse had been remade with the stuff of the Abyss. Reeling, Cale struggled to comprehend what had happened. He turned circles and gawked.

"Dark," Jak breathed. "What happened?"

Cale placed his hands on his hips and shook his head, dumbfounded. "I don't know. Where are we, Jak?

"How should I kn—"

Jak's abrupt stop pulled Cale around in alarm. He turned to see Jak's eyes glued to the demon's corpse on the floor. The same demon's corpse. Relative to Cale and Jak, the twisted body lay exactly where it had been previous to the motion.

"How—"

Jak waved Cale silent, eyes still on the demon. "Let me think a minute."

Cale watched his face and waited, and wondered. How did the demon's corpse move with us? What was going on?

So far as he could tell, the abyssal guildhouse seemed an exact copy of the real guildhouse. To be safe, he drew his long sword and kept his eyes on the stairway above and below.

"Gods, Cale," Jak said. "I don't think we've moved!"

Cale turned around to face him. "What?"

"We haven't moved," Jak said again, nodding. "I'm certain of it."

Cale didn't get it. They had been in a desert, and now they were in the guildhouse—of course they had moved.

"How can we not have moved? I felt us move."

"That wasn't motion," Jak replied. "It was . . . reality changing."

Involuntarily, Cale's eyes fell to the demon's corpse—exactly the same distance and direction from him as it had been before. He pulled his waterskin from his belt and had a gulp, glad now that he had thought to bring water. "What do you mean?" He offered the skin to Jak but the little man declined.

"This plane is nothingness, Cale," Jak explained. "Literally, nothingness. The gray wasteland from before—that was me. I expected the Abyss to be a wasteland and it was. The plane shaped itself to my expectations. Or my expectations shaped the plane. You see? Just before the guildhouse appeared—"

Cale nodded in sudden understanding. "I said, 'we've got to get to the guildhouse.'" He looked over at Jak, still not quite believing. "You're saying that I made this, then?"

"You made it," Jak affirmed with a nod. "Your desire made it. Your expectations, your will, whatever. You made it."

Cale tried to make sense of that. His mind rebelled, but he slowly got his intellectual hands around the idea.

In the end, it really didn't matter whether they had physically moved or had themselves moved reality. Here they were, and they still needed to find a gate back, fast. The golden auras still sparked and sizzled, at war with the energy of the void. There was no telling how long they would last.

"So what now?" Jak asked. He reached for his pipe out of habit but stopped himself before reaching the drawstring on his pouch.

After a moment, Cale made the only decision he could. "Let's move," he announced.

"Where to?" Jak asked.

"To the basement," Cale said grimly. "Just like we had planned before. Let's see if anyone's home in *this* guildhouse."

❧ ❧ ❧ ❧ ❧

Cale led as they warily descended the stairs, blades held ready before them. Silence reigned—the silence of the dead. Their breathing, sharp and tense, sounded to Cale as loud as a scream. The stairs evidenced no warping on this side of reality. Like the gates, the warping seemed to be only one way. He kept his back pressed to the inner wall as he spiraled down the stairs.

As with everything on this plane, a dim light with no apparent source illuminated the interior of the abyssal guildhouse. Through the gray, Cale could see clearly for only a short span, beyond he could only make out blurred shapes and movement.

"Light spell?" Jak whispered from behind him.

"No," Cale softly replied over his shoulder. If there were anything at home here, a light spell would only draw its attention. Gripping his enchanted long sword in a sweaty hand, he advanced. Ahead and below, the archway that opened onto the long hallway in the basement beckoned.

He turned to Jak and spoke in a hushed whisper. "That archway opens onto the main hall. The shrine is to the left. To the right, the hall ends with the storeroom. I'm thinking left."

"Left," Jak agreed with a nod. "But remember Cale, you're looking for a gate back to our plane, not the demon."

Without reply, Cale briskly turned to go—if he saw Yrsillar, he intended to put the bastard down—but Jak grabbed him by the arm and pulled him around.

"Listen, Cale, godsdammit," the little man whispered sharply. "Demons are stronger on their own planes. We don't want to face Yrsillar here. We don't. Burn me, but we don't want to face *anything* here. We need to get back to our own plane first."

Cale stared expressionlessly into the little man's eyes. Again he made no reply. He could make no promises. If an opportunity to fight Yrsillar presented itself—here or back on their plane—he would not pass it up, not unless it meant putting Jak in unnecessary danger.

Seeing his expression, the little man apparently understood his resolve. He released Cale's arm. "I'm with you either way, though," he said with a sigh.

Cale tried to reassure him. "I want to find a way back too, little man. I also want Yrsillar dead. I'll try not to let the one get in the way of the other."

Jak seemed to accept that. "I want him dead too, Cale." He hesitated a moment before adding, "If we kill him on his own plane, he's dead forever."

"What do you mean?"

"I mean that if we kill him on our plane, we only kill his manifestation there. That doesn't really kill him. It just prevents him from returning to our plane for a century or so. But if we kill him here . . ."

"We kill him for real and forever," Cale finished.

Jak nodded. "But it's harder, Cale, much harder. Like I said, he'd be more powerful here, not as easy as that shadow demon you killed before going through the gate."

Cale leaned against the wall while he digested the information. It probably did not matter much. He had no reason to think that Yrsillar moved back and forth between this plane and their home plane. This guild-house was probably empty. They had to find a gate back.

"What will a gate back look like?"

Jak shook his head. "I don't know for sure. But I think we'll know it when we see it."

Cale gave a nod, and with that, they descended the rest of the stairway. When they reached the archway to the main hall, Cale stopped short and peeked around the corner. Jak squirmed between his body and the wall and did the same. Their simultaneous intake of breath was as sharp as a blade, but neither could look away.

As would have been the case with the main hallway in the real guildhouse, the hallway here stretched left to the shrine and right to the storeroom. Doors dotted the walls, some open, but most were closed. No garbage littered the floor here, and the smooth, unwarped floor was bare except for some twenty or so indistinct gray forms.

Positioned at intervals along the hallway, they crouched low to the ground as though hiding behind something Cale couldn't see. If not for their occasional movement, he would have thought them an illusion, a trick of his eyes in the twilight. But they did move, and they were real.

Composed of swirling gray vapor, Cale could distinguish no facial features, could barely make out the rudiments of a man-sized bipedal form. The beings waited in absolute silence. Though Cale and Jak stared in amazement, the beings showed no signs of having seen them.

Abruptly one stood and loped back down the hall toward another pair that flanked the shrine doors.

It loped.

Cale recognized the movement. His eyes narrowed.

Jak must have sensed his sudden tension, for he asked in a whisper, "What are they?"

Afraid one of the creatures would hear, Cale grabbed Jak by the collar and ducked back behind the archway.

"Ghouls," Cale replied in a whisper. He held his blade ready and kept his ears attuned for the sounds of the approaching pack.

Rather than fear, Jak looked at him with a furrowed brow. "Ghouls? Those aren't ghouls." He peeked back around the corner. Cale did too.

"Wait until one moves," Cale said. "There."

One of the figures rose and crossed the hall. Though indistinct and vaporous, Cale couldn't mistake its low crouch, hunched back, and loping stride. Neither did Jak. The little man gave a start and both again retreated into the archway.

"Trickster's toes," Jak softly oathed.

"What kind of ghouls are those?" Cale hissed. "What is going on here?"

Jak looked as dumbfounded as Cale. "Let me think," he replied softly, and stroked his whiskers. "Let me think."

While Jak considered, Cale looked into the hall and kept his eyes on the misty forms of the ghouls. He did a headcount, twenty-six, all of them crouching low, all of them trying to hide in plain sight. Cale began to work through the rudiments of an attack. Though he could not distinguish features, he felt certain that some of the ghostly ghouls looked right at him. Yet none moved to attack. Their unnatural silence sent a chill up his spine. He ducked back. There was nothing to do but to attack head-on.

"It's like they're waiting to ambush us," he said to Jak, and readied himself for a charge.

Cale had anticipated an ambush in the guildhouse basement—in the *real* guildhouse basement—but he hadn't expected so many ghouls. Between the battle at Stormweather and Cale's necklace of missiles, Cale figured over thirty already had been killed. The Night Knives had numbered no more than forty men all told. Yrsillar must have transformed more Selgauntans into ghouls than just the Night Knives. He shuddered to think of what might have happened at Stormweather if the attack had succeeded, if he had not driven off the shadow demon.

"They *are* waiting for us," Jak suddenly exclaimed, and snapped his fingers.

"Quiet," Cale hissed, and looked in alarm around the corner. Except for an occasional shift of position, the ghouls hadn't moved.

"They can't hear us," Jak said aloud. "And they can't see us either."

Before Cale could stop him, the little man stepped brazenly out into the hallway. Cursing, Cale leaped out beside him, blade ready for the swarming pack.

The ghouls showed no sign of noticing anything amiss. Though Cale and Jak stood in plain sight, they continued to crouch and wait.

With one eye still on the misty ghouls, Cale looked to the little man.

"They're like the shadow demon, Cale, but in reverse. This vapor shape is their manifestation on *this* plane. Like the shadowy form of the demon is its manifestation on our plane." He stated it as though it were obvious, but Cale's confusion must have shown on his face.

"The transformation from man to ghoul must result in some sort of dual existence, part of them here, close to the Abyss, but most of them—their corporeal form—on our plane." Jak tapped his chin and went on, "But they aren't powerful like a demon, are they? No, they have a dual existence, but must not have a dual consciousness. They can't see into this plane, which means that they can't see us." He looked up, smiling. "Cale, this guildhouse must *correspond* to the real guildhouse. Back on our plane, these ghouls are waiting for us in the real basement, but they can't see us here in *this* basement." His hand went from his chin to the luckstone at his belt and he smiled broadly. "Mask isn't the only one with us tonight, Erevis. The Lady's decided to come along as well."

Cale couldn't argue. He looked around at the ghouls crouching, lurking, ignorant of their presence mere feet away. The little man's theory fit the facts. Cale could picture the ghouls' fleshy forms back on their plane with their stinking, rotted skin, filthy claws, and vicious fangs. He realized that the ghouls crouched like this because they were hiding in the real basement, behind toppled chairs and debris that didn't manifest in the abyssal guildhouse.

They couldn't see or hear him, but he could see them. He had only one question.

"Can we kill them?"

Jak's pleased expression grew more serious at the thought of killing. "I don't know."

Cale advanced a few steps down the hallway, vengeance for Stormweather on his mind. "Only one way to find out."

Jak grabbed him around the wrist. "Wait, Cale."

Cale stopped, looked into his friend's green eyes.

The little man looked uncertain. His gaze looked past Cale to the misty ghouls. "Erevis. How can we do this? I can't fight a creature that can't defend itself."

Cale placed a hand on Jak's shoulder. "They're *evil*, Jak. We'll do it quick and clean."

Jak still looked unsure so Cale gave him a slight shake, knelt down, and looked hard into his eyes. "I know they were men once, Jak. But what they *were* doesn't matter now, only what they *are*. They're evil, and we have to do it."

Jak looked back at the ghouls, then at Cale. He gave a slow nod.

Cale patted him on the shoulder and rose. "You wait here, little man. Leave this to me."

With that, he walked past Jak and into the hall. The ghouls did nothing as he closed, merely waited in an ambush that would never occur. After a moment, Jak fell into step beside him, short sword and dagger bared.

"I said I'm with you, Cale."

Cale gave a hard nod and together they advanced on the nearest ghoul. Still no sign of alarm. Cale stood over the crouching creature with enchanted blade held high. It looked right at where he stood, unseeing, ignorant of the threat.

Gritting his teeth, Cale cut through its throat with a powerful forward slash. He needn't have swung so hard. The feel of the blow reminded him of the way it had felt to wound the shadow demon back on their home plane, slight resistance, then sudden give. Like slashing a pudding.

No flood of purple spilled to the floor, and no scream of pain resounded in the hall. The ghostly ghoul clutched its throat, writhed silently on the ground, and suddenly disappeared. Cale wondered if back in the real guildhouse, purple blood had pooled about the nearly beheaded corpse of a ghoul.

Must have, he thought, because the hallway erupted into motion.

Misty ghouls lurched from their hiding places and charged to the point where the body would lay. There they stopped, confused. Seeking an unseen foe, they turned about and clawed at the air. So many surrounded Cale and Jak that they seemed engulfed in the morning fog that rolled off the Elzhimmer River—located off the far shore of Selgaunt Bay—most autumn mornings.

Cale gave Jak a reassuring glance, then the two friends set to work.

Grim-faced, Jak ran one through with his enchanted short sword. It buckled, clutched its gut, collapsed to the floor, and disappeared. He stabbed another one through the face with his dagger, to no effect.

"The dagger won't bite," he announced, unnecessarily loud in the otherwise silent hallway. "Only magical weapons will work." He sheathed the dagger and gripped the short sword with both hands.

Mercilessly, Cale sliced the head from a ghoul, then another, then another.

Confused and falling dead without explanation, the pack milled about in the hall. They jumped at one another, clawed and bit at the empty air. In the chaos, individual creatures became difficult to distinguish. Cale now saw only a swirling fog. He knew the hallway back on their home plane must be awash in purple blood, gray bodies, snarls, and guildhouse debris. Here, there was only silence.

He sliced indiscriminately at the mist and killed every ghoul within reach. Unable to defend themselves, unable even to see their attackers, the ghouls died one after another. Without mercy or remorse, Cale cut them down. He felt no guilt, only grim satisfaction. The ghouls that had attacked Stormweather, had preyed on the defenseless, had cut down men armed with dinner utensils and women armed only with screams. They deserved what they got.

For Stormweather, he thought with each slash, for Thazienne.

The survivors swirled around him, confused, close to panic. He raised his blade high—

A sudden realization hit him like a bolt of lightning. He stopped in mid-stroke and looked beside him to Jak.

"Yrsillar doesn't know we're here," he said, certain. "He thinks we're still in the real guildhouse."

"What?" With his short sword, the little man ran through the ghoul Cale had spared. It collapsed, writhed, and dissipated into nothingness. "How do you know that?"

Cale took no time to explain. The panicked ghouls started to mill down the hall toward the shrine.

"Don't let any get away!"

He ran down the hall and ripped one of them in two with an overhand slash. The misty body split neatly down the middle and dissolved into nothingness. He cut down another, and another. Jak leaped into their midst and did the same. None escaped.

Afterward, he and Jak took in the spotless hallway, their unbloodied clothes. Back on their own plane, the hallway must be littered with carnage. He and Jak had administered a slaughter and yet remained clean. He found that thought unsettling.

"Yrsillar must not know we're here. He knows his ghouls are vulnerable to attack from this plane. If he had known we were here, he would have been waiting for us himself, not allowed his ghouls to be slaughtered this way."

Jak winced at his choice of words.

Pretending not to notice, Cale waved his blade around the hall to indicate the implied carnage. "They were waiting to ambush us in the *real* guildhouse. They didn't have any idea we were here. Neither does Yrsillar."

Thoughtful, Jak scratched his head and finally nodded agreement. "Makes sense. We've only been here a quarter-hour or so. That's not very long. He must not yet have learned that we passed through the gate and survived, much less stumbled onto the planar correspondence."

Breathing hard, flush with their success and eager for more, Cale nodded, "We need to find a way back home quickly. He's vulnerable now. We killed the shadow demon and we killed the ghouls. Yrsillar will have to face us alone." Cale felt confident about the result of that confrontation.

"Agreed," Jak said, rallying himself. "We find a way back and hand that bastard his guts." The little man shot Cale a grim smile, but his confidence gave way to nervousness when he eyeballed the golden aura that protected him from the Abyss. "Let's move fast, though. I don't know how much longer this spell is going to last."

Cale held out his arms and checked his own protective spell. The golden light seemed to have faded somewhat, and the soft sparks and pops sounded less frequently than before. If the unrelenting energy of this plane fully drained their spells, he and Jak were dead.

His hand went to his pocket, and he ran his fingertips over the felt mask. Just a while longer, he hoped, just a while longer.

"Let's move." Cale strode for the closed shrine doors. The shrine to Mask seemed the center of this whole affair. The worship hall of the Righteous Man, the place Cale had first encountered Yrsillar, the home of the god for whom Cale seemed called as a Champion.

It was as likely a place as any for a gate back home.

Before they reached the doors, the telltale ripping sound of sundered reality stopped them cold. Without words, they fell into a wary crouch. Back to back, Cale watched the shrine doors while Jak watched the hall behind them.

A thin red line appeared in the air three paces before Cale, a bloody slash that hung unsupported five feet up in the nothingness of the Abyss's air. A gate.

"There," Cale said excitedly.

Jak turned and stood beside him. Both watched as the glowing line expanded to the size of a small window. Colors! Colors poured from the hole like a waterfall and overwhelmed the drab gray of the Abyss. The colors of their own plane. The colors of home. Cale had never seen anything so beautiful.

"That's a gate back!" Jak exclaimed.

"I know!"

"They must open and close randomly," Jak said, as both stepped toward it. Because it sat so high in the air, Cale knew he would have to lift Jak through and then jump—

A shadow blotted out the cascade of hues. A head appeared in the midst of the gate and moved toward them, corrupting the colors with its emptiness. Nauseatingly, the scene called to Cale's mind a giant womb giving birth to a horror. Involuntarily, he and Jak stepped back. The head of a shadow demon crowned. As it did, the shadowstuff solidified into a bluish-gray oval of flesh, featureless but for two malice filled, milky-white eyes and a slit that might have been a mouth. Two powerfully clawed hands appeared to either side and gripped the edges of the gate as though to rip open the birth canal fully.

A shadow demon, Cale realized, another shadow demon.

It saw them, and the baleful look in its pupilless eyes pierced Cale like a stiletto. The milky-white orbs narrowed to slits and it hissed through the slash of its mouth—the first actual sound Cale had ever *heard* one of the creatures make.

"Another shadow demon," Jak said, and sounded tired. "Gods." Cale could hear the fear in his friend's voice. The little man began to ease backward.

The demon eyed them evilly, hissed again, and began to squirm through the opening. Its twisted, winged form took shape and fully eclipsed the rainbow colors of home pouring through the gate.

"Feed on you," it whispered through the lipless hole in its face. Its voice grated like fingernails on slate. "Eat your soul. Feed on you as I fed on the others." It was through the gate up to the shoulders. A wave of supernatural fear went before it.

The others. Was *this* the demon that had attacked Stormweather, and not the other that Cale had already killed? Remembering the slaughter in the feasthall, recalling Thazienne's wounded spirit that might never heal, Cale's anger flared white-hot and chased away his fear.

It doesn't matter which one did it, he thought. For that sin, they would all pay. I'll wipe out every godsdamned one of them. He had already killed one, and he could damn well kill another. He *would* kill another.

Without another thought, he charged.

"Feed on this!" he shouted, and raised his enchanted sword high to strike.

With only half of its body clear of the narrow gate, the demon raised its claws defensively, hissed in alarm, and lurched backward. With all his anger, Cale slashed downward into the creature's shoulder and chest. The long sword struck with a satisfying *thunk* and went a handwidth deep, opening a bloodless, meaty gash in the demon's gray flesh. The demon screamed and writhed in pain. Though in the throes of agony, it nevertheless swiped a retaliatory claw rake toward Cale.

Cale dodged a heartbeat too late. The claw struck him along the arm. Golden light exploded in his eyes, knocked him backward a step, and nearly blinded him. The demon shrieked louder still and jerked back its clawed hand, now blackened by contact with the protective spell. Cale stood unscathed, body and soul, by the attack, though the protective aura that surrounded him had dimmed to a soft yellow.

"Cale, the gate!" Jak yelled from behind.

Screaming in pain, the demon pulled itself fully back into the gate. As it retreated, its flesh grew increasingly opaque, its body grew smaller as though the gate was a tunnel over a bowshot long. One of its claws—the unwounded one, Cale noticed—still clutched the edge of the shrinking portal. The demon's arm seemed to stretch for miles, half shadow, half blue flesh. The gate shrank as the demon shrank, diminished with each heartbeat. The demon was pulling the gate closed behind it.

Desperate, Cale slashed crosswise at the demon's exposed hand. The enchanted blade bit through the demonic flesh and severed two long, claw-tipped fingers. They fell to the floor of the abyssal guildhouse and for a nauseating moment squirmed and flopped like thick worms. Cale *sensed* in his soul rather than heard with his ears the demon shriek as it released the edge of the gate and retreated farther within. Its screams grew more and more distant until they finally tapered off to nothingness and it vanished from sight. The portal stayed open, albeit smaller now, and the demon was gone.

Alive with the colors of home, the swirling gate

hung in the drab air. Only as wide as a man's forearm, Cale realized that he and Jak would have to go through one at a time. He turned to the little man—

Jak's wide-eyed gaze went from the demon's fingers to Cale's face. "Trickster's hairy toes, Cale! You're not afraid of anything!"

Cale ignored the compliment and indicated the gate. "You first," he said. "I'll lift you through." Jak began to protest, but Cale cut him off. "I'll be right behind you, little man. I can make the jump up by myself. You can't." He looked into Jak's eyes. "This could be our only chance out of here. You saw, the demons open and close the gates themselves. It's not a random event. We need to go now."

After a moment's consideration, Jak nodded and stepped beside him. "All right. Let's do it."

Cale gripped him under the armpits and lifted him halfway toward the gate. In one hand Jak held his short sword, with the other he clutched his luckstone.

"Wait, Cale, Yrsillar must know we're here now. What if he and the other shadow demon are waiting on the other side?"

"Then we kill them right there," Cale grimly averred. "Don't worry. I'll be right behind you." In truth, Cale hoped the demons were waiting for them. He would welcome the chance to put an end to this.

"All right," Jak said, but didn't sound convinced. Cale lifted the little man toward the portal home. Jak led with his sword.

Before he got Jak fully into the gate, a sudden pressure assaulted his eardrums, like the thickening of the air that occurred before a heavy storm. The sensation affected his equilibrium and he nearly lost his balance.

"Cale?" The tip of Jak's blade already stuck through the gate.

"I feel it," Cale acknowledged with a grimace.

"Put me down. Hurry," Jak ordered.

Nodding, Cale set the little man down and tried to get his bearings.

A charge ran through his body. The hair of his arms rose and stood on end. His breath left him. A wave of nausea washed over him and he retched.

"Cale . . ."

Abruptly and without warning, the sensation vanished.

Jak bent over and held his stomach. His breath came hard. "What was that?" he asked.

"Don't know," Cale replied. Intuitively though, he *did* know. Another gate had been opened, opened by something more powerful than the shadow demon.

He felt a presence manifest. A palpable wave of malice radiated out from behind the closed shrine doors. Hate rained down on him like a sleet storm.

"Cal—" The sheer power of the presence lurking behind the shrine doors choked off Jak's words. Breathing hard, the little man turned to face the shrine. Cale placed a hand on Jak's shoulder and did the same. The doors began to pulse like a heart.

"Yrsillar," Cale hissed through gritted teeth. The demon's hate seemed so substantial as to be a physical thing, the *only* physical thing on this plane of emptiness. Cale answered the demon's hate with a rage equally substantial. Here was the cause. Vengeance was at hand. He took a step toward the doors.

Jak clutched his hand, pulled him to a stop, and fairly jumped into his arms. "Lift me through, Cale," he said urgently. "Lift me through!"

Eyes on the pulsing doors of the shrine, Cale made no response. Anger consumed him. He felt no fear. Yrsillar was waiting for him.

Jak gripped Cale's hand in both of his own. "Erevis!

Cale! Dammit, you can't fight him here. He's strongest here." Jak shook his arm as though to bring him to his senses. "Let's go through the gate and fight him on our own plane. Erevis! Don't."

"You go, little man," he said, and lifted Jak toward the gate. Cale wanted to fight Yrsillar here.

"What? Wait, wait." Jak squirmed in his grip like a fish. Cale turned the little man around so they could look into each other's eyes. Cale's resolve must have been evident from his expression, for Jak's protests fell silent. The little man visibly wilted.

"Why, Cale?" he softly asked.

"Because when I kill him here, he's dead for good." Nothing less could satisfy him now.

Jak said nothing for a moment, merely hung in the air between Cale and the gate home.

"Put me down," he said at last.

"You don't need to—"

"Put me down, godsdammit," Jak ordered. "This is *our* fight, Cale, not just yours. Those bastards hurt me too." Jak looked at him meaningfully. Fear had given way to resolve, or resignation. "I said I'm with you and I am. Put me down."

Cale did. Both drew blades and turned to the pulsing doors of the shrine.

"He's waiting for us," Jak observed. "He thinks it'll make us more afraid."

Cale started for the doors.

CHAPTER 11

CONFRONTATION

Cale strode boldly for the pulsing double doors. The wooden slabs beat faster as he neared, as though in anticipation of his touch. From behind the doors he heard only silence, but he could feel Yrsillar's brooding presence. The demon was waiting.

Beside him, Jak's breathing came in fearful gasps.

"Easy," he said, and reached down to pat Jak on the shoulder.

The halfling nodded, struggled to get himself under control. "I'm all right," he said, though his breathing still came hard.

Cale saw that Jak had sheathed his dagger. He now held his magical short sword in one hand and his holy symbol in the other.

Frightened, the little man had fallen back on his god for strength. Jak had sheathed a weapon of steel to draw a weapon of faith. Cale envied him.

The felt mask in his pocket brought him small comfort. Perhaps someday faith could be a weapon for him, but for today he would rely only on his steel.

Standing before the doors, he took a breath and kicked them in.

The moment the doors flew open, a wave of terror blew from the shrine like a black wind. Cale's throat constricted and fear threatened to overwhelm him. With great effort of will, he fought down the supernatural terror and stood his ground. It's not real, he told himself, it's only magic.

Beside him, Jak let out a soft moan.

"It's magical, Jak," Cale said, and shook him by the shoulder. "Resist it."

"I know," Jak replied through bared teeth. He clutched his holy symbol in his fist so tightly that it must have cut into his palm. Cale saw blood squeezing from between Jak's white knuckles, but the little man held his ground.

"We'll provide you no amusement, Yrsillar!" Cale shouted into the gloomy shrine.

"Damn right," Jak echoed with as much bravado as he could muster.

No response came from within.

They shared a solemn glance and walked through the open doors.

The shrine here looked much the same as the actual shrine back on their home plane. They saw rows of pews that led up to a raised dais and an altar.

From the opposite side of the room, Yrsillar's voice boomed, the deep bass of distant thunder. "You've grown some since last we met, Champion." His voice dropped so that each syllable dripped with enough malice to make Cale wince. "Some, but not enough."

Cale scanned the room toward the altar. He saw nothing but shadows and darkness.

"There," Jak softly said, and pointed to the left of the altar.

The shadows and gloom suddenly unfolded, vomited forth the titanic form of Yrsillar. Cale's breath caught in his throat.

The demon lord looked majestic. Where the lesser shadow demons had been lean and wiry, Yrsillar was a mountain of bluish-gray flesh. Powerfully muscled, the demon lord's mammoth chest and rippling torso sat squarely atop a pair of tree-trunk-sized legs. He towered over Cale. Naked, but seemingly sexless, a nauseating spiderweb of purple veins pulsed visibly beneath the hairless, leathery skin of his body, each beat keeping time with the pulsing of the shrine doors, each beat no doubt keeping time with the pulsing of the gates back in the real guildhouse.

Overlong, powerful arms ended in bony, three-fingered hands, each digit capped with a black claw as long as Cale's hand. Membranous wings sprouted from his back and spanned the room. He stood still as a statue, a nightmare carved of stone. The voids of his eye sockets, each as large as a Sembian fivestar, stared holes into Cale's soul.

From the darkness around him emerged the shadow demon that Cale had wounded earlier, a miniature version of its master flitting about Yrsillar like a moth flitting about a flame.

Silently, majestically, Yrsillar stepped to the altar and regarded them coldly.

"Not enough," he said again. From behind the demon lord's shoulder, the shadow demon hissed.

"This is just how Yrsillar chooses to appear to us," Jak whispered through the side of his mouth. "To heighten our fear, but he's made of nothingness, Cale, nothingness. Remember that."

Cale nodded grimly, his eyes on the demons. "We give him nothing," he whispered in reply.

"Damn right," Jak said, and sounded as though he meant it.

They stepped forward into the main aisle, blades ready, and walked halfway to the raised dais and altar. Yrsillar regarded them in unconcerned silence, hate embodied. Cale felt the demon lord's hunger for them as an itching between his shoulders. He ignored it and spat on the floor in defiance.

At that, the shadow demon hissed, pawed at the air, and flitted about in agitation. Yrsillar said nothing, did nothing, simply stood before them and let their fear build.

Silent seconds passed. They seemed an eternity. Though his heart pounded, Cale braved the blizzard of hate and held unflinchingly Yrsillar's baleful gaze. He refused to bow to his fear.

The stress became too much for Jak, however, and he began to lose composure. His breathing sounded like a bellows and he shifted anxiously from foot to foot.

"Dark," he oathed under his breath, "Dark and empty."

Cale placed a hand on Jak's shoulder and shouted at Yrsillar. "You'll get no fear to feed on from us, *ecthain*." Defiantly, he held forth his enchanted blade. At that, Yrsillar's wings beat once—and he began to laugh in a booming, mocking chuckle.

"Once more you face me, Champion of Mask, and once more I smell the fear you try to hide. You stink of terror." He shifted his gaze to Jak. "As do you."

The little man let out an alarmed peep. "Trickster's toes," he muttered like a chant, "Trickster's hairy toes."

Cale grabbed a fistful of the little man's cloak and gave him a single shake. "We give him nothing," he hissed. "He wants you to be frightened. Give him nothing."

At that, Jak started to rally. He slid a step closer to Cale so that his shoulder bumped Cale's thigh. The touch apparently gave him strength.

"We give him nothing," Jak softly agreed, and his voice sounded steady. Shaking only slightly, he returned Yrsillar's stare. The shadow demon hissed in rage. Yrsillar beat his great wings in anger and looked sharply at Cale. His mocking tone turned deeper, heavy with hate and dripping with hunger.

"I'll savor your soul, Erevis Cale. As I will that of the other Champion."

Jak's breath caught at that, but Yrsillar did not so much as glance at the little man. "Both of you will live out the rest of your lives in pain. I will hold your souls in thrall, feasting at my leisure." He stepped from behind the altar and down the dais, graceful despite his size. Muscle rippled with every move he made.

As though by prearranged plan, the shadow demon darted like an arrow for the ceiling.

"I will force you to watch impotently as I swallow the souls of the ones you love."

Cale thought of Thazienne *defiled* by this creature and his rage doubled. Guilt, self-loathing, and hate for Yrsillar fueled his anger. He gripped the enchanted long sword with both hands, knuckles white with anger.

"Leave him to me," he said to Jak through gritted teeth. "You keep an eye on that thing," he indicated the shadow demon, "and watch my back."

Jak nodded once, vigorously. "*We'll* watch your back," he replied, and held up his holy symbol in a bloody hand. His gaze went to Cale's pocket and he added meaningfully, "You're not alone, Cale. Remember that. If you accept the call, you *are* his Champion."

Cale nodded and gripped his shoulder. Jak smiled and looked up to watch the shadow demon.

If you accept the call . . .

Tentatively, Cale reached for his pocket, for the symbol of Mask, but stopped halfway.

I won't do it this way, he thought to the Shadowlord. Staring death in the face, most everyone turned to the gods. Cale had never consciously acted out of fear. To turn to Mask now would be to surrender too much of himself. He wouldn't.

You make the first concession, he thought to Mask.

He received no reply, no stroke of divine lightning.

Unsurprised, Cale looked down the aisle and regarded the demon lord.

Yrsillar stood at the end of the center aisle, near the base of the dais. Briefly, Cale wondered what happened to the body of the Righteous Man while Yrsillar manifested here. Was he in stasis? Dissipated? Nothing? He didn't know, and had no time to consider the matter further.

He stared into the voids of the demon's eyes and held his gaze. Yrsillar said nothing but the veins beneath his leathery skin began to pulse faster. His wings fluttered intermittently, filling the room with gusts of fetid wind. He held the slit of his mouth partly open, a half-moon carved in the face of a nightmare. His claws glistened despite the gloom. Cale sensed his hunger, sensed his growing anticipation.

Cale took a step toward him—

Inexplicably, Thamalon's words suddenly rang in Cale's brain—*Unbridled aggression can sometimes be an enemy*—but he pushed it aside. Unbridled aggression was all he had.

Snarling, he gripped the hilt of his blade in both

hands and strode toward the monster that had murdered so many.

❧ ❧ ❧ ❧ ❧

The gray-skinned shadow demon eyed Jak evilly as it flitted about the ceiling rafters. Willing to take his eye from it for only a moment, Jak spared a quick glance over his shoulder to shout encouragement to his friend.

"Cale! Remember that you're not alone! Mask is with you if you ask!" Cale showed no sign of having heard him.

Jak looked back just in time to see the demon streaking down for him.

"Dark!" He dived to the side and used the back of a pew for cover. The shadow demon's claws screeched across the wood and tore his cloak, but did not reach flesh. He regained his feet in an instant. The demon had already darted back into the air. It hovered near the ceiling, willing to wait for another opportunity.

"Feeeeed," it hissed at him.

❧ ❧ ❧ ❧ ❧

Cale's fury propelled him forward. Feeling nothing but hate, he walked resolutely toward Yrsillar. He felt apart from himself, numb, as though he were watching the scene unfold from above. With each row of pews that he passed, his anger increased. Yrsillar's veins pulsed faster, his claws opening and closing in reflexive anticipation.

Undeterred, Cale's hate demanded that he advance. His walk turned to a run, his run to a charge. Yrsillar crouched on his powerful legs and held his claws out wide.

As Cale closed the last few strides, he held his blade high and shouted years of pent-up rage into the rafters, sent a lifetime of self-loathing careening into the nothingness of the Abyss. Yrsillar answered with a terrible roar so full of malice that it would have blown Cale to his knees but for his forward momentum.

Only then, in that final moment, did it occur to Cale that Mask had long ago made the first concession, had made two, in fact—the darkness back in the real shrine, and the golden aura that protected him now.

Too late, he realized, as he bent against the demon lord's roar like a man in a snowstorm. He would have to stand or fall on his own.

Yrsillar made no move to retreat, he merely crouched and held his claws at the ready, a giant predator awaiting its prey. His veins bulged beneath his skin, tracks of livid, sickening purple.

Cale lunged forward and swung his blade toward Yrsillar's chest in a vicious upward arc, the stroke so powerful that it cut through the air with a whistle.

As fast as a hunting cat, the huge demon bounded back a step and hopped atop the dais. Cale pursued, reversed his stroke, and chopped downward. Impossibly fast, Yrsillar jerked back. Cale's long sword rang sparking off the altar block.

Little more than a gray blur, a claw streaked for Cale's throat. Using the altar as cover, he dropped beneath the blow and slashed upward with his long sword. The blade cut a swath through empty air. Yrsillar's arm had arced before Cale ever got his blade into position. He jumped back to his feet, held the long sword before him like a pike and lunged over the altar for the demon lord's chest.

Yrsillar swooped up and under with one of his claws. Caught in mid-lunge, Cale's momentum prevented a dodge. Golden light flashed brightly as his protective spell flared out of existence. The power of the spell seared Yrsillar's flesh but the demon lord did not recoil. Cale whiffed the meaty odor of charred skin. The powerful, dagger-length claws tore through Cale's cloak and split his leather armor from abdomen to throat. A shallow gash opened along his entire torso. The blow stunned him. Warm blood coursed from the wound. Without the protective spell, his soul began to seep from his body. Unable to defend himself, he reeled on the altar, an ironic offering to Mask awaiting the sacrificial knife.

Yrsillar roared, balled his hand, and drove his fist into Cale's chest.

The blow crashed down on Cale with the force of a maul.

Cale careened backward off the altar and flew through the air, arms flailing. Only the remnant of his enchanted leather armor kept his ribs from shattering.

He crashed four rows deep among the pews and collapsed in an awkward heap of bones and wood. His sword flew from his grasp and clattered away.

Battered and gasping for breath, he knew then that he was a dead man. He had failed Thazienne, had failed Mask, had failed himself. Yrsillar would finish him before he drew another breath.

❧ ❧ ❧ ❧ ❧

The shadow demon swooped for Jak. Ready, and still clutching his holy symbol, Jak spat the magical words to a spell, *"Inre luxos,"* and pointed at the diving demon.

Instantly, a glaring light flared in the demon's eyes, turned the milky-white orbs into glowing opals. Blinded in the middle of its headlong descent, it clawed wildly at its face and tried to pull up.

Nimbly leaping pews, Jak dived to the side as the enraged creature crashed to the floor and sent pews flying. Still hissing in anger, it climbed to its feet and flailed about with its claws in a mad effort to locate him.

"Feed on you," it hissed, enraged. "Feed."

It swept wide arcs with its claws. Jak scrambled over and under the pews to avoid its reach, but it pressed him relentlessly. His spell would last for hours, but he would run out of room to run long before that.

The shadow demon sniffed at the air as it lashed about, like a vile hound searching for the scent trail. Jak knew that despite its blindness it could somehow sense him. He had been invisible in the Soargyl bedroom and still one had sniffed him out. He kept moving, dodging over and under pews.

It stayed on him, always one step behind, but never giving him time to plan a course of action. Jak could sense its hunger for him. It hissed and beat its wings in angry frustration. Purple veins pulsed beneath leathery skin. Its rancid-meat smell made Jak want to gag, but he dared not make a sound. He hid behind a pew, gasping, mind racing, and tried to think.

He dared not close to attack, even from the rear. An inadvertent strike by one of the enraged demon's claws would dispel his protective aura. He could cast the same spell again, of course, but that would take time. Time that he wouldn't have if he were in hand-to-hand combat with the demon. If he went too long without the protective spell, the plane would kill him.

"Feed. Feeeed."

It closed on him. He readied himself and pulled two of his throwing daggers free.

Might as well see if plain steel can hurt it in this form, he thought. He touched each blade to his luckstone, raised his arm, threw, and darted away.

When the demon erupted in a pained squeal, Jak smiled. Thank you, Lady, he thought to Tymora. The blades had struck home.

Feed on that, wretch, he thought with a grin.

"Feeed on you, little creature. Feeeed."

Leaping behind another pew, Jak placed his holy symbol in his belt pouch and jerked another dagger free of its sheath. Pumped full of adrenaline, and focused only on the demon, he suddenly felt no fear. The realization changed him. He had been frightened only moments before and he remembered being utterly terrified back at the Soargyls the last time he had faced one of these creatures.

I'm getting more like Cale every da—

Abruptly, the demon's hissing ceased and gave way to a series of softly muttered words. Jak didn't recognize the language, but he recognized the intonation and cadence of spellcasting.

By the gods, spells?

He peeked over the pew.

The opalescent glow had vanished from the demon's eyes. The creature had dispelled Jak's cantrip, and now it could see him. Its milky white eyes instantly discovered him.

It stalked forward, wings beating.

"Dark," Jak oathed.

He rose from behind the pew, dagger and short sword ready. The demon's hunger hit him like a bitter wind, but he vowed not to give in to fear, vowed to give this demonic bastard the fight of its life. The last time he had faced one of these creatures, he'd frozen up, humiliated himself by wetting his pants.

"Not this time," he promised himself.

"Come on," he said through gritted teeth, and beckoned it forward with his blades—

At that moment, a victorious roar from the front of

the shrine jerked his head around. He watched as Yrsillar swiped a claw through Cale's midsection, followed by a crushing blow to the chest that sent his friend flailing through the air to crash among the front rows of pews.

"Cale!"

The shadow demon took advantage of Jak's lapse and leaped forward, quick as an adder to strike the little man.

Though the strength behind the claw nearly knocked the blade from his fist, Jak managed a parry with his dagger. A second claw rake followed. Jak leaped backward out of range then immediately lunged forward with his short sword. He was too slow. The demon backed off in a crouch and hissed, its claws weaving hypnotically through the air.

Jak saw his death in those claws. The demon was too fast, and when it hit him, his protective aura would flare out—

"Burn me," he said, an idea dawning.

The demon's touch *would probably* dispel the aura, but in the process its energy would hurt the creature, the original intent behind Jak's spell.

The beginnings of a plan took shape in his mind, a desperate gambit. He would probably die, but if he did, he hoped to take the demon with him.

❧ ❧ ❧ ❧ ❧

Cale righted himself and scrambled to all fours, expecting Yrsillar to thunder toward him at any moment. His lungs ached and his head throbbed. Dazed, he crawled for his sword. When he closed his fist over the hilt, he saw the white vapor of his soul bleeding from the skin on his hand. It billowed back toward the altar, back toward Yrsillar. Already he was beginning to feel the effect it had on him. He was growing weaker by the instant. In minutes he would be dead. He lifted his increasingly heavy head and looked out over the pew.

Surprisingly, Yrsillar remained on the dais. The voids of his eyes focused on Cale and he began to laugh. Cale quailed before that terrible sound and ducked back behind the pew, breathing hard.

"I can taste your despair, Erevis Cale," Yrsillar said. "Only now, at the very last, do you realize your folly."

Summoning his courage, Cale again looked over the top of the pew. Yrsillar made no move to come finish the fight. Instead, he seemed content to let Cale die slowly. With the protective aura dispelled, the gray vapor of Cale's soul flowed into Yrsillar.

While he watched, the great demon sucked in the streams of his life-force. The demon's great body shuddered in ecstasy with each mouthful. Cale wanted to vomit. He was watching his soul be devoured piecemeal.

Yrsillar laughed as he feasted. "Your weakness is apparent to you now, is it not, Erevis Cale?" He gobbled in still more. "So fares the so-called Champion of Mask. So fare any who rely on gods for salvation."

Or course, Cale had not relied on Mask for salvation, had not relied on Mask for anything. He did now. Prayer came hard to him, but he quelled his pride and did it.

Lend me strength, Shadowlord, he thought. *If I'm to be your Champion, lend me strength.*

His body suddenly grew less sluggish. Shielded from Yrsillar by the pews and invigorated by the prayer, he crawled along the row until he reached the center aisle.

"I will not give up," he vowed, the words hollow in the face of his weakness. "I will not!"

Yrsillar's laughter mocked his resolve. The demon lord continued to devour his soul, piece by piece.

Cale knew he had to retrieve Jak and get the Nine Hells out of here. The little man had been right all along—they should not have fought Yrsillar on his home plane. They needed to get back to their own plane fast or they would both die here.

I let my anger and pride blind me. He should have heeded Thamalon's advice—unbridled aggression *had* been his enemy. His fear of losing himself had been his enemy.

The sudden understanding brought him to reach into his pocket and pull out the felt mask. Its touch brought him comfort. He realized now that espousing a faith did not mean surrendering himself; it meant the possibility of *bettering* himself. In a flash of inspiration, he realized that his lifelong derision of religion had its true origin not in his fear of losing himself but in his own self-hatred. He had pretended to despise religion because he had deemed himself unworthy of it. But his own standards had been too high, Mask had *called* him, and Mask knew Cale's flaws.

He thought of Jak and Ansril Ammhaddan, both of them priests, and both of them flawed men, but both *good* men, too. For the first time in his life, Cale realized that the one did not exclude the other—he could be both flawed *and* good. With that, he took the final step toward faith.

I accept, godsdammit, he thought to Mask. He only wished he had done so sooner. He had become Mask's Champion only to die at Yrsillar's hands. The irony almost drew a smile.

Still, he'd be damned if he'd die without a fight. He jumped to his feet.

Yrsillar's laughter immediately ceased. "You are going nowhere!"

Cale didn't dare turn around. He ran back toward the double doors as fast as his weakened legs would carry him.

❀ ❀ ❀ ❀ ❀

From the corner of his eye, Jak saw Cale sprinting toward him. His protective spell was gone! He trailed the mist of his soul behind him like smoke from a flickering candle.

With Jak momentarily distracted, the shadow demon raised a claw.

Jak staggered backward out of reach. Cale shouted to him as he closed.

"I'm coming, little man!"

The shadow demon turned its head toward Cale.

Seeing his opportunity, Jak charged, arms wide in an embrace. Too late, the demon tried to bound backward. Jak crashed into it and wrapped his little arms around its leathery midsection in a great hug. Brilliant golden light flared blindingly bright. As the protective aura dissipated, its energy exploded into the shadow demon. The stink of charred demon flesh filled Jak's nostrils. The creature screamed, spasmed, and tried to pull away, but Jak held on. Absently, he noted the feel of the creature's skin, cold and flabby, like a wineskin filled with ice water. A claw tore painfully across his back. He screamed but held on. Another claw gripped him around the head, lifted him into the air, and flung him away like a rag doll.

He grunted, hitting the ground awkwardly. Jak looked up to see the demon standing over him, its abdomen and torso horribly burned and smoking.

Cale appeared behind it, long sword overhead. He chopped across and neatly swiped the demon's head off. Milky-white eyes widened with surprise, and the shadow demon soundlessly collapsed. Thick purple liquid trickled from its neck.

"Cale!"

"Little man." Cale extended a hand and helped him to his feet. "We're leaving."

"Good," Jak said. When he gripped Cale's forearm, he saw their souls bleeding from both of them. The gray mist rose from their skin and floated back toward the altar where Yrsillar still stood, eating. Jak felt weakened already, but whether from the drain or the bleeding wound in his back, he couldn't tell.

"You cannot escape me," Yrsillar boomed, but remained on the dais.

Cale steered Jak for the door. "Let's move."

Behind them, Yrsillar began to mouth the words to a spell.

"Dark! I didn't know they could cast spells, Cale. I swear I didn't."

They ran.

Jak glanced behind them to see that a *distortion* had formed in the air before Yrsillar. In a voice as loud as thunder, the demon lord spat the final magical syllables of the spell and pointed a clawed hand at Cale and Jak. At once the distortion spread out and took on the shape of a wave, a tide of pure nothingness. Pulsing with power, it undulated toward them like a great worm. Picking up speed, it swallowed pews, floors, and ceilings, and left only *blankness* in its wake. Yrsillar and the dais sat amidst an ocean of absolute emptiness.

Jak found the emptiness hypnotic, the oblivion tempting.

"You're going nowhere!" the demon lord boomed again.

"Run!" Cale ordered, looking over his shoulder and pulling Jak along. "Run!"

Jak ran. Trailing wisps of soul in their wake, they ran down the rest of the aisle as quick as they could, crashed through the doors, and sped down the hallway for the gate that led back home.

Right behind them and gaining, the wave burst through the door, wall, and floor. It consumed everything in its path. They reached the gate. Cale lifted Jak to throw him through.

"No," Jak said. "We go together or not at all."

The wave sped toward them. Cale didn't argue. He nodded, picked Jak up, and slung him over his back. "Hang on."

The wave closed in, swallowing everything. Looking into its emptiness, Jak felt dizzy. He closed his eyes and clutched Cale around the neck.

"Go!" he screamed. "Go!"

Cale backed up a few steps, spun on his heel, and sprinted forward. The wall of nothingness seemed about to engulf the colors of the gate, to swallow them in emptiness.

"Cale!" Jak was face to face with the void. Bile raced up his throat. They wouldn't make it!

Cale took a final stride and leaped into the air.

❦ ❦ ❦ ❦ ❦

Jak's final shout resounded in his mind but Cale could make no reply. He felt his body stretched as thin as parchment and a tingling that quickly grew painful, as though tiny needles had been driven into his pores. There was light and color.

"Oomph!"

"Dllarlk!"

They toppled from the gate and collapsed to the floor in a heap. They quickly disentangled themselves from one another and tried to recover their bearings.

Above them, a pulsing void of emptiness swirled in the air—the other side of the gate that they had just traveled through. With each pulse, it pulled the hairs upright on Cale's arms and head, like a tide trying to pull him back to sea. The pull of the void.

He took a deep breath, inhaled the acrid and coppery air of the real guildhouse. He sat up and looked around.

Corpse after bloody corpse littered the hall, over twenty of them, all gutted and decapitated. They were the ghouls he and Jak had slaughtered in their vaporous forms back in the Abyss.

Jak stared at the slaughter. "Dark," he said in wonder.

Looking upon the carnage, Cale felt no horror, just a distant, grim satisfaction. The ghouls were twisted evil creatures—irredeemable horrors—and he and Jak had done what they had to.

He surveyed the rest of the guildhouse, the *real* guildhouse—wood plank floors, piles of broken furnishings, heaps of filth. The whole was lit by the familiar flickering of torches. They had made it back alive.

He was surprised to find his strength returning, the energy of home apparently replacing that sapped by the Abyss. With the return of feeling came a heightening of pain—his ribs ached sharply and the gash in his torso throbbed with every beat of his heart.

The pain of being alive, he supposed. The pain of the human condition. He welcomed the sensation. Better that than the oblivion of the void.

Revivified, if not quite whole, he looked at Jak with raised eyebrows.

"Jak?"

The little man nodded. "I feel it too. It's replacing the life we lost to the Abyss." After a thoughtful pause, he added, "But it can't replace the life-force consumed by Yrsillar."

Yrsillar. He'd be coming as soon as he realized that his spell had not killed them. Cale climbed to his feet, one hand holding his blade, one hand holding the felt mask.

"Let's do this," he said, and helped Jak to his feet. "He'll be coming."

Jak nodded, pulled out his holy symbol. "First some healing. We're both wounded."

Without waiting for a reply, he chanted the words to a spell and laid a magically charged hand on Cale's arm. Cale's bruised ribs instantly stopped aching and the gash in his torso closed. Jak cast another on himself, sealed the slash in his back and the scratches about his face and head.

"That's it, Cale, that's all I can do," Jak said as he pocketed his holy symbol.

Cale nodded, held up his blade. "We'll make do with only these, then."

Jak chuckled softly, indicated Cale's shredded cloak and torn leather armor. "Not exactly in the best shape for this though, are we?"

"We'll be all right," Cale reassured him. "We've got an extra ally now." He showed Jak the felt mask he held in his hand.

The little man took in Cale's meaning, nodded knowingly.

"You've accepted then?"

"I've accepted. Let's go."

Together, they turned and walked for the doors that opened onto the shrine of Mask, his god. Jak fell in beside him.

Before they had taken five paces, the sound of an opening gate from within the shrine gave them pause. The voice of the Righteous Man, the voice of Yrsillar, came through the doors.

"Erevis Cale! You *will* face me!"

"I want nothing more," Cale muttered, and made for the doors.

As they walked, Jak grabbed Cale's forearm. "Remember, he's weaker here, but he'll still have magic. We need to be careful."

"We will." He looked down on Jak and held up the felt mask. "I have to face him in the shrine. We fought him on his turf. Now we'll fight him on mine."

Jak eyed the mask, nodded in understanding, and the two friends strode for the shrine.

As he walked, Cale thought of Thazienne, of Thamalon and Stormweather, of the warped Night Knives, the uncountable dead inadvertently caught in this demonic nightmare. He gripped his blade and the mask tightly. A reckoning was finally at hand. He jerked open the shrine doors.

Burned pews and charred ghoul corpses lay scattered about the room, the aftereffect of the magical globe Cale had exploded in the shrine two days earlier. The rest of the room remained intact, and Yrsillar, now in the form of the Righteous Man, stood in the center aisle halfway between the shrine doors and the altar to Mask. A gate swirled behind him, the doorway through which he had transported himself back.

Having seen the awful majesty of the demon lord in his true form, Cale could hardly conceive how the guildmaster's body contained such a being.

As though in answer to his thought, a distortion began to take shape around the Righteous Man's slight frame. Flickering tongues of nothingness danced around the Righteous Man's body that obscured his human form and suggested the awful magnificence of Yrsillar's true shape. To Cale, the Righteous Man's body seemed ready to burst at the seams, to vomit forth the truth of Yrsillar's being from the lie of the guildmaster's form.

"Come, then," the demon hissed.

Without hesitation, Jak jerked free two throwing daggers. Silvery blurs in the torchlight, they sliced through the air for Yrsillar's throat.

Casually, Yrsillar sidestepped the first blade, then shot forth a thin arm to snatch the second dagger out of midair. Quick as a striking snake, he hurled the blade back at them.

It streaked past Cale's ear before he could move, missing by sheer luck, and sunk all the way to the hilt in the wood of the doorjamb.

"Dark," Jak breathed.

Cale nodded agreement but said nothing. The strength behind that throw had been superhuman, demonic. That meant that the frailties of the Righteous Man's body did not limit Yrsillar in this human-demon form. The realization alarmed him because it meant Yrsillar would not be as weak as they had hoped. It also exhilarated him because it perhaps meant that the demon lord could be killed, not simply transported back to the Abyss.

He had no more time to ponder. Yrsillar advanced, strode boldly for them, the limp of the Righteous Man no longer in evidence. The distortion about his body became increasingly defined as he neared. The terrible form of Yrsillar expanded with each step and dwarfed the human body that struggled to contain it.

"Your death will be long, Champion of a paltry power, long and painful."

Cale and Jak spread as far apart as the aisle permitted.

"Be careful," Cale said out of the side of his mouth.

"I'm always careful," Jak replied.

Yrsillar ignored Jak and headed directly for Cale. He bore no weapons.

Cale backed off, drawing him in, blade held defensively before him. "Come on," he breathed. "Come on."

From behind Yrsillar, Jak rose up and charged, short sword aimed straight for the creature's back.

Yrsillar whirled halfway around, sidestepped Jak's stab, and backhanded the little man's jaw. Blood and spit flew from Jak's mouth.

"Unngh." Jak flipped head over heels from the force of the blow and crumbled to the shrine floor.

Cale lunged forward and stabbed Yrsillar through the abdomen. He drove the long sword through the distortion and all the way into the Righteous Man's thin body until the tip of the blade burst out the other side his ribs. Blood poured from the wound.

"Arrrgh!" Yrsillar sagged. The demonic distortion faded, shrank back into the body of the Righteous Man. Cale grimaced and twisted the blade. He felt the metal shear at the demon's organs, gave his anger free play.

"That's for the Uskevren, *ecthain*," he hissed into the wrinkled face of the Righteous Man.

It was Yrsillar's voice that groaned with pain. The demon still had possession of the Righteous Man. Cale drove the blade in farther, pushing the body of the Righteous Man across the aisle.

Yrsillar spat blood and grimaced in pain.

Cale smiled grimly, satisfied and victorious. This was over.

Even as that thought crossed his mind, the body of the Righteous Man suddenly jerked up straight. The voids of Yrsillar's eyes regained their focus and their glare sent a shiver up Cale's spine. The demon lord's grimace of pain twisted into a mirthful leer. He closed a hand around Cale's wrist and began to squeeze.

"Not so easy, Champion."

Though the distortion no longer played about the

Righteous Man's form, the old man's slight body never-theless exhibited the terrible strength of the demon lord.

Desperate, Cale maniacally jerked the long sword around and opened a hole in the Righteous Man's flesh. Yrsillar laughed into Cale's face and *squeezed*.

"Ahhh!" His wrist snapped. Still Yrsillar squeezed.

"Ahhhhh!" Bone grated against bone like grinding millstones. Dizzy, he thought he would pass out from the pain.

Unable to stop himself, he released the hilt of his blade. Yrsillar still gripped his wrist.

With all his strength, Cale balled his free hand into a fist—a fist that enclosed the felt mask—and punched Yrsillar in the face. Again and again he struck power-ful blows that broke the Righteous Man's nose and split his lips.

With blood streaming down his battered face, Yrsil-lar only laughed. He lifted Cale by the wrist and shook him in the air like a child's doll. Cale screamed in agony.

Disdainfully, Yrsillar flung him aside. Cale flew through the air and crashed amongst the pews and charred ghoul corpses. Wracked with pain, he righted himself and looked up to see Yrsillar looming over him. Cale had no weapon. He crawled crabwise over the ghoul corpses, cradling his broken wrist.

"I told you that you cannot escape me," Yrsillar taunted, and spoke a word of magic. Five glowing bolts of energy streaked from the demon's extended fingers and slammed sizzling into Cale's chest.

The impact knocked him flat on his back. His chest was on fire. His breath left him. He rolled over onto his stomach and tried to crawl away. Yrsillar followed him. Cale could feel him, could feel the empty holes of the demon's eyes burning into his back.

"And you thought to challenge *me!* You and your ridiculous god." He laughed evilly. "I have eaten more souls than you have lived days, Erevis Cale.

Then with another magical word, another wave of energy seared Cale's back.

His vision went blurry. He struggled to stay conscious. Desperate, he clutched the felt mask in his spasming fist. Its soft touch brought him a moment of clarity.

He would die with dignity.

I'm your Champion and I won't die like a groveling dog, he thought to Mask.

Another blast of energy sent stabs of pain along his spine. He clamped his mouth shut and walled off the scream of pain that tried to burst from behind his teeth.

Though the effort nearly made him pass out, he flipped over onto his back. Yrsillar stood over him, frail with the Righteous Man's form, but awful for the power he contained.

"Damn you," Cale croaked.

Yrsillar stopped laughing, bent down to regard him with narrowed orbits. "It is you who are damned, Champion," he said. "Your soul is mine. I'll devour most of it, but leave you with just enough to remain sentient, enough so that you can appreciate your fate."

Cale tried to spit in his face, but only managed to dribble saliva down his chin. "The gods damn you," he croaked again.

Yrsillar stood upright and regarded him with amused contempt. "The gods do not damn, fool, nor do they bless. They manipulate. This is where those manipulations have brought you," his mouth twisted into a snarl, "*Champion.*"

Yrsillar reached for him.

Though it took a supreme effort of will, Cale did not

try to squirm away. He would not give Yrsillar the satisfaction of seeing him afraid. He would die defiant.

Reflexively, he threw the only thing he had left. The felt mask.

"To the Hells with you," he said.

A bird of cloth, the mask fluttered through the air and softly struck Yrsillar on the chest—

Without warning, the air around the demon lord exploded in a blast of silvery-gray light. A roaring sound filled Cale's ears. A sphere of energy encapsulated the demon lord, sizzling and burning him. He roared in pain, reached for Cale in a rage, but the energy held him shackled.

Shielding his eyes, Cale scooted away.

Yrsillar's roars grew more and more pained, his promises more and more dire. The sizzling intensified. "You will suffer an eternity of pain, Erevis Cale! I shall peel your soul like an onion and devour you over the course of millennia. I shall—"

The cascade of silver energy grew brighter and brighter until it reached a sparkling, sizzling crescendo.

"No!" roared Yrsillar, and swung his arms wildly against his confinement. It was a futile effort.

With the suddenness of a lightning strike, the demon's translucent form was torn from the suddenly slack body of the Righteous Man. The mortal separated from the demonic with the sound of ripping cloth. The guildmaster's body fell to the ground unmoving. Yrsillar's writhing demonic form, still contained in the silver energy, was blown across the shrine and into the gate. His screams of rage and pain diminished as his body grew smaller and smaller.

The gate snapped shut with a sudden pop, the sound as final as a funeral dirge. Another such pop sounded from the hallway outside the shrine as that gate closed. Within seconds, the ubiquitous pulsing had ceased. All the gates in the guildhouse must have closed.

Cale looked around stupefied, dazed. The shrine was empty and silent.

It took a few moments to register. Yrsillar was gone. They had won. The realization affected him strangely. He fell back and tried to laugh, but managed only a pained grimace. He wasn't yet ready for laughter. Emotion flooded him though—not happiness, but something he couldn't quite put a name to. His eyes welled. He blinked away the tears.

How? he wondered, but already knew the answer.

Mask had banished Yrsillar, or Cale had banished Yrsillar with the power of Mask. It no longer mattered which. He was now a man of faith.

I accept, you bastard, he thought with a half-smile. I accept.

He lay still and let his emotions run their course. After a few moments, he recovered himself enough to climb unsteadily to his feet. Jak needed him.

He staggered along the aisle, past the body of the Righteous Man. The guildmaster's abdomen gaped from where Cale had slashed it open. The rest of the body looked shrunken and dried out, sucked empty. The felt mask lay on the floor beside it. Cale stooped to retrieve it.

"Caaale," the Righteous Man croaked.

Startled, Cale jerked back.

"Cale . . ." A thin arm tried to move, failed, and instead a bony finger beckoned.

After a moment's hesitation, Cale moved forward and knelt beside his former guildmaster. "I'm here."

The Righteous Man's eyes fluttered open. Cale gave a start—the sockets sat empty, mere pink holes in his sunken, wrinkled face.

Cale resisted the impulse to touch him, to give him

comfort. He felt no affection for the guildmaster, only a distant anger. "What happened? How—"

"You're the Champion," the Righteous Man whispered.

"I am," Cale acknowledged. With his good hand, he picked up the felt mask and placed it in his pocket. "I am." There was nothing more to be said. Jak needed him. He started to rise, but the Righteous Man gripped him by the forearm with surprising strength.

"Wait, Erevis," he wheezed.

The Righteous Man's touch was dry and cold.

"I'm not afraid to die. I'm at peace with the Shadowlord now. I see his plan." He coughed a bloody foam onto his chin. "But I want to be at peace with you, Erevis, Champion." Another round of coughing. He pulled Cale closer. "I didn't mean for Yrsillar to go free. . . ."

Cale waited another moment but the guildmaster said nothing more. Cale gave him what absolution he could; no one should die with guilt on their soul. "I know," he said, disengaged his hand, and started to rise.

The Righteous Man jerked to consciousness, coughed, beckoned Cale closer. "No, that's not what I meant. I *didn't* free him. . . ."

Cale stiffened at that. If the Righteous Man hadn't freed Yrsillar, then who?

The guildmaster struggled to say something. A word hung on his blood-flecked lips. Cale leaned forward, clutched the guildmaster's tattered robe with his good hand—

"Riven," the Righteous Man softly hissed. "Riven and the Zhentarim set Yrsillar free."

❖ ❖ ❖ ❖ ❖

Cale knelt over Jak, probed his jaw with gentle fingers. Not broken, though the little man had lost several teeth. His cheeks had swollen enough to distort his face. His head would be fuzzy for hours.

"Jak," he called, and gently nudged his friend. "Jak."

After a few moments, the little man's eyes fluttered open, focused blearily on Cale.

"Cale?"

Cale smiled. "Yrsillar's gone. We won, my friend."

Despite his words, he didn't feel like he had won. He felt little more than tired and angry at Riven and the Zhentarim.

"Gone." Jak's small hand found Cale's arm and squeezed. The little man sighed and closed his eyes. "How?"

Cale quickly related the story of the combat, of the mask and Yrsillar's banishment. Afterwards, he looked at the mask he held in his hand. "I'm his Champion, it seems."

Jak regarded the mask for a moment, looked into Cale's eyes, and nodded knowingly. "You're his Champion. But you're still your own man, Erevis." He chuckled and said, "That's probably why he chose you in the first place."

"I am still my own man," Cale affirmed. He knew now that he could have his faith and his individuality. Smiling, he used his good hand to help the little man to sit upright. Careful not to jolt his broken wrist, he took his waterskin from his pack and offered it to his friend.

Jak took a sip, swished it around in his mouth, and spat blood. Afterward, he eyed Cale shrewdly. "Can you cast spells?"

Surprisingly, Cale did not find the question alarming. "I don't know. How would I know?"

Jak took another gulp from the waterskin. He swallowed this one down. "You just *know*."

Cale considered the mask. *My holy symbol,* he

reminded himself. He didn't feel any different—certainly didn't feel like a priest, or a Champion. "Then I don't think so. No, I can't."

"Try it," Jak said.

"How in the name of the gods do I try it? I've never cast a spell before."

Jak looked at him as though he were a dolt. "Dark, Cale, you're not a mage. You don't need years of training. It's a divine gift. You will it to happen."

"Will it? That's it?"

"You will it," Jak said with a nod and a pained wince, "then pray to your god to realize your will."

Cale was incredulous. "That's it?"

"That's it," Jak replied. "Now try it."

Though he felt an idiot, Cale held the mask in his hand, closed his eyes, and *willed* his wrist healed.

Nothing happened.

"You have to pray," Jak said. "You can do it silently if you need to."

Cale saw Jak's smirk but chose to ignore it. He calmed himself and for the second time that day, prayed silently to Mask, this time for the power to heal. At first nothing happened, but then his consciousness flew open. A dam had burst in his brain.

"Dark," he whispered, awed. A warmth filled him, a presence joined with him and made its will his own. He knew then the feeling of serving something greater than himself, knew then the transcendence of the divine.

His wrist began to tingle. Suddenly, bones and tendons knit back together. The pain ceased. He opened his eyes, held his hand before his face, and rotated his wrist—no pain. The pain in his back and chest, too, had vanished. He had healed. The realization humbled and exhilarated him.

"You're still your own man," Jak reassured him.

"I know," he replied. Mask had made no demands. Cale would have done everything he had done with or without Mask's involvement. A convergence of the mortal and divine interests, Jak had called it.

So be it, he thought. Touching Jak, he prayed, and willed his best friend healed. The swelling in the little man's face diminished until it had all but vanished. Jak's bruises disappeared. His color returned and he shot Cale a grateful smile.

"This is going to be an interesting time, Cale," he said, and rose to his feet.

"Indeed," Cale replied. He gently tucked his holy symbol into his pocket.

Jak's smile fell when he looked around the shrine— ghoul corpses, charred pews, the stink of death. His eyes lingered long on the corpse of the Righteous Man.

"I guess you're finally out of the guild."

"I am," Cale replied. He had, however, entered into a brotherhood of a different sort.

"And I'm out of the Harpers."

"You are."

"So what now?"

Cale too looked around the shrine. The whole guild-house had become a slaughter-pen, an abomination to man and god.

"We burn it," he said. "Gut the entire place. The sewer entrance too. There's oil in a storeroom upstairs."

❧ ❧ ❧ ❧ ❧

They spent the next hour soaking the basement in lantern oil. Cale had seen many such fires set by Night Mask arsonists back in Westgate—he knew how to ensure a good burn. Afterward, he threw a torch on the kindling point. The fire would gut the basement before the flames were even visible from the street outside.

And by then, the building would be lost. Selgaunt's fire-crews would spend their energy preventing the flames from spreading to the buildings nearby. The Night Knife guildhouse was dead. The Night Knife guild was dead, and Cale had been reborn.

Side by side the two friends walked upstairs, from the darkness and toward the light.

"I can't believe it's over," Jak said. The smell of smoke was already strong in the air.

"It isn't," Cale said, and left it at that. This end was only a beginning—his whole life had changed in the course of only two days. He now had to return to Stormweather and face Thamalon with the truth, the *whole* truth, no more lying. He had to face Thazienne, who by now must have read his note and learned his feelings for her. His life would be different from now on, harder in some ways, but at least he'd be able to face himself.

"We never did find out who Yrsillar meant by 'the other,'" Jak observed, as they emerged onto the street.

Cale nodded. His mind had already turned to his next task—Riven had set this entire nightmare into motion.

CHAPTER 12

THE END OF THE
BEGINNING

Riven rose and dressed in silence. Behind him on
the feather bed, Iris lay amidst a sea of sweat-
soaked sheets, still breathing heavily. Her dark
hair pooled on the pillows. Small but nicely pro-
portioned, her shapely legs stuck tantalizingly
out of the blankets. The soft candlelight high-
lighted the curve of her thigh, the smoothness of
her skin. He felt the stirrings of arousal again
but sublimated them—he had too much on his
mind to spend all night with a whore.

The Night Knife guildhouse had burned to
the ground two nights ago. There had been
rumors about peculiar remains found in the
charred ruins, but he didn't know whether
Yrsillar and the shadow demons had been
caught within the flames or had used the

arson as cover to hide themselves. As usual, Malix, who finally had returned from Zhentil Keep yesterday, could offer no insight. Riven had come within a bladewidth of splitting that self-satisfied dolt on the spot. Malix had foreseen nothing, and his *plan* to let Yrsillar slay the Zhentarim's enemies—while it had wiped out the Night Knives—had gone very bad very fast.

In typical fashion, it would fall to Riven to pick up the pieces. The aftermath of this misadventure would cause unrest in the underworld. The various gangs would be scrambling for position. The Zhentarim had lost so many men—including Verdrinal, Riven thought with a satisfied sneer. It was far from certain that the Zhentarim would come out of this better off than they had come in.

This might be the time to get out, he thought. With the Zhentarim as weak as they now were in Selgaunt, old grudges would resurface. Carrying the black and gold badge of the Network might be the quickest way to a bloody end—

Iris interrupted his thinking with a giggle.

"What's funny?"

"Nothing," she playfully replied in her lilting, singsong voice. "The smoke from the candle made a mask around your face. You looked like a bandit just now."

Riven waved the black smoke from his eyes and grunted at her foolishness.

"Come back to bed," she pleaded. He found the offer tempting, but resisted.

"No, I've got things to do yet."

She writhed around on the bed with an exaggerated sigh.

He ignored her, grunted a goodbye, pulled on his scarlet cloak, and strode from her flat.

Due to the late hour and bitter cold, Ironmongers

Lane stood empty and dark. All but one of the street torches had been extinguished by the wind and the city's linkboys didn't concern themselves with relighting the lamps on back streets.

Thoughtful, Riven crunched through the ankle deep snow.

For the next month or so, he would have to keep an eye on Malix. With Verdrinal dead, Malix likely would try to pass responsibility for this operation to Riven. He might even try to kill him and attribute blame posthumously. He thought again about getting out.

Movement a block ahead drew his attention. Out of habit, he backed into the shadows of a nearby building and peered up the street.

A short, cloaked form was staggering down the street. A drunk halfling, he recognized. Not especially unusual at this hour. A feathered cap—

Recognition dawned and he exhaled a cloud of frozen mist sharply. Fleet. Riven could count the number of halflings in Selgaunt on both hands, and only one of them dressed like a peacock even in the depth of winter. Jak Fleet.

He snarled silently and his hand drifted to his back. He still bore a scar from the backstab that little whoreson had dealt him a month ago. Malix had forbidden him to hunt Fleet down for fear of Harper retaliation, if Riven even had been able to find the little puke. Fleet went underground as well as anyone.

But now here he was—drunk and alone. If Riven had worshiped a god, he would have thanked him for this.

Time for payback, he thought as he stepped from the shadows and silently trailed after the halfling. He drew both his enchanted sabers.

Fleet turned right on Larawkan Lane and headed east, toward the Warehouse District. Still staggering, the little bastard hummed as he walked.

You're sloppy, little whelp, he thought. And it's going to cost you.

Gradually, he closed in, careful to maintain silence. Fleet had no permanent residence in the city. That's what made him so hard to locate. Riven assumed he was making for a Harper safehouse. The Zhentarim knew the Harpers kept at least one safehouse in the Warehouse District, but they didn't know where. At the moment, Riven wasn't concerned with finding that out. He wanted Fleet's blood, not his hideout.

The wind picked up, whipping Riven's cloak behind him. Fleet lost his hat and turned to retrieve it.

Riven ducked into the darkness, held his breath, and didn't move.

Fleet skipped clumsily after his hat, at last caught it, tucked it under his armpit, and headed back off toward the brick towers of the Warehouse District. He showed no sign of noticing Riven.

Riven emerged from hiding and followed.

Fleet moved deeper into the district. Silently, Riven closed to within twenty paces. He felt the thrill the hunter feels as he closes on his prey.

Near Drover's Square, Fleet looked both ways and ducked down an alley.

Drover's Square was the place Fleet had given Riven his scar. Appropriate that he die here, Riven thought.

He followed the halfling down the dark alley, using carts and refuse heaps as cover. Ahead, Fleet continued to weave uncertainly. He stopped periodically, confused, and muttered to himself. With the acoustics better in the alley than in the windswept street, Riven could make out his words.

". . . thish hash a back door?" He giggled in that annoyingly high-pitched halfling way. "No? Darksh."

The halfling trekked on. Ahead, Riven saw the alley

hit a dead end. Too drunk to realize it, the halfling walked forward. The prey was trapped. Sneering, Riven let his foot scrape the street. Fleet froze, but didn't turn.

Riven stepped from the darkness and walked forward. "Jak Fleet, I've been looking for you."

The halfling whirled in alarm. Riven put on his most contemptuous sneer, expecting to see Fleet wide-eyed with fear. Instead, the halfling wore a sneer of his own and spoke without slurring.

"And we've been looking for you, Drasek Riven."

We?

Too late he caught motion out of the corner of his eye. Ambush! Riven whirled to see a tall, bald specter slide from the shadows and cut off his retreat. Cale! The towering bastard held a long sword in one hand and a piece of black cloth in the other.

"Cale!"

Fleet giggled.

Riven's lips peeled back in a hateful snarl. Quickly, he got his back against the alley wall and lowered into a fighting crouch. He could take both of them in a straight fight.

"Come on, then," he challenged. He whirled his enchanted sabers before him with easy grace. He'd give these whelps more than they could handle.

"You're an idiot, Riven," Fleet said.

Riven glared at him, but watched Cale—the more dangerous opponent—out of the corner of his eye.

Cale kept his distance. He regarded Riven with an expression as cold as the air. Riven had never seen such an expression on Cale's face before. He looked not merely angry, but . . . hateful. The expression made him nervous.

"Come on, Cale," he said again, to hide his discomfiture. "This has been a long time coming."

"Long time coming is right," Cale hissed. He lowered his blade, rubbed the piece of black cloth between his fingers like a talisman, and stared into Riven's face. "You were responsible for freeing the demon."

He stated it as a fact, not a question. Riven saw no point in denying it. "Correct. So?" He sneered. "Part of the game, Cale. Business. That upset you? You miss the guild? Nine Hells, I did you a favor."

Cale's eyes narrowed. "Business, is it?" he whispered, soft and angry. "Part of the *game?* So is this, then."

With that, he closed his eyes and began softly to *incant*—incant!—as though he could cast spells.

Dumbstruck with disbelief, it took Riven a moment to realize what Cale was doing. Casting a spell? Cale? When he finally recovered himself enough, he lunged forward with both blades and tried to disrupt the spell.

He was too late. Before he had taken two strides, Cale had already finished. A spark shower erupted in Riven's brain. On the instant, his body froze, immobile.

He couldn't move his head, couldn't even blink, but he could see into Cale's narrowed eyes.

How in all the levels of the Abyss can Cale cast spells?

Cale folded the piece of cloth—a mask, Riven saw, and thought of Iris's words—then placed it in his pocket. He looked to Fleet and said, "Nice work, little man," then turned back to Riven. The look in his eyes would have made Riven turn and run, if he could have moved.

Cale walked up and stood nose to nose, stared into Riven's eye. "Do you have any idea of the damage you've caused?" he hissed.

Riven could do nothing but breathe. Of course he knew the damage he had caused; causing damage had been the point. "Of course you don't," Cale went on. "You're nothing more than a Zhentarim lackey."

Riven bristled inwardly. Lackey!

Quick as a striking snake, Cale gripped him by the throat, turned his head, and put the long sword beside his throat. Cale's voice rose as his anger escaped his control. "A lackey and nothing more. And no one cares whether a lackey lives or dies."

Here it comes, Riven thought, the sharp flash of pain as iron ran across his throat.

But it didn't. Cale got himself back under control. A fact that alarmed Riven all the more.

"I'm making you the first, Riven. The first of the Zhentarim to die. The first of many." Cale gripped him by the cheeks so hard that Riven's teeth cut into the inside of his mouth. He could make no sound. He could only endure the pain in silence.

"You're all going to pay for this. You understand? By Mask, every godsdamned Zhent in Selgaunt is going to answer to me for this. Starting with you."

Starting with you. Cale *was* going to kill him, then, and he could do nothing but stand here and take it. Inexplicably, his mind turned to Verdrinal—to the nobleman's panicked expression as he bled to death.

At least I won't go like that, he thought. Even if he had been afraid—and he wasn't—his frozen expression could not have shown it.

Cale tensed as though to draw the long sword across his throat. Jak Fleet's words halted him.

"Let him live, Cale. He'll know he's alive only because we let him walk away. He'll let the rest of them know we're coming. We want that."

Riven could see Cale's inner battle written in his expression.

Listen to the halfling, Cale, he thought. Listen to him. It would gall Riven to know that Fleet, of all people, had saved him, but at least he'd be alive. He'd have his revenge on Cale, sooner or later.

Cale hesitated, stared into Riven's face, and finally lowered his blade. He leaned in close.

"You tell them I'm coming for them," he hissed. "Every Zhent in the city. I'm bringing them all down."

Riven would have laughed if he could. The whole Selgaunt organization. How absurd! The Zhentarim had infiltrated every high office in the city, and most of the noble houses. No one man could bring it down.

"After you tell them, get out." He rummaged through Riven's pockets until he located his small Zhentarim badge in the inner lining, the badge that had replaced the one Riven had tossed at the Righteous Man's feet when this operation had begun.

"If we meet again and you've got another one of these, then I swear by Mask—you're a dead man, and I'll kill you ugly."

He pocketed Riven's badge and punched him in the face with all of his strength.

Riven heard his nose break, the same sound his boots made when they crunched the snow. Light and pain exploded in his head but he could not cry out. He collapsed to the ground and blacked out for a heartbeat. The next thing he knew he was staring up at the rooftops and night sky. Still unable to move, blood and snot streamed unabated down his face.

Cale's head appeared above him, blotted out the sky. "Part of the game, you bastard." He moved out of Riven's field of vision. Riven heard them walking away.

Cale's voice carried from somewhere down the alley. "I meant what I said, Riven. I'll kill you if I see you again. By Mask, I'll kill you."

Riven would have laughed if he could have moved his jaw. *By Mask?* Who did Cale think he was? The Righteous Man?

FROM BELOVED AUTHOR
ELAINE CUNNINGHAM...

FOR THE FIRST TIME TOGETHER AS A SET!
SONGS AND SWORDS

Follow the adventures of bard Danilo Thann and his beautiful half-elf companion Arilyn Moonblade in these attractive new editions from Elaine Cunningham. These two daring Harpers face trials that bring them together and then tear them apart.

Elfsong
Elfshadow
Silver Shadows (JANUARY 2001)
Thornhold (FEBRUARY 2001)
The Dream Spheres

AND DON'T MISS...
STARLIGHT AND SHADOWS

Daughter of the Drow
In the aftermath of war in Menzoberranzan, free-spirited drow princess Liriel Baenre sets off on a hazardous quest. Pursued by enemies from her homeland, her best hope of an ally is one who may also be her deadliest rival.

Tangled Webs
Continuing on her quest, drow princess Liriel Baenre learns the price of power and must confront her dark drow nature.

FORGOTTEN REALMS

COLLECT THE ADVENTURES OF
DRIZZT DO'URDEN AS WRITTEN BY

BEST-SELLING AUTHOR

R.A. SALVATORE

FOR THE FIRST TIME
IN ONE VOLUME!

Legacy of the Drow
Collector's Edition

Now together in an attractive
hardcover edition, follow Drizzt's
battles against the drow through
the four-volume collection of

THE LEGACY, STARLESS NIGHT,
SIEGE OF DARKNESS,
and
PASSAGE TO DAWN.

The Icewind Dale Trilogy
Collector's Edition

Read the tales that introduced
the world to Drizzt Do'Urden
in this collector's edition
containing *The Crystal Shard,
Streams of Silver,* and
The Halfling's Gem.

NOW AVAILABLE
IN PAPERBACK!

The Dark Elf Trilogy
Collector's Edition

Learn the story of Drizzt's
tortured beginnings in the
evil city of Menzobarranzan
in the best-selling novels *Homeland,
Exile,* and *Sojourn.*